The Marriage of the Sword

By Ami Kathleen

PublishAmerica
Baltimore

ISBN: 1-4241-2846-3
PUBLISHED BY PUBLISHAMERICA, LLLP
www.publishamerica.com
Baltimore

Printed in the United States of America

This book is dedicated to Virginia and Maryrose and in loving memory of our Tyson.

The Treachery....

Four generations ago, when the world was young and the lands were in strife, the Great Goddess Danu called upon the Lord of the Elements—Tuatha Dé Danann— to bring forth four treasures.

With these four treasures, she entrusted the people of Thaumatur to resolve their differences and educate the people of good and beautiful things.

And so it was, that the Lord of Fire brought forth the Claimh Solais to Findias. The Lord of Water bestowed upon Murias the Undry. The Lord of Earth blessed Falias with the Lia Fáil. Finally, The Lord of Air gave to Gorias the Gáe Assail.

The Elders of the kingdoms were content and at long last, Thaumatur had order. In the act of love and loyalty to Danu, the Elders and the Tuatha Dé Danann constructed a great temple in between two rose covered hills in honor of the Four Season Daughters. To consecrate the Temple, a Golden Skylight was forged with all the elements and amber, and it was placed in the ceiling so that it could absorb the blessings and magic from the sun.

For many years after, the Elders weakened with desires to grasp the Powers of the treasures. They were used in vain, tainted by the very ones trusted to protect them.

But the Elders were deceived by one of their own. In the last generation, a young prince, greedy and malevolent, charged an army across Thaumatur, destroying all that was good and desecrated the Temple of the Seasons. They shattered the Golden Skylight and scattered the shards among them. In turn, the four great kingdoms were imprisoned in four different seasons.

When the twentieth fifth year comes to pass, the darkness of the moon will obscure Danu's sun. Findias will burn. Murias will drown. Gorias will disappear. Falias will crumble. The veils between the realms thin and demons will rise again unless the Bearer of weapons, a son of royal blood, returns the treasures from whence they came.

-Tuatha Dé Danann-
After the Great War

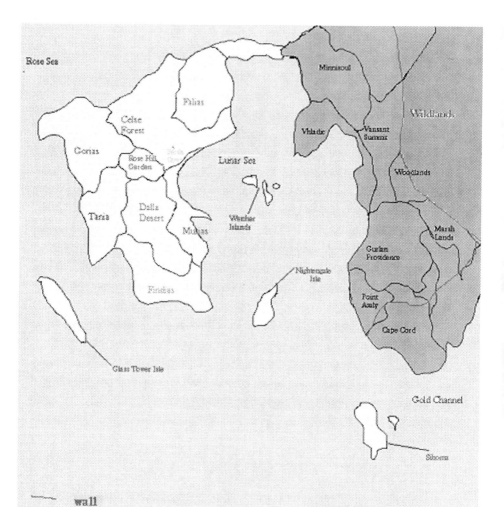

Rose Sea

Celse
Forest

Falias

Minnisoul

Wildlands

Corias

Rose Hill
Garden

Vilade

Vansant
Summit

Lunar Sea

Woodlands

Taras

Dalla
Desert

Mutas

Weather
Islands

Marsh
Lands

Finolas

Nightengale
Isle

Gurlan
Providence

Point
Analy

Glass Tower Isle

Cape Cord

Gold Channel

Sihorra

——— **wall**

BOOK ONE

Thaumatur, Land of the Mages

PROLOGUE

The Beginning

Eyes of blue-violet glimmered behind the curtains of sun-golden hair. She stood upon a Stone of pale flames, a Sword at her back, a Spear at her waist and a Cauldron in her cupped hands. An inferno fanned around the figure's head, her lips twisted into an accusing frown.

"You have forgotten me. I, who will save you from the sins of our Elders, have answered the Call to the Circle. Save me…" She wailed.

A blast of flames devoured the girl into nothing.

High Priestess Janella DeBurke darted from her sleep. Sweat poured from her brow and her eyes burned with the vision. She pulled on her robe and fled down the misty corridors to the tiny chamber at the end of her flight. She flung open the door with little care of courtesy and met the wide eyes of her First Priestess Sierra. The woman shook with fear. Janella could see the confirmation in her eyes. They saw the same vision.

"Come!" Janella cried and tossed a burgundy cloak to her, "It is time."

Sierra flung the cloak over her shoulders, grabbed the nearby lantern, and followed the High Priestess deeper into the caves. An old door was a temporary obstacle. Sierra waved a hand through the air and the door swung open.

Four globes of jade light illuminated the cavernous room. Janella lowered her head in silent prayer before opening one of the orb's tops. The last four of the Earth Crystals and they were to be used sparingly. She pulled out the diamond-shaped jade and placed it around her neck. Sierra was at her side in seconds, clinging tightly to her hand.

The thunderous clang of metal shook the cave beneath their feet. Janella met eyes with Sierra. "Dear Goddess, it cannot be!"

She gathered her skirts, Sierra at her heels, and fled the passage to the upper level. A cacophonous hissing breeched the common serenity of the atmosphere. Janella gasped.

Horror stood at the threshold of the caves. A mass of black and steel clad figures cornered them. The tyrants were restless in their deliberately slow approach and their eyes burned with crimson hatred through the chasms of their hoods. Janella gripped Sierra's frail hand and retreated.

"I know another way out!"

The passage was dark, but the pulsing jade of the Earth Crystal lent some light. Once they entered the sacred garden above the caves, they could use the Earth Crystal to transport. It was too powerful to be used the condensed Brosia Cave's passages.

Janella cast a glance behind her and, though she saw nothing of the vile creatures, she didn't risk slowing down. They slammed into the arch door and spilled out onto the moonlit garden. She squeezed Sierra's hand and touched the Earth Crystal as she moved her fingers in swift incantations.

A shadow divided the two women ripping apart the link of hands. Janella lifted her eyes. Axes and spikes of twisted metal gleamed above her. Pale faces of translucent skin snarled and spat venom in their rancorous song. She managed a glimpse of her priestess companion and cried,"Run, Sierra!"

Sierra ignored her, fighting them off in a whirlwind of kicks. A clawed hand yanked the High Priestess up by her hair.

A sudden stir caught the creatures' attention. Janella's captor thrust her to the ground in a painful thud and spun about.

"*Enivid Nus!*" A deep voice cried.

An explosion of white light ignited hissings and wailings. The light was gone and so were the creatures. When Janella met eyes with her defender, relief washed over her.

With a twirl of dark robes and a wand clutched tightly in his hand, Darius Percival leaped down from the standing stones and rushed to her side.

"Priestesses," He said in a steely voice, "don't tell me that what I just saw were Demons!"

Janella gasped for air and met his onyx eyes, "I'm afraid they were."

"How is this possible? We've much time before Solar Eclipse." Darius tugged Janella to her feet and supported her against him. Sierra quickly took up the other side of her.

"I'm not certain, Darius. We must call the knights of the Circle. I want someone to go to Findias and learn what we can from the queen there." Janella withdrew from their support.

"What of the Elders? We cannot do anything without the consent of the Sun Order." Darius asked lowly.

"Leave them to me." Janella turned to meet Sierra's eyes and then Darius'.

"There's something more, isn't there?" Darius raised his brows.

Janella couldn't hide such a thing from the knight, not only because he was a Mageborn of Danu's Circle, but because he was a Mind Mage. A very *strong* Mind Mage. And she wouldn't resort to the secretive tactics of the Sun Order Militia. She wasn't an *Enchantra*; she was the High Priestess of Danu and the Brosian Ministry. The secrets would end now.

"The Prophecy was wrong," Sierra spoke before Janella.

Darius nearly gasped, and that was a rare thing for the normally expressionless knight. He fixed his confused gaze on her.

"The Bearer is a girl."

CHAPTER ONE

Fire Magic

Your time has come…

The noon sky swirled with different shades of grey. The snow fell, and then would come the hail. A storm approached and the market below was evacuated with its first warning. It always snowed in Falias.

The smell of the baker's work wafted up in the air and the speckle of lights added a cheering stroke to her viewing, but Miarosa Maladinto was distracted by voices. She stood tall on her balcony in a pool of woolen cloak and shivered. It was not the first time she heard strange voices. For weeks she ignored such ghosts. She was going crazy, she was sure of it. And with good reason too.

Mia was bound to the selfishness of her King Brother, Aiden. He forbade her much of the world beyond the castle walls and left her with only a governess to describe the other beautiful kingdoms of Spring, Fall, and Summer. But she was grateful for her governess, Nan. It was Nan who Mia looked to when her own mother shunned her coldly. Merle hated her. And the one person in her family who loved her was dying in the heap of his own soil. Lucian, Mia's father, had been ill for many years and was forced to give his son the throne prematurely. She loved him beyond all.

Mia wrapped the woolen cloak more tightly around her and carried herself away from the haunting afternoon. She lowered herself deep between the cushion pillows of blue velvet in front of the hearth, and summoned her companion, Oxanna. The sleek black cat with eyes of amber brushed a furry cheek against her hand and rumbled with delight before curling into a ball upon her knee.

There was a slight stir from behind the door of her chambers, and then came a tiny knock. For a moment Mia froze and prayed that the disturbance hadn't come from her bodyguard, Jacob. He was an ill-mannered Barbarian who wasted no time to ruin her mood.

In the early part of the past year, Jacob was sent to Thaumatur as the Barbarian Emperor's envoy, and he settled in Falias alongside the Winter King. But Jacob handled the mission of peace as if it were an undesired order. He didn't at all appear to be free of bigotry toward the Thaumaturi despite his ruler's aspiration for peace among the races.

The knock came again and Mia sighed heavily. The knock wouldn't have been so gentle if it were Jacob. She rose from her comforts, careful not to disturb Oxanna, and smoothed her skirts. "Enter."

A maid dressed in a grey frock curtsied before her with the urgency of a scared rabbit. Mia stifled the urge to tell the maid that it wasn't Merle she stood before.

"My lady," The maid said in a squeaky voice, "The King wishes to hold audience with you at once."

For a moment there was silence, and the maid wouldn't take leave unless she was dismissed. But the wheels were turning in Mia's mind. She was reluctant to send the maid forth with an answer. It wasn't often that Aiden wished for her company.

"Very well. Inform my brother that I'll be there in a moment." Mia sighed and the maid scurried from the room.

The entry way was muffled with activity in preparation to receive dinner guests. Fresh silver and blue banners embroidered with wolves—the crest of Falias—were hung in the corners of the hall, the enormous hearth blazed beside the golden statue of the Goddess.

Aiden awaited her in the entry way, pacing the floor in his sweeping sapphire robes with his hands clasped tightly behind his back. His eyes burned as bright as the fire in the hearth when he fixed his gaze on her. Black hair framed his flawless expression of annoyance. He was much older than Mia, being twenty upon her birth, but he was so well kept that one could hardly tell. Some would even say he was beautiful.

Aiden's favorite mistress, Lynn, hovered over his shoulder with a broad smile and eyes as narrow as a cat. Whatever brought the smile to Lynn's face couldn't be good for her. She was a shameful wench in every sense achievable and viciously jealous of anyone or anything that could possibly divert the King's attention away from her. Mia chose to ignore Lynn and turned her gaze to Aiden. "You wished to see me, Brother?"

Aiden cleared his throat to dismiss Lynn. She lingered, her smile etched for a moment before wandering off to aid the servants in preparations.

"Yes, Mia, I have requested your presence." He began, "I've been alerted to certain circumstances in Gorias that raise my concerns about your security." He paused long enough to let Mia's mind settle on his meaning.

Again and again it happens. You never keep your promises.

"You see, sister, there were several attempted assassinations in Tania." He continued, "The Viscount and his daughter were taken to a hidden safeguard and they've both been under protection for nearly two Moons."

"How does this pertain to the masquerade in Gorias, my lord?" She grabbed his hand.

Aiden drew in his breath and wiped his brow with an embroidered sleeve, "It's believed that the criminals are mercenaries revolting against the treaties of peace between the Thaumaturi and the Barbarians, not to mention Tania borders Gorias. The House of Allegiance suspects that the masquerade is their next target. It will not be safe."

"That is absurd! I'll be at your side every moment, and surely Jacob will guard me. It's his duty," she tightened her grip on his hands. Aiden pulled his hands free and turned a cheek to her.

"There's something more, isn't there?" she asked suspiciously.

Mia could see it in his eyes that he didn't wish to answer, but he also knew he had no choice. "Jacob informed me of these matters and has advised me against bringing you. He, as your bodyguard, isn't willing to place you in that kind of danger." Aiden said.

Of course that prejudice Barbarian is behind this! Brother, are you not King? You are as spineless as a newborn without its mother!

"He could care less about me!" Mia rolled her eyes and threw her head back in laughter. "And how did he learn of this news? Is he not a Barbarian? Maybe he's in contact with our enemies."

"That's enough!" Aiden thundered and spun on her, "It's that kind of bigotry that keeps our kinds at war!"

And it is men like Jacob who drives hatred into our hearts! She thought, but held her tongue. It wouldn't aid her in her case.

"How could you forbid me from going after you have promised me, Brother?"

"In time you will understand, Mia." Aiden turned away from her attempting to end the dispute.

"Mother has something to do with this too, doesn't she?" Mia cried.

"It doesn't matter who says what. I've the final say and I forbid it!"

Mia buckled in her ire. A blast slammed into her, weakened her, and at the same brought forth omnipotence. Fingers branched out from her stomach and a sensation seduced her into reaching deeper within to grasp, what? She was self-combusting with her fury!

Fear closed her throat, and she froze, trying to understand what possessed her. She closed her eyes tightly and slowed her breath forcing the ugly feelings aside. When she opened her eyes, she exhaled recognizing her natural senses return her to control, but barely. Aiden was facing her again with a steel expression and she was thankful he didn't notice her condition. If he did notice, he most likely waved it away as her temper.

"Mother has poisoned you against me." Mia replied slowly, her voice teetering with her temper. "I'm eighteen years old, an age in which most women are married! It's about time for me to make my own decisions. I'm going!"

"You will not!" He roared with his own anger in which *he* had very little control over. His eyes were wild with anger, but they were clear enough to see that he wouldn't yield his decision.

"Don't make me lock you up again!" He warned, "You know how I hate to do so, but I will! So do not push me!"

The thought of being confined frightened Mia. Fear was her downfall to control. The fervor returned with an even more commanding presence. Chills prickled her skin and the back of her neck, and beads of sweat tickled her brow.

"You are just her puppet! I hate you for that!" Mia spat trying to ignore the burn beneath her flesh, "I hate you!"

As soon as the words shot from her mouth, the hearth behind them erupted into a firestorm. Fire circled around the room in a hungry ring shouting its infernal roar and disappeared as quickly as it came. Mia clasped her throat against the fiery flow from within her body. Aiden jumped and spun to see what happened. When the smoke cleared the servants were on the ground covering their heads, while others scurried to their feet and fled. Perverse fascination danced in her brother's eyes when he looked at her.

After a few moments of frantic stares from the remaining servants, she flew up the stairs. By the time she reached the peak of the staircase, she felt fatigued. Her knees bowed and she grasped the railing to support her. It was as if she befell a fever, and her eyes were weak with sight.

Jacob stood tall and broad at his normal post before Mia's chambers. His lips were pursed sourly, a glittering silver stud protruded from his neatly trimmed beard. His fair hair fell below his shoulders decorated with scattered braids. Mia scowled at him and slammed the door closed behind her.

She collapsed on her bed and stifled her angry screams with a pillow. Her body was alive with fire, and the pain stimulated her more than hurt her. But she didn't have the strength to control it, or the vigor to rise from her bed. Her own hearth was a cold and dead pile when she first entered. It was now a raging blaze, crackling its presence. She didn't look to see it, but she knew it was there. The magic was coming from her, she concluded, and she cursed it. Then she cursed Aiden for his weakness and her loath for her mother deepened.

"Demons are among us." Janella stormed through the vast hall of the Sun Order's assembly.

Some of the Elders jolted from their seat with her abrupt approach and some scowled. They were not happy to see her. So be it.

The Sun Order, consisting of sixteen ruling Elders, was one of the three bodies of rule in Thaumatur alongside the House of Allegiance and Janella's own ministry. The Elders of the Order acted as if they had complete power.

"What is the meaning of this intrusion, Priestess?" Karenna Bell, the white-robed Grand Paladin's voice cracked like thunder.

Janella lowered the hood of her burgundy robes and placed a slender jeweled hand on the table before her, "I and my First Priestess were attacked by Demons last eve. I hope you had no knowledge of such threats and kept it secret from the Ministry."

A trail of gasps circled the room. Karenna's hand fluttered to her heart. "You've no right to come in here with such accusations."

King Valance Llewellyn of Gorias placed a hand over Karenna's and rose to his feet in folds of autumn bliss. Janella could at least rely on him to pay mind to her.

"Lady Priestess," Valance knitted his thick silver eyebrows together with concern, "Are you well? Has Sierra been harmed?"

"Nay, Valance, Darius of the Circle came to my aid and managed to banish them with an illumination spell." Janella said.

"Darius of the *Circle?*" *Enchantra* Llew snorted incredulously, "You still cling to such foolish ideas?"

"It is inappropriate to speak ill of Danu's Circle." Janella turned her burning gaze on the *Enchantra*, "They are the promised Mageborns."

"Impossible!" Llew bellowed, "We are the last since the Tuatha Dé Danann retreated to their exile in the Glass Towers generations ago."

Janella opened her mouth to rebut, but Valance, to avoid further conflict, lifted a hand. "I have trained them alongside of the priestess, my friends. And I have told you before, these knights are Mageborn."

"Valance, you know that I have never questioned your judgment before, and I wouldn't do so now, but," Karenna shook her head with the animation of her point, "you claim that two mariners from Murias are Mageborn. How far do you think you can honestly trust *them*? Mariners care for nothing but their own gain. And as long as they have their ships and waters to sail them in, they could care less if the land around them crumbles into the sea."

"I agree with Karenna, Valance." *Enchantra* Scatha replied huskily, "Mariners have been known to bargain with the Barbarians allowing them to freely come and go across our borders as they please. It wouldn't surprise me in the least if the mariners were held responsible for the missing treasures."

"The Barbarian Emperor has come forth peacefully, yet you make such comments about them. The world has changed, Scatha." Valance placed a hand on her shoulder and she stiffened, "Is it not the right of the Barbarians to voyage to our lands?"

"True," Scatha pressed, "The Barbarian Emperor has attempted a peace treaty, but he isn't our ruler though he seems to think he is."

"I believe we've gotten off of the subject." Valance sighed, "It's clear to me that the High Priestess has a more important matter to discuss."

"I do." Janella began, "I wish to send one of my knights on an investigation to Findias. I'm merely extending a courtesy by asking you for your accord."

"As if your knight could get through the gates there!" Karenna laughed, "They have the Summer Kingdom sealed up like a tomb from Thaumatur's dealings."

"It's imperative that the Summer Queen is questioned about the events of last night. She is our best option." Janella pressed, "It will be done with or without your support."

"Are you quite certain you saw *Demons*? It is impossible to summon Demons before Solar Eclipse." Karenna fixed her steel grey eyes on her, "Perhaps you have been deceived by one of your visionary dreams."

"I know what I saw." Janella snapped, "They were Demons. And we all know what that means."

Silence enveloped them. Indeed they all knew too well what it meant.

With the shards of the Season Temple and two of the four weapons missing, it drew them to no other conclusion. One of the relics had fallen into the wrong hands.

"The treasures have been discovered?" Scatha interceded.

"Call them what they are, *Enchantra*." Janella replied sharply, "They are weapons."

Karenna slammed her hammer on the table and hissed, "You speak of the gifts in vain! Your words are blasphemy, Priestess!"

Janella didn't flinch from the outburst, but an accusing flame danced within the wise pools of violet. *So pious and with little cause!*

"It wasn't the ministry who took the treasures in vain." Janella didn't raise her voice but it seemed to reverberate throughout the chamber, "It wasn't *my* lips that tasted the Cauldron's blessed gifts with selfish intent. It was an Elder of *your* Order who did so. And it was that simple act that made the treasures vulnerable to the Power. They were all used to murder, steal, and gain supremacy." Janella withdrew from the table, "The treasures became weapons the moment they were tainted."

"Send your knight, Janella." Valance shared a warning expression with the rest of the Elders, "It is better to be safe than sorry."

Janella nodded and retreated from their irritating presence. Valance followed her out. It was then that she revealed her vision to him.

"You and the Circle must find her. It is time things come to order before it's too late." Valance advised her and then kissed her cheek, "I am here if you need me and don't let them get to you. You know how they fear the loss of control."

Janella smiled and embraced him quickly before she left to do the will of Danu.

Aiden stormed through his mother's tower and flew up the winding stairs. He was angry and impressed at the same time with Mia's reaction. The inferno was the sign his mother awaited, yet he felt a cramp of jealousy and even intimidation. He knew Merle would be pleased that Mia possessed Fire Magic, but Aiden wasn't about to let the girl use it to her favor.

The story Aiden told Mia wasn't entirely false, but the truth in it was indeed stretched. Jacob had nothing to do with it, but the escalating dissention between Mia and the Barbarian was perfect for blame. Actually, he wasn't even sure what his mother's reasons were for forbidding the girl to go. Maybe bitterness, but who cared. Aiden planned on enjoying himself and it would be done a lot easier without Mia there.

When he reached the top of the stairs, he sighed with annoyance at the darkness his mother insisted on living in. The smell of burning incense and wax filled his lungs. It was the smell of secrecy spells. Everything was a big secret with Merle.

Aiden noticed his mother's silhouette against the north wall beneath the only torch lit in the quarters. She wasn't alone, which meant only one thing.

Falcon placed himself in Merle's favor and possibly bedded her with his dark arts. But he claimed that he was under no such influence as the Legion was known for.

The reign of the Legion was impossible to forget, although Aiden was just a youth when it ended. And it was an even more unforgettable reign to fall. His brother, Ahriman, was banished from Thaumatur, along with his devotees, because of his blasphemy against Danu and his attempts to solidify a dark empire over all the lands, Barbarian soil and Thaumatur alike. It was the seed of the Barbarian's vehement racism.

Ahriman broke the ancient seal, defacing the temple that honored the Season Daughters and used the shards as weapons to open the gates of the Underworld, releasing Demons to be controlled by his Legion. The rituals and invasions failed. However, the outcome left the four kingdoms frozen in four separate seasons.

It was hard to believe that Merle didn't get tangled up in the banishment, for she openly supported her eldest son, and even harder for him to swallow Falcon's proclamation of transformation. Aiden had his own opinions concerning him and one of them included treachery.

As Aiden strode forward, the sound of his boots clanking along the stone floor stirred Falcon, but his mother didn't move an inch.

"My lord, what a pleasant surprise." Falcon welcomed in a cynical voice and inclined his head.

Aiden brushed past him and put himself in front of his mother's view. She didn't look up to him, for she never looked up to anyone. He broke the silence when he cleared his throat and she stood from beneath his shadow. It was then that their eyes met.

"You spoke with her about the masquerade, have you?" She hissed.

"I have." He replied evasively. He enjoyed testing her patience.

"Well?" She questioned, her eyebrow lifted into a sharp arc.

"What do you think happened, Mother?" he began leisurely, "She was angry. Once again she figured out that you were behind my restrictions, only this time she expressed her bitter feelings toward *me*. I'm sure that pleases you."

Merle smiled crookedly to confirm her satisfaction. She ran a jeweled hand through her ebony hair and adjusted the black snake she always carried close to her throat. It was a wild snake unless held by Merle, with its venom smile and flopping forked tongue. Aiden shrank from the hideous thing. Merle swung her dark eyes to Falcon, whose smile matched that of the snake.

"That explains it, Falcon." She announced and he nodded his agreement.

Aiden rolled his eyes and awaited his mother's explanation. *Speak already woman, so that I may be out of this tomb you call a chamber!*

"I felt the use of the Power in my castle. She has broken through." Her words were like a triumphant whip, "How did this come about? Hatred for me, I hope."

It was Aiden's turn to smile now. He lifted his chin to show his control once again and rocked on his heels before he granted her an answer.

"No, Mother, it happened when she expressed her hatred for *me*." His smile widened as the victory melted away from her face. "You see, Mother, she's used to the disappointment of you. Where as I, on the other hand, showed her kindness. She has genuine care for me—"

"It is because you have spoiled her and given her more than she deserves when she was meant for the dirt beneath our fists! That wasn't the initial intentions here!" She reproached. Her eyes were glowing with rage and her fists were clenched at her side. Aiden knew Merle wanted nothing more than to hit him. Yet she controlled her urge.

"I don't spoil her, Mother." Aiden huffed.

"Yes you do!"

"If it were up to you, Mia would be in a dungeon to never see the light of day!"

"If it suits my purpose—"

"You know that it doesn't." Aiden paused with his mother's behavior. She managed to look like a child throwing a temper tantrum if she couldn't win a disagreement. *It cannot be.*

He cocked his head to one side and widened his grin. This infuriated her, he knew, because she couldn't stand him either. "Mother, please tell me that you don't still cling to *that* grudge!"

Her face went red and her eyes narrowed. Falcon took a cautious step back from her. Realization dawned on him through his joy.

Could this woman, who prides herself on control and power, not overcome the memory of another woman!

"It's true then," Aiden stabbed her with his arrogant tone. "Your vengeance was quenched, or at least I had thought, with *her* death!"

Her hand coiled up at him and connected with a hard blow. This time she couldn't control her urge. His laughter evaporated into a growl, but he didn't dare strike her back in front of Falcon. He spit blood from the side of his mouth. "What's the matter, Mother, the truth hurts?"

"How dare you? I've given you everything you wanted! I handed you this kingdom and all of its power! You would be nothing if it wasn't for me." She hissed.

"I never asked for it, nor wanted it! You gave me your burden so that you can master some infallible plan away from watchful eyes! Take it back, for then I wouldn't have to hear *you*." He growled.

Falcon strode forward and placed himself between the two of them before Merle could rebut. "Perhaps we should focus on something else, shall we? Tell me about the girl's first experience with magic since we now know she is Mageborn."

Aiden's eyes never left his mother, but he felt the anger diminish slowly between them. Finally he was able to speak. He explained everything and stormed off not caring to discuss their reactions any longer.

Chapter Two

Mageborn

"My Child, you look horrible!" Nan flew to Mia's side urgently. She guided Mia to the large chair before the hearth and drew a blanket over her.

"I feel it too, Nan." Mia replied and shuttered inside of the coverlet.

"You poor thing, I'll tend to you at once." Nan made a swift movement to the door, but Mia stilled her with one hand.

"Please, stay with me, Nan."

The stout woman nodded, although the worry didn't leave her face. She pressed a cooling palm to her forehead. "You've no fever."

"You heard, I mean, you saw what happened, Nan?" Mia questioned, hoping she wouldn't be fearful around her.

"Aye, my little rose, I saw and heard." Nan replied softly.

"What's happening to me?" Mia cried out in frustration.

"There, there," Nan stroked her cheek, "It'll be alright. It is a gift from the Goddess, Danu," She began. Her eyes danced with enchantment. "You are a Mageborn, Mia."

"What is a Mageborn?" Mia asked bewildered.

"The Mageborns possessed the Elemental Rites. Some of them were born with the Power of Water, or Earth, and some with the Power of Air or Fire. The element lived in their blood, in their organs and in their souls. No wand, no incantations, and by no typical means of the Thaumaturi craft was needed."

"You speak as if they no longer exist, yet you've told me that I'm one of these Mageborns." Mia asked unable to understand.

"That's because I'd thought them extinct all accept the Elders. But the Elders are only a shade of what they were. All elements had abandoned them during the time of the tyranny. It is said that they were the last.

"I could see the magic within you, but I'd not fully understood until this day. I was born with a special ability as well, although it couldn't compare to the Power of a Mageborn. I'm what you call a Watcher, you see, but don't ya let anyone know I admitted to it." She giggled softly.

"A Watcher, what is that?" Mia asked resting her elbows on her knees with great inquisitiveness.

Nan chuckled a little and too leaned forward with joyous animation. "We Watchers can see magic as clear as you see a tree, even when the magic is as old as time, or suppressed. We were often called upon during the times of threat to aid the Sun Order in the searches for the ones who posses the Power. I never told you of this before, because I wasn't certain you were ready to know. So don't go and be upset with me. I was only trying to protect you." She said raising a stubby hand.

"I could never be upset with you! You're all I have, Nan." Mia looked down at her feet. She wondered to herself why Nan remained behind instead of using her gift where it was needed. But then again, she felt a selfish part of her happy that she didn't leave her.

"He disappointed you again, I know. But the Barbarian Nations' pride hasn't completely healed from the great war. Some have yet to be civilized and educated on reason. You need to be protected."

"What is this Power you speak of?" Mia question half enthralled and half leery.

Nan crinkled her nose and for an instant a chill seemed to affect her, but she regained her warm smile.

"It's a bit of a complicated matter," She began, "but I'll tell you a little, child." Nan paused and shook her head, "Not all of the Mageborns were saved from the seduction of their element. Years ago, when the Mageborns were plenty, some lost sight of their true purpose and in time their weaknesses consumed them. They used their Powers for personal gain. Some even went as far as raising the dead and summoning Demons.

"They turned their gifts, twisting them into something evil in which became known as the Power." Nan's eyes grew dark and distant, "These dark Mageborns, later called the Necromancers, destroyed our bonds with the Barbarian Nations in their obsession for control. The Barbarians understood nothing of magic and witnessed the ugly side during the invasion."

"Am I a dark Thaumaturi, Nan?" She asked self consciously." Perhaps that explains Jacob's attitude towards me."

Mia was aware that her guard didn't like her, and he stiffened into ice whenever they were together. She disliked him just the same, but it wouldn't be so if Jacob was civil in the first place. She supposed it even hurt a little when she saw him cringe with repugnance at the sight of her especially when she was quite taken with him the first time they met. She would never let *him* know that.

"Of course you aren't! Jacob is just a big goof who finds pleasure in nothing but battle and beer." Nan laughed and rushed to her side. "And no matter what anyone tries to tell you, not all magic is bad."

Mia, not completely clear, was happy to know at least someone cared enough for her. Nan stood and smiled down at her. Mia found herself looking back with such emotion that she could hardly swallow.

"Come now, Mia, it's almost dinner time. I'll leave you to wash up."

She paused casting her eyes to the corner of the room at a cluster of green illuminating beneath a lantern, "Caring for healing plants affirms our union with Danu. So be certain you care for them well."

Mia nodded and watched as Nan shut the door with Oxanna at her heals meowing softly. Quickly, Mia sprinkled the beautiful healing plants with water. Once she was through, she drifted onto her balcony with the blanket around her.

When Nan spoke of the evil, it wasn't foreign to Mia. She heard bits and pieces of that time from the gossips of the waiting women that served her. She also knew that her oldest brother, Ahriman, was banished for his involvement before she was born. Curiosity struck her more than once about him, but whenever she asked questions they were left unanswered. Even Nan was evasive. In time she grew tired of drawing blood from a stone and ceased to ask about him.

You have a gift beyond any simple Mageborn.

The whisper sang into her ears, or at least she thought she *heard* it. She spun around and saw no one lingering in her chamber. She spun back and cast her eyes into the twilight kissed sky.

Nothing. She gripped the edge of the balcony and looked down into the snow covered streets. The village was vacant.

Look from within your heart and not within your mind.

The sound was loud and sweet, femininely musical. Mia wasn't hearing the voice with her ears, but from within her. A methodic beat of wings came closer, so close that she had a sudden urge to duck. Then she saw it.

At first it was only a blotch in the sky, but as the wing-song grew louder, the blotch took form into a silvery white owl. With a shriek, the owl swooped down as if it were on the hunt, and landed on the balustrade of the balcony before her. She took a cautious step back and gasped.

Never before had she seen an owl so large and beautiful. It perched before her coated in silky layers of white and sparkling silver, fussing with its feathers until it was content. Eyes of gold and jade not quite animal and not quite mortal gleamed up at her.

Do not be frightened, Beauty.

Mia jumped back with sudden fascination. The creature could talk to her through its mind?

And please, Beauty, do not think of me as a creature. The owl cocked its head as if it were a mischievous child.

Mia felt her cheeks burn and she bowed humbly, "Forgive me, Great Owl. I shall call you what you will, if only you tell me what you are."

A rumble or a purr—maybe a little of both—that sounded much like laughter came from the owl. Mia arched her brows.

I am what I am, Beauty. In time you will understand why I have come to you. You needn't fear me for I am loyal to Danu. It's my voice you have heard in your solitude.

"I am not going crazy!" Mia exclaimed.

Nay, you are not. The owl sang delightfully. *You are not the last Mageborn.*

Others have been born this age. You are the Circle of the Goddess. Redeemers of the Seasons and the weapons of Danu.

"I don't understand—" The sound of the door slamming snatched Mia around.

Time to go, but I shall return.

When Mia looked over her shoulder, the owl was gone as if it was never there. She stomped through balcony arches to confront whoever dared enter her chambers uninvited.

Jacob was looming in front of her door sneering. His hands could easily fit themselves around her throat if he willed it, but she wouldn't shrink before him.

"You dare enter so boldly?" She spat and embraced herself as if she were totally naked before him, "I might not've been decent!".

"What have you been talking about with your old crone?" He said contemptuously.

"What are you talking about?" Mia sniffed.

Was he eavesdropping on their conversation? Mia raked her mind for something, anything. She couldn't allow Nan to receive punishment for her pressing curiosity. She stood her full posture fixing her gaze deeply on him. He shivered with disgust and focused his eyes anywhere but her face. He hated her.

"What I speak to my maid about is of no concern to you! I have the right to privacy!"

"I'm going to ask you one last time, wench. What did you and the old woman speak of that kept her within the chambers so long?" Jacob commanded.

Mia didn't back down. The newborn moonlight swept across the room drawing a line between them. His face and pale hair glistened between the combs of light. He was a fearsome form but she would knock him down from his pedestal of barbarism promptly.

"Need I remind you of your position here in my brother's castle? Don't overstep your boundaries with me," she huffed. Jacob reared his head back in sadistic laughter.

Mia drew her breath in and slapped him. The blow only fueled his cruel pleasure. He caught her second swing firmly in his grip. His laughter came to an abrupt stop. His grip tightened sending a shooting pain up the length of her arm.

"Let me go, Jacob," she ordered, "I mean it."

"I'm no fool," he hissed, "I'm watching you, girl!" He threw her arm down and spun to leave, but Mia surprised herself and took hold of his sleeve.

"Tell me, Jacob," she began, "Why do you hold such a stupid grudge against me?"

"I am your bodyguard," he replied venomously, "Not your lap dog." He tore away from her and slammed through the door.

I am no fool, either, Mia thought. *Your grand words are hiding something and in no time I will find the truth behind them.*

Jacob hurried from the wench's chamber before he decided to beat her senseless. He never before felt the urge to strike a woman, but she held so much arrogance, he couldn't stomach it. If he believed in hitting a woman, she would've been a bloody mess a long time ago. She was a spoiled brat who was never taught to properly hold her tongue. Had she shown such disrespect in his lands, she would've been put in her suitable place. But he wasn't in his lands. He was stuck here by the order of his Emperor to maintain a solid ally in Thaumatur.

The old woman maid was up to something, he knew it. And despite his bitterness, he *was* responsible for the girl's safety. He would see to it.

He loathed the *magicians* and their ridiculous ways. Everywhere he turned someone cried about prophecies or collected oddities for their ridiculous little potions. Talk of Demons rising from the Underworld and the end of times weighed heavily on his brain. And to top it all off, he was stuck guarding this annoying wench who relished in materialistic things basing power on beauty. She wouldn't soften him. Every time he looked at her, he saw nothing more than a *magician*. When he decided to settle down, *if* he decided to settle down, it would be with one of his own who would find value in moral things.

The servants were occupied with dinner preparations so the corridor was vacant from any distractions. There was no time better than this to head for the upper library. He opened the arched gold trimmed door and fled through the rows of bookshelves to a secluded table that had a tube of ink in the center of it. The room was soundless and empty, and for the first time in many days, Jacob was able to release some of the tension in his neck and shoulders. Yet the solitude didn't wipe away his anger completely. He needed to divert the rage in some way.

He hated feeling so bitter. He hated this foreign land. Anger was always a strong emotion within him, but it evolved into something ugly. Something that he wasn't. He couldn't even try to be civil with *her.*

He reached in his pocket and pulled out a piece of parchment, grabbed the quill, and began to write. Once he finished the letter, he rolled it up and stamped it with his personal seal. The Barbarian Emperor needed to open his eyes and put things in order once and for all.

Jacob flung the chair from beneath him and stormed back out to the corridor. One of the tower's maids cowered with the sudden abruptness of Jacob's emergence, but managed a small smile. Her name was something like, Eve or Eva. What did it matter anyhow? He knew she was watching him longingly, despite his obvious rejection. It matter not to these women in Thaumatur. They were free with their love and relied on their love potions to get them what they desired. He found himself angry again and thinking of Miarosa. *Damn that* magician!

In one rapid motion, Jacob grabbed the servant's arm and dragged her off to a vacant chamber in the tower. Before the door was even shut, he had her firm against the wall, kissing her, grabbing her tiny breasts, and burying his groin between her legs with all the rage that fueled him. The servant clung to him with long awaited hunger and tugged at his breeches with clumsy fingers. She hissed provocative words in his ears, but he didn't care to make out what she said. He was limp and nothing could rouse him. His forceful manner was driven by hatred and not from the heat of his manhood. Suddenly, he pushed himself away and dropped the servant to the ground in a thud. She looked up at him with a fire that didn't die when she hit the floor. She wanted more of him, but he wiped his mouth and left her alone with her blood racing.

He had another way of releasing his anger. He would speak to Aiden and his Demon-loving mother about Nancy Prall, the oh-so-ever-loving maid.

Aiden was lounging on his throne when he found him, but he wasn't his usual drunken self. The golden goblet sat beside him still full with white wine. His eyes were red and narrow fixed on something beyond the invisible. Jacob cleared his throat to draw Aiden's aimless mind back to the now. Aiden forced a thin smile and adjusted himself to converse and nodded. "Jacob."

"My lord," Jacob hissed, "If I may have a word with you in private."

Chapter Three

The Unveiling

Nan tossed an arm full of logs on the cooking fires and wiped the sweat from her brow. The cooks were almost through with the dinner feast, so she decided to take a moment's rest on the kitchen porch. She inhaled the cool spiced air and leaned back against the stone wall. She couldn't help but to think of Mia.

Mia was always restrained from having a normal life. She was never permitted to leave the castle and was forbidden to have friends. Sure she had everything materialistic a girl could desire, but it was meaningless to her. She was a precious dove caged in the middle of some controversy she was clueless to.

Nan took great care in nurturing Mia from childhood, teaching her the jobs of women, and planting the seeds of love and kindness within her that, with each passing year, flourished with her outer beauty. The princess was special, born utterly strong with magic. The aura flowed around her in blends of all the elements. It was hard to determine from which her magic would ignite until this day. It was something Nan was sure the Queen Mother awaited, despite her ignorance to the girl's desire to see love in Merle's eyes.

She cast her eyes to the twilight sky. Another night before the feast. Jacob had ruined Mia's first chance to be free of this place. What was Aiden thinking placing such trust in a prejudice Barbarian?

"Nancy," a servant boy whispered from behind the porch door, "The Queen Mother and the King request your presence in the receiving hall."

He was a lanky little boy, no more than six or seven, with a patch of brown stubble over his head. He would never know a good life and if he made it to manhood, he would still be here, trapped in the duties of a piss boy. Nan felt she was lucky in her duties compared to the other servants. She placed a hand on the boy's shoulder and thanked him.

The request came as no surprise. She knew it would only be a matter of time before they would send for her. Things were getting too wrinkly and the possessiveness of the young princess was closing in like a hungry viper.

Nan strode through the kitchens into the foyer and pushed through the side doors of the hall. She curtsied before she even looked at the Queen Mother. Merle's eyes were cold and her smile was a frozen tight line. She was garbed in a black chiffon gown and upon her ebony head she wore a crown of silver and black roses. Her posture was straight in the throne giving her a much taller appearance than usual and her snake coiled the length of her arm resting its head just above Merle's heart.

Of course the cold-blooded beast fancied the nearness of a freezing heart! Nan bit her lower lip in scolding of her silent vile thought.

Aiden sat in the highest throne beside Merle. Sermino, Aiden's advisor—a dark and gentle man who was much too good for the likes of the Maladintos—stood tall in folds of amethyst and gold a step below Aiden. To the far right of Aiden, the Barbarian Jacob leaned against a pillar.

"Nancy Prall," Merle spoke coldly, "It was brought to my attention that you have served here in Falias for nearly two generations. Is that correct?"

"Yes my lady, but it's not by mistake. I've willingly stayed on even after I was given my leave," Nan replied in a strong but respectful voice.

"I see," Merle replied "And why is that?"

Merle brought her hands up to her lap, intertwined her fingers, and leaned forward. The snake slithered its way to the base of her neck. Nan turned from the sight of the creature and met eyes with Jacob. His face was always imprinted with a scowl, but she saw a triumphant glint in his hard eyes. For a moment, Nan hesitated in answering. But she took a deep breath and lifted her chin proudly.

"Because I wished to look after the Princess and because it's an honor for me to serve my King and the Queen Mother."

"Ah," Merle pressed back into her throne and gripped the jeweled armrests, "Very well spoken, Nancy."

"You see, servant, we feel that you've done a great service already. We would like to grant you a reward as well as your freedom," The King interceded.

"The Majesties are most gracious, but I'm quite happy in servicing the Princess."

From the corner of her eye, she saw Jacob shift his jaw with annoyance.

"The Princess will soon be matched for marriage. She does not require your services any longer," Merle confirmed coldly. "Now, first thing in the morning, I will arrange for your transport to a cottage just outside of Tania and before the harbor of Murias in the providence of Rose Hill Gardens. It's quite lovely there, within the cusps of the spring and fall climate, and I know you will just adore it—"

"Mother!" Mia strode passed Nan in the mist of flowing violet sparkles to the foot of the throne. The anger twitched around the young girl's lips and she planted her hands firmly on her hips. Jacob glared at her, but she didn't yield as most women would. Merle darted upright.

"You dare intrude with such insolence?" Merle's voice echoed throughout the high-ceiling hall.

"How dare you make decisions for my woman?" Mia argued.

"Nancy isn't your woman, girl," Merle looked down her nose at Mia with even more bitterness than Jacob, "She was a servant to your father long before you were born. Stop being so childish and selfish and let this fine servant be free to live the rest of her days out in peace!"

"Don't try to turn it around on me, Mother! If Nan wishes to remain with me, then that's exactly where she'll stay," Mia spat and took hold of Nan's hand guiding her out of the throne room.

Nan stopped Mia in her flight. She placed a hand on her cheek and whispered, "My little rose, you mustn't go against your mother. I'll always honor the queen's wishes."

"Nan, no," Mia whispered breathlessly, "You cannot leave me."

"And I never will. If ever you need me, I'll be there for you, no matter how far apart we are," Nan promised her putting a mask of courage on her face. *No matter the case my little girl...*

Inside, she knew that she was losing the only daughter she ever had. But Mia was playing at a dangerous game with her rebelliousness.

"She will be here for one more night, Mia," Aiden was at their side before Nan even knew he moved, "You cannot go against Mother."

"I don't want her to cast Nan out as if she is meaningless!" Mia exclaimed.

"The queen has offered me a nice place to call my own. She's not casting me out," Nan cooed, "It's a generous gift."

"You wish to leave?" Mia asked ill-concealing her disappointment.

"I'll go and be content, Mia," Nan lied for the sake of the girl.

Mia nodded, biting her lip in defiance and swayed her eyes toward her Barbarian guard. A look of pure contempt shadowed her face. The air was stagnant and the tension was so thick, that even Merle shifted restlessly. Mia shoved by the King and headed straight for Jacob. She could hardly meet his face without arching her head back.

"You're behind this, aren't you?" her words were short and low, "Aren't you?" she then shouted.

Jacob said nothing. He just glared.

"Let us go to the dining hall. Dinner is nearly finished," Aiden rushed forward putting himself between them before it grew uglier than it already was. "We have some honored guests with us today."

The two of them ignored the King's words and battled each other silently.

"You are a cruel man!" Mia wheeled around shooting daggers at her mother before leaving.

"You are dismissed, servant!" Merle growled and retreated through the back of the hall.

Nan downcast her eyes and took leave with great relief, but not for the child who had so little to desire in the years to come.

The aromas of dinner filled the corridor, but Mia lost her hunger. The guests would just have to dine without her company. She couldn't stomach to look at Jacob while she ate tonight.

Oh, how one good thing came from Aiden's restrictions. I will have no one to stop me when I confront that Barbarian!

She hastened to her chambers but the corridors were not entirely empty. She felt a shadow upon her back and the heat of another's stare. With annoyance she whirled, but stopped before she spoke with the harshness of her tongue. Her cheeks flushed when she saw him, his hair so fair and thick, and his eyes sparkling like ice-blue diamonds. He wore green and gold robes, a tunic of black and charcoal breeches that accented his long muscular legs. He was a head taller than she and she blushed even further with the memory of his strong arms around her.

Vastadon DeLucible was no prince, but a political advisor for the House's Viscount. He was well liked among all who he met, despite the fact that the blood in his veins were of both Thaumaturi and Barbarian. She met him one year ago and the connection between them struck like a bolt of lightening. Vastadon stretched his arm out to her and she took his hand without hesitation. Mia often prayed that Aiden would match her to Vastadon for marriage, but her brother's grip on her had tightened of late.

"My lady, what sends you away from the dining hall? Have you not missed me as I missed you?" He said with a deep and smooth voice.

His smile was wide and it revealed an endless row of brilliant white teeth. Mia couldn't deny him anything, and suddenly her anger dropped into the bottomless well, forgotten.

"But of course I've missed you, my lord," She quipped.

They were walking now, her arm through his, in the direction in which she was running away from a moment ago. He smelled of fresh spring when she playfully leaned her head against his shoulder, his breath hot upon her brow.

"I truly hope to see you at the feast of the New Moon. I plan to steal you away underneath the starlit sky, beneath the apple blossoms of the Gorias orchards," He promised.

"I'll not be attending the masquerade. My brother fears for my safety at this time to go anywhere," Mia said softly.

"You are jestng, my lady, aren't you?" Vastadon exclaimed.

"Nay, my lord, I wouldn't jest about something like this."

"It would be absurd for the King to leave you home when you would be much safer by his side."

"I know, but he doesn't see it that way."

Vastadon stilled them in their flight and scooped her hand in his. He pressed his lips against her knuckles and fixed his eyes on her. "I will that I may have a word later with your brother. Perhaps he'll see reasoning through the eyes of an officiator."

Mia nodded but Vastadon caught her up in his arms and brushed his lips against hers. It was a small lingering kiss, almost punishing. He drew back, his face alight with hunger. Her mouth still tingled from where his lips touched.

"You've stolen my heart, Princess," He whispered in her ear.

She smiled, unable to free her tongue. He didn't wait for an answer. Instead he guided her to the dining hall.

The high board was filled with guests, all except Merle. Beside Aiden, sat a Barbarian garbed in elegant furs and beads. He was crowned with an onyx and gold circlet that matched the gauntlets he wore at his wrists. Two less elaborately dressed Barbarians sat beside him wearing simple vests of fur. A large golden plate embossed with a thorn-crowned panther was pinned on the left side of each of their vests. Their manes were fair with a hint of red fancied with several scattered braids of their heritage. All three men wore studs at their chins like she had seen on Jacob.

Aiden's eyes locked onto hers and quickly rose to summon her,

37

showing no indication that he remembered the confrontation of Nan's fate or the disagreement that he had shared with her in the late afternoon.

Vastadon escorted her with haste to Aiden's side and pulled out her chair. The dining hall's décor was rich with sapphire candelabra's and satin drapes curved the walls with exotic elegance. Indeed these guests were of great importance for such a reception.

Platters of honey dipped duck, hard cheese, and bread were being served to the lower tables. Servant maids ran to and fro with pitchers of cold milk and wine, and one young boy was dishing out apples imported from Gorias drenched in a cream sauce sprinkled with cinnamon and sugar. Flutes and harps added a soothing stroke to the atmosphere.

"Miarosa, I'd like you to meet Emperor Aldrich Hilliard of the Barbarian Nations. He has brought his people to civilization as no other ruler could!" Aiden bragged, but the big man paid no mind and plunged his hand toward Mia.

"Very pleased to meet you, my lord. I hope you enjoy your stay here among the bitter cold of our kingdom," She delicately placed her hand in his.

He lifted her hand to his lips and she felt the tickle of his mustache. "It's truly an honor to meet such a lovely girl and with great spirit too!" he said in a husky voice, "And I must say that it is wonderful weather here, for soon in my lands, when Beletene comes, I'll be yearning to return here for refreshment."

The men laughed at the Barbarian Emperor's humor, but inside Mia's head, questions raised about the meaning of this dinner. Despite the handsomeness of this stranger, her brother couldn't possibly think of matching her with this man who could be her own sire! She looked at Vastadon who was smiling along with the others. He kicked his chair out from beneath him and embraced Aldrich firmly.

"Welcome back, Father!" he said joyously.

Father? Mia almost choked on her wine. *How come he was slow to tell me that he was son to the Emperor of the Barbarians?*

Vastadon didn't return his attention back on her, but it was all the same. Unlike her brother, she had become quite good at obscuring her expressions. Yet this was beyond a surprise.

The Emperor was taller than his son and his hair a bit redder. Vastadon preferred to keep his chin clean from hair and studs. Aside from that, Mia could see the resemblance now that they stood so close. They shared the same handsome nose that fell perfect in proportion with their high cheekbones. She shifted her eyes down and picked at her food with a strong ear. She'd always given her brother reason to believe she cared nothing for the talk of men. It gave the men ease to speak politically while she was within earshot.

"It seems that you have become quite a demand in these lands, son! I'm proud that I can rely on at least one of my kin to work for peace!" Aldrich said, "Come Vastidrich, and sit here beside me at table so that we may talk of the developing things in our new worlds!"

"I'm now called Vastadon, for the name is a compromise to make both of my kinsmen comfortable," He replied and fell into the seat between Aiden and Aldrich, "But I'll not deny my birth name from your lips, Father."

"Catchy name," Aldrich raised an eyebrow, "I'll be joining you and Aiden at the feast of the—full moon, is it?"

"Nay," Vastadon chuckled, "It's the feast of the *New* Moon."

"Nevertheless, I shall show my interest in the Thaumaturi customs and quench my curiosity all at once," Aldrich replied and shifted his eyes to the entrance. "Will he be going as well?"

Mia followed the Emperor's line of sight. Jacob made his entrance and met eyes with Aldrich. There was no sign of joy in Jacob's eyes as he strode to the high board.

"Jacob will not be going, Aldrich. He is guarding the princess in my absence," Aiden added gnawing on a piece of bread.

Forgotten resentment gushed back into Mia, but she held her tongue and silently prayed that Vastadon could speak plainly to Aiden and charm his favor.

Vastadon…the son of royalty…prince regent born to an emperor.

Possibly a marriage match between them wasn't so inconceivable after all.

"My Lord, I didn't know you were here. It's good to see you," Jacob's monotone voice drew her mind back to the table.

"But of course, Jacobane. You look well. It seems that Aiden has treated both of my kin with kindness," Aldrich replied and embraced Jacob in the same manner as he embraced his son.

Aiden shot his head up in confusion and looked from Jacob to Aldrich. "I beg your pardon," Aiden said smoothly, "Did you say both of your kin?"

A hush fell over the hall and all attention was fixed on the head table's conversation. Even the harpers halted their sweet melodies. Mia pretended to pay no mind, but she was just as curious. Aldrich interrupted the silence with a hearty laugh and slapped Jacob on his back.

"I cannot believe you didn't tell Aiden, Jacobane! Seriously, you've gone far with this one track mind of yours!"

"It isn't important. I've no such privilege in these lands, nor do I want them," Jacob huffed.

"This here is my younger brother, Aiden, although he has forfeited his rights to the throne if by some chance I would pass to the world of souls prematurely. You see, Jacobane meddles in battle and military issues and shows no interest in sitting high upon any throne. The High Prince is a great commander of armies, I must admit. He keeps the Tribes at bay in Vansant Summit behind the great wall. The Clawclan and the Gravens are only two of the few uncivilized that has taken a liking to Jacobane where as they have displayed their dislike for me."

"It's only because you have insisted on changing their way of living. They're happy with the way things are on their side of the wall," Jacob rebutted in his cool voice.

"I've not forced an entirely new lifestyle on them, Brother. I've simply set a few laws. We cannot allow our kind to turn on each other and rape innocent women, burning their homes down from beneath them while their men are away from their keeps," Aldrich said in annoyance, despite his remaining smile.

"Only few are so bold," Jacob growled, "And I've kept things under control while I'm *at* my keep to manage the wall."

"A few too many occurrences," Aldrich said, "I can see that you have lack of understanding. Perhaps it is better that you chose to hand my son the throne."

"I find the welfare of my people more important than playing a game of tug of war with your half-blood for power."

"You dare!" Vastadon jolted upright and looked down on Jacob angrily.

Mia swallowed hard and her insides tensed, but to her relief, Aldrich interceded.

"Come, Vastidrich, sit" he said calmly, "I've not come all this way to see you and your uncle quarrel. Let us enjoy our healthy feast here in this beautiful hall."

After a moment, Vastadon eased back down. Jacob was sitting on the other side of Mia, where she could easily slap his face for his ill manner. She smiled at the thought. Unfortunately, she could not act upon it before all of the court.

"Tell me of the Tribes from behind the wall, Brother. Are they content, or do I have to deal with another mess when I return home?" Jacob hissed between clenched teeth.

"There has been no change in the activity around your wall or I would've been informed. The Gravens and Clawclan have aided us from their side and prevented many battles. It was a great blessing from our Gods that you and these two Tribes have aligned yourselves. I don't know how you managed to get them to sign a treaty, but it was quite clever anyhow. The Tuskans are where our problems lie, but they no longer are a threat to us because of your intelligence." Aldrich said proudly.

"I did nothing so special." Jacob said flatly.

Aldrich said nothing more, and turned his attention to his meal. The talk between the brothers attracted the entire hall's silence. Mia was in awe at how smoothly the emperor handled his ill mannered brother. Aldrich continuosly complimented Jacob, yet he was the one who behaved like a spoiled child.

"So, my lady, you won't be attending this great feast in the Fall Kingdom?" Aldrich asked Mia, after he finished his food.

"It's my liege's wish that I remain behind by reason of security," Mia answered.

"How is it, Aiden, that you don't feel guilt in leaving behind your lovely unwedded sister while you trollop in the night's festivities. I believe that she's of a marriageable age. Don't you think it's time to match her?" Aldrich questioned.

"Of course I've been considering several suitors, but she is very valuable to me. I mustn't make a haste decision. My younger sister Arabella is Queen in Findias and has bore two sons. Aside from the fact that the princes are too young for marriage, they are too close in kin. King Valance of Gorias is childless. That leaves only the Murians of Spring, there are three princes to think on there, but my mother doesn't wish to unite with them. I've had offers from the House officials, but it's untraditional that a princess should marry one not of royal blood." Aiden shook his head, "Then you have the Dukes and the Landowners, not to mention a gypsy king from the Rose Hill Garden providence," Aiden crinkled his nose at that.

Mia shifted in her seat uncomfortably in hopes to remind the men that she was indeed present. How could they discuss her future right in from of her as if she was invisible!

"Well, perhaps your mother would be pleased to match her with a Barbarian prince, if not one of my own kin," Aldrich rubbed his chin.

Mia's restlessness melted and her heart sailed with those words. Vastadon was close as kin to Aldrich as one could get. She looked up and Vastadon captured her with his jovial eyes. She could hardly suppress a smile let alone the excitement she felt at the idea of being his wife.

Aiden cleared his throat and said, "We shall discuss the matter later, when Mother is well enough for an audience. She decided to take another journey and won't be going to Gorias, although she hasn't told me where she is to go. Typical of her."

Aiden took a gulp of wine to camouflage the bitter attitude he had towards Merle, "She claims that she needs solace away from the kingdom and its demands. I, at first, didn't think it wise that she leaves, but I believe that Jacob will be quite able to handle the kingdom in my absence. He has become one of my most trusted companions."

"Ah," Aldrich replied and glanced at his brother sideways, "Perhaps you've come around to acceptance better than I thought, Jacobane."

"Aiden doesn't rely on the tricks of light to make a decision," Jacob murmured from the side of his mouth before drinking his wine.

"Well, let us say that we've overcome our different views and learned to get along quite well. He is indeed my sister's bodyguard. A task that I don't take lightly," Aiden quickly recovered but Jacob frowned.

"Who looks after Vansant Summit during my absence?" Jacob persisted.

Mia never saw Jacob this adamant about anything before. She almost felt sorry for him. Why should she? Did he not deserve what he gets? She gritted her teeth. He would certainly share no compassion with her or with Nan, for that matter. She also noticed that Jacob's conviction was riding on his older kinsman's nerves.

"It's left in the hands of Fershius Cornict," Aldrich commented.

Jacob nearly spat out all of the wine from his mouth. "You've left command to that murderer!" Jacob thundered, "And you've not sent reinforcements to see how my people fair?"

"You are overreacting, Jacobane. You have maintained the wall for a long time before your leave. I'm sure the Tribes don't even know you are gone."

Jacob slammed his fist against the table and pierced his brother with small eyes of rage. "Have you forgotten what Duke Fershius did? And you left our sister's wellbeing in the hands of that man?"

"Sasha and her children are well and *Brother* Fershius has converted to the religion of our Chaplains. He's been absolved of whatever crimes he committed and took on the sufferance of penance when he joined the Brotherhood. I believe that a man is worthy of a second chance. Besides, Sasha suggested his name despite all that he has done to her. As far as I am concerned, if she is willing to forgive him, then we can learn to also," Aldrich replied in ignorance to Jacob's outburst.

"He's a traitor to his own people and now you ask that I trust him! The man who left Sasha widowed with three children!"

"He's changed. That is that," Aldrich continued, "You must trust in me, Jacobane."

"I must return to Vansant Summit and the wall before the Tribes who do not care for peace gain advantage on us," Jacob continued forcefully.

Aldrich put down his cup heavily and drew in his breath. "You'll not rest until our words grow with anger, will you, Brother?" Aldrich shook his head, "You are *needed* here. Aiden has become dependant on you and so has the Princess. Until I say further, you'll remain here."

Jacob opened his mouth but Aiden was quick to respond.

"Are you not happy here, Jacob? Have I provided you with less than the best comforts?" he whined.

"I've no complaint but my people are surely yearning for my return and protection," Jacob said flatly.

"The Princess needs you too. I cannot make my time available to protect her in the way she should be protected."

"Sermino is a great protector. He could do my duty just as well," Jacob continued and glanced at Sermino.

Mia would be overjoyed to have Sermino as her guard. He was as gentle as he was wise, and he'd been a loyal bodyguard and advisor to Lucian. His dark-gold eyes twinkled when they fell on her, but his expression remained stern and compliant to whatever Aiden decided.

"Sermino hasn't the time, for he is at my side always. I cannot spare him and you know this. Who am I to trust in your leave?" Aiden was just about whimpering.

"Forgive me Brother. You all seem to have forgotten that I *am* here," Mia spoke against her better judgment. "And I see no problem with Jacob's request. Let him go." She waved her hand toward the door.

"You say this because you dislike him, for whatever reason. You know nothing," Aiden snapped.

"I don't deny that I've been unhappy with Jacob, but since we now know that he is High Prince and protector of this great wall then we should let him go."

"I needn't you to defend me, girl!" Jacob growled at her.

"I'm not defending you. What is right is right. And to be rid of you would be an added benefit!" She reproached.

"Jacobane!" Aldrich bellowed, "You dare speak to a lady this way! You embarrass me!" He slammed his fist on the table and darted to his feet. His eyes were on fire as he bore them into his younger brother.

Jacob returned the gaze unflinchingly. "She's nothing to me, Brother, but a nuisance!"

"It matters not to me what the boar thinks!" Mia jabbed a finger in the direction of Jacob.

Aiden raised a hand and shook his head. "Enough with the two of you! Mia, since Mother has retreated to her chambers unwell, I'll need you to call your women once you're through with feasting. Have them prepare baths and beds for these men. They have traveled long and I will not have them insulted by poor hospitality especially here where we are looked upon highly for the care of our visitors."

"As you wish, Brother. I'll make certain Lynn sees to the proper care of our guests." she stood and inclined her head to the men at the high board. "I bid you all good night. I'm exhausted and wish to seek my bed early. It was a pleasure, Emperor Aldrich, to make your acquaintance." She curtsied and made her way to leave.

Jacob followed her as he always did to see her safely to her chambers. *Danu forbids if I have a private moment in my anger! As if an attacker could make way through the sentries at the gate and safely into the corridors of the spell protected castle to bring harm to me!*

"What kind of duty is this?" Jacob mumbled. "I'm nothing more than a puppy at the heels of a spoilt *magician*!"

Mia wheeled about and felt the sourness spread across her lips. He was trying her patience, that boar. His cold blue eyes focused on her for the briefest second before he averted them. He acted as if he would catch the disease of magic if he looked too long into the eyes of a Thaumaturi.

"Stop that!" she yelled.

"Move forward, I haven't the time for delay!" he said giving her a tug.

"You always call me a *magician*! It's improper and prejudice. One word to my brother and you—"

"He hasn't the power. I don't abide by your kind's laws!" he interrupted drawing the attention of the servants.

"Is everything alright, my lady?" Lynn strode from one of the quarter rooms.

Her face was fairly shadowed by the dimness of the corridor, but Mia knew that sleek voice anywhere. She could see enough of the woman's lusty eyes flicker over Jacob as if he were a piece of meat. She refused to tell Lynn the details of her falling-out with Jacob. She wasn't about to give Lynn the satisfaction of spreading gossip to the other women.

"Nothing is wrong, Lynn," Mia began in a stern tone. "Have my women prepare four guest chambers and baths with oils for the lords of the Barbarian Nations. They're almost done with their feasting and will be ready to bed for their journey was long and trying."

Lynn nodded and said with a sarcastic smile. "Are you to prepare the Lord Vastadon's comforts?"

Mia sneered at Lynn's suggestive remark. The woman pushed her limits.

"No, Lynn," She replied so uncharacteristically bitter it made the slave shrink. "I'm retiring to my chambers for the night. Once you have called on the ladies, I would like for *you* to come to my chambers and settle me."

"As you wish, my lady," Lynn replied boldly. "But you don't wish for Nan to attend you, my lady?"

"Not on this night, Lynn. I wish for you and don't send Eve in your place either. I'm not up for idle chit chat tonight," Mia said sharply and then headed for her own chambers.

A few hours later, long after Lynn had come and gone, Nan came to her door. Quickly the old woman pressed a finger to her lips and brushed by her with a bundle tucked neatly beneath one of her stubby arms.

"I'll take my leave at dawn's first light, child. I wanted to give you something before I go," Nan whispered.

To Mia, those words were the most horrible thing she ever heard. Tears streamed down her face, and her stomach was hollow. Nan pulled a handkerchief from her pocket and tenderly rubbed her cheeks.

"I don't know how I'll go on," Mia threw her arms around the round woman.

"This isn't goodbye, my little rose. We'll cross paths again," she squeezed her. "I'll do you better away from Falias."

Nan handed her the bundle. Mia unraveled the thick wool with shaking fingers. Within the folds, she saw the gleam of a sword. The golden hilt, bejeweled with four ambers and silver knots, was beautiful and looked to be made merely for the eye to admire. The sword vibrated softly beneath her touch sending a humming song to her ears. It was in the likeness of the owl's voice from earlier, but instead of hearing words, she felt energy. The owl, Mia thought, was more of dream. This was solid within her grip, bonding with her spirit. She turned her bewildered eyes to Nan.

"This sword must be worth a fortune, Nan. I cannot accept this." She pushed it back. Nan stilled her hand and grew serious. It was as if the veil of some divine wisdom fell upon her.

"This belongs to you, and no other. Can't you feel its connection within your grasp, child? You must accept it and let no one know of it," Nan demanded.

"I don't understand." Mia whispered.

"You will, Mia, when the time is right." Nan answered quickly and pulled her into her arms, "And that time isn't now. Tuck it away like a lost treasure and forget you have it. The Sword of Light will Call you when its use is necessary. You must never use it otherwise, for I fear it'll taint you. I must go now, but remember, I'm always here for you. You can find me in the Rose Hill Gardens."

"Nan," Mia lightly touched her hand, "I wish to give you a gift as well, so that you remember me."

Mia reached down and cradled the sleeping Oxanna. She kissed her gently on the forehead and rubbed beneath the rumbling beauty's chin. She smiled and handed Oxanna to her. Nan gasped and her eyes watered with tears. She shook her head in protest.

"I cannot take her from you. You love her so." Nan whispered.

"As you do. She will keep you company in your lonely home and remind you of me." Mia smiled knowing Nan would love Oxanna's companionship, "I want her to live in a happy home. A place of love not sorrow. Please, take her with you."

Nan nodded and took Oxanna in her arms. "Thank you. It's the most wondrous gift anyone could give me. I must go." Nan paused, "I love you, my little rose."

She gave Mia one last squeeze and left the chamber and Mia with her own tears.

CHAPTER FOUR

The Arrangement

After Jacob escorted Mia to her chambers for the night, he couldn't bring himself back to the hall right away. He wandered out into the cold and planted his feet deep in the snow, overlooking the ice crackled sea that separated him from his homeland. What would it take for Aldrich to see that his time here in this foreign and strange land was done?

If peace is what the lands wished for, so be it. He had no disagreement with it even though his prejudice views were obvious. Now it didn't seem to matter. Not even the arrogant ways of the princess could stray his attention from such apprehension. All that he wished for, all that he needed was to return home. And Sasha…oh poor Sasha is faced with the command of the very traitor of the worst kind who left his sister's children fatherless. *Yet she forgave him.*

Jacob felt a stream of warm liquid flow from in between his fingers. He hadn't realized he'd clenched his fist so tightly that he drew his own blood from the jagged ancestor ring he wore.

Duke Fershius Cornict came from a reputable Barbarian family, a civilized life, and his fortune was boundless. Yet all of his luck didn't win him the hand of Emperor Luthros Hilliard's daughter in marriage.

Fershius fell madly in love with Sasha before she was married, but the duke's strange beliefs were looked down upon by the late Emperor. So Luthros betrothed Sasha to a Barbarian King, Harrick Sylvinick of the Minnisoul Providence, as an answer to Fershius' request. With this, Fershius went mad, leaving the comforts of his golden life and disappeared.

Six years after, a band of Tuskans invaded the Minnisoul Providence, the Duke among them, and murdered the King. The Tuskans retreated once they realized their defeat, but Fershius didn't flee with them. Instead, he clung to the bloody throne of the murdered King, weeping like a child and professing his love for Sasha. At this point, Aldrich was the crowned emperor, and he rested the authority of punishment upon Sasha. She couldn't bring herself to call an execution, so she sentenced him to life imprisonment. Had Luthros lived to see that day, he would've put Fershius down like a sick animal.

Luthros despised the Thaumaturi and taught Jacob to never trust or accept them. A memory flickered in the back of his mind from his childhood….

The tall grass swayed gently alongside several patches of jeweled wildflowers beneath the blue skies of the broad valley just outside of Vhladic. It was over, the great war of the dark Thaumaturi, yet the blood of a thousand Barbarians tainted the valley, and even further along the coast of the Barbarian Nations.

A tall Barbarian man, crowned with onyx in a fur robe that danced around his ankles, stood on a mountain that overlooked the ruins. His face was carved with lines of worry and anger and his white beard was braided with sliver beads. His long hair was weaved into a thick plait that fell midway down his back. A young boy clung to his hand tightly, his eyes as hard as stone. The big man squeezed the boy's hand and glanced down at him.

"Remember what you see here, my young son." Luthros Hilliard said to Jacob, "For when I die and leave my empire to your brother, he will need you to remind him of this day. Aldrich is weak-minded. He fights for a world that will never exist."

Jacob nodded, but he didn't lift his gaze to his father. He stared down beyond the ravine at something illuminating beneath the sun. It was a blood tainted sword strewn beside a cluster of dark specks. Luthros growled and slammed his sword against the craggy earth, but it didn't draw his son's attention back to him. The dark specks, crows,

49

flapped away shrieking in protest to the clamor. They rose into the sky like a funnel, leaving behind the remnants of two dead women face down and stripped of their entire garb.

"Look what they've done!" Luthros thundered, "Thaumaturi. The embodiment of greed and immorality. They are filthy magicians, who care not what they do to the innocence of women and children, even to their own, so long as they can conquer foreign soil with their Demons." Luthros paused and lowered his body to his son's side, "Peace will never be, my son! Never, no matter how Aldrich wishes for it. You must protect our people from them and whisper in your brother's ear when he is emperor! Magic is evil unless it comes from our own chaplains, the true followers of the Trinity of Gods."

His eyes were wide as he looked into his son's expressionless face.

"I shall remember, Father," The boy replied vaguely, "I shall not let him forget what the magicians have done."

The corner of Jacob's eye stung with the threat of a tear. He set his jaw and replaced the memory's pungency with anger. He studied his signet ring, a jagged thorn crowning a panther. The thorn represented his mother's family. The panther was of his father's family, a rapid and stealthy force, with keen eyes and a sense of honor.

Fragments of his younger life fluttered back into his mind of a time when he was a young adolescent. Aldrich, because he was twenty-one years older than Jacob, had cared for him, taught him all the skills of battle and took him under his wing like a father. Aldrich *had* been the only father Jacob knew. Luthros was more of a respected pragmatist and Jacob was his thirsty pupil, until the day his father died from a festering plague that swept through the imperial city of Vhladic induced by the magic the Thaumaturi left behind with their defeat. Yet Aldrich was driven into a passion for peace and even fell in love with a *magician* despite their father's ill fate.

Aldrich told him that not all magic was bad and if it hadn't been for the good side of that very magic, the tyranny of the dark *magicians* would've over run the Barbarian Nations until there was nothing left. Jacob knew better. When the era of the Thaumaturi fell, it wasn't the end of the poor Barbarian people's suffering. Jacob had seen too much of what magic did to the people of his lands and the children who had suffered, starved, died...

No...I will never forget, Father, and I'll never change my mind over it. My brother has always been weak minded and trusting.

For now he needed to focus on convincing Aldrich to allow him leave, so that he could hurry back to Vansant Summit.

When Jacob returned to the dining hall, Aiden, Vastadon, and Aldrich were all that was left of the feasting, save for two servants who clung to jugs of wine and ale. His kin and Aiden were drunk from their indulgence in booze and laughing together like they were childhood friends.

"Brother!" Aldrich bellowed merrily with a wave of his hand, "Come and loosen up some with us!"

As for Vastadon, his blue eyes were on fire with the sight of Jacob and his body was hunched in his seat like a panther about to pounce. The anger was still there, but it would always be until the day came where a fight couldn't be avoided.

Jacob walked past Vastadon sparing him not even a look. Instead, he studied the scene before him. Aiden hung his arm over Aldrich in a brotherly manner and smiled lazily. Jacob might gain advantage with the manner in which they all were in now.

"Jacob," Aiden began in a voice thick with drink, "It indeed has taken you a long time to return from my sister's presence. I trust I needn't worry about the loss of her maidenhead with *you*?"

The two of them erupted in laughter and it was clear to Jacob just how drunk they were. Aiden was quite the unnaturally possessive one when it came to Miarosa and would've never jested about such a thing if he was sober. Vastadon's nostrils flared and the left side of his mouth lifted sardonically.

"Of course you wouldn't need to worry of such a thing. My uncle is far from a ladies man and a bit oafish if you ask me," Vastadon spat.

The men once again laughed robustly at the remark, but Jacob found no amusement in Vastadon's *banter.*

"Some men don't fancy themselves to chasing every skirt that turns a pretty eye on them," Jacob said with no sign of humor. The laughter ceased and for once the other two men realized that it was no time to jest.

"Someone sounds jealous," Vastadon retorted.

Aldrich, upon seeing the developing fight, took hold of Jacob's robe and yanked him into the vacant seat beside him.

"Now come boys, is there no time for enjoyment? Please stop making such fools of yourselves here before this fine king!" Aldrich commanded.

There was a sudden stir in the room. Merle entered with a viper about her neck and didn't at all look like she was as ill as she claimed. Jacob tended to think she was throwing a tirade in private because of the earlier display of defiance shown from her youngest daughter. Like her shadow as always, Falcon followed concealed deep in his robe. He carried his serpent headed staff like a walking stick, steely-eyed and expressionless.

Gods, I can deal with Aiden and even his little brat better than this Demon-loving wench and her minion! Jacob thought to himself, but forced as much of a nod as he could in greeting. He was never one to pretend.

"My lady, you are as refreshing as the gentle cool rain in the smoldering summer!" Aldrich greeted slurring.

Merle's smile was wide and brilliant and extremely fake as she glided forward to take Aldrich's outstretched arm. He flung a chair out for her and ignored Falcon's presence.

"If only I had such a beautiful face to greet me every evening in *my* keep!" Aldrich continued clinging to her hand like a stable boy with a crush. Jacob's blood boiled. *Must you make such a fool of yourself, Brother?*

Jacob noticed Aiden roll his eyes. He was sure that Aiden couldn't stand to see his mother so complimented. Jacob knew all too well the feuds within these castle walls.

"Why thank you, Aldrich," Merle replied and let out a short low laugh that sounded more like a cat's purr, "But I fear that Falias' fine ale has softened you." Her eyes sharpened and she slipped her hand from Aldrich's clutch. He didn't appear to notice.

"Aiden tells me that you were feeling unwell earlier, although I couldn't tell by the looks of you. Are you feeling better now, my lady?" Aldrich creased his forehead with genuine worry.

"Slightly better, but I couldn't miss the chance to pay you a small visit before your leave. It's a pleasure when you come to Thaumatur. I trust you have met my youngest daughter then, my lord?"

"I've met the little beauty and I've heard that Aiden is having a difficult time matching her up for marriage." Aldrich replied.

"He has, not only because we are reluctant to give her up, but because we've been faced with little option. I'm not quite ready to unite with the Murians, nor do I wish to hand over my daughter to a gypsy king."

"Well if it suits you, my lady, I'd gladly match her with a prince in my lands, or even a caste king."

Her eyes lit up with the prospect, "That may very well be the best choice for us. And it would display a great effort in making peace among our kinds. Mia appears to be quite taken with your son, here." Merle leaned her head in Vastadon's direction.

Vastadon nodded with an arrogant grin and said, "She has, my lady queen, and she would be well treated if we were to marry."

"Let's not get ahead of ourselves, Vastidrich," Aldrich intervened, "You still have much to do here and you may be too occupied on other things. It could be unfair if you take a wife now. Besides, haven't you made an intimate acquaintance with the daughter of the Viscount? It's said that her beauty is beyond any."

"I find no one more beautiful than the princess of this castle, Father," Vastadon reproached.

"Still," Aldrich tightened his jaw, "We shall see."

Merle quirked an eyebrow and leaned forward to look at Jacob. Her smile wasn't a warm one, but the kind of grin that sent tiny icicles down the length of one's spine.

"I understand that Viscount Birch has already agreed to a match between your son and his daughter. That man is quite fond of him. Vastadon would be much better matched with Camille Birch for his attention *could* be shared with a wife so close to the heart of his dealings." Merle said to Aldrich, but her eyes remained on Jacob while she spoke, "Match Mia up with Jacob! He is High Prince and it would do Mia some good to get accustomed first hand to your ways. Perhaps if he brings a bride from Thaumatur back with him to his country lands, the idea of a truce would settle in better there."

"What?" Jacob dashed to his feet, "That is absurd! You provoke civil war with such ideas!"

Not with her! He would rather marry a lowly Barbarian servant than that spoilt *magician*. For the first time in his life, he was afraid. He couldn't bring her home and show his people the very thing he has so long looked down upon. He worked hard to gain the favor of the Graven Clan beyond the wall. If they heard such a thing, they would definitely withdraw their aid against the malevolent Tribes. The Thaumaturi were hated among the Tribes.

The demon-woman wanted her daughter unhappy! She thrived on it. The wench was no fool and knew more of the happenings in the castle than her own son. It took her no time to learn of his royal birthright when it was revealed this very night. She knew the feelings of bitterness that Miarosa and he held for one another.

She can play this game with her daughter if she desires, but by no means will I allow her to include me in on them!

"I agree with Jacob, Mother," Aiden shook his head. "She'd be miserable and would much rather wed a stranger than Jacob."

Merle glared at her son, and Jacob noticed the woman's fingers twining.

"I know that you are fond of Mia. But it's now time to let her go. You are too possessive," Merle warned softly.

Aiden swallowed and didn't answer her, like the good little puppet he was.

"Well I think the idea has merit! I consent to it!" Aldrich said and embraced Merle as closely as he could without aggravating the snake she carried.

Witch! Jacob thought viciously.

"She'll never marry him, Father," Vastadon interfered rebelliously, "She is in love with me."

"And you cannot have two women at once, and since you've found it difficult to make a choice, then I shall make the best one for you!" Aldrich thundered, "You'll marry Camille Birch!"

"I choose Mia then! Camille is merely a friend to me! I look to her as I'd look to Aiden!" Vastadon thundered.

"Hardly, Lord Vastadon, unless you prefer to broaden your sexual preferences. I've seen you with the Viscount's daughter and it looks like much more than an acquaintance." Merle grinned wickedly.

"It is too late! I've asked you time and time again what you wanted. And now that I have made the choice for you, you rebel against it. Done is done!" Aldrich tossed the chair from beneath him and loomed over the table.

Jacob took hold of Aldrich's arm and turned a pleading eye on him. It was the last straw. "Brother, pray tell me you are not serious?"

Aldrich pulled his arm from Jacob's grasp and said jaggedly, "The time for jesting has just ended. I'm only one man, Emperor, but still only one man. I've done everything I could for the both of you, yet it seems that I never measure up to either one of your needs. I'm tired, Jacobane, of trying to compromise. You want to go home to the wall? So be it. But you return with your bride!" Aldrich was staggering from the hall but turned back one last time. "You better warm your bride, Jacobane, so that she will be eager for you on your wedding night," he turned and left.

Jacob felt a cold hand of anxiety trace down his body. How could he even bear to call this woman wife when he could hardly look at her? Acid rose in his throat with the mere thought. An arm draped over his shoulder and gave a reassuring squeeze.

"I'll speak with him in the morning, Jacob, after our visit with Lucian. Maybe then I can calm him and make him see reason," Aiden said calmly.

Jacob wasn't fooled. There was no changing Aldrich's mind when he ordered something. And it would be a fate that both he and his nephew would suffer. Vastadon looked truly broken-hearted. But he would obey his father to gain his favor and word as his successor, no matter the price, and most likely grow to live with his fate more easily. Jacob could never be that lucky.

He looked down the other side of the table and met eyes with Merle. Her face was expressionless, but her eyes mocked him, laughed at him with malicious pleasure. For once in Jacob's life, he'd met someone who was even more prejudice than he. Only that the witch before him hated Barbarians and Thaumaturi alike.

CHAPTER FIVE

The Summer Queen

As rosy dawn reached across the rolling sand dunes, a knight wrapped tightly in a dark purple cape and a priestess in emerald robes approached the eroded stone fortress gates. Two sentries dressed in grey leather breeches, dirty green tunics and dangling white turbans guarded the gate, only one fully awake. The one that was awake shielded his eyes from the gleam of the knight's chained helmet and spat from the corner of his mouth crudely.

"Halt there, sir knight," the guard said in a raspy voice and inclined his head to the priestess. He gave a toothless smile and scratched his sand spitted beard with a torn gloved hand.

The knight came to a deliberately slow halt, holding a hand protectively across the priestess and looked down on the dirty guard from atop the prancing war steed. With a heavy hand, the knight patted the russet beast on its side to calm it, but remained silent.

"State your business here, sir knight, in Findias," the guard spoke forcing dominance in his voice.

The knight's shoulders lifted with annoyance and with swift fingers, removed the helmet. Hair of blue-chestnut bounced freely along a thin sun-touched face. A *female* face.

"I am no *sir*, sentry," the knight said with a grin and eyes that lit up like a ray of sun, "I am Diamond Lunistar, *Lady* Knight under oath to the Goddess and I hail from the Sun Order." She jerked her head toward the priestess, "This here is the First Priestess of the Caves, Sierra."

The dirty guard softened with surprise when he focused on the priestess, but he didn't let his suspicions down entirely. Diamond laughed at the man and reached into the collar of her cape thrusting forth a medallion. It was the emblem of her brigade designed intricately by a Brosian druid blacksmith. The medallion was embellished with an owl perched upon a lion's back, encircled with gem stars and flames of vibrant ruby and sun-blazed gold. The guard faltered, but quickly bowed with swift recovery.

"My lady, I don't dare interfere with the business of the Order, or the sanctity of the Ministry. However, it is my obligation to inform the king of all those who cross our gates here and the business in which they bring. The raiders have become more than a problem. It has left my liege no other choice but to practice such precautions," he said in a much milder tone.

Diamond nodded and wound her fingers through the steed's caramel mane with tattered patience. Her cape billowed behind her in a tangle of sand and wind. The sun was burning a whole into her head and she prayed that the palace was cool and refreshing. Then she prayed that her dealings would be short here, because there was much business left undone back home in Tania.

"Tell your king that we've been sent by the High Priestess of the Brosia Caves and that we've no interest in speaking with him. We seek an audience with his queen," she replied in a flat voice. "Now, if you don't mind, we wish to at least enter your city to purchase beverages from the market. We are by no means used to this kind of climate!"

"But of course, my lady!" The man hustled to the long thick rope in which controlled the lifting of the gate.

He nudged the sleeping guard and spoke to him sternly. Their dirty suntanned muscles twitched as they pulled the rope down until finally the gate was lifted to a height in which Diamond and her steed could ride through easily.

The inner city was the running colors of beige and brown that blended quite well with the desert she recently swept across. The streets were sandy and the homes that lined either side of the street were short stone foundations with flat tops. The city was waking slowly and very few tent-roofed stands were set up for the day. The City of Summer, enchanting as it was, had always been secured behind the walls of separation between the kingdom and the rest of the world.

Diamond urged her steed forward with a squeeze to its sides and nodded to a young girl veiled in black who was standing meekly by a well. She held a wooden goblet in her hand and stared up at Diamond with wide eyes. Diamond tossed a gold coin in the goblet and smiled. She knew that the money would feed an army of children the size of this little girl. She felt a pang at her heart and generously tossed another into the goblet.

"Thank you, my lady, for your kindness!" The girl exclaimed and quickly put the coins into her pocket. The girl filled two goblets with water and reached one up to Diamond with two small hands.

"Thank you, little one for refreshment," Diamond replied and passed the first one to Sierra, and then drank deeply from the second cup. "Do you know how to care for horses?"

The little girl nodded, "Yes my lady Knight. There's a stable down the way where your horses may rest and feed." The girl pointed behind her.

Diamond leaped from her horse in a jingle and patted the girl on the head before passing her the reigns. She held a hand out to steady Sierra's dismounting, for she was a little woman. The priestess grasped her hand and climbed down with the gracefulness of a spirit.

Sierra lowered her sharp eyes to the child, who returned the gaze with awe. The innocence of children allowed them to stare into the eyes of a priestess unflinchingly. It was less often these days that an adult could do so with ease.

"You are a beautiful girl," Sierra spoke with a thick gypsy accent and gently cupped the child's chin. "The Goddess Danu bless you, child."

The little girl beamed, appearing unaccustomed to the gentle caress of an adult, and her eyes sparkled as if she was given the greatest gift. She bowed her head and took hold of the second sets of reigns. She called over her shoulder and a young boy appeared from behind the curtains of an orange tent beside the well, his dirty face was pinched with the signs of first morning wake. When he looked up at the knight, his eyes widened and his cheeks flushed with embarrassment. With jittery movements, the boy grabbed the reigns of the mare.

"His name is Thatcher and the mare is called Stardust. Care for them well and I shall give you twice the gold as this," Diamond promised placing two more gold coins in the child's hand. "One for you and one for your friend."

The girl led the horse away, the young boy followed, and said, "They shall be well treated, my lady! Very well treated!"

"My lady," the familiar voice of the sentry bellowed, "Lady of the Caves, the king is ready to receive you now."

Diamond frowned and expected half as much. Men such as King Foridazzle couldn't help but to force dominance on their women. It wasn't always the ways of the Thaumaturi. Men had grown bold with their egotistical attitude towards women.

She shifted her eyes to Sierra. The Priestess was calm and patient. She could sense it even though Sierra concealed her entire face—except her eyes—with the silk embroidered emerald of her veils. Irritation and fatigue invaded Diamond's tongue.

"But, guard, did you not hear my words? We haven't at all asked to be received by the king, but by his queen," Diamond replied harshly.

Sierra placed a gentle hand on Diamond's arm to calm her. It worked, but only to a certain extent. The guard's brown cheeks turned crimson and he stumbled over his own tongue when he tried to respond. She hadn't the time to play games with the stumbling fool.

"Never the mind with you, guard. Take us to your king," She snapped and strode forward.

When they reached the Findias Palace entrance, Diamond was gaping at its beauty for it was the first time she laid eyes upon the kingdom. Unlike the bland brown colors of the city, the palace was dotted with vibrancy. A limestone fountain spat water into arches in the center of the walkway and erotically dressed women danced around it with veils of colorful silk and sheer skirts. The front of the palace erected into two narrow towers accented with glittering jewels that were woven into the

AMI KATHLEEN

architecture like a spider's web. The doors in which the sentry led them to were domed and appeared to be made from solid gold. An eagle with outstretched wings and a sword at its crown was emblazed across the door in gold and amber—the emblem of Summer Kingdom—the light and distant creature with keen eyes and senses. It fitted Findias quite well.

The door swung open soundlessly, as if it merely floated across the surface of the grand portico, and a rotund man with a coarse dark-bearded chin garbed in a tan and orange wrap emerged smiling wide with the contrast of his white teeth against the rich bronze of his complexion. The man wore a golden turban crowned with green petals and he smelled of peppermint indicating he was in high standings among the court. He extended his hand effeminately.

"My lady knight of the Goddess, welcome to the Summer Palace!" He said airily.

Diamond took his hand with a strong grip, but quickly pulled it away before he had the urge to kiss her hand. She was a knight and a mage of the highest arts. Such a gesture is left for the ladies of court. The man's eyes became alive with excitement when he settled them on Sierra. He bowed lowly and then grasped her hands, kissing them.

"My lady, Priestess of the Caves, how honored we are to be graced with your presence!" He squealed delightfully.

Diamond rolled her eyes and thought he was quite an actor. The man cleared his throat and looked at the guard who had originally brought them there. As he slowly scanned the guard, his lips curled in disgust. Diamond's innards cringed from the rudeness of it.

"That will be all guard!" The man snapped and sent the guard scurrying away.

He returned his attention to Diamond and swung his hand to the side inviting her to enter the threshold.

A cool breeze swept across Diamond's skin when she stepped through, cooling the sweat she had accumulated at her brow. She inhaled deeply with slight indulgence and then advanced forward. The noble man was a small man, now that she stood beside him. He was almost a head smaller than her, who was at an average height for a woman. He didn't exceed the slightness of the young priestess. He quickly looped his arm through Sierra's and strode ahead of Diamond. He chattered nonsense, which Diamond blocked out, with Sierra all the while.

The entrance hall was narrow and filled with light from the painted glass windows in the ceiling. Closed doors garnished with green leaves lined the wall decorated with the eagle of their king. The corridor wound into a large room rich with refreshing steam and spices. A square of white pillars cradled an opened garden of brilliant green spine-like leaves and vibrant yellow and pink flowers. A waterfall spilled over five layered rocks into a lily pad pool.

"Oh, my," the short noble said and halted interrupting her wandering whims, "Forgive me, but I haven't yet told you my name." He chuckled like a little boy, "I'm King Xavier Foridazzle's right hand man and advisor, Kalabu."

"It is good to meet you, Kalabu, and quite *inspiring* to hear one speak proudly with such little accomplishment," she jested but he didn't seem to catch the irony. "Yet I don't understand why the queen hasn't sent one of her women to greet us at door."

"It is because the king himself wishes to greet you before he allows an audience with his queen," The man said aloofly.

Diamond couldn't decide whether Kalabu held his nose high because he attempted to gain height or he simply relied on his arrogance to make his appearance more appreciated. He irked her and even more so with his badly presented dialogue.

"*Allows?*" She derided.

"It's only proper," he said shortly and pushed open two large doors. "May I present to Your Majesty, the Lady Knight from the Sun Order and the most holy Priestess of the Caves," he announced, kissing Sierra's hands once again, sliding his fingers from her with a poor attempt at charm, and left them before the king.

King Xavier sat comfortable on his throne with several dark haired women at his feet. They were gossiping and pampering the king and didn't acknowledge their entrance. The king however straightened his posture and smiled handsomely at them. His dark eyes glittered with curiosity and scrutiny suddenly making Diamond aware of her travel wearied appearance. He wore a sleeveless white wrap that was clasped at the shoulders with embroidered gold pendants, crowned with matching leaves. Soft ebony ringlets strayed across his brow and along the base of his bronze neck and shoulders. His chin was neatly trimmed into a pointed goatee. He was handsome for his age and was only touched with silver around his ears. It wasn't the size and sight of the king that left Diamond unnerved, but the dark eyes that now looked upon her lustily. He was an indulgent pig, she could tell.

"Welcome, my ladies, to my court," he sang jubilantly finally catching the attention of the women at his feet.

He looked down to them and somehow through his wide smile, the women knew enough to leave. Sierra turned her head slightly and smiled with silent encouragement. She departed the throne room soon after the women, leaving Diamond to the investigation and most likely went to give blessing to those who wished for it.

Xavier stepped down and approached Diamond with a more serious look once all were gone from earshot.

"So they decided to send a woman. To allure me perhaps?" He said tipping a gold pitcher over two goblets.

"My business isn't with you, King Xavier. I summoned an audience with your wife," she replied forcing down her irritability.

He turned rapidly and thrust a goblet into Diamond's hands. He grimaced after sipping his wine.

"What concerns my wife concerns *me*."

"Not in the matters of the Goddess."

"But you are a knight from the Sun Order, not a priestess, correct? The priestess wandered away," he said scathingly waving a hand to the door.

"It seems that you've been so long gone from the councils of Thaumatur that you have forgotten that the Secrecies of Light include the Order *and* the Ministry. One in the same, therefore making all purposes the will of the Goddess, my lord."

"The rest of the land has excluded me, offering me no aid in my time of need when raiders and thieves have overrun my kingdom," He rebutted bitterly.

Xavier took one long swig from his goblet and slammed it down on the table. If his forceful temper tantrum was meant to startle her, he would be disappointed.

"You are mistaken, my lord. You have isolated yourself from even your own people while you live in comforts and riches here in these towers. It seams you have struck luck with the abundance of water you have here. Surely the good people who struggle beyond the fortress of this palace could rely on you to graciously bless them with your good fortune," Diamond said angrily remembering the poor condition of the young children by the well.

"You dare insult me in my own dwelling?" He bellowed dangerously.

"And you dare speak ill of the Secrecies of Light?"

He was silent and paced with his back turned. She could feel his anger give way to fear.

"Anytime a great knight from your Order comes sweeping across the desert to Findias, it's usually something ill-fated. Is it wrong for me to try to protect my wife from your news? I just want to know what is going on now," he said defeated.

"I understand your concerns, but I assure you that no harm will come to your wife with mere conversation. She at one time has taken an oath, as all women do, before the Goddess, Danu," Diamond reminded him.

"I suppose I've been gone for far too long then."

Diamond didn't like this king at all, but she knew there needed to be some form of a truce to get by him in order to finish the task she was sent here to do.

"Perhaps I was a bit hard on you," Diamond commented biting her lip. "I have grown grumpy on this blasted ride. It's damn hot out there!"

Xavier took a deep breath and smothered a laugh. He signaled for her to follow him into a large cavity adorned with several decks and silk draped gazebos. Around every turn there were scattered steaming pools and fountains embellished with lilies, palm trees, and roses. This kingdom, Findias, was by far the richest in the lands.

The room was vacant, but she imagined the way it would be while people gathered here. Dancing, singing, and laughing maidens delivering all of the luxuries this kingdom had to offer. Oh, she was sure the queen had her share of indulgences to forget her dark childhood in Falias. She *was* the sister of the tyrant.

The king glided across the cream marble floor and swayed before one of the bubbling pools. He side stepped from Diamond's view spreading apart two yellow sheer drapes. Behind the curtain a fair middle aged women with long ebony braids woven into flowers and green ribbons lounged in the foaming waters of the pool. Arabella's eyes widened with the sight of Diamond and she reached for a robe on her side wrapping it around her. She darted upright indignantly. Beneath her scowling expression, Diamond sensed she was fearful.

"Husband, could you not warn me?" She said between her clenched teeth.

He ignored her, briefly smiling at Diamond before leaving the two of them alone. A sense of satisfaction swam in the Xavier's smile. This union wasn't as amazing as the palace they called home. It was a matter of convenience for the both of them.

"Queen Arabella," Diamond greeted and inclined her head.

Arabella didn't answer, but slowly climbed out of the pool. Diamond knew it would be difficult to face the hard woman.

"What do you want?" Arabella hissed.

"My name is Diamond and I'm here to speak on an important investigation, Queen Arabella."

"What will you take from me *now?* Another son, perhaps," She spat back.

Indeed Diamond was prepared to expect this kind of reaction from Arabella. The Sun Order had taken all royal-blooded sons that year as a precaution to the Prophecy of the Bearer. Arabella's first son, a son many would call a bastard, was such a son.

The Bearer wasn't a boy, but a girl. Diamond thought ironically as traces of the High Priestess' revelations etched her mind. *It was all a big error. An error too late to correct.*

"The Prophecies of the Goddess wished it so. You weren't the only one," Diamond softened her voice. "He is alive and well, as all the first sons of that age are."

"He must be a grown man now," Arabella said distantly and threw a glance Diamond's way, "Probably about your age."

"Probably," Diamond agreed although she wasn't old enough to remember the time of the Prophecy.

Suddenly Arabella clutched at Diamond's cape, from her eyes sprang tears of loss and her expression twisted with pain.

"Where is my son? Tell me for I must look upon him one time."

Diamond gently cupped Arabella's cheek and forced her own pity to the back of her mind remaining firm and strong as was expected of her. "I'm sorry for your sorrow, my lady, but I cannot tell you where he is for I'm not permitted to know. Only the High Priestess can hold that knowledge. It's sacred."

"Damn that Priestess! She plays with our lives like we are puppets on her golden strings! Her great secrets and magic should only disgrace her name before our Goddess!" Arabella cursed. Diamond knew that she spoke out of pain and not of heresy.

"I know you've suffered, but you shouldn't speak so of the High Priestess. She has sacrificed her very self to spare our lands from the bloodshed we suffered before now. She means well. It's she who has sent me to you."

"You are but a child," Arabella snapped. "What do you know of this world?"

"I know what I have learned. I honor you, lady, for your sacrifice," Diamond said looking down into the sad eyes of the queen.

Arabella's sourness slowly melted into appreciation of Diamond's compliment. It made Diamond hopeful to see what decent respect and gratitude could do for one such as Arabella. *A Maladinto.*

Arabella's eyes cleared from the clouds of tears and she offered Diamond a seat beside her on the plush chaise. The rushing sound of water smoothed the stiffness from between them and soon Diamond felt as if she would drift far away somewhere. She was tired and thought she might even stay if invited for the night to revive.

"High Priestess Janella sends her blessings and this," Diamond said pulling from her pocket a bundle of silk.

Arabella took the bundle in her hands and unraveled it carefully. Inside was a small firestone. Arabella smiled curling her slender fingers over it and closed her eyes lightly.

"The Priestess said you would know what it means. By the looks of it, she was right." Diamond grinned.

"Yes," Arabella whispered, "She has reminded me of a time with this stone. It seems so long ago. Her destiny was much different than mine was, but until it claimed her we were very close. We met in the schooling of the Brosia Caves where I learned to service Danu unselfishly under Janella's guidance. It was funny, because, she who was my teacher was only five years older than me. I chose to school there because I needed to heal my heart from…much," she paused worrying the bottom of her lip before continuing. "We went to the Barbarian Nations one year during Luthros Hilliard's reign, on a mission of peace," Arabella chuckled. "What a time to go and believe me, the retreat wasn't lengthy. Oh, some of those brutes were as crude as pigs in mud, but there were too some gentle big men. One in particular Barbarian was very kind to us. He gave us each a stone like this so that we might always remember at least one friendly brute Barbarian." Arabella laughed again, "I think Janella was quite charmed by the fellow."

Diamond listened to Arabella with genuine curiosity. She hadn't known that this richly pampered queen was a dear friend to the High Priestess in her youth. She watched as Arabella's giddy smile melted with each turning thought.

"Then my mother thought it best that I forget about becoming a Priestess. My brother's banishment damaged my mother. She loved Ahriman, I think, best of all of us. Soon after, I learned that it was Janella's order to take my son. I was cruel the last time I saw her," She said sadly.

"I can see that it's hard for you to speak on your past. I must ask you for your courage one more time," Diamond said placing a hand on Arabella's.

It was cold and soft, trembling with fear. Arabella said nothing, but nodded her consent to the questioning.

"The High Priestess has detected Demon activity that long ago died with Ahriman's legions," Diamond began. "Is it possible that your mother, Merle, could somehow be involved in this? I know that she wasn't held responsible for your brother's actions, but do you think she might've been in contact with him?"

"Merle is too distraught and cold to have such knowledge of her beloved son's whereabouts. Like I said before, he was her very pride and joy, even through all of his black wizardry," Arabella replied scornfully. "I can't say how far she would go to find him. As for me, I believe him to be dead. He has disappeared for far too long."

"What of your other brother, Aiden, or I believe you have a very young sister, right?" Diamond asked.

"Yes, I do have a sister," she paused for a moment. "I don't think Aiden gives her enough breathing room to even know the history of our *precious* little family. Miarosa is like a flower amidst weeds. Yet she is strong somehow and is always by my ailing father's side when permitted. Lucian was a good king when he was well. I can still remember him as he was..." Arabella's voice cracked with emotion.

"I'm sorry, my lady. Take whatever time you need." Diamond squeezed Arabella's hand apologetically.

"Oh," she waved her hand, "It is okay. I've grown used to his condition. I'm sometimes ashamed of myself for abandoning him. Where was I?" she flung the tears from her eyes as if they were never there. "Oh, yes. As for Aiden, well he is just a fool who lives his life in oblivion, a dazzling world as king and with the women who want nothing more out of life than to fall over each other at his feet. It's a wonder that he doesn't have a thousand bastards banging down his door for a piece of the Falias throne. If something has come from my family, I'd have to say Merle. But I'm truly doubtful. Perhaps there is a new generation of black mages, who only hope to recapture the glory of my brother. They will be sorely mistaken, for it seems that the Order and the Ministry haven't turned a blind eye this time." Arabella stood and laughed, "Come, let me call my women to refresh you. I extend my hospitality for as long as you need it."

Diamond too stood and smiled widely, "I think I will take you up on your offer. But at dawn I will ride back to Gorias. I must retrieve the First Priestess who has come with me. She felt that she needed to leave our meeting private."

"A priestess, you say?" Arabella's eyebrows lifted, "Well, I must ask for her blessing, since she is already here. I have not received the Rites of Danu for some time."

"Sierra would be pleased to give you what you ask." Diamond smiled.

"Very well, Diamond," Arabella laughed, "It has been too long since I've received personal visitors. Dinner will be served on the tented deck. You will be called, but for now, you are due for bath!"

"Of that I am certain!" Diamond laughed and strolled beside the Queen, "I feel like a man!"

CHAPTER SIX

The Locator

Sierra was already bathed and sitting on the patio that overlooked the grand hall's fountains. She wore a gown of gold and burgundy, with flared sleeves. At her waist and her forearms, thick silver braided ropes dangled. Her dark hair was covered with a floral veil, but her face wasn't concealed as it usually was. Her olive skin glowed from within her body. She was beautiful, but vanity was a sacrifice she made to Danu. Sierra had said nothing, but smiled knowingly that it indeed went better than expected.

After Diamond bathed and changed, she set about washing her riding gear and the purple tunic patterned with fiery tongues that marked her as a Sun Knight. The dress the queen had chosen for her to wear was elegant and soft, made from pearl colored silk with sea-green sleeves and flowing mesh veils.

When she glanced at her appearance in the mirror, she burst out in laughter. "Why, I could pass for some great queen in this get up!"

Sierra laughed as well at the jest. It was a wondrous sound, for the priestess hardly ever spoke, let alone laughed.

Soon after, a maid led them down to the tented decks in the rear of the palace. The night was sapphire blue with speckles of diamonds around a bright moon.

Diamond pulled her eyes from the clear night sky and scanned the fully alive deck for Arabella. Dancing candles and ribbons of greens and reds fluttered about the chimes and flute tunes. People were laughing and drinking merrily and for a moment, Diamond felt herself ease into the festive atmosphere. A dashing dark-skinned man dressed in gold from head to toe grinned charmingly at her as she weaved through the crowd. She nodded politely and then spotted Arabella on the far side of several dancing ladies, sitting delicately among her women.

Arabella's eyes connected with hers and she fluttered her hand in the air waving her over. Diamond squeezed through the stunning garbed dancers, Sierra close at her heels, and they took a seat beside Arabella on her chaise. One of the women poured wine into two gold goblets and offered it to them bowing.

"Thank you," Diamond said and took a sip. Sierra politely declined.

It was a peculiar tasting wine with a hint of cinnamon, yet it wasn't as sweet as the grape wines in the Rose Hill Garden providence, Sierra's homeland, where they were renowned for their vineyard brewed wine. Another woman offered them a tray filled with many different treats. Diamond didn't recognize any of them, so she randomly took one to avoid offending her hostess. The treat was a rounded flaky shell with open ends that had cream dripping along the edges. It was drizzled in what Diamond thought could be chocolate. Chocolate was a delicacy, commonly found in Tania. Expensive. She took a small bite from it and was grateful that the taste wasn't sour or disgusting. The cake was delightful actually.

"It is called flazium, and yes it's topped with chocolate." Arabella leaned into Diamond's ear, "Good isn't it?"

"Absolutely," Diamond laughed. "It's truly beautiful here. I can see how one wouldn't care to know the woes of the outside world while here."

"Yes it is. Even if my husband is not!" They both giggled.

Arabella looked at Sierra, her eyes glittering with curiosity or maybe amazement.

"How lovely you are, Lady Priestess. It isn't often you show your face. I've heard the maidens chatter about you. They say you have the most exquisite eyes, although you chose to wear a veil about your face," Arabella commented admirably.

"It is a vow I've sworn to the Goddess Danu," Sierra began. "I'm permitted to remove my veil at important outings, but only the highest occasions."

Arabella gained color in her cheek and her smile stretched even wider. She was speechlessly flattered. "I am honored, Lady Priestess." Arabella lowered her head with respect, "Will you bless me?"

"Of course, Lady Queen," Sierra said softly and circled her finger upon her forehead, lips, and heart.

The blessing was silent, but Diamond saw the white orbs dance around Sierra's hands and disappear into Arabella's aura.

It was Sierra's gift.

There was movement at the front of the deck that silenced the feast.

"You are not to enter here!" A guard bellowed.

All fell into a struggle and from what Diamond could see there was a huge wild like man with dark skin garbed in pale breeches pushing his way through the crowd. No guard could restrain this man as he headed straight for Arabella. Diamond reached for the dagger strapped at her ankle, unsheathed it and stood protectively in front of Arabella and Sierra. The man showed no interest in the queen, but focused his big brown eyes on Diamond and then his gaze fell on Sierra. He didn't attack and it wasn't because he feared the little dagger she was now holding like she held a sword between her fists. She met his eyes with the fierceness of a warrior, but soon the caution melted into confusion. She knew instantly that he didn't come here to harm anyone at all. He was just as confused as the entire court was. Diamond slowly lowered her dagger.

He was Called…

"Why have you come here?" She asked, but the man remained silent.

The entire court was watching intently and the sound of silence ringed through the air.

"Did you come here to raise a fight?" Diamond asked more sternly.

The man shook his head "no" slowly. Diamond lifted her brow and

71

tried to focus on something that tugged at her instincts. Her magical senses were alert, but not in warning.

"Can you speak, sir?" Diamond asked and felt the priestess's touch.

The man shook his head again, but took hold of Sierra's hand and knelt. The guards lifted their weapons in defense, but Diamond waved them away. The man pressed Sierra's palms to his cheek and kissed them. His tears drizzled down Sierra's fingers.

"Carry on," the queen commanded from behind her, "all is well now."

The crowd slowly stirred up again and within moments, Arabella was beside Diamond, whispering in her ear.

"You are of the Circle, aren't you?" She exclaimed. "I have heard of the Prophecy when I was at the Caves."

"Yes," Diamond confessed. "But how did he know?"

Sierra didn't pull her hand from the big man, but instead placed the other tenderly on his bald head. She took hold of Diamond's hand and placed it upon the man's head as well. When Diamond touched him, she felt the familiar bond she shared with six other Sun Knights. He belonged with them in the Secrecies of Light, inside of the Goddess' Circle.

At that very moment Diamond realized her purpose for coming to this kingdom. She came for *him*, a missing link to the Circle, the Locator. She cast her eyes down into the man's big innocent pools of brown and gently pulled him to his feet. She smiled at him and an eagle soared above her head crying. The sound of his name silently drifted into her mind.

"Alabaster is it?" Diamond asked.

He nodded vigorously.

"You kneel to no one, Locator. For you are part of the Goddess' Circle," Sierra chastised him. "We will leave for Brosia at dawn, so go on and prepare for a long journey home. Do you have a horse?"

He looked down and shook his head.

"Then I'll buy you one before our leave, Alabaster. You finally found your belonging," Diamond quickly added.

The smile that lightened his face displayed his youth and in a leap, he turned to hurry away.

"We shall meet you in the city's stables at dawn's first light!" she called after him. "Don't be late."

Diamond retreated to the comforting company of Arabella, but her mind wasn't quite at ease. Sierra had already departed for solitude. Diamond lingered behind so that the priestess could have some privacy in her worship. She chattered with Arabella about women things for an hour and politely excused herself to bed.

"It has been a wonderful visit, Arabella," Diamond said.

"I agree, Diamond. You are like a breath of fresh air to me on this day. You remind me so much of Janella. Please tell her I somehow understand now and that I forgive her. I think that one day she will reunite me with my son when this is all over with," Arabella said through a half smile. "You've cleared my mind, Lady Knight and have given me strength I have long ago abandoned."

"I know that the High Priestess will find comfort in your words, Lady. Please, Arabella, come to the festival of the New Moon in Gorias. You've been away for too long and I know that Priestess Janella would be absolutely delighted to see you again. Besides, I've grown rather fond of you myself during my visit here," Diamond urged hopefully.

"Perhaps I shall, and make something of it," she grinned mischievously. "I'm going to see about stealing my younger sister away for a Moon Cycle. They keep her cooped up in there like some dark secret. Then again, it would be unlike Mother to be upfront."

They embraced and Diamond went to the sleeping chamber.

The next morning was even hotter then the one prior. Just as the little girl promised, Thatcher and Stardust were well taken care of. She paid the girl what she promised and also purchased a steely grey stallion for Alabaster. Alabaster was waiting for them in the stables wearing a turban and a robe of light brown to shield the sun from his already tough skin. She put a set of reigns in his hand.

"I hope you know how to ride," She said and winked at Sierra.

Alabaster nodded and leaped onto the horse's back and took off.

"I said ride, not race," Diamond muttered to herself and charged Thatcher after him.

At the sentry's gate, Kalabu greeted the three of them with over exaggerated joy. Diamond rolled her eyes. Beyond him she saw Arabella sitting upon a mare beneath a rider's canopy of ivory colored cloth.

Not a bad idea, Diamond thought.

Arabella's smile was wide.

"Mount your steed Kalabu. We will ride with the Lady Knight and the Lady of the Caves to Falias," Arabella commanded.

Diamond was pleased with the queen's decision despite the inability to use the Earth Crystal Janella had given her for swift transport, but she had another plan.

"I will escort you to your destination, but I must then part with you. I'm summoned to the Caves upon return," Diamond winked and pulled a pouch from her pocket.

They watch Diamond with great curiosity as she leaped from her steed. She closed her eyes, gripping the pouch tightly, and cleared her mind. The wind blew strong upon her face and lifted her hair and cape with vigorous life. Behind her eyelids, a purple speck pulsated and spun until it exploded into an aura of brilliant purples.

Come to me. Her mind called out.

The reigns of the horses jingled and the muffled sounds of slow-paced hoofs approached her. She smiled when she felt five wet noses nuzzle her.

Great Stallions, the treasures of transport you are. I ask you permit me to enhance your performance with the magic of my spell. Diamond bowed as the words rolled around in her head.

Yes, Lady of the Circle, Beast Mistress of Danu. Five angelic voices answered in unison.

A small smile touched her lips and she flung her eyes open to see Kalabu panicked and Arabella awestruck with appreciation. Diamond returned her attention to the horses.

"Thank you, horses," Diamond said aloud and reached into the pouch.

She sprinkled the manes of each horse with Crysallop—a rare and enhanced herb with the likeness of sandalwood—and silently said an incantation.

"Now," Diamond spread her smile between all of them, "Our horses will run with the speed of an eagle. Your eagle, Arabella. We shall be at our destinations before nightfall."

Arabella laughed nervously, "I suppose I should hold on for dear life then."

"Aye!" Diamond said and leapt back onto Thatcher.

Within moments, they were just about flying through the vast desert.

CHAPTER SEVEN

Last Breath

The morning snow fell gently to the Winter ground in large fragile flakes. Mia and Aiden glided down the glass walled corridors to a desolate chamber in the west tower. It was a commitment neither of them could break. The room in which they entered was dim with a blue hue from the crackle glass orbs that were scattered about the floor. The high ceilings were made of dark stained glass and it looked like an evening sky with glittering patterns of silver against the lighting of the early sun. There was a canopy bed with lace draping and two high back chairs. One of the chairs was near the bed, while the other looked out the single mosaic window that had a mural of a full moon surrounded by several swords. The floor was polished grey marble that echoed each foot step ten times the normal sound.

It was the time of the month in which Mia and Aiden visited their father, Lucian. He was lying in the bed buried beneath olive and cobalt satin and was sleeping peacefully. Mia almost hated to wake him, but he would be disappointed if he knew he missed their visit. Aiden was composed coolly while Mia clung to his arm. Perhaps she feared what she might find upon entering. The guards and Jacob halted at the threshold of the chamber and were not permitted any further. The sole guard that constantly remained at Lucian's bed also took his leave during their visits.

Aiden guided Mia to the chair nearest to Lucian and took the seat by the window. He was usually without words during his time with their father. Mia did most of the talking. She placed a hand on Lucian's face and spoke softly to stir him.

"Father, we are here now," She whispered

Lucian looked worse than the last time she visited him. His face was sunk in and his skin was the color of cheese. His chest rose slightly with shallow breaths, so she was relieved to know he still lived. When he finally focused his eyes on Mia, they brightened with the strength of a healthy warrior. He smiled slightly and cupped his bony hand over hers.

"It has been too long, child. I missed you so. Is my Aiden here with you?" he asked in a small gasping voice.

Mia nodded slightly and turned toward Aiden. Aiden didn't tear his gaze from the window.

"I'm here, Father," He said in a monotonous tone.

Mia drew in her breath and covered her annoyance with Aiden's careless manner and forced a smile upon her face when she looked down at Lucian.

"How do you feel, Father?" She whispered.

"Well, as good as can be expected, my little rose." His voice was a little stronger but still raspy. He tried to sit up, but Mia pulled the blanket up to his chin and eased him back down.

"Rest, Father, you need your strength."

"Oh, stop fussing girl," Lucian scowled but didn't put up too much of a fight. "Now tell me what has been happening in my kingdom this Moon? I certainly hope my son is handling things well. Is all well, Son?"

Lucian shifted his eyes in the direction in which his son sat. Aiden made no effort to reply. Mia felt disapproval ring in every part of her body, yet still she was careful not to upset Lucian.

"You know how it is, Father." Mia began diverting his attention back on her, "It hasn't been too busy. Last night we feasted with the Barbarian Emperor. Peace is at hand now. People of the court are content and the only other visits were from a courier or two. They usually bring news of little importance."

Mia was weaving her way through a conversation on subjects she knew very little about. It was only to please Lucian in what little time he had left. Mia remembered when he was strong and he would come home from his journeys with his arms outstretched. She would fling herself into them and hold him so tight in fear that he might float away. He would sit on his throne and bounce her on his knee telling her stories of the foreign kingdoms. Now it was her turn to tell him the stories even though she couldn't dream of being as talented as he was.

A tear threatened to fall, but she slammed her eyes shut. She bit her lip and turned away from Lucian cautiously and met eyes with Aiden. His face was unreadable and it left Mia wondering why he felt the way he did towards their father. After a moment, Aiden rolled his eyes and tore his gaze from her. He had very little patience for tears.

"You look so tired, Father. Is there anything I can do to help?" Mia asked hoping to sway her mind from memories.

"Nay," he mumbled, "A visit from my children is all I need. Has my Arabella called on me?"

"She hasn't returned since her marriage to King Xavier Foridazzle. Her vows are new Father and it's a great responsibility to settle in another land, as queen no less. I'm sure she has been very busy," Mia recovered and chastised herself for the lie.

In truth, Mia couldn't begin to count the years since Arabella had come home to see their father. Four?

"Oh, my daughter managed to keep her time occupied when she was home," He grunted. "This is Arabella for you, I suppose."

Mia only nodded in reply. Arabella was in her fifteenth year when Mia was born, so the difference in age wasn't as large as her and Aiden.

"She is wallowing in her riches and position, no doubt. Let her. The less of a nuisance she is to me because of it," Aiden growled his criticism.

"I miss her too, Father," she impressed disregarding Aiden's ignorance.

Mia spent the remainder of the visit telling him some of the stories her women chattered about and she spoke about her visit with Vastadon

DeLucible and the Barbarian Emperor in a little more detail. She deliberately let out the bickering between the family and the sad departure of Nan. Nan, after all, was his woman too.

Mia decided as the new hour approached that he needed his rest. She stood and kissed him gently on his pale cheek. The small spark in his eyes when she first arrived was gone when he looked up at her. He clung to her hand in a manner that wasn't the same as any other time. There was urgency about his hindrance. His tired eyes shifted to Aiden who was about sleeping and then back to her. Mia wanted to ask him what was wrong, but her mouth didn't move. She lowered her cheek to his lips, but instead of that vague kiss, he pressed his lips to her ear.

"My Mia," he whispered breathlessly, "There is a chamber in the south tower always forbidden to you. Do you know the tower?" he asked and she nodded quickly, "Find it and see what you were never told. Don't let them trap you here, as I have been trapped. We are only flies tangled in the bitterness of *her* spider's web. You are too special for that."

Mia's pulse quickened and she could feel the crease etched in her forehead. His words weren't clear, but they were familiar. She could feel it in his grip and she could see it in his eyes.

With suddenness, he shuddered from one last gasp of life before falling limp. Panic ceased Mia as realization dawned on her. She drifted backward into Aiden's arms. For a moment she couldn't move and the sound of a thousand bells echoed in her ears. It was a blur to her. All accept one thing. The only person in her family, who loved her truly, was now dead. She never felt such grief.

"Guards! Jacob! Someone come and prepare the body for burial! Lucian is dead." Aiden announced with the voice of a whip.

Mia could've sworn she heard a hint of relief in it. She pulled from Aiden's hold and fled from the sight of her precious father, the cold aura of her brother and from the pain of her loss.

"Mia!" Aiden called behind her.

Mia ignored him and continued fleeing. She screamed her denials with each stride. She was truly alone. First Arabella had left her, then Nan. And now her father was dead!

Aiden caught up with her and wrapped his arms around her from behind, steadying her, hindering her from her grief in solitude. She kicked and struggled to break free but his grip was too strong. Her heart burned with such pain, yet she couldn't cry. She couldn't speak. Finally, she grew faint from her struggle and pressed back against her brother's torso. She collapsed into a loose embrace and buried her head in Aiden's chest. But it wasn't her brother she clung to.

"Come Miarosa, your brother wishes me to see you to your chambers," Jacob said flatly.

"Be reasonable, Aldrich! You want to marry the only man who'd stay true to your father's path to a Thaumaturi Princess?" Aldrich's first general, Claude, paced the heavily rugged floor of his guest chamber. "They were never meant to live among us. And now you want to put one of them on our throne?"

They had been at Aldrich's door since the first crack of light split the dark sky. Displeased and annoyed as usual.

"It's why the Gods have made them so much different," Claude continued ranting. "Their lands are punished by our Gods. Their climate is distorted and confused and their prophecies are only the base for deception and magic. Man controls their own fate. It's why the Gods have given us the will to choose. Now you slap Them in the face with your defiance over what? A *magician* whore?"

"Watch your tongue before you ruin your life!" Aldrich bellowed and snatched his general around by the metal chains of his armor.

It was more often than not Aldrich found himself in this very predicament. Claude was a good man and brutally honest with his opinions. Aldrich cared for him deeply and trusted him, but their views clashed and Aldrich was unusually easy to provoke when it came to the woman he loved. *The mother to his children.*

Claude willed to follow Luthros' visions of separation, and Aldrich was desperate to fulfill his mother Cordelia's lifetime and final dream of peace. The difference spawned arguments, but Aldrich knew his general would remain loyal to him in his choices. But he feared he had pushed too far this time. It needed to be done. He was emotively certain of it.

Sidian placed himself in between the two but he clearly sided with Claude.

"We bleed our man power in Thaumatur while your own kind is forced to stay behind a wall. The Brotherhood runs our lands in your leave, under your nose," Sidian shook his head. "You've separated us from ourselves and then invite the *magicians* to our land? Thank Gods for Jacobane. If that day ever comes that the High Prince can no longer negotiate with the Tribes, which could very well happen now since you've made such a poor judgment in arranging this union, Gods help you Aldrich, because I'll not. I loved your father as I love you, and it is because of him that I stayed loyal to you, but how far do you think you can push us?"

"The Tribes behind the wall are savages. They are blood thirsty creatures who rape and murder woman and children!" Aldrich pounded his fist against the wall, "We're not those kinds of monsters!"

"Aldrich I've known you since you were a little a boy and I supported you at your father's death," Claude hissed ignoring Aldrich's outburst. "At least for the sake of the Gods and the Senate who remain steadily loyal to you, please choose a Barbarian heir. Call off this marriage arrangement. And give the empire a Barbarian heir and not the son you have born to the woman who has weakened you."

Aldrich spun his back. Silence enveloped them, but Aldrich wouldn't yield in his decision. He would have to face not only these men, but the harsh scrutiny of the High Chaplain and the Brotherhood of the Gods. It would show weakness to crack beneath his piers.

"Return home. After the wedding I'll follow you there," Aldrich ordered. The two of them grunted their annoyance and in return, Aldrich's irritation enflamed. "What makes us so much better than them?" Aldrich banged his fist into the wall, "What disturbs me most is your contempt for these people."

No answer came. Aldrich had expected that much.

"He doesn't love the girl, does he?" Sidian jabbed the question like a spear. "Because even that would be a small logical reason for such a union!"

"My lords," Lynn popped her head through the door after a brief knock, "The former King Lucian is dead!"

The argument was forgotten. Aldrich leaped to his feet and followed Lynn's lead. His sympathy didn't fall upon Aiden or Merle. It nestled upon his heart for Miarosa.

With heavy sighs, Claude and Sidian followed their beloved Emperor, as they always did and always would despite their disparities.

The afternoon came swiftly. Aiden stood before his mother inside of her clammy towers. She looked light, as if a weight was lifted from her shoulders. Lucian's death was something she anticipated, for it was known that she and Lucian never saw eye to eye when he was sound. It was as if she was shedding unwanted clothes, or burning old pictures that were too tattered to keep.

"Let Mia handle Lucian's arrangement, Aiden," Merle said coldly, her eyes bitter shot. "She loved him most, anyhow."

"How do you think it will look to the rest of the kingdoms if I am absent during my own father's funeral?" Aiden paced before his mother.

"It'll not look good if you refuse to escort the Barbarian Emperor to the masquerade either," she snapped. "I don't want Aldrich to form a stronger alliance with any of the other kings, or worse yet, the Elders!"

"Mia couldn't bare it all alone, Mother. Even I know that much. You are so cruel to the girl!" Aiden rebutted.

"She'll not be alone. Jacob can help her. Let it be the first of many they bury *together*." Merle's words were deep and apparently amusing.

Her blood red lips twined about her face wickedly giving them the look of the viper she loved so much. Aiden looked at her with scorn and shook his head. As shallow and unfeeling as he considered himself to be at times, he wouldn't be this cold.

"That is another thing. How are we supposed to order her to marry a man she hates now?" He argued.

"*We* are not going to order her. *You* are."

"You arrange this façade and let me deal with the hard part? How noble of you Mother," Aiden snarled tossing his hands in the air.

"That's what you get for favoring her," she replied running the tip of her long red nail down the back of the black snake.

"Did it ever occur to you that the reason I am so against this marriage is for the sake of Jacob? I've befriended him, you know."

Merle's eyes narrowed and the morbid amusement on her face gave way to a grimace. "You are so soft. Not at all like Ahriman. And blind too. Don't think I haven't figured out what the ever-so-humble Barbarian Emperor is up to. He plans to stretch his empire over these lands if he hasn't already planted the seeds in the House with his half-blooded son. I've just taken measures to secure our portion of the power. I know you think I'm cruel, and maybe I am. It isn't like I have another *daughter* to offer up for marriage to the Barbarian," Merle reproached. "Although, I *am* now a widow and it is said that the Barbarians are extremely good lovers. *I* could marry the boar." She laughed wickedly.

"Be serious." Aiden rolled his eyes at his mother's insane jest. "And you say that I've lost my head! Jacob has forfeited his rights to the throne. Vastadon will gain control when the time comes, not Jacob!" Aiden cracked a smile pleased with himself.

"And if you believe that Jacob will just hand over the throne to his half-blooded nephew when the time comes, then you are even more foolish than I thought. Jacob hates our kind, no matter how you wish to ignore it. He'd not stand for an emperor that has the blood of a Thaumaturi flowing through him." She said.

Aiden simmered down into a confused state. She, although he hated to admit it, was as wise as she was malevolent. If an empire was at hand, then that would put the two of them very close to the heart of the power. He nodded his submission and stared up at her.

"All that I ask is this. Let me tell Mia after the ball. Give her some time alone to mourn Father and then I promise you, it will be taken care of," he said.

"Very well," She sneered.

"Has someone informed Arabella that her father is dead and it's now safe to come home for his funeral?" Aiden said contemptuously.

"I have sent Falcon…"

"I am already here Mother," A cool voice echoed in the desolate tower.

A familiarly cool voice.

Aiden spun to see Arabella brilliantly poised in a wave of almond colored silk, beside her stood a short rotund man wearing a tight blue turban with the same colored robes. She wore her hair concealed behind a crown encrusted with scattered jewels and the veils of a graceful queen. She folded her hands close to her middle and glanced from Aiden to Merle with steely eyes and a face of stone. He could sense she wasn't too pleased to be here.

Why did she come? Aiden thought. *She couldn't have received word of Lucian's death already.*

"So you are," Merle regarded her coldly and leaned back lazily.

"Welcome home, sister," Aiden's lip curled into an impious grin.

Arabella sliced her hand through the air sending her companion scampering away.

"I was on course for Gorias but decided to come home first. The guard at the door greeted me and then told me that Father is dead," Arabella said grimly. "I trust that the two of you are relieved."

Aiden noted that the women who stood before him was different from the sister who had left five years ago. There was anger in her once gentle and bleak eyes. She grew strong in her exile and Aiden wasn't sure he liked it much. In their youth, he considered himself close to Arabella, until Father grew ill. She adorned him and heeded his word over all. Now that she had her riches and high position, she looked down her nose at him. He opened his mouth to comment on her remark, but his mother was the quicker to respond.

"You speak to me as if I'm heartless, Arabella. Indeed I am relieved but only because your father no longer suffers," she said in an exaggerated hurt voice.

"It is only us here now, the sordid family that we are. Nothing to

84

encourage such a frontage Mother!" Arabella snapped. "Now, where is Miarosa. I'm sure she will need a woman's comfort at such a time. And we all know that Mother will not be of use. I must go to her at once."

Aiden strode forward and scooped his sister's hand up. He embraced her and inhaled the odd fragrance she wore.

"I will take you to her momentarily, sister. But she needs time alone, now. She did, as you assumed, take it very hard."

"You will not disturb your sister, Arabella!" Merle bellowed darting from her seat. Her eyes were glittering red from her anger and she was scowling so much that it looked as if her face would at anytime sink into her mouth.

"As if you care, Mother! You hate her for reasons that are not her fault. I don't suppose you will ever tell her the truth, will you?" Arabella pointed her finger at Merle.

Merle clutched the arms of her chair as the snake around her neck became wildly alert, flapping its tongue viciously. "No one will, including you! Done is done, Daughter! You will never speak of it again in my dwelling!" Merle said shifting her jaw. "Now tell me the real reason why you have come after all of these years you have chosen to ignore your side of the family!"

"I am attending the Moon masquerade in Gorias, as I told you already, and I figured I'd visit poor Mia. I can see nothing has changed." Arabella said scornfully.

"Is King Xavier Foridazzle with you as well?" Aiden asked in attempt of diverting the subject into another direction.

"No," She replied quickly keeping her eyes fixed on Merle.

Someone stirred behind the door, and Aiden released the breath he was holding in welcome to the interruption.

"Enter," Merle growled.

One of Aldrich's Barbarians entered and nodded his greetings. He stepped aside while the Barbarian Emperor stepped through in a sweeping brown robe. Aldrich nodded to Merle and when his eyes fell on Arabella, they lingered with a mysterious light. She too was immobile before she smiled softly.

"Please, my lady, I offer my highest regrets for your loss. My men and I will do all that we can to honor your husband," He offered.

"Thank you, my lord," She said in her sickly fake voice. "I don't want to place a burden on you, however. I know that you must take leave this evening for the masquerade."

"Nonsense!" He reproached. "I'll have it postponed. It would only be just to honor the great king of Falias, my lady."

"I don't see how that is possible," Merle replied hastily.

"I've already sent Vastidrich with word to the Viscount when I heard of his death," Aldrich replied.

"I don't know what to say," Merle said softly.

Aiden was deep in thought and remembered the words his mother spat earlier. If Aldrich could postpone a ritual masquerade without even so much as a days notice, then he already had power in Thaumatur. He isn't expanding his empire, he already ceased it.

Damn I hate it when Merle is right! How could I not see this coming?

Aiden kept his bitter thoughts hidden behind the straight smile he was showing.

I best keep peace with this foreigner so that I may keep everything I have. So what if the marriage arrangement isn't what Jacob and Mia want. At least they will be heirs to an empire.

And if Mia had such power, Aiden would want to be in her favor. That meant that he would weasel his way out of the blame for the marriage arrangements.

CHAPTER EIGHT

The Emperor's Will

The late afternoon was grey with threatening wisps of clouds violently waving across the sky. It was Lucian's wish to be incinerated, his ashes cast upon the winds. Mia clung to the arm of her older sister and supported herself against Jacob. He offered no comfort, but he did his best to avoid conflict. Suddenly the fights between her and her guard were of no importance now.

Merle stood in a pool of black lace, as still as stone, across the way beside Aldrich and his two men. Her face was downcast, but Mia wondered if she was crying or smiling. Aiden was hardly visible behind the Barbarians. The castle's priestess glided around the circle of the royal family placing clove necklaces over their heads and then moved swiftly to the middle of the white garden, her eyes wide and her cheeks vacant from tears. She cried her prayers to the Goddess for the safety of Lucian's soul during the final journey to the Heavens and then tossed the remnants of his body to the sky.

Mia couldn't feel her heart beating. There were no tears aching behind her eyelids. The world seemed to stop moving and time was stretched beyond the boundaries of reality. Then the words of her father entered her mind with a force as strong as the Whispers that called to her.

Do not let them trap you here. You are too special for that.

"Father…" her lips barely moved when she spoke his name. It drifted away with the wind and the ashes it carried.

Arabella gently squeezed Mia's shoulders and guided her away from the white garden into the palace while others followed in a silent procession. From the corner of her eye, she had thought she caught a glimpse of flapping silver and white wings, but when she looked again, she saw nothing. She just about convinced herself that the beautiful owl was a part of her tired mind's overactive imagination.

Hyacinths and candles lined the walls of the hall and jasmine incense were lit in honor of the deceased king and with the intent to comfort the bereaved. It didn't work for Mia. Servants stood in the shadows eagerly waiting to serve with their hands filled with trays and pitchers of refreshment. How simple it must be to live their lives to serve others.

Mia took a seat at the high board between Arabella and Aldrich. Aldrich placed a large hand over hers and looked at her with sincerity.

"I'm sorry, my lady. I only wish I could've known him better," he said sadly.

"Perhaps it's better this way," Mia swallowed her wine. "The less he suffers now." She could hear a trace of ice in her voice. It wasn't driven by some seen motive, but from a numbness that she couldn't explain.

Deception, Control, Betrayal…

A Whisper grazed across her ears that sounded much like the whimsical voice of the owl. She didn't know where it came from or why, but she took it as a sign. It wasn't the first time something reached her without the vision of an imagined creature. It was time for her to follow the path laid before her, whatever it may be.

Betrayal…

The Whisper repeated with the sound of an ocean rushing through her ears, pushing her head and eyes around the tables, searching for something.

Then it struck her. Vastadon was nowhere to be found. On this day of all days he couldn't stand by her side? Heat rushed to her cheeks, pushing some life into her frozen body. She took a long quenching sip of wine and pushed Vastadon from her mind. If she didn't, it would place her in a bad position with his father.

As the hours past, Mia felt dizzy and bold from the sweet wine. She drank a little heavier than normal. Every goblet she put down made her yearn for more. She wouldn't sink entirely into the clouds of booze. She didn't speak for most of the night, and it seemed that those who were nearby knew enough not to attempt conversation. The court was louder and freer with their words. It was as if nothing changed and the memory of Lucian's death was a mere dream.

"Sister, I *will* be taking you to the masquerade, I hope you know," Arabella whispered drawing her attention.

"And I *will* be going with you," Mia replied coldly.

"Then I will request that you come to Findias with me for a little while," Arabella said in a firm voice. "This place will do you no good but preserve you in bitterness."

Arabella wasn't directing the finality of her words toward Mia, but toward their mother and Aiden.

"Good," Mia answered and stood. "Anywhere is better than this damned place!"

Mia hadn't realized the volume of her voice until she saw all of the court gaping at her. She scowled at them and turned her fiery eyes on her brother, who held his cup halfway to his lips. He shifted his eyes from her to the hearth nervously.

The crackling flames were elevating with enchantment. *Her* enchantment. The flames ran through her blood into her heart and up her throat in a tide of the magic that she was born with. She had no clue how to control her magic and at this point, she didn't care. It wouldn't take much to cause a scene.

"I am accompanying my sister and Emperor Aldrich to the masquerade, no matter what you or mother say. It's final," Mia narrowed her eyes wickedly as the flames leaped higher and higher in the hearth.

Mia knew Aiden feared nothing more than embarrassment and Merle was so secretive that she wouldn't want any to know just how much magic her daughter was born with. The embarrassment Aiden felt now with her clear defiance would be nothing if she turned the hall into an inferno.

Horrible things raced through her mind. Dark things. Things she would never have dreamed of doing. But here she stood; ready to embrace the shadow that threatened to darken her heart. Merle shot to her feet wordlessly, her steel posture was bent from apprehension. Mia was thrilled to have placed her in such a position.

Oh, yes, Mother. I will uncover your secrets soon. The south tower, my father said?

A smile spread across Mia's lips as she studied the two of them sweating. "Try to forbid me!"

"Mia, come, sit…you are fatigued and in a state not of your own…." Aiden fumbled with his words.

"Then you don't forbid me?" Mia asked pushing her limits without care.

"Of course you can go, um, if you are up to it that is," Aiden replied shifting his eyes across the onlookers fretfully.

"I'm up to it. I'll prepare now," Mia gathered her gown, and turned her eyes on Jacob. "Come, if you wish to escort me."

Jacob took a swig of his ale and kicked the chair out from under him. He was trying to hide his amusement when he looked at his brother.

"I'll return momentarily after I tuck the brat in," he said in a voice thick from drinking. Aldrich stared up at him showing no sign of his thoughts and nodded. Jacob stumbled off behind her.

Mia was so angry that she was able to find her way through the dark corridors by instincts. Jacob's footsteps sounded behind her, and, unlike any other time, she welcomed the sound. Perhaps a good fight would shake the wickedness from her. Once they reached the doors of her chamber Mia took hold of Jacob's wrist and pulled him inside instead of shutting the door in his face.

"I despise you!" She spat at him.

"Then why did you drag me in here, when I could be on my way back down to put away more ale?" He laughed.

"You are drunk!" Mia scowled.

"And so are you," he said pointing a wavering finger at her.

He was staggering and his eyes were lazy beneath the soft glow of the candlelight. She wanted to see anger, not this.

"Some bodyguard you are! If someone were to attack me, my cat could've been a better defender than you now!"

"Like an attacker would get close enough to you, you little spitfire *magician*," he said mockingly.

"Get out of my sight!" Mia ordered with a wave of her hand.

"As you wish!" Jacob said and turned to leave.

Mia threw herself in front of the door before Jacob could leave. Her mind was spinning, as her room was now. "Where do you think you are going?" she cried arching her head up at him with a vicious sneer.

"You are crazy!" Jacob shook his head.

The smile on his face remained and the normal bitterness he held for her was nowhere to be found. The drink softened him into a stupor. He grabbed her by the waist placing her out of his way, but she clung to him like a cat clung to the edges of a pail of water. They struggled until they both fell onto her bed. He was huge and if he had put the full of his weight on her, she would've been crushed. He smelled of man and wild spice, a hint of the potent ale on his breath, and his hair was soft against her cheek. For a moment, her struggling ceased and she contemplated how it would feel to lay in his arms. To absorb the strength always carried within his warm body. To forget the obvious bitterness between them. Her body reacted to him, but her intelligence was winning the battle. His muscles were tense and firm around her, and for a brief moment he too seemed to relish the feel of their bodies' proximity. She set her jaw in aggravation against her own absurd drunk thoughts. She wiggled her hand free and slapped him hard across the face. "What's wrong with you? Say something, anything! Don't stand there and take it!"

She hit him again and again until finally he pulled himself free of her grip.

"Go to bed and sleep it off!" he growled looming over her like a mountain. He was irritated, but it wasn't to her expectations.

Mia was breathing heavy and felt the sting behind her eyelids for the first time since Lucian died. Was she going mad? Damn Vastadon, damn him for not being here. She needed *his* arms around her, pulling her tightly against *his* skin. She sat up angrily, and almost asked Jacob to stay. Instead she spoke begrudgingly.

"Tell me, Jacob, where's Vastadon on this night? Of all nights, he leaves me alone."

"My nephew cares only for the wellbeing of himself. I would've thought you were bright enough to figure that out by now," Jacob said frankly.

"He cares for me, Jacob. He'd never hurt me," Mia rebuked and crossed her arms over her bosom. Even as the words shot from her mouth, some uncertainty lingered in the corners of her heart.

. "Believe what you want." Jacob shrugged his shoulders and wiped some blood from the corner of his mouth.

Mia sobered a little, and felt some guilt in beating Jacob up. Some guilt and some humor. She must've caught him with her fingernails. How could she have been so vicious? She didn't want to hurt anyone.

She got to her feet and broke a leaf off of one of her healing plants. She went to Jacob and wiped the leave across his cut, while he swatted her away.

"No magic!" he growled.

"You are being stupid. It's not magic. It's a plant leave," Mia snapped and continued applying the healing substance. "I'm sorry. I don't know what came over me. I thought that if you fought with me, I might forget things…" She apologized after a few moments of silence.

"I am drunk! I'll fight with you tomorrow!" He stomped to the door.

"On the way to the masquerade, you will have plenty of time," she replied. "Please, send my sister up, for I need a companion this eve."

"Sure I will."

Fifteen minutes later, Arabella was there.

The booze was wearing off and the fogginess of Jacob's little dance with the *magician* carved across his memory. Had he been in his right mind, he would've given her the fight she wanted. Or perhaps a little more… He ground his teeth and erased his moment of weakness. After all, she was a woman, and he was a man no matter the race. And he was drunk.

She apologized and proceeded to wipe me with that slime.

There would've been a lot of things prevented had he been of sound mind. He had to admit that he rather enjoyed the bold display he saw in the hall earlier on. The demon-loving queen was speechless for once. It was odd that she would allow her daughter to speak so freshly before the eyes of so many.

Aldrich refrained from drinking all night, and his eyes were drawn with exhaustion. Yet he lingered in the hall, without words. Jacob was bitter from the night before. However, he still worried for his brother. He nudged Aldrich and jerked his head toward the enclosed portico just outside the hall.

"What troubles you, Brother?" Jacob asked him once they were alone.

Aldrich sighed heavily and gripped the balustrade before him.

"Something is very wrong," He replied distantly. "I feel it. The darkness within this place is well hidden. The High Chaplain warned me of such things. It's why he refused to take the journey."

"And you wish for me to bring a piece of it back to my home, where the people rely on me to keep such things out," Jacob shook his head. "Sometimes you make no sense."

"A war is a war, Jacobane, no matter who is involved. I know what our father believed, yet he wasn't free of guilt either. He allowed the vengeful Tribes to run rampant across the valleys and the waters of this land, to murder Thaumaturi women and children alongside of the men. It goes both ways," Aldrich spoke with wearied irritation.

"Yet you tell me now that you sense evil in this land. An evil that Chaplain Hector Altorius warned you of?" Jacob rebutted.

"Not in this land. In this castle," Aldrich shifted his tired eyes to his brother. "You're the only one who can marry this princess. She is different from the others. I fear that she is in grave danger here."

Jacob grimaced and folded his arms. The night air was cold, but it wasn't the wind that sent chills down his spine. He too felt the darkness, only he'd grown accustomed to it during his long disruption here. Mia wouldn't help the situation, nor was she any different than those who dwelled here. Aldrich needed to let go.

"When are you going to see that the Thaumaturi aren't our problem?"

Jacob growled. "I'm not you and I'll not find love with a Thaumaturi as you have. You cannot go back in time through me!"

"You misunderstand me, Jacob. A war is coming," Aldrich confirmed. "A war in which both Barbarian and Thaumaturi will be subjected to."

It was as if somebody dumped a pail of ice cold water down Jacob's back giving him the uncomfortable feeling that Aldrich spoke truth. War was something he wouldn't embrace easily. And now it seemed that his brother spoke in twisted riddles, just as the *magicians* wailed in the streets of the market. He turned his back in denial.

"And your woman has told you this?" Jacob scoffed throwing his hands in the air. "It's about her? You let her toy with your mind, Brother."

"It's not about her. It's about protecting the existence of the world."

"Why not let your son marry Miarosa. It's what they both want."

"I trust no other more than you. I love my son, but I cannot see his position on things clearly. I fear for him. It must be you. And that comes from me, not my woman. Princess Miarosa is a naïve girl. She isn't corrupt."

"Just like the Queen Mother of this place?" Jacob shook his head.

"I'm no fool, Jacobane," He replied slowly. "I know Merle isn't to be trusted. It's my intention to appear unthreatening and enthralled. She doesn't serve the Goddess of this land, or our Gods. She is a servant to some unspeakable evil. And I believe she plans to use her own daughter to benefit her."

"Then why did she agree to send her so far away," Jacob shook his head skeptically.

"Merle wishes for the girl to suffer resentment and animosity. She knows the way the two of you despise one another and wants to use it to her advantage. What she does not count on is my secret knowledge. I know that the marriage union between you and Miarosa will be the key to something much greater. You'll be my successor to the throne alongside your Thaumaturi wife. Unity will defeat all evil, Barbarian mercenaries and dark Thaumaturi alike."

"I've no interest in the throne. I wouldn't follow your path," Jacob protested.

"You're a fair man, and despite your bigotry, you have honor. You wouldn't slaughter innocent people no matter their race. I need you to accept the throne and I need you to marry her," Aldrich spoke desperately.

"Vastidrich is eager to replace you."

"Vastidrich is a fool!" Aldrich roared.

"Father would look down on this if he still lived."

"He birthed you with his hate! Let go of your hate, Jacobane! Love and will peace among this world. You must promise me," Aldrich grasped both of Jacob's arms tightly. "It was Mother's wish for you to be my successor. Just as she yearned for the peace I am working so hard to obtain now."

The determination in Aldrich's eyes was so fierce that it made Jacob flinch. He couldn't deny the brother he loved so much this. His heart wrenched with the memory of his mother. "Please. Don't speak to me of our mother."

"You carry a blame that isn't even yours." Aldrich shook his head but he knew enough to return to the original subject. "I will ask you one more time."

"I will honor your wish. However, things always change," Jacob submitted.

The exhaustion miraculously lifted from Aldrich with his promise. Jacob would agree to anything his brother asked to protect him.

"Say nothing of this promise and continue to show your disinterest in the throne. It will protect you and her."

Jacob nodded and whispered, "It makes no sense."

"I know, but it will to the two of us in time," Aldrich replied and cast his eyes across the white fields.

For a moment it felt as if they were the only two left in the world as they let the silence captivate them. Then, as if an apparition took form, Jacob saw a glowing white owl soaring across the moon. He blinked and the ethereal bird was gone.

CHAPTER NINE

Earth Magic

The journey to Gorias began at dawn's first light. Mia rode in a litter with Arabella as far away from Aiden as possible. Her sister napped most of the way and when she didn't, she complained that her back hurt and how battered her appearance must be. Mia shared her prayer that they might have a chance to freshen up before the masquerade.

Mia stuck her head out between the drapes to look outside. There was no snow on the ground and the air was cleaner and clearer then in Falias. Tall grass swayed in the wind along side thin stemmed yellow flowers. Oak and spruce trees lined the road in brilliant gold, crimson, and browns. They were at the edge of the forest, but Mia couldn't see too far ahead as to how close they were to the Fall Palace.

"Knight," Mia called to a man garbed in the blue robes of her kingdom. "How much further?"

"Not so far. Over the hill into the valley and we are there," The knight replied and returned his attention back to the road.

"Word has it that your champion is a High Prince in the Barbarian lands," Arabella giggled from inside the litter.

Mia pulled her head back in to see Arabella playing with her fingernails and eying her with a mischievous grin.

"Jacob is hardly my champion, Arabella," she said rolling her eyes. "And yes, he is High Prince that boar!"

"I was wondering what took him so long to return after you commanded him like a dog to follow you last night," Arabella began. "When he returned, he was quite sober, and *bleeding*."

Mia's cheeks flushed. She did make quite a fool out of herself the night before. "He picked a fight with me," Mia replied falsely. "Is it my fault he picked a fight me?"

Arabella lifted her eyebrows and shook her head before returning her attention to her polished nails. For awhile they didn't speak. The hooves trotting against gravel and jingling reigns filled the air, and in the distance, Mia heard the cries of little birds. She looked back at Arabella, who was snuggled in a pool of white and beige silk skirts, her eyes barely open.

Dare I ask her…?

"What is it, Mia?" Arabella asked her lightly as if she read her mind.

Mia swallowed hard and said, "Nothing."

"You're lying to me. Sisters can tell those sorts of things. What troubles you?" Arabella asked with her eyes now fully opened.

"It's just that…well," Mia looked down at her feet.

Arabella pulled herself up and studied her with concerned eyes. "Yes?"

"Father told me something just before he…" Mia said softly.

Arabella's eyes widened and the color left her face. She darted her eyes away from her and fumbled with the sachet on her lap. "What did he tell you, Mia?"

"He mentioned the south tower." Mia watched her sister's reaction.

Arabella stilled her hands for a brief moment.

"Have you mentioned this to Aiden or Mother?"

"No," Mia said firmly.

"Good. What do you suppose Father meant?" Arabella asked more at ease.

"I was hoping you would be able to answer that—"

The caravan halted abruptly sending Mia and her sister tumbling forward. The sound of the horses' cries shrieked outside of the litter.

"What has happened?" Mia asked breathlessly and went for the curtain of the litter. Arabella gripped her collar and yanked her back wrapping her arms protectively around her.

"Stay close to me and don't invite trouble in here," Arabella commanded and spread her outer skirts to reveal a curved blade at her hip.

Mia jolted to the sound of an explosion of metal mixed with the wild cries of men. She clung to Arabella while the litter shook forcefully.

"An attack. Possibly raiders, but that would be suicide for them to attack a caravan so heavily guarded," Arabella mused. "Perhaps Outlander Barbarians, but we have in our care the royal family of their native land."

"Brother mentioned something of mercenaries," Mia said.

Arabella released her grip for a moment and another rattle of the litter sent Mia rolling through the drapes and onto the ground at the foot of a large brown boot. When she looked up, a toothless man with a silver eye and a feral beard looked down at her wildly. He held a spiked club over one shoulder and dragged her up by her hair.

"I got me a wench, boys," The man leered maliciously, spittle running down the side of his mouth. He took hold of her cheek roughly and raised his thin lips in a lusty smile. From behind the gruesome man, a thunderous battle raged and disarray masses rolled down the distant hills screaming savagely. The organized knights of Falias met them with swift precision.

Mia's heart hammered as the man's hands tightened on her face, and then she shuddered from the feeling of magic. Her body grew rigid, and for a moment, she thought she might have turned to stone.

The earth shook beneath them. The man teetered backwards loosing his grip on her. She kicked him in his groin and ran from the sound of his agonizing howl. She lost her footing again and tumbled to the ground hard. Before she could blink, another large man was charging her, his gleaming contraption of twisted metal raised above his head. The scream that erupted from his mouth paralyzed her escape. Jacob dodged in front of her driving his sword deep into the attacker's exposed middle. He spun with ease and turned his sword on her. His blue eyes were wild and blood stained his face. He swung his sword over her head slicing another warrior's throat. At the same time he unsheathed a short sword from his back. In a whirlwind of blades he killed two more. He reached a massive arm down and snatched her up.

"Return to the litter!" he thundered and when she didn't move, he shoved her, "Go now!"

Mia shook her head and ran as he commanded but she put herself behind the litter—she wouldn't risk having one of those beasts follow her right to her sister—and watched the rest of the wild men fall to the ground. Her eyes did not leave her bodyguard and his mesmerizing fluid movements. She saw Jacob bury his sword into several more men and spun with an uncommon grace for a man his size slicing one man after another with great precision. He saved her life. No other had done such a thing and no other would've had he not been there. It was his duty.

Mia's heart hammered once more, and this time the earth's tremors split the ground in two, swallowing any in its path of separation. Then she noticed a hand reaching up from the earth's split, a ring with a sapphire wolf gleaming beneath the sun.

Aiden!

She flew past a group of fighting men and fell to the ground before Aiden. He was looking up at her, his eyes filled with terror, his cheeks pale with fear.

"Mia," he gasped.

"Grab on to my hand!" Mia commanded with an outstretched arm.

He took her wrist and tried to pull himself up, but instead, she slipped downward. She used all of her might to tug upward. Her knees burned from scattered stones beneath her. Her skirt tore, and liquid oozed from her legs easing the burning from her fresh scratches. She couldn't let go of him. Despite her anger toward him, she loved him and would never see to his death.

"Mia, you cannot do this! We'll both fall! I'm too heavy! Call someone over!" Aiden bellowed on the verge of tears.

She nodded but didn't let go of Aiden's arm.

"Somebody help!" she cried but her voice was so breathless she could hardly hear herself.

The faint feeling of her heart hammered again, but she bit her lip to force the feeling down. The tremors were coming from within her, she knew. If Aiden fell it would be her fault. The top half of her body now hung over the gorge, leaving her no leverage. Her eyes widened to what was below. It was an endless pit of darkness.

"Leave me!" Aiden cried.

"No, I'll not let you go!" she exclaimed.

An arm clutched her waist and pulled her backward. She hit the ground with force and was relieved to see Aldrich pulling her brother up safely. Aiden rolled on his side and twitched with horror.

The battle was over and several bodies lay on the ground in puddles of crimson. Arabella came fluttering out of the litter and skid across the ground to Aiden's side, holding him in a mothering embrace. Aldrich and Jacob stood side by side shaking their heads at the carnage before them.

"These men are not mercenaries! What in the hell are the Tribes doing here?" Jacob asked Aldrich angrily. "The wall was breached during my absence."

Aldrich crouched beside a body and pulled a medal from beneath the bloodied tunic.

"Tusk Tribe," Aldrich said ripping the medal from the corpse's neck. "It must've been an assassination attempt on me or even you. They don't like you either."

"I know this. They hate Thaumaturi and your cause, Brother," Jacob pointed out.

"They hate anything, even each other," Aldrich corrected and met eyes with his two Barbarian companions. They were approaching holding captive one of the attackers. "Is that all of the survivors?"

"Aye. The rest are dead, all except a few that fled," Sidian snarled. "What is your will my lord?"

Aldrich paused a moment. The man before him was wounded, but he would live. He looked upon the Emperor with hatred, his eyes a burning pyre of clear defiance. He resisted the men who held him captive, though futile his efforts were. "Speak for yourself, Tuskan. I want to know the cause of your comrades' ambush."

The grizzly Barbarian sneered, but remained silent as his eyes slid over the men that circled him until he caught sight of Mia. He roared lunging with all his might. He didn't get too far with two large men securing him. Mia's heart beat fiercely, but she remained unflinchingly in her spot. She would not show fear, only pity for the captive. To allow such hatred to devour one's soul and mind…

"*Magician* lover….failure spawn!" The man thundered and looked beyond Aldrich at Jacob. "Too busy humping your brother's leg to keep your word, little prince?"

The man barked laughter. Jacob dodged for him. Aldrich hindered him with the palm of his hand. "Your savage remarks are meaningless to me and my kin." Aldrich circled the prisoner, "Who sent you, and why?"

"Your *Magician*-loving mother from the grave." The captive scoffed and spat at Aldrich.

This time, Aldrich reacted with a hard blow that broke the captive's nose. The captive howled. Aldrich looked at his companions. "Return this traitor to Vhladic at once and make certain he is kept behind bars until I return."

"But, My Lord Emperor—" Sidian's protests were silenced by the lift of Aldrich's hand.

"You are relieved. Once in Vhladic, send word to the High Prince's First Warrior to come at once. You will find him close to the Imperia Hall."

Jacob grew urgent, "Jovich has not been in Vansant Summit during my leave?"

"I have assigned him to be seated in the Senate on your behalf," Aldrich looked at him briefly. Before Jacob could respond, Aldrich told him, "I trust him completely."

"There are so few left to be trusted," Jacob murmured without argument.

"Someone has betrayed us, Jacobane. But who?" Aldrich queried, his chiseled features were pinched.

"I have a good guess," Jacob threw a glance at Mia before stomping away.

I know you don't like me, Jacob, but do not dare blame such a thing on me.

Mia clenched her fists and chased after Jacob. Aldrich put himself in her path.

"He doesn't mean you. Have patience with him. He has been through great trials and wants nothing more than to return home to his people. I've prevented it because I thought he would ease up on his prejudices by being here. I see some change."

"Well I don't," Mia huffed.

"Is there nothing you find good in my brother?" Aldrich asked quickly.

Mia detected anxiety and hurt feelings within Aldrich's voice. She sighed because she didn't like to be cruel. "Forgive me, Lord Emperor. I don't mean to hurt your feelings. If only Jacob wouldn't react to me with such revulsion. Despite our differences, it hurts me how someone could actually shutter with disgust from the mere sight of me." Mia lowered her head.

Aldrich cupped her cheek and tilted her head back up. He smiled handsomely, keeping his eyes completely focused on her. Mia's cheeks reddened a little, not only from the kindness of the gesture, but because he was careless to the onlookers that would take the scene as something much less innocent than it really was. A servant's entertainment for many Moons.

"I think you are beautiful."

What a sweet, compassionate man to say such kind words, Mia thought as her blush deepened. She wasn't accustomed to compliments unless she was in the presence of his son, whom she barely saw. It was a surprise he had no woman to call his empress.

"He is fearless," Mia grinned and when Aldrich arched a thick brow she laughed. "I admire Jacob's unwavering courage. He doesn't fear a thing, does he?"

"I think he fears women," Aldrich quipped.

"Some how I might agree with you on that," Mia burst her question out. "Why would your own people want to kill you?"

"It's complex, Miarosa. The Tribes east of the wall don't accept change very well," Aldrich said sadly and turned from her.

"What do you plan on changing?" Mia questioned.

He stopped in his tracks and called over his shoulder, "The world."

He continued walking away. A part of her wanted to embrace him, for she felt in her heart that he spoke his true desires. Something in his words brought comfort, yet a streak of apprehension prickled her spine. He would die trying, she knew it. When or if it did happen, it would be a horrible loss for all humanity. Then her mind shifted to the wise words of Nan.

Some of them were born with the Power of Water, or Earth, and some were born with the Power of Air or Fire.

What if a Mageborn possessed two Elemental Rites? Because she not only possessed Power from Fire, she possessed the Powers of Fire *and* Earth. It would be a secret she shared with no one.

CHAPTER TEN

The Fall Kingdom

When the caravan arrived at the Fall Palace, people poured from the castle gates with anticipation. After the rush load of curious onlookers subsided and the travelers' horses were taken away for resting and grooming, the royals were escorted into the council hall so that the Viscount and Gorias' King Valance Llewellyn could hear the details of what happened. Mia sat in her sister's shadow while Aldrich, Aiden, and Jacob stood at the head of the table.

The hall was as grandeur as the beautiful ruby crested palace's exterior. The room was bright from the clear skylight, and there were several floor standing candelabras, golden glass orbs of light, and jewels, scattered throughout the hall. Three tall windows dripping with embroidered crimson drapes looked over the ocean on the west wall.

A warm silvery-haired man, who looked miniature in between Aldrich and Jacob, listened to the details of the attack intently. Mia presumed him to be the Fall King.

"It was clearly an assassination attempt," Valance mimicked the words Mia heard from Aldrich at the end of the battle. "I don't see any possible way the Outlanders could've slipped so far through our defenses."

"Someone made it easy for them," Jacob snapped. Mia saw Aldrich's hand slide down to Jacob's wrist to hinder his temper.

"What my brother means to say is that, it's quite possible the Tusk Barbarians have established a treacherous alliance here, somehow," Aldrich said politely.

"What do you think, Viscount?" Valance's eyes shifted to a balding man on the far right of him.

Viscount Eamon Birch lifted his round body from his seat and scowled as much as he could through the layers of fat that jiggled beneath his chin.

"If there is a traitor among us, I shall find out whoever it is and wring his or her neck for the attempt on the life of the Good Barbarian Emperor, here. This man has done nothing but offer his hand in peace and pledge his military to protect our people from an act such as this. We need a supporter like him, because we aren't accustomed to such barbarism. I fear that we would fall under if Emperor Aldrich hadn't intervened as many times as he did." Viscount Birch banged his fist on the table hard.

"Calm down, my friend," Valance said in a soft voice and nodded in Mia and Arabella's direction, alerting the men to the presence of women, "The Goddess will see that justice is served. What we will do now is prepare for the masquerade and enjoy ourselves! My guards will inform me of any disturbances, if there will be any." He turned his attention on Mia and Arabella both, "Queen Arabella, I'm thrilled you were able to make it this time. And this must be your sister, the lovely Miarosa. I'm so sorry for the ordeal you have been through, my ladies, and for the loss of your good father. I will do my best to offer you as much comfort as you need during your stay here. Dougal, send for my women so that they can escort these ladies to refresh!" Valance bellowed and a tall red haired man with a full beard nodded and left.

Mia felt a strong liking toward the Fall King, a connection of something strange. And his home was as warm as the sun itself, not like her home at all. Jacob was at her side before she even knew he moved. He placed a heavy hand on her shoulder for a moment, and she reached her hand up to cover his. With her touch, she felt him tense and it brought a smile to her face. She didn't know why she felt the urge to touch him, but it was as if she couldn't feel any bad things within the Fall castle. She cherished everything, even Jacob, the man who put his life on the line to protect her…a woman he despised. She looked up at him. He looked away from her, and she felt his hand slide from underneath hers.

The corridors were wide and carpeted with plush crimson over polished white marble floors. In every corner, there were golden statues of the Goddess and the Four Season Daughters, flowers of vibrant colors, and random rubies, pearls, and diamonds. A raider's dream would be to enter the riches of this castle.

She followed a brightly dressed woman with braided caramel hair. Mia wouldn't have thought she was a servant by the looks of her. Jacob was close behind her, gripping the hilt of his weapon.

It must be quite a difference from home, Jacob.

"My name is Opal," The servant spoke as freely as a noble. "You must be very lucky to be guarded by a *prince*," Opal whispered. "A very *big* Barbarian Prince."

"I hadn't known he was a prince until a few days ago," Mia whispered back and giggled when she looked at Opal's astonished expression.

Mia took hold of Opal's forearm when she saw a large archway that lead out into the open. A brilliant tree, crowned with leaves, swayed in a gentle wind beyond the arch striking her curiosity. A refreshing breeze grazed her cheek and stirred her hair. With the fingers of the breeze came a Whispered song of allure.

Go see…

"Please, Opal, I would like to see what is through there," Mia said as she pointed.

Jacob grunted in annoyance, but followed the two women out onto a cobblestone walkway. Mia gasped at the splendor before her. It was a garden full of unusual looking plants and rows of ruby roses sweeping along a small brick bridge.

The gentle sound of a rushing brook and the chirping of little birds swept Mia away from the world in which she lived. To the far end of the bridge, figures of cornstalks bowed in a circle of orange dotted moss. She closed her eyes and inhaled deeply the sweet-smelling scents of apples and spices mixed with the aroma of the roses.

Slowly, with the guidance of the wind, she knelt before the rolling bushes of crimson and reached her hand out to touch the rippling face of a rose. Her eyes flew open when Jacob snatched her hand away.

"It is safe, my lord," Opal explained, "She may pick one if she likes. These ruby roses where given to our king as a gift from the Spring Kingdom of Murias. They are enchanted roses that never die no matter the condition of the weather."

Jacob eased his arm away, releasing her hands. With a slow light finger, Mia stroked the rings of soft petal. Something about the feel of it required her to pray softly for permission to cease one. Recognition, or perhaps an unspoken permission, encouraged her to grasp the stem. Opal rushed to her side nearly tripping over her skirt to help.

"Like this, Princess. If you aren't careful in capturing such beauty, you might be pricked by one of the thorns," Opal smiled.

The sage words of the servant had a meaning that went far beyond the picking of a rose. Mia would keep such philosophy in mind.

"Thank you," she replied when Opal placed the single red rose in her hand. "What is this place?" Mia asked looking around.

The haze that spellbound her didn't release its grip fully, but it wasn't such a sensation that Mia wished away.

"If you cross the bridge a little, you will see a cottage."

"I see it," Mia said lifting up on her tip-toes.

"It's the servant's quarters," Opal replied gleefully.

"Servant's quarters? My Goddess, it's so beautiful! How wondrous your King must be to offer such kindness!" Mia exclaimed with admiration.

"Our King's kindness is legendary. There isn't a soul in need he would turn away, no matter the caste or race."

Mia studied the apple trees intently. She had often read about how fruit grew on trees. Nothing compared to actually seeing such an enchanting sight.

A body crashed into her, knocking her off of her feet before she had a chance to see what was coming. She shook the stars from her head and saw Jacob was looming over her with his sword unsheathed. There were two others standing in front of them, a blonde haired man and a flame haired woman.

"My lord, please put that away. It was mere clumsiness on our part. We mean no harm to your mistress," the blonde haired man said with a light tone.

The man then turned his attention on Mia, and extended his hand out to help her to her feet. When he looked at her, his hazel eyes locked onto her. She grasped his hand and gasped. A vibration, passion, and pure heat slammed into her entire form. Her body jolted, but it didn't falter. His support prevented that. It was as if she could feel his essence inside of her. No matter how she tried, she couldn't tear her eyes from him. She could feel the recognition he had, but in what she couldn't be certain. A Whisper came....

You are one with the Goddess's Circle.

"Jacobane?" the female's voice broke the strange lock from her eyes, "Jacobane, is that really you?"

Jacob's eyebrows arched quizzically, as he considered the red headed girl. "Anne?" He asked with surprise.

"Yes, it's me, Uncle!" the girl replied excitedly and threw her arms around Jacob.

Jacob embraced her just as warmly. Mia gaped at the two of them. It was as if a curtain of gloom was lifted from her bodyguard.

"People here call me Aunyia, however," She smiled and looked at her blonde companion. "This is my friend, Horace Ebonis. He is a knight in my brigade. Horace, meet my Uncle, the Barbarian High Prince Jacobane Hilliard."

As if Horace snapped out of a dream, he released Mia's hand quickly to shake Jacob's. The heat whipped from her leaving her cold and naked.

"Very nice to meet you," he said. "And I must apologize for startling your mistress."

"Jacobane and I grew up more like brother and sister than uncle and niece. He taught me how to fight as soon as I was old enough to hold a sword," Aunyia winked and than locked her eyes onto Mia.

Aunyia was speechless for a moment, and her face softened. She was a tall woman, about her height, dressed gracefully in sleeveless velvet with a cross-laced bodice. She poised herself with the grace of a queen, and her jade eyes spoke in volumes of kindness. The intensity of the woman's gaze sent a shudder through her. Mia swallowed hard and quickly looped her arm through Jacob's.

"I suddenly feel ill, Opal. I'd like to settle in a chamber of some sort if you don't mind."

"Of course, my lady, come," Opal said worriedly and took hold of her free arm.

"Excuse me, Anne and Horace," Mia nodded politely.

"It was nice to meet you, Princess," Horace called after her.

It would've been a normal parting, but she never told either of them who she was. It seemed as if they had met before some how. No, that was impossible. Mia never traveled so far from her home before this. Actually, she never left the castle courtyard until now.

How did he know I was a princess?

Opal led them through another similar corridor and up a grand stair case to the second level of the palace. She then led Mia to a door that was set off to the side from the others in a corner that could pass for a small hallway. Opal curtsied and left promising to check on her a little later. Mia couldn't stop thinking of her connection with Horace. She *wanted* to feel it again. Her cheeks reddened when she imagined intimacy between her and a total stranger. Except he didn't *feel* like a stranger. She swore she knew every crevice of his body and mind. She shook her head and when she spun around, she noticed Jacob was still in the room. He frowned.

"What's wrong with you?" Jacob asked.

"It will not look good for you to be in here alone with me when everyone now knows that you are a prince, Jacob," Mia said ignoring his question.

"Is it because she is part Barbarian?" Jacob snapped.

"What?" Mia said, her mind clearing from the elation she felt.

"You were rude to my niece," Jacob snapped.

"I don't know what came over me, Jacob. I was overwhelmed with a sick middle! I would never intentionally be rude to anyone. Not everyone is like you," She huffed.

"You seemed to welcome, the boy *magician* okay," Jacob spat.

"Please, Jacob I don't want to argue with you about this. I don't know what you want me to say. I will not lie and say that I'm prejudice when I'm not," Mia replied.

"Perhaps it's because you despise me. I assure you that my niece is a gentle woman with a good heart. She must be hurt by your treatment," Jacob growled.

A smile spread across her face. "It enlightens me to see that you actually feel affection for someone. And I don't hate you. At least I don't hate you *here* for some reason. You have to admit, dear Jacob, that the enchantment of this place summons fulfillment in ones soul," she said and twirled around perhaps a bit too energetically. She clung to a wall as a wave of nausea quivered in her stomach. It passed thankfully.

Jacob rumbled and turned to leave.

"I will make it a point to converse with her at the ball so that she does not feel insulted!" she called after him.

Mia took a deep breath and studied the room with admiration. The high ceilings were hand painted images of the Goddess and beautiful depicts of each Season Daughter. Two large panel windows draped in red velvet curtains and embroidered with golden flowers opened up to the view of the orchards below. The four poster bed was covered with scarlet silk sheets and two large pillows rested on top of a matching woolen blanket. Several lace folds of crimson, gold, and white dripped from the posters.

What drew Mia's attention was a picture of a beautiful maiden set atop a large cherry wood bureau surrounded by ruby roses and candles of white and red. She had curls of rich chestnut kissed with gold tones that swept across a creamy and smooth complexion. Her violet eyes expressed happiness and her smile was so warm and radiant that it seemed to produce an aura around the photograph. Mia felt herself drift closer to the picture with great interest.

"She's very beautiful, isn't she?" A soft voice came from behind.

Mia wheeled around to see a slender woman veiled in the burgundy robes of a priestess. Mia didn't even hear her enter. The Priestess drew back her hood and it fell into a single ripple with her draped neckline.

Multi-toned chestnut hair strayed across her rosy cheeks and her gentle eyes rested on Mia tenderly. The woman before her resembled the maiden in the picture strongly. Mia nodded slowly.

"I am High Priestess Janella DeBurke. Welcome to your first visit to Gorias."

Mia widened her eyes and swept the Priestess' hand up to respectfully kiss it. A High Priestess was considered the closest mortal to Danu. She was to be respected as accordingly.

"Forgive me, High Priestess, for my ill manners. I didn't expect to be honored by your presence. I am Miarosa Maladinto, Winter Princess," she humbled.

"It is alright, my child," Janella laughed softly.

"Is that you in the picture?" Mia queried.

Janella cast her eyes somewhere beyond Mia, into a memory maybe, and shook her head.

"She is Cassiandra DeBurke, Eldest Princess from Murias, sister to the Spring King. My sister..." she sighed and held her arms out to her sides, "This was her room for many Moons. It is the Fall Majesty's wish for you to occupy this room. Cassiandra was very special to him, so take it as a gift."

"My brother's wife..." Mia looked at Janella quizzically.

Ahriman's wife...

Janella didn't remove the smile from her face, but the cloud of Ahriman's memory somehow darkened the brilliantly lit room. Mia rarely thought of her eldest brother Ahriman, because she hadn't known him. His name was only whispered in her home. She heard the random gossip of the servants in Falias and that is how she came to learn the name of Ahriman's wife.

"Yes," Janella replied sadly.

"I understand that he was banished from these lands for dappling in black wizardry. I know nothing about his wife. Only her name and how beautiful it was to my ears whenever I heard it," Mia said.

"She was a beautiful and strong woman. I wished you could've known her," Janella whispered bleakly.

"Some say she followed Ahriman when he left."

"No, she did not," Janella said, her eyes hardening, "She was murdered."

"Who would murder such a lovely woman?" Mia asked angrily.

"Dark forces, Mia," Janella said forebodingly, "Don't let the darkness sweep over you."

"Never," Mia replied quickly. A chill crawled beneath her skin with even the notion.

"Good," Janella smiled, "I'll let you refresh."

The High Priestess drifted to the door, her burgundy robe sweeping behind her along with the unsettling feeling of a history Mia didn't yet know about her family.

Merle circled her neck loosening the tendons. Her journey would be a quick one, and in order to cover the vast distance between Falias and her destination, she chanted a Shape-Changing spell to transform herself into a crow. It was a painful procedure, but Merle rather liked pain.

She wasn't a Mageborn, but the Power she possessed was a gift from the Darkgod who she devoted her entire life too. However, the strength and extent of her gift evolved through her. She nurtured the Power, breathing Fire, Earth, Water, and Air into it. And she would use it to bring all existence to its knees before the One she served.

She stood in an abandoned temple awaiting her contact to show his face. The inky-black temple reeked of rot, but it was secure and private. Both qualities were most necessary. It was a covered ruin, tattered from battle and blood, strong with memories of a time when she was content. A time when she could look upon her oldest son's face.

The faint sound of movement caught Merle's attention. A hooded figure emerged from the shadows. Merle found herself laughing at her contact's overactive anxiety. They were so well hidden that, even during the bright light of day, no soul would stumble upon them. No soul that mattered anyhow.

"Merle Maladinto," he said in a joyous voice, "I was beginning to wonder when you would show up again."

She studied what she could see of him. He was a tall man, though not muscular, and his presence, among most, had a way of commanding attention and possibly fears. She feared him not, for she feared nothing. She knew what he looked like beneath the concealment. She *knew* who he was and used it to her advantage.

"I wouldn't trouble myself with unnecessary journeys. Only when I learn something of importance, I come," Merle replied stridently.

"What have you learned?" the hooded man asked.

Merle laughed wickedly. The fool had yet to learn the ways of a woman with the Power. She wouldn't deny that he was a prevailing influence in her plot, but she by no means trusted him. He was known for his treachery.

"I shall tell you my secret if you tell me yours," Merle replied in a taunting voice.

"I've no secret," the hooded man growled and turned his back on her. The joy evaporated from his face and his voice in one instant.

"But you do. You live your life behind a barricade of clandestine, *Chaplain.*"

"You know what I do," the High Chaplain replied sharply, "So why do you insist on playing this game every single time we meet. I have much to do and cannot waste my time with this."

"Do you have them?" Merle snapped.

"What are you talking about, woman?" he replied.

"The shards, the weapons?" Merle's voice was jagged and strained with impatience, "Do you have them?"

"I have the shards, and they will not leave my hands," he laughed, "But you knew this."

The questions appeared to him as games. That was her intention. To her, the questions were tests, challenges to root out trickery and half-truths. Merle searched him for any deception. To her disappointment, she found none.

"Damn. I want those weapons!" Merle spun her back to him and clenched her fists, "We must locate them. Have you no knowledge of their locations?"

113

Then my son can return where he belongs!

"If I did, don't you think I would've recovered them by now?" he said sarcastically.

The tone of his voice set Merle ablaze. She turned back on him. His eyes lit up with malicious pleasure when he stepped closer to her into the illumination of the moon.

"Do not be sarcastic with me!" Merle warned, "All of the information I have on you would send you straight to the execution block!"

"As if they would believe you over me," he grumbled, "My reputation hasn't been dulled from *that* war."

"You shouldn't underestimate me. Remember, it was I who found you out," she hissed. "I can see it now. Thaumaturi sacrificed to the forbidden Darkgod by the hands of the Barbarian Brotherhood. You couldn't flee fast enough nor far enough away could you? Defiling your own Gods and murdering Thaumaturi in cold blood," she clucked. "Your Emperor would be devastated."

"Do not threaten me!" he bellowed, but his voice calmed and his face loosened into horrible joy, "I had thought you less foolish than your firstborn. He wasn't so wise to break our agreement. I truly hope you would know that it would be unwise to betray me."

"And you say that the Darkgod favors you over all?" she laughed mockingly, "Yet you couldn't give him what I have."

"Enough of this bickering, woman!" the chaplain bellowed, "Tell me of your secret."

"Perhaps I should go forth and leave you alone with your wonderment. After all, I know your views on women. Yet it's women that you've needed most when things fall apart. Is that not what you do now?"

"I've learned to view you as something very different than a woman," he said and waved his hand through the air as if he were swatting away unwanted recognition. "I have no use for women."

"I am flattered by your compliment, but it's a bit hypocritical, considering your newly found friendship with the Emperor's sister. It seems that she is the only royal descendant that pays you much attention." Merle smiled satisfied with her shrew remarks.

She could feel the heat rise off of him, and he was losing control of it.

It was what she did best. Pushing buttons and limits were a form of amusement for her.

"The Lady Sasha," he tightened his jaw, "looks to me for comfort. And in return, she has kept me well informed about what goes on surrounding that wall. If any threats would arise, I am confidant that she would provide me with fair warning. In other words, we use each other. I need her not."

"Then I suppose you care not about another woman, a girl in fact," she paused and saw him shudder. "Then I did waste my time with this journey." Merle brushed past him.

"Wait!" he bellowed, his eyes were wide with desire, "Tell me about her. I wish to know."

"I'd thought you would," Merle smiled. "Sometimes I feel that you may be using me as well. I would hate to think you ungrateful."

"Don't be foolish. You know I am grateful for you. I always have been," he murmured, "Now, tell me, I must know."

It was so easy to pinpoint the weakness in every man. They were allured by desires. And for a man who had no use for women, he certainly desired them. She strode back toward him, her expressions took on seriousness.

"The girl has found her magic. She is a Mageborn who possesses Fire Magic," Merle confirmed. "Her magic is strong. She will be the one."

"Good," he said with wicked pleasure, "How soon will you bring her to me?"

"Patience," she replied. "It is too soon."

Disappointment befell him, though he tried to conceal it. She wasn't handing over her precious gem so easily. Much time and development were needed before anything could be done.

"I hope you can oversee things properly with the girl," he replied anxiously.

"I have already begun. She must progress, but progress to darkness," Merle grinned. "I have planted the seeds of poison already. We just have to wait until the time is right. Then we will strike this world like a viper. You, on the other hand, have much work to do concerning the Emperor and his peaceful nation. Stir things up a bit."

"It isn't hard to do with this Emperor. Luthros was much more difficult with his compulsive bigotry and tight boundaries," the Chaplain paused for a moment placing a hand under his chin, "Yes, a battle would indeed scatter the forces. It will be done."

"That is the spirit," Merle quipped.

She then took leave and headed back to Falias to oversee her plans. She would too work from her side of the world and whisper in the ears of those she could bend. First things first, it was time to prepare for a wedding.

CHAPTER ELEVEN

Shattered

The Gorias dining hall was covered with banners of every lord, king and nobleman known in Thaumatur as well as the fierce panther and thorn of the Barbarian Empire. Jubilant music filled the hall and servants danced to and fro with arms full of trays and pitchers. The food that was offered varied from lemon fish to candy glazed mutton and baked hen. The wine and ale flowed freely and dashing men and glamorous women of all sorts laughed and danced together arm and arm. Alluring jewels and golden streams were strewn in every corner, and a multitude of candles suspended in the air above them.

In the center of the grand hall, a golden statue of the Goddess rose, crowned with silk veils and adorned with rubies. The hall was mixed with the delicious aromas of food and the fresh snap of roses and frankincense.

Arabella wore a backless gown of teal satin that spanned out at her feet and she held in her hand a mask with peacock feathers. Arabella also chose the costume for Mia.

"You never wear white or silver," Arabella had said earlier that evening. "So I figured I would bring you a gown that had both."

The gown was beautiful, a bodice of the purest white seamed with sparkling silver. The skirt fell endlessly to the floor in silk waves of white and silver with patterns of golden stars, the back was laced with gold and flowing white chiffon. Arabella also crafted Mia a crown of diamonds and stars to match, as well as a mask with feathers that resembled a dove. When she was dressed and Opal finished delicately braiding the hair at her temples, Arabella squealed with delight when she saw her.

"My little dove," she exclaimed, "The very symbol of peace!"

King Valance feasted among his people at a table with several youths as opposed to taking a seat above the court at the high board. Among them sat Jacob's niece, who was dressed in a shoulder-less red gown embroidered with black and gold cords. She wore a rose behind her ear, which blended nicely with the fiery tones of her hair.

Holding true to her word, Mia excused herself from Arabella and walked over to the table.

"Hell,." The girl smiled warmly up at her. "You look striking tonight, my lady."

Her voice sang with joy, and her warm welcome made Mia feel less awkward.

"Hi, uh, Anne is it?" Mia smiled.

"Call me Aunyia, my lady. Please," She said extending her hand inviting her to sit beside her.

Mia nodded and sat saying, "I must apologize for my rude behavior earlier. I didn't mean to rush off. I just felt—"

"Ill," Aunyia finished the sentence for her, "It is quite alright, Lady. I wasn't offended in the least."

"Mia," she said and offered her hand.

Aunyia took it firmly and sang, "Mia."

You are one with the Circle.

The recognizable words captured Mia along with the hand that touched her. The same unwarranted elation of familiarity encircled her, and the clout of it affected Aunyia as well. Confusion filled Mia because she couldn't imagine a passion so deep shared between women, nor did she find a woman appealing in such a way. But the girl's touch ignited something within her though it wasn't accompanied by the same lust she felt when she touched Horace. Their gazes locked in a timeless struggle to hold tight to the enchantment between them.

"My lady," A man's voice interrupted them and Mia released Aunyia's hand quickly.

Horace was wearing a white mask that concealed the top part of his face. He was dressed in a pearly white tunic and white leather breeches threaded with golden squares. His blonde hair framed his soft, boyish face, and fell past his shoulders freely. Mia was captured by his hazel eyes. Desire to stroke his fine skin and silky hair slammed into her once again. A knowing twinkle danced in his eye.

"I am glad to see that you are feeling better," he said through a half smile and then scooped Aunyia's hand in his.

"Welcome back to the table Horace. You have been bouncing all over the place with great vigor. I do hope you are having a grand old time," Aunyia jested.

"But of course. However, I never depart for too long. I find it difficult to stay a way from such a beautiful little rose," He winked.

Little rose…Nan. Mia winced. How she missed Nan. How she needed her now more than ever.

"What is wrong?" Aunyia asked.

"What, oh nothing," she replied struggling with her thoughts on Nan.

"It looks as if your face melted into a puddle of gloom," Aunyia replied. "What troubles you?"

"Oh, it's just that my governess use to call me her little rose," Mia forced a smile.

"How nice. You cared for her didn't you," Aunyia commented.

"Very much," Mia shook her head, "I miss her."

"You are the Winter Princess, aren't you? My Father and Uncle mentioned you to me," Aunyia smiled. "They speak highly of you."

"I know you're uncle, but I don't believe I met your father." Mia furrowed her brow.

"But of course you did! My father is the Emperor of the Barbarian Nations!" Aunyia laughed.

"My Lord Aldrich is your father?" Mia asked with excitement. *Vastadon is your brother?*

"Yes!" Aunyia laughed.

"Forgive me, Aunyia, I didn't know! I suppose I thought Jacob was your uncle by another sibling," Mia said feeling a bit foolish. "Aldrich is a wonderful man!"

"And he is quite fond of you too."

"Jacob spoke highly of me?" Mia said disbelievingly.

"Well, he didn't show any signs of disagreement when Father talked of you. And my father said that you were as lovely as the morning dew."

The girls both laughed, and Mia discovered that she liked Aunyia a great deal. She was a joyous girl, and as Jacob assured Mia earlier, she had a good heart.

"Well, Aunyia, your father demands that his lovely daughter dance with him at least once before the night's end. And he wanted me to remind you how long it has been since the two of you seen each other," Horace said.

Aunyia sighed and rolled her eyes as she stood. She kissed Horace on the cheek quickly, excused herself, and glided off with her gown flowing behind her.

Horace reached out and grasped Mia's hand. She clung to it as he pulled her to her feet. The sensation of familiarity was vague with his touch, but it was still there.

"Would you honor me with a dance, my lady?" Horace smiled widely and gracefully kissed her hand.

"Of course, my lord," Mia curtsied.

Horace twirled her out onto the white marble floor, never letting go of her hand. They swept, looking much like a blur of white and silver-gold at a smooth pace. It was as if they had coordinated their attire for this dance. His warm smile was frozen, and his handsome hazel eyes studied her with an impish twinkle.

"So, Princess, I was wondering when your brother would share you with the rest of the world. Although I must say, one can not blame him for hiding such a beauty," Horace quipped and dipped her body, sweeping her back up.

Mia could tell that his charm was like another sense, much like sight or sound. Yet there was something very honest and noble about him. She enjoyed his company and the way it felt to be in his arms. It was a comfort that was so powerful, that her conscience reminded her of Vastadon. A screen of guilt covered her heart.

"Well, I am quite happy about it, my lord. One can become very restless if cooped up for too long," Mia replied lightly. "Are you a knight?"

"Aye, as the lovely Aunyia is. Our brigade within the Sun Knighthood is special. We only share it with few others."

"I see, and so you say that your brigade is so superior, that you need no others," Mia laughed.

"Nay, it would only hinder our talents," He said and grew serious. The music was coming to a stop, but he didn't release her. "Mia, this may not make sense to you now, but we have been trained skillfully and perfectly to protect *you*," He whispered in her ear his breath hot and his lips soft. "You are one with the Circle."

He caressed her cheek with his thumb and placed a gentle kiss on her forehead. He released her, leaving behind the intoxicating smell of ginger, and floated into the sea of people. Mia was speechless. The Circle and his words laced together in her mind flawlessly, making eccentric sense, but she couldn't possibly understand their meanings.

She returned to her sister's side and remained fairly silent. She was trapped in bewilderment of how the crazy things Horace said to her felt genuine and real.

"I saw you dancing, Mia," Arabella whispered puckishly. "The two of you looked absolutely beautiful out there."

Mia blushed and swatted at her sister, "Stop that!"

"I am serious. All eyes were on you, even the dancers stopped and watched," Arabella continued.

Mia listened to her sister point out all of the flaws of the women who passed until she spotted Vastadon DeLucible toward the front of the hall. Her nerves frayed when she saw him. From where she sat he couldn't see her. She was hurt because he didn't come to her father's funeral, yet she cared deeply for him all the same and would offer him a chance to explain. He was sitting across from a man she recognized to be the Viscount and an extremely beautiful woman. The woman's platinum hair was swept up elegantly in a mass of uneven curls at the crown of her head. She was dressed in an emerald sleeveless gown that dipped down accentuating her form, and she wore no mask. She was perfectly stunning. The woman looked to be a great deal younger than the Viscount, so she surely couldn't be his wife. Mia leaned into her sister's ear.

"Who is that sitting with the Viscount? The blonde woman, I mean," Mia whispered.

"Oh, that must be Camille, his daughter. My, she is all grown up," Arabella sniffed. "Absolutely beautiful, as she always was."

Mia swallowed the jealous feeling down. Camille Birch threw her head back in laughter as she playfully swatted at Vastadon's hand.

I wonder what is so funny over there. Mia thought bitterly.

She excused herself and decided to get a closer look at them. Before she moved two feet from the table, a big hand clamped down on her shoulder. It was Jacob. His eyes were narrowed with suspicion. He didn't wear a mask and he remained in his usual attire. Poor sport.

"Where have you been, Mia?" Jacob hissed in her ear, "I have looked everywhere for you!"

"Now you have found me," Mia replied and put a finger to her mouth then pointed in the direction of the Viscount who stood from his seat and waddled to the center of the hall.

"It is a splendid night for a ball, isn't it?" The Viscount bellowed.

The crowd howled their agreements smacking goblets with one another merrily. Once the crowd again hushed, the Viscount continued his speech.

"As you all know, we have in our presence here tonight, a great man not of our own kind," Eamon slurred slightly from a great deal of drink. "An Emperor to his lands and an ally to all of us here. Aldrich Hilliard has generously offered his protection to our women and children from the bands of wild mercenaries who have on more than one occasion invaded our coasts. They spare no one." The Viscount paused enough to allow the crowd to murmur their agreements. With a wave of his hand to indicate that he wasn't through with words, the crowd fell silent.

"Aldrich has also given me the best gift of all and I am going to share my joy with you tonight. A marriage between our kin and I invite you to celebrate the union of my beautiful daughter, Camille Mesa Birch to Vastadon Hilliard DeLucible!"

The crowd erupted joyously, all but Mia. She felt as if she was slapped in the face with the thorn of Vastadon's kin. Tears filled her eyes as the sounds around her diluted into senseless murmurs.

Betrayed...

The Whisper reminded her of its prior warning. Vastadon stood and embraced the Viscount warmly, his future bride clinging to his arm like a trophy. Then the two of them collided in a long kiss. Mia could no longer take it, so she grabbed her mask and met eyes with Jacob. "I wish to return to my chamber," she said distantly

Mia gaited forward and when she reached the end of the hall, she glanced over her shoulder. Vastadon noticed her for the first time, and in his eyes she could see panic revealing that he hadn't expected her to be there after all. His intentions to speak with Aiden were never true. Traitor! His grin melted from his face and he began to excuse himself from the people around him. Mia turned away.

"Let us go quickly, before he catches up with me. I cannot stand to look at the turncoat now, for I fear I may spit on him," she told Jacob and jogged up the stairs.

Arabella was sprinting alongside of her, her hair loosely falling from the veils. Mia filled Arabella in on her relationship with Vastadon while they sat together in the litter earlier on their journey. Her older sister was thrilled and curious of the entire prospect of newly found love. It wasn't love at all, but the bittersweet drumming of resentment deep inside of the most precious parts of her.

They entered Mia's chamber and Arabella bolted the door behind them. She noticed Jacob was still in the room.

"Well it's too late now," Arabella snapped. "I am not risking letting that pig you call nephew in here just to let you out."

Jacob didn't respond, but carried his large form out onto the balcony away from the two women. Arabella wrapped her arms around Mia.

"Oh, darling, I am so sorry!" Arabella cried rocking her younger sister gently. "I only wish I were by your side sooner, and then I could've determined whether or not he was good! I should've been here for you!"

"I leave tonight, sister," Mia said flatly. "I will not risk a confrontation with him."

"Then I shall leave with you. And together we will gather some things from your home and return to the Summer Kingdom. Within my dwelling, the pig will be long forgotten." Arabella smoothed the younger girl's hair and then squeezed her even tighter.

"Mia!" Vastadon's bellow came from behind the rattling door, "Let me in! Mia!"

"Go away! You have done enough for one night, pig!" Arabella yelled back at him.

"Please, my ladies, I only want one word!" Vastadon pleaded.

"No!" Arabella snapped and squeezed Mia closer to her.

He sounded so desperate. Mia couldn't deny her feelings for him and how hurt she was from the announcement. The truth remained; he wanted to play two sides of a coin. She would have never known the truth. He knew how Aiden isolated her from the world.

"I still love you, Mia! I didn't want this!" Vastadon thundered and pounded the door, "You were supposed to be *my* wife not *his!*"

"What?" Mia's surprise was barely a whisper.

She tried to stand, but Arabella hindered her. "He is drunk, Mia, and grasping at anything he can to get you to open that door. Trust me, I know his kind," Arabella snapped. "Don't you think he had his chance to marry you? Of course he did, but he wanted a more influential wife, one who is closest to the heart of power. Pay no attention to him."

"I never wanted this!" Vastadon rambled on and on.

Jacob flew from the balcony, with his hand gripped on the hilt of his sword beneath his tunic and whipped open the door to stare at his nephew.

"Get a hold of yourself, Vastidrich, and take yourself downstairs to face the choice you've made."

"You sneaky bastard!" Vastadon spat at him, "What the hell are you doing in here! Hypocrite!"

Jacob turned his angry eyes on Arabella and barked, "Lock the door behind me!"

He darted from the chamber and so did Vastadon's voice.

"Keep quiet and sober up Vastidrich!" Jacob ordered once they were well away from Mia's chambers.

Vastadon clumsily swung at him, missing completely. Jacob grabbed him by his robe firmly. He was far beyond anger to focus on striking Jacob, who was highly trained in combat skills. And he wouldn't dare use his magic so openly.

"You are vermin, Uncle!" Vastadon spat and struggled to get his hands around the big man's throat.

The younger man's handsome face was red and twisted, his nostrils flared rapidly. Jacob stared back at him with emotionless irritation.

And to think he was the successor to the empire. Jacob stifled a laugh, and for the first time, he understood Aldrich's desires to keep his son from the throne. The boy would play with the empire as if it was a game board.

"It isn't set in stone, nephew, so get a hold of yourself!" Jacob growled and after a few moments, Vastadon's features eased, "You will now have to marry Birch, I am afraid, but, believe me when I tell you that I will do all that I can to change your father's mind about my arrangement."

"I hate her!" Vastadon began and pushed himself away from Jacob, "but I love her all the same."

Jacob assumed he was speaking of Miarosa.

"You cannot have both women. It's inappropriate even among the *magicians*," Jacob replied coldly.

"I am part Thaumaturi too, you know. Maybe you should watch what you say," Vastadon shot back and smoothed his ruffled cape.

"The better part of you is Barbarian and you know this."

"There you are, love!" A sleek voice interrupted, "I have searched everywhere for you."

Camille Birch slid a slender arm around her future husband's waist and pulled him close to her. She was smiling widely. There was a certain arrogant lift in her chin. Vastadon's face immediately melted into a charming smile when he looked at her.

"Uncle," his voice took on an irritably warm tone, "I would like you to meet Camille, my fiancée."

She extended her hand and met his eyes with a flirtatious glint and said, "Charmed, my lord. I must admit, love, that I can see where you get your good looks from."

Jacob grunted and left the two of them alone. Their laughter chased him in his flight.

They are made for each other.

Jacob turned a corner too quickly and nearly collided with a priestess in burgundy robes. She wasn't alone. A simmering fire ignited inside his stomach when he looked to see his brother, Aldrich, clinging to the priestess' hand. The woman turned her face away and snagged her hands from Aldrich, but it was too late. Jacob saw it all.

"So is this the woman you start wars over," Jacob hissed.

The hurt and embarrassment on his brother's face made him wish he bit his tongue. The priestess drifted away, but Aldrich hindered her with his hand.

"High Priestess Janella DeBurke, meet my brother Jacobane. He is my closest friend and most trusted confidant."

"Yes, Aldrich has spoken highly of you to me," Janella said in a soft but commanding voice.

When Jacob met her gaze, he felt the singe of her eyes upon him. He turned his eyes from her quickly.

"I will leave you too it, then." Jacob swept away.

CHAPTER TWELVE

Forbidden

High Chaplain Hector Altorius paced restlessly within the dimness of the temple's cellar. It was there that he could go to think, to feel, and to receive the direction of his God. The people in Vhladic revered him, believed his words and promises as if *he* were a god himself. And some even valued his voice over their own emperor. It was how he liked things, and besides he viewed himself as the closest mortal to a god one could get.

Hector's last visit with the self-esteemed Merle excited him and worried him all the same. The girl was past womanhood and she would soon be his to mold, to consume, and to use. But he found that he questioned Merle's delay in the plot. He was no fool, and she knew that he wouldn't yield in his design.

In the end, Merle would align herself with power. And he would be the one who held it. If the girl's Power was as great as Merle said, he would have much persuasion to do. He had the Darkgod with him, all around him. Vhladic was the Darkgod's domain.

Hector was neither Thaumaturi nor Barbarian—his kind had faded ages ago—although he could pass for either. He was a tall man and preferred to wear the braids of the Barbarian heritage, but his eyes spoke in mysterious volumes that only a true Mageborn could pick up on.

Hector had festered for many years in solitude, beneath the grounds of Vhladic's holy palace, behind his public face, remembering the days of glory and power. The Goddess' attempt to bring forth the perfect being was flawed. The Mageborn had two sides of her soul, so contrast to one another, like day and night. Light forces and Darkness. He laughed aloud. The sound of his voice echoed ten times its resonance in the hollowed chamber. He knew that it would only be a matter of patience and time before he could indulge in a reign of tyranny again. Once the girl was where he wanted her, she would bring forth the remaining weapons he failed to acquire.

Ahriman became arrogant, as is common with youth and triumph. It was his arrogance that caused him to fail the Darkgod. Hector wouldn't allow Ahriman's kin to fail for a second time. He would enchant her with his seductive magic, and she would sire his children. It was her purpose after all. And his as well. Merle didn't need to know that, nor did she need to know the knowledge of his plans with the weapons. As it was she pried too deeply into his dealings and she would use it against him. No, he would keep the witch's favor until he got the girl.

The Thaumaturi served his purposes differently, and this time the Barbarians would be his pawns. He wanted to strike from all sides, but the Barbarian Emperor could know nothing of his plans. Had Aldrich discovered what was buried beneath his harbors, he would either fall dead with shock, or have his chaplain's head.

Hector was no fool. He wouldn't openly oppose Aldrich. The man was still well loved and held too much influence in the Senate, yet he was easily deceived in his good nature. It was a weakness he would face all too soon.

Hector stopped his pacing and darted to the foot of the altar. He fell to his knees, the emerald and ebony robes encircled his bent form. He lowered his head in silent prayer, inhaling the potent incense and the candles that blinked vigorously with the dark spells of vision and the Power. Only the Darkgod could bestow patience upon him.

"You punish yourself with your devotion, Chaplain," A recognizable voice breathed in his ear. "You should save such punishment for the *magicians.*"

The voice stirred within him, and desires burned beneath his robe for the touch of one such as her. Slowly, he pulled himself up from his prayer, and studied the woman before him. Sasha, the Emperor's sister, was tall and well formed with toned muscle that a lesser man might envy, but her bosom was full and soft beneath the restriction of her bodice, so he imagined. She was middle aged, but her image didn't betray how many years she lived. Pale strawberry hair spilled across her shoulder and framed her round creamy face. He followed her features, with imagination, secretly hoping his prize was so luscious. Desire was to be rewarded at the end of all things. He looked away from her.

"What brings you here, my lady?" he asked joyously, "Has things become too hard to bear in the High Prince's land during his absence."

"Things have been let go. My younger brother will not be happy when he returns, *if* he returns. Until then, I will not go back," Sasha pouted.

"What of your children, my lady?" Hector said and walked farther into the shadows.

She followed him, but stopped short before the tiny sliver of a window. A ray of light traced the smooth curve of her throat down to the deep cleavage of her nearly exposed breasts. She arched her back against the stone wall and sighed heavily. In that instant, the chaplain believed she deliberately tried to arouse him. It worked, but he restrained himself from acting on it.

"They didn't wish to leave," she twisted a finger around a strand of hair. "My oldest daughter has become wild for all of her fifteen years. She entertains herself with ideas of battle. I almost feel like I am looking after Jacobane all over again. I think she wills for the Tribes to bring forth war. The little ones wanted to stay with her, so I left them," she shifted her eyes to him. "Stop looking at me that way!"

A bead of sweat formed at Hector's brow and he held his breath with her outburst. A feeling of embarrassment invaded him, and that was uncommon.

"What do you mean?" he replied coolly.

"I can feel the disapproval in your eyes." she began and he exhaled all of his anxiety, "I didn't abandon them to fend for themselves. I left them in the care of Lucia. I couldn't force them to leave, could I?"

"If you believe that they are safe, then I trust your judgment, my lady. And besides, Brother Fershius would see to their safety."

Sasha threw her head back in laughter, "Brother Fershius finds it hard to part with me. He has it in his mind that the two of us are connected at the hip."

"He returned with you?" Hector questioned ill-concealing his disappointment.

"Of course he has. Not all of the Brothers restrict themselves as you have," Sasha sniffed. "He may have been absolved by your Brotherhood, but he still is a man. And men desire what they cannot have."

"And through him you have acted out your greatest sin," Hector's words were smooth and cutting.

Sasha stiffened for a moment, allowing the silence to taunt him as she did with her languid manner. Sasha was spoilt as a child, the love and center of her father, Luthros' world. There was nothing she wouldn't do to gain his attention, and still after his death she didn't cease. She was a rebellious youth, wild and untamed, never accepting responsibility for her actions. It was in her most heinous acts that she acquired what she wanted. Exactly the type of woman Hector enjoyed.

"I have confessed to you in confidence, for forgiveness of the Gods. A man of the robe isn't allowed to judge what is to be judged by the Gods' alone," she snapped pointing her finger to the ceiling, but her frigid smile remained. "I have done the Empire great justice by ridding it of that man. My husband became nothing more than a *magician* lover."

"The arrangement of your husband's murder has been absolved within the eyes of the Gods. And I haven't betrayed your rights to confession," he smiled, "Come, and tell me what I may do for you, my lady."

Sasha loathed the Thaumaturi, but was a true follower of the Barbarian Gods, neither Hector truly served. In truth, he favored neither of the races, for it wouldn't matter soon who would win this petty little war of bigotry. In the end they would all fall the same unless they embraced the ways of the God he served. The Darkgod and the Demons of the Underworld would be released within this generation. Hector would see to it.

"It concerns political matters. Although I am fond of my brother, his reign couldn't end soon enough. He spends his time tip-toeing around the *magicians'* lands, begging for peace when he should be bringing them to their knees at his mercy. They are not what they once were. It seems that most of their magic has abandoned them. My brother has the forces to conquer them! Yet he relinquishes to the skirt of a *magician!*" Sasha's face was sour with her thoughts.

"Tell me, you do not plot to kill the Emperor?" Hector asked.

"Never! I am insulted!" She drew her head back.

"Forgive me, Lady," Hector stifled a chuckle.

"You play with me, Chaplain!" Sasha turned her back on him.

"Nay, my lady. I am truly interested, go on," Hector soothed her with his voice.

He would only be so lucky. Aldrich's day was coming. She softened the dramatic expression of her face and spoke again.

"I will not have to kill him. It will only be a matter of time before the *magicians'* tire of him. And when he dies, who does that leave us to control the Empire? A half-blooded brat who I have always despised, or my younger brother Jacobane, who despises the Thaumaturi enough, but will he gather enough enthusiasm to rule in Vhladic as he should," Sasha pouted once again. "Jacobane was never fond of politics. He'd sooner wallow in the mud with the militia."

"Who do *you* wish to see as Emperor in his place?" he questioned.

"If I had to choose between them, you know who it would be! My choice would be the Thaumaturi hater, my brother, who would never follow the path in which Aldrich has laid. It's a pity that a woman cannot become sole empress."

Hector, for the first time, forgot the desire she coaxed in him and looked at her with renewed interest. The absurdity of a sole empress was beyond credibility. It would never come to pass.

Give her false hope. For then she will be of some use. Hector thought maliciously.

131

"It isn't impossible. If Aldrich *names* you successor, would that not be honored by the Empire?" Hector grinned.

"You tell me. It seems that the Brotherhood has more influence on the Empire's people than its own Emperor. You would do the Empire justice if you'd only speak to Aldrich about this matter. He wouldn't listen to me, but in your guidance, he trusts," Sasha replied with her eyes ablaze in the way that they always did when she set her mind on something she wanted.

They were the eyes of a child.

Death… Death

The foreboding Whisper filled her ears with such might that the color drained from her. Even to the High Priestess of the Brosia Ministry, the dismal sound of such a word couldn't be ignored. Its connotation could mean a number of things from a change in the winds to the destruction of the lands. But she saw what it meant. The vision soon followed after the wind song warning. Streams of crimson flowed before her eyes. It poured down the face of the man in front of her like a poisonous waterfall. Janella's heart wretched at the sight. It was difficult to accept, but she recognized the omen.

Goddess, I pray to you. If anyone is to be punished, let it be me. Aldrich cannot die!

Janella was so overwhelmed with the severe vision, that she didn't give much attention to the company of Aldrich's younger brother. She sensed enough in him to know that he was rather disturbed at the fact that he was among the Thaumaturi. His piercing blue eyes were no longer innocent and compassionate as they once were when she saw him as a child. Life had not been gentle to him. He was in a sense a casualty of the war. The young man left as quickly as he arrived.

Before Aldrich caught up with her, she was silently watching the masquerade from the shadows of the stairway balcony. She couldn't help but to smile when she saw and *felt*, the fascination of Horace and Miarosa dancing gracefully across the floor. Joy and love, pastel auras, illuminated the room with their beauty. Janella nearly cried when she saw her daughter, Aunyia, dressed in the colors of roses, dance with her father. It was the first time they were reunited since Aunyia was a seven year old girl. Yet it seemed to Janella that the years melted into nothing between them, and that they were never separated at all.

Once Vastadon, her oldest child, was announced to be married, a chill traveled up her spine. The room began to weep silently to all but her. Aldrich whipped his head toward her as if he knew her discomfort and knew she was there. She flew from the scene and prayed she wasn't noticed. She didn't intend to speak with him, but it was inevitable. Their souls were linked in such a deep way, that they could feel each other, like the tide of an ocean, their bodies pulled to one another. It had been that way from the moment they looked into one another's eyes.

The Barbarians, fresh with bitterness, hated her kind in those days, but not sweet, gentle, Aldrich. In the last years of the tyranny, when Janella was a young priestess, the Brosian Ministry journeyed through the dangerous war zone dodging the scattered battles to the city of Vhladic on a mission of peace and petitioned the Empress Cordelia Hilliard to join forces against the Legion. The Empress was known for her compassion and kindness to her people and Thaumaturi alike and she was every bit as wondrous as her reputation.

The war was nearly at the imperial palace's door, yet Cordelia bravely sat among the people of the city, her youngest son, Jacob stood protectively before her. She expressed her agreement with the Brosian Ministry's suggestions, but Emperor Luthros quickly declined. Aldrich argued in support of his mother's decision unsuccessfully.

It was the first time she saw him. His young face was strongly handsome, yet his eyes were brave and compassionate. She found herself staring at him, and he returned her admiration with glittering eyes. It took sometime for Aldrich to penetrate her otherwise strong demeanor. Before her leave, however, she was swept away with the tide of his love. Their romance deepened every time they secretly met. Janella made herself available for all of the retreats to the Barbarian Nations. But after the birth of her first child, she took up the robes of the High Priestess. It was then that she limited herself from seeing him.

When Luthros found out about them, he expressed his rage vividly, embarrassing Aldrich before the eyes of the lower caste Barbarian kings and their people. Yet Luthros was shamed to announce to the world the affair. The secret was so well kept that not even her children knew who their true mother was. He labeled Janella a whore *magician* among his closest kin, and only allowed her to remain secretly in Vhladic until she gave birth to their first child. That did not keep them away from each other.

The relationship finally came to an abrupt end once the Barbarian High Chaplain learned of the second child.

With the death of Luthros, Aldrich sent their daughter, Anne, to her so that she could learn to service the Goddess. She trusted Aldrich with her life. He was the only one, aside from King Valance, who knew of the *entire* discrepancy in the Prophecy.

The Bearer was a *girl*.

"There isn't much time," The Priestess whispered pushing her thoughts from her.

It was her duty to appear strong.

"I know this," Aldrich replied. "I will do all that I can to abet you, for I know that the outcome will benefit all of us."

"Demons have been sited. The darkness stirs. It was always there, but merely a festering sore, until recently," Janella said and dropped her voice to a whisper. "I am certain that the young Falias Princess will be a factor in all of this. She is the one I overlooked many years ago."

"You are trembling," Aldrich whispered when he took her hands in his. "Are you fearful?" His face contorted with great worry.

Although she yearned to absorb the warmth of his fingers, she slid her hands away. The bloody vision still lingered in her sight. She wanted so desperately to protect him from all of this. She was torn between his love and the will of the Goddess.

She was unfaithful to her vows, yet Danu still spoke to her, guided her and embraced her with Her wisdom. She couldn't disappoint Danu a second time, but she was drawn to this Barbarian so powerfully, that she couldn't bear to feel him near her. The love and passion, forbidden for so long, was still unreachable now, at this moment. He had never married despite his Senate's encouragement.

Aldrich fixed his pain-filled eyes on her. He fought the feelings too, even after all of the years. He fought them for her sake. He could take her now as his wife, for he was Emperor, yet he refrained from asking her to flee with him. He did all of that for her, because he knew the importance of her position, and he knew that it would be difficult for her to leave behind the life she was born to live. And they both knew that she would leave with him if he asked.

"You mustn't get involved," Janella whispered. "If it becomes public, you will be in danger. The evil does not stop here. It invades the land of your Gods too."

"I am careful, Janella," he replied softly and pulled her into his strong embrace.

His sturdy arms were a blanket of comfort, solace. She could float away on the feeling, but she couldn't allow her mind to be clouded by such things. Yet she didn't remove herself from his embrace this time.

"There is so much we do not know," Janella said softly. "I only have knowledge through the Prophecies of the Tuatha Dé Danann."

"Share with me your knowledge," Aldrich urged, with his breath hot against her ear. "I want to know all about your kind."

Janella nodded slowly, "Very well, but no man must gain the knowledge I am about to reveal. No man, no woman, unless they are trustworthy."

Janella withdrew from his arms and took hold of his hand. She guided him into a parlor vacant from any possible intrusion. She dropped down into a fine cushioned seat and Aldrich took one across from her.

"The Sun," Janella began, "a circle of never-ending force with the point of individualism in its center is the ancient source to our continued existence, which we call the Spirit. The Sun engenders life and vitality, and it represents guidance, resolution, dignity, creativity, generosity, compassion and love," Janella paused and could see the vague lines of confusion fold on his face.

"In other words, our world without the Sun's Spirit could fall into chaos, corruption, greed, and famine. The Prophecies predicted the first rise of evil correctly, yet the new Prophecy to pass was flawed," Janella whispered.

"So it could be very possible that the Prophecy is false," Aldrich commented.

"It was my thought, until this day." Janella eyed him, "Miarosa is the last of the Mageborns, of that I am certain. I could feel the untamed magic within her when I was near her. The blazing emotions and the elements collide inside of her, battling. It has two sides to it in which could be very dangerous either way."

"She is but a child, Janella. She could be taught and sheltered," Aldrich murmured.

"But it is what alarms me the most." Janella sighed deeply and continued, "She does not understand and she may become frightened by the ethereal turmoil. She has the power to manipulate the Sun."

"Mia has control of the Sun?" Aldrich asked incredulously.

"In a matter of speaking, Aldrich," Janella answered evading the topic of the weapons, for in fact the Bearer could very well turn on the Goddess and use the weapons maliciously, "Sun Magic in combination with all four of the Elemental Rites could predominately change our existence. She could summon a Solar Eclipse and that is our most dangerous time. During a Solar Eclipse, the veils between the realms are weak. It is how the gates to the Underworld could open. I know that the young princess hasn't a cruel bone in her body, but trials and tribulations she will face. And for one so young, seduction is sometimes too strong to resist. So," Janella said standing from her chair, "I have taken my own preventative measures. A small brigade of Sun Knights is assigned to secretly protect her from what may appear to be threats."

She was moving for the door, because she needed solitude to figure things out more clearly, but Aldrich beckoned her to wait. When he looked at her, his eyes were heavy with inquisitiveness."Tell me more of the Maladintos, mainly the one who was banished."

Janella drew in her breath, partially because it was painful times for her and her family. Ahriman was the husband of her own half-sister, Cassiandra. The love, the happiness, the very breath was ripped from Cassiandra when she was taken by him. It was a forced treaty marriage that was arranged to spare Murias from annihilation during the tyranny. It was a stain on her brain that spread like a disease whenever she thought about it. But she retained her seat by the crackling fire.

"Ahriman Maladinto was barely twenty years old when he conquered these lands," Janella said sadly, "You see, nearly four generations ago, the Lords of the Elements—Tuatha Dé Danann—aided the Elders in the discovery of the physics of our magic, and with their unearthing, they raised a temple to house the Daughters of the Seasons' beauty and essences, a temple so beautiful that it looked as if it were the house of Danu Herself. And to preserve their sanctity and the Sun's Spirit, they gathered Crystals of Amber and Calcite, and by the powers of the four elements, they forged a Golden Skylight.

"The Golden Skylight maintained the order of the Seasons and absorbed the magic of the Goddess. But one of the Elders deceived them, although the traitors name wasn't known. This nameless traitor, later called the Cryptic Oracle, festered for generations, plotting his greed and darkness, until he found the perfect perpetrator.

"Ahriman was a greedy, powerful man who failed to see the Goddess' way. An army was raised with Ahriman's great wealth, and from that point, they defiled the Daughters' temple and shattered the Golden Skylight. He seized the ancient shards and held the Power, using it to conquer. The shards were not only forged with ancient magic, but they were designed to absorb limitless forms of magic. Eight long years of Barbarian and Thaumaturi bloodshed, Ahriman spread his evil, until the day came when the Rebellion defeated him. All but two shards were found and placed back into the temple. It's why the seasons to this day cease to rotate as they should in our lands."

"What do the shards have to do with your Prophecy?" Aldrich asked.

"The shards can be used to summon Demons," Janella said softly. "Beyond that, I do not yet understand. However, I believe the missing shards have fallen into hands that should not have them. It's where this hungry darkness is coming from."

"How can we retrieve them?" Aldrich asked vividly concerned.

"The Goddess has shown me how," Janella smiled a little impishly. "She has given me her Circle of Mageborns, the last to be born and the very brigade I appointed protectors of our young princess. Once this masquerade is over, I shall devise an intricate plan to recover the shards with them."

Aldrich grinned, and Janella found herself lost for a moment within his eyes. She wanted to taste his lips, make love to him one more time. She couldn't. He was a distraction. He caught her up in his arms and kissed her. And she fell into his sweetness for a dizzying moment before drawing back. He was hurt. But he knew she was too.

"Are you going to tell Mia who she is?" Aldrich inquired.

"For now, she must be protected until she matures into her magic. The Goddess will provide me with the right time for her to know."

How long that would take, Janella couldn't tell.

Mia stared at the crackling hearth, hugging her knees. Although she loved the enchantment of Gorias, she couldn't return home soon enough. The soreness that settled around her heart began to numb, her eyes stung liquid sorrow.

It was dawn when they returned to Falias, but the journey home was much swifter than their first voyage out. Instead of riding in a litter, Mia traveled on the back of a horse along with Jacob surrounded by five guards. He was warm and strong to ride with, comfortable. Silence does wonders. At Mia's insistence, Arabella agreed to stay behind.

"Mia," Jacob startled her, "Here." He shoved a tray at her containing a bowl of soup and a small tea pot. Then he plopped down in the seat near the fire. "The servants are still in bed, so I did the best I could," He grumbled.

Strange, Mia thought, for him to be so thoughtful. She studied the clear broth contents in her bowl and wondered if there might be poison in it. She shoved the bowl aside.

"Thank you, Jacob, but I am not hungry," Mia whispered. "I think I might lie down for a little while."

"Eat, I didn't poison it, and I wasn't trying to be considerate either,"

Jacob murmured as if he read her thoughts. "I have a reason for coming here. We need to talk."

Mia raised her eyebrows and lifted herself from the floor to take the chair across from him. The urgency of his words sent beating wings in her stomach. Since when did he want to converse with her.

"What is it?" she asked.

The hearth sparked and spewed a visor of shadows across the Barbarian's face. His forehead was creased with worry, but the rest of his face was unreadable. His blonde hair looked like a flame from the glow in the room. An impulsive urge to stroke his strands caught her off guard. She swallowed hard, embarrassed with her own thoughts.

"Eat, and then we will talk." he ordered.

Jacob watched as Mia spooned the soup into her mouth. He knew how her mind worked, and he wouldn't let her think him soft now just because he brought her a little food and tea. He wouldn't see another hungry or weak, even if that person was *her.*

He was pleased to leave early from the festival. He was uncomfortable among the decorated formalities and masks of such a grand event. He chose to live in the country, not Vhladic, for such reasons. He enjoyed the festivals of his land, where the bonfires roared into the night sky, ale flowed freely, and all who attended dressed in a casual manner. He yearned for his home and the smell of the fresh forest air, the simple markets, and the company of his own kind. Summer was approaching the hills of Vansant Summit. Beletene. It was a time rich with liveliness, quite the contrary of this bizarre kingdom.

When Jacob and Mia rode back to Falias, he was deep in thought. His promise to Aldrich was hard to ingest, but he couldn't break his word to him. Mia sat in front of him on the russet horse nearly falling asleep. He had clutched her tight against his torso to keep her from collapsing.

While they rode together, he inhaled the floral scent of her. He had tried to feel comfort with her in his arms, enjoyment, even passion with the nearness of her. But he felt nothing but the nagging twists and turns of his innards.

This woman would be his wife, unless he could somehow change Aldrich's mind. It was then that it had come to him. If he was to change his fate, he would have to tell her.

She spooned down about half of the soup and pushed it aside. Her deep blue violet eyes were wide with interest when she set them on him. He turned from her gaze.

"Aldrich wants something to happen," Jacob began with no clue how to say it.

"Well, that is good I suppose. What is it?" she laughed that arrogant laugh.

"He has consulted with your mother about an arranged marriage," Jacob stared ahead at the flames, "An arranged marriage between you and me."

Silence fell upon them. Not even the sound of the fire seemed to be audible.

"You are kidding, aren't you?" Mia asked disbelievingly.

"I wish I were," Jacob replied.

"We cannot marry!" Mia shouted now, "Mother is cruel and vindictive! If she were here, I would wallop her for such a horrible thing."

Mia darted from her chair and smacked the stone wall. Probably imagining Merle's cold face. Jacob, for once agreed with her. He wasn't so sure, however, why he disliked the way she rejected the idea. He shifted restlessly in his seat and looked at her.

"Tell your brother that you will not marry me," Mia said more calmly, "Surely he wouldn't see his brother unhappy."

"I have tried, but it is of no use. I've already given him my word," Jacob mumbled.

"You did?" Mia put herself between the fire and him, "You *want* to marry me, the spoilt *magician?*"

"I didn't say that," Jacob snapped. "It is hard to say no to my brother because he *usually* asks very little of me. He told me if I agreed, I could return to Vansant Summit."

"You would take me to the Barbarian Lands where they loathe my kind?" Mia placed her hands on her hips and shook her head.

"It is my home," Jacob replied sharply.

"It's as if no one cares about how I feel! People just make plans for me as if I were a puppet!" Mia's voice cracked and a tear glistening on her cheek, "Was Vastadon forced into marrying another, as well? Did I treat him poorly for something he had no choice in doing?"

Jacob could hear it in her voice and see it in her face. She yearned for a justification to his nephew's actions. But he wouldn't dare lie to her. Vastadon had double sides and he enjoyed the company of women. *Many* women. Sure he finally made his choice, but it was after he was nagged about it for over a year and finally forced into a decision. He wanted both women, but he couldn't have his way this time. Anger seized Jacob and tore at the scab of an old wound.

"No!" Jacob growled, "It was because of his choice that we are faced with this predicament! I curse him for it!"

She drew her head back from some invisible blow, and for the first time he felt something for her. Pity. Pity, because she was spawned from a family of deceivers and pity, because she was weak. Pity, because she was a Thaumaturi. It was the same pity he felt for those of his own kind and nothing of what he felt for the *magicians*. Yet he couldn't stop the instincts within him. He paused a moment before he spoke again.

"If we don't convince Aldrich to change his mind, then I will stay true to my word," Jacob said. "I'll not lie to you and tell you that I'll be happy with it, because I'm not and never will be. As my wife you will be well protected and properly treated. I am loyal, and wouldn't dishonor you. Never expect more than that."

"You are more willing to marry me than a man who I thought loved me? You would sacrifice all you believe just to return to your people?" Mia asked, her voice trembling.

"Right now, there is a man who oversees my home that cannot be trusted. I need to return as quickly as possible. So if you believe you can change Aldrich's mind, you must hurry."

"I will change his mind and not only will I change his mind, I will make sure my mother regrets her interference." Mia plopped on her bed.

Jacob rose from his seat with intent to leave, but he found himself studying her for a moment. Her golden hair fanned across the sapphire pillow. Her pale skin shimmered from the tawny glow and a curtain of thick lashes fluttered with the escalating fury inside of her. He could see the fullness of her pouting lips. She hardly knew what the world was about, and when she finally was free for the first time outside of her decorated prison, she suffered the first hard lesson of betrayal. Vastadon had that affect on many people. For a tiny insane moment, he yearned to take her in his arms and absorb the sadness that dimmed her common arrogance. He wanted to taste those pouting lips and stroke her golden hair. He would not.

Jacob pulled his eyes from the fairness of her face. She was beautiful in a way that didn't seem to fit among this world, almost ethereal. But she was a Thaumaturi and he was a Barbarian. They were too different to find comfort and passion within such an arrangement.

He turned on his heels and left wordlessly.

Merle was despicable. Yet Mia couldn't help but think she did her a favor. Had she married Vastadon, she would've expected his love and loyalty. And by the looks of things, she would've been mistaken.

How could she marry the very man she last expected? He was a Barbarian who made no secret of his contempt for the Thaumaturi. And he most certainly wouldn't be happy to know that his future wife possessed the magic of a Mageborn.

He would sacrifice his entire beliefs to return to his people.

She was afraid to live in the foreign lands, afraid of the strange magic that grasped her, afraid of being diverse, and she was afraid of the strange feeling stirring her up when she thought of Jacob and his selfless promise. She was too damned afraid of everything. Jacob was afraid of nothing, though it seemed. He walked with self-assured purpose and valor, as if the world was nothing more than a disturbance. To Mia, no man or woman would openly challenge him. Except her.

There is so much more you do not know.

Her lungs hurt and her heart ached from the misery she had endured the past couple days. Nan was gone, Lucian was dead, and now she was unable to marry the man she wanted because he turned out to be a traitor to their love. Now she was faced with a marriage that would drag her from her home into the wilderness of the Barbarians.

The thoughts were too heavy and soon she felt the drunkenness of sleep take her from this world. And from this world she fled with eagerness.

Chapter Thirteen

The Circle

The High Priestess stood garbed in folds of white robes in the center of a rounded room. Beside her, she held tight to the hand of her successor, Sierra of the Rose Hill Gypsies, who took up the burgundy robes. The chamber was beneath the ground of Gorias lest any rebel or spy could access information. It held councils for generations, back when the first Elders learned the secrets of magic.

The memories and ancient enchantment of the oldest Thaumaturi thickened the atmosphere with static and light, churning with the Power of Air. The pastel swirl marble beneath her feet was smooth and solid, rooted with the Power of Earth. The crescent moon hearth roared with yellow and orange tongues, burning with the Power of Fire. And the gentle roll from a heart-shaped fountain soothed the chamber with the Power of Water. A ring of silver stars surrounded her position before the sphere-shaped table, painted with the auras of the infinite circle of the sun. Eight swords were placed before each knight setting, their points aimed to the center of the table.

Janella released Sierra's hand and stretched her arms before her, palms facing outward. She closed her eyes and searched out the loop of enchantment that weaved in and out of each Mageborn knight and through the central point of the table. The sensation was flowing with the strength of all the elements. She had never felt their magic so strong. Her hands burned, and tingled with the presence of the Goddess. The thunderous voice was also sweet and soothing.

My Circle is forever. The magic hasn't entirely abandoned My children.

Janella smiled gently as the words filled her ears and she opened her eyes to look at the knights before her. If they had heard the Goddess' words, they showed no sign of it. Their eyes were glowing with wisdom, the purple hue of their skin was faint and possibly invisible to a lesser trained priestess. Clad in the tunics of their knighthood—violet with fire blazed across their waist—their appearances were sharp, aware, and focused. Patiently, they awaited guidance from her. Yet she felt only a fraction of their size. Eight knights, eight points that encircled the Sun and with their own lives, they would protect the Spirit.

The Bearer…Miarosa Maladinto

Once Janella adjusted to the tide of their omnipotence, she cleared her throat to speak.

"The Bearer is not corrupt. We still have a chance to bring her home to us, and to us we shall bring her at once. Together and united, the Goddess' Circle will bring justice to the darkness that stirs!" Janella exclaimed.

In unison, with the swiftness of an eagle's soar, the knights ceased their swords and angled them inward with the clamor of steel upon steel. The sensation heightened, becoming visible to the eye for the briefest of an instant. The swords pulsed with the aura of violet, and a laced web of gold branched through them in a flash. As soon as the beautiful sight of it appeared, it dissipated into a clear cloud.

For a moment they froze as if they were only part of a painting. Janella glided slowly around the table taking the knights medallions embedded with their individual jewels in her hand and kissing the face of them. It was a custom blessing given to the Sun Knighthood before they served in battle.

Cole Alexander's grey eyes fixed fiercely ahead. His hair as black as coal, his handsome face was the incarnate of a deity. He was the son of the

Duke in Tania, but he left all of the wealth and his rightful succession four years ago. Cole felt he was Cursed with the unusual feelings of magic that flowed through him and sought aid from Valance, who had a reputation of healing such things. Valance explained to the young man his gift and gave him an option to stay under his guidance to nurture the Elemental Rite within him of Fire Magic. Cole never returned to his estate. He was the Circle's Defender.

Janella moved on to the next knight. Diamond Lunistar was the smallest of them all aside from Sierra, but mighty in strength and willful in manner. The mariner's eyes were speckled with the tiniest hints of gold against honey, and her blue brown hair was braided in three plaits that looped to the crown of her head. The girl had arrived at the Brosia Caves nearly two years ago, alongside her brother. The two came from a poor fisherman family and suffered much before they sought the counsel of the High Priestess. Janella took particular notice to the girl, for she had been damaged as a child physically. During her time, she progressed nicely into her Air Magic and became partner to Cole's unyielding bravery despite whatever pain she suppressed. She was the Circle's Beast Mistress.

Next she met eyes with the newest member of the Circle before she pressed her lips to his medallion. Alabaster Talon was a large dark-skinned man, handsome with great innocence, but powerful in his Elemental Rite of Earth Magic. Diamond had explained to her earlier how this young man searched her and Sierra out in Findias. He was the Circle's Locator Mage.

Aunyia stood to the right of him, graceful and dignified. She was tall with the Barbarian honor of her father, and slim with delicate features of the royal DeBurke family. She was her second child, her daughter. Although it was never openly mentioned, she suspected that the Healer knew the truth of her maternal side. Janella was proud to see her daughter flourish in Healing gifts and Earth Magic. She was the Circle's Healer.

Janella glided to Horace who was never too far from Aunyia's side.

Horace was mysterious and he had seemed to appear out of nowhere. When he arrived at the Brosian Caves a Moon Cycle before the mariners, he simply blended in with no questions and no explanation. His powerful presence was alluring and left those who came near him enthralled with him. It was a perfect natural magic that became quite handy with his special duties of espionage, but he constantly placed wards on himself when he was near his friends. Water Magic was strong with him. He was the Circle's Emissary.

The next knight was probably the most powerful of them all. Mysteriously distant from the others Darius Percival was, yet one with them. His ability to dismember the mind was unreachably advanced. The Fire Magic enabled him to move objects with his mind. He was a young orphan before Valance fostered him and as he grew into adolescence, Valance brought his Power to Janella's attention.

A sheet of dark hair concealed the sides of his face and his onyx eyes were cold and narrow. He had seen much more darkness than the others.

Janella kissed the medallion and glided to the final knight. Phoenix Lunistar, a Murian mariner as his sister Diamond, yet he was gentle and patient. His red hair was tied back in a ponytail, and his face was tanned from earlier years spent upon the sea. She placed the kiss upon his medallion and then rejoined Sierra in the center of the star ring.

The knights withdrew their swords and placed them back on the table in the traditional manner. Then, with uneven shuffles, they took their seats.

"What is the will of the Goddess, High Priestess?" Darius spoke first, his voice flat.

Janella folded her hands and rested them just above her naval. She didn't sit, and neither did Sierra.

"I have a plan, and although the Circle is strong with unity, we must take on separate missions. However, as long as you wear the sacred medallions of your brigade, there will be no break with your spirit's connection," Janella said.

"Tell us what we must do to retrieve the Bearer," Cole asked.

"In the morning, I will journey to Falias and have a word with the king. I plan to ask him for his permission to bring his sister back with me to the Brosia Caves so that she may further learn the ways of the Goddess. Darius will accompanying Sierra and I."

Darius nodded, but his expression remained unreadable.

"As for the rest of you," Janella began, "I am sure that you all have felt the ripples of something dark. And the minions of the Underworld's gates have been summoned by strange magic. It's only a matter of time before more are released. I am afraid these acts have left me with no other conclusions. The two missing shards have fallen into the wrong hands. Now I have said this to no one, but I feel that the evil isn't coming from Thaumatur. It comes from the north and east of the Lunar Sea."

"I have felt it the strongest when I was in Vhladic," Horace announced.

"So you have told me," Janella replied.

"We all are sensing what you are, Lady Priestess. Tell us your plan," Aunyia interceded.

"Cole, I want you to lead a voyage to Vhladic where you will stay until my contact meets you. There is an inn on the south side of the city beyond the harbor called Vizan Inn. You will know the woman when she finds you there and she will be your city guide. Locate and recover the shards if possible, though this will be no easy task. Alabaster should be a great aid in the search, and Aunyia knows the lands well. The three of you will leave by the end of this week. During your mission, use your Elemental Rites only if in dire need. Frivolous use of it will draw unnecessary attention to you."

"It will be done!" Cole bellowed nearly leaping from his seat.

Janella suppressed a chuckle. The knight was as fearless as he was handsome. And his beauty suppressed almost, if not all men.

"Diamond and Phoenix, rumors have reached my ears about Thaumaturi missing, never returning from the sea voyages they take. You are well trained knights and equally experienced mariners. Return to Murias and learn as much as you can about the comings and goings of the Thaumaturi and the Barbarians. I'll send word to you if you are needed elsewhere." Janella then turned her attention to Horace.

"I am afraid you will not be going on a voyage," Janella laughed, "But a mission you shall have. I want you to place yourself within the social ring of the House. Root out all of the suspects that could possibly have something to do with this. Sadly, I find that I trust scarcely. Greed has become an influential force that diminishes the values of our old ways. And some of that greed has found a home in the Viscount's council." Janella lowered her head.

"Well, it seems that I have the most pleasurable task of all," Horace laughed and the others joined in, all except Darius.

She spoke truth, for the House did become merely a casing of what it once was. Wealth was an issue and some used it to their advantage as well.

Janella delved into her thoughts, while the knights took on a lighter conversation. What if her plan failed and Aiden of Falias refused his consent? Would she even be able to reach the castle hall for an audience? It mattered not, because she would stop at nothing to save the girl from herself.

The knights laughed at some joke Janella didn't hear. Her spirit soared when she saw them so joyous. But it wouldn't be long before the sorrow and tribulations shadowed them. She met eyes with her successor and dismissed the meeting.

"Priestess, I wish to go with you on your journey tomorrow," Aunyia whispered in her ear.

Janella smiled softly and knew exactly why the girl requested permission. Aldrich was to stop at Falias before his leave.

"Very well. I cannot know when you will have the chance to see your father again."

The girl thanked her and returned to Horace's side. Aunyia was growing rather fond of the young Emissary, but Janella sensed that their relationship would be tested like no other.

CHAPTER FOURTEEN

The Mirror

Lucian's face was pale, but it wasn't haggard as she remembered. He glided toward Mia, hovering above the ground like a spirit in cerulean robes, and his watery eyes glittered with joy. He sat beside her and caressed her cheek and hair. Warmth spread throughout Mia's body of happiness and safety.

"Father!" She cried and threw her arms around him, but when she drew back to see his face, Horace smiled back at her.

He pressed his lips to her palms and smiled, and soon his face faded into the sweet face of Aunyia. She stood, still holding Mia's hand, and looked down at her.

Aunyia dissipated into a cloud of white feathers. The Great Owl zoomed out through the balcony doors. Mia followed the owl to a golden floor length mirror. She saw her reflection change, and she gasped when the image transformed into the beautiful woman she saw in the picture just yesterday. Ahriman's wife smiled back at her with such love. Mia drifted closer to the mirror. Cassiandra stretched her hand forward and as the smooth surface of the mirror rippled, her slender hand protruded. In her grasp she held a picture. Mia took it and smiled back at the mirror. But the image of Mia's face quickly returned to her.

It was similar to the very picture she saw in Gorias, only the woman wasn't alone.

She sat beside Lucian and another man, who resembled Aiden, but had the strong features of Merle.

Ahriman…

As she studied the picture, the faces began to melt behind an eruption of flames. Quickly, Mia dropped it and fled to her bed, grabbed a large blanket, and ran back out to the picture attempting to smother out the fire. It didn't work. The blanket had caught on fire as well.

"*No!*" *Mia cried and ran back to grab a pail of water.*

She fumbled with the pail finally dumping the water onto the spreading fire. It was as effective as if she had drowned the flames with wood. No matter what she did the inferno grew into a raging blaze. Once she realized there was no saving the picture, she ran to the door and tried to open it.Iit was locked. She banged ferociously, crying for someone to let her out.

"*Somebody please, help me. Let me out! Jacob!*" *she screamed until her throat burned.*

Nobody came.

She was forced to face the fire and covered her eyes from its brilliance. The smell of burning wood filled her lungs as the fiery tongues reached out to grab her. She turned her face away from it, her heart racing with panic, only to see a dark figure looking back at her through the mirror. Her eyes widened and she screamed as the mirror began to crack slowly. A red light spilled through a split and an ominous figure emerged creeping toward her with his arms outstretched. Large shadows expanded behind his back that looked like wings on a bat. She could hear a hissing noise echo in her ears. An inhuman voice spoke to her.

Mia….

Come to me…

He came closer and closer, captivating her with his malign seduction…

The south tower, daughter!

Mia opened her eyes startled from the dream and the indistinct message from her father. It wasn't only Lucian that called to her, but a chorus of distorted droning, unworldly voices. She rubbed her eyes and saw that darkness had fallen. There were no noises save for the pounding of her heart and the quickened breath from her lungs

She reached for her robe and went in pursuit of the tower. It was time to find out what her father wanted her to know.

Mia climbed the large winding stairs of the south tower when something seized her. She spun on her heels and was faced with two large wooden doors tucked within the corner of the stairwell. Mia reached out and touched the faces of the three vipers that glittered animatedly beneath the dim glow. Her hand grew cold from the touch, and a wave of eerie tremors coursed through her body.

The door swung open and dust filled her lungs. An already lit oil lamp sat upon a small table to the right of the threshold.

As she inched deeper into the wing, she traced the light along the walls and saw a variety of old paintings. There was one in particular that caught her interest. It was of a dark-haired man crowned with silver snakes, his eyes full of hatred. He wore armor chain mail and in his grip he held a pointed staff across his chest in military fashion. Something about him frightened her, but much more, it filled her with yearning. Somehow, she felt love for him. Could he have been her brother, Ahriman? She tried to visualize the features of Ahriman in the picture from her dream. It was a blur. She looked up into the dark painted eyes of the man. He was evil, she was aware of it.

She continued to the next picture. This was even more intriguing, for the same man that looked so evil was in this picture as well. But a hint of love dimmed the darkness in his eyes. He was holding something in his arms. She wiped it with her scarf, however it did no good. The bundle was scraped away from the painting. Fueled by her desire to know who he was, she wiped at the picture vigorously, hoping to find a name.

Suddenly, she heard something crash behind her. She swallowed hard and spun on her heels. The widening circle of light revealed to her an old door slowly creaking open.

At first Mia gasped when she saw a girl looking back at her. Then she realized it was her reflection in a cracked mirror. She chuckled at herself and entered the room slowly.

An untouched, perfectly made bed with violet and silver satin blankets took up most of the floor space in the room. A large dressing table covered with perfumes and toiletries was beside the bed. Curious, Mia went closer to the table.

"Ouch!" A sharp pain invaded her heel. She fell onto the bed and pulled a piece of glass out of her skin. She lowered the oil lamp closer to the floor and noticed an overturned picture frame surrounded by shattered glass. She reached down to grab it when a brilliant light exploded from the cracked mirror. The mirror was an aura of soft colors that reached out to her. A soft voice called to her.

Come, Miarosa, and discover the truth they have been keeping from you....

When Mia drew closer to the floor length mirror something strange began to happen. A funnel of blue diamonds expanded outward, pulling her deep into the glass. Visions took form in her mind.

There was a small child before her of no more than five, a child that she merged with. Through these new young eyes, the whole world was nothing short of a wonderful dream surrounded by glowing warm faces and gentle kisses. She closed her eyes and accepted the fragment images that stirred within her soul.

Mia traveled down the twisted and winding corridor of her memories to see a beautiful woman bathing in the aura of sunlight, beaming and reflecting through her smooth and flowing chestnut hair. Garbed in a long white lace dress, she danced within the wind's gentle sway. Her soft violet eyes shined with love and compassion. The familiar warmth of her whispers echoed in Mia's ears, her arms outstretched to embrace her.

Mother....... Cassiandra.

With a sudden turn, the images faded. Her whispers diminished and were replaced with a rumble of bellows and a blinding angry blaze. Choked by her screams of fear and defiance, before her very eyes, Cassiandra stood bound with thick ropes and was mounted against a stake. At her feet rose a ferocious inferno devouring.

Mia tumbled through the maze of hooded zombies, twisting and spinning. The accusing pale faces grimaced at her as they continued their chants toward Cassiandra.

"Burn you traitor, Burn for your treacherous hand to our lord!"

The fiery tongues smothered Cassiandra, stifling her cries for mercy. That was when the crowd turned on her with hate in their blank stares. Their accusing grins and their clammy hands clutched onto her tiny shaking frame. Her heart raced, her head pulsed, and her breath was taken with panic. An old wrinkled face peered down at her, a woman with a rotting smirk and breath that stank of fish. Her distorted expression spat venomous words into her little ears.

"My Child, behold the woman who betrayed your father, our wondrous king, Ahriman! Your mother will suffer for what she has done!"

Her laughter pierced Mia's mind, leaving her numb to her surroundings. All went dark…

She found herself floating somewhere else, somewhere silent…

Her lungs filled with the smell of must, her ears perked with the strum of raindrops. Slowly she awoke to blackness. The air was so still. Was it all a dream? Her raspy voice managed a small, weak cry.

"Mother…Mother, where are you?"

No answer came, only the booming clad of water dripping above. Her tiny body felt non-existent, numb with the shock of her predicament. Then she realized she couldn't move. Her wrists were bound by cold metal, a warm liquid substance dripped from her wrist.

A million presumptions twisted inside her head. There were so many unanswered questions. Tears streak her face. How long had she been here? Her lips were dry and her thirst left unsatisfied.

Her twisted pondering was interrupted by a swift clank and a creak of a heavy door opening. She squinted against the flickering light that spilled in through the crack of the door.

The source of the light was that of a candle in the grasp of a maiden. She was dressed in black rags, her hair concealed by a veil of brown. But there was something familiar about her. The maiden's eyes were full of compassion. Mia's adult mind tried to place the face. It was Nan. Nan leaned over her and whispered softly into her ear.

"It is alright child. this will be a forgotten memory now, for we are leaving this eve."

Nan unbounded her and lifted her into her arms, gently rocking back and forth.

"You are returning to the castle were you belong, little rose," she cooed.

Tears erupted from her eyes as she clung to the only kindness she had felt since her mother was ripped from her. Nan tightened her embrace.

Mia slammed back on the hard floor before the mirror panting and shaking from the overwhelming feelings she had just endured out of her mind. Did that really happen?

Lady Cassiandra is my mother? Cassiandra was unjustly murdered before my eyes, my mother?

She felt a simmering rage like she had never felt before, for if what she had discovered was true, then her whole life had been a lie. And what hurt her even more than the stinging pain of her back was the fact that the one person she indeed trusted had said nothing.

"Oh Nan, How could you!" she cried barely finding her voice.

Mia climbed to her feet and decided to confront her brother as soon as he returned, if he hadn't already.

Or uncle.

Before she left, her attention was drawn back to the mirror to see, not the overbearing radiance that hypnotized her earlier, but her eighteen year old reflection. The entire splendor of its magic was gone. It returned to its original jagged appearance and ignored her as if it was satisfied with the outcome and had no more intentions of revealing anything further.

Mia regained her bearings and turned to leave, but she jumped backward not expecting to see someone in the room with her. She fell into the mirror nearly crashing it to the ground as Jacob swiftly grabbed her with one hand and the mirror with the other.

"Well, what do we have here?" He questioned.

"Has my brother returned?" she asked forcing calmness in her voice.

"Just now. He sent me for you and that is when I heard the clamor in here," Jacob replied flatly.

"Good, I need to speak to him now," Mia said sourly and pushed by Jacob, "Alone, Jacob." She glanced back at the huge Barbarian when she heard the shuffle of his feet.

He appeared to understand, offering no reprimand or disagreement. Unusual, but Mia was gracious nonetheless. She hurried back down the winding stairs.

Mia hustled through the corridor passing by the looming presences of the guards and pushed through the double doors of the grand hall. The room was nearly empty, save for a few servants cleaning the evidence of pitchers and goblets, and a bard before Aiden playing songs with his harp and singing merrily. The bard didn't cease, nor did Aiden acknowledge Mia's approach. He was leaning lazily upon his silver and sapphire throne, plucking grapes from a golden bowl placed beside him. She stifled a derisive laugh with his supercilious manner. The man could sit there, knowing the secrets he knows, without a care in the world.

How can you do it brother? How can you even smile with what you have done to me?

Mia stormed to the foot of the throne. It was then that Aiden noticed her. He leaned forward and placed his hands firmly on his knees.

"There you are!" he exclaimed, "I have sent the servants to search everywhere for you! Where have you been?"

"Leave us!" Mia bellowed and cut her hand through the air.

The hall cleared out in a scurry leaving Mia and Aiden to solitude. A silence stretched between them. She bore her eyes angrily into him, and for the first time in her life, she saw the man she most feared, loved, and respected flinch.

"How could you?" Mia demanded pointing a finger at him.

"How could I what?" he snapped back.

"I know the truth. I went to the south tower, into the old wing you shut off from the world," Mia said.

Aiden lifted himself from his throne and turned his back to her. His chest rose and fell with escalating anger. He had no right to be angry.

"You have defied me!" Aiden thundered. He coiled his fist beside him and thrust it forward knocking the table and all of its contents to the marble floor.

"And you have lied to me!" Mia cried, "I would've expected it from Mother, but you?"

"You had no business. Why did you go there, the very place that no one was permitted to go?" He spun on her his eyes glittering with the blaze of his fury.

"Father, or should I say, Grandfather told me of it, with his very last breath. And when I found myself before it, something within the wing itself beckoned me to enter. It wanted me to know what you were hiding! Maybe it was my true mother, Cassiandra's spirit who willed me to enter!" Mia shot back.

He scowled deeply and rolled his eyes. However, she saw beyond his mask of annoyance.

"You are punished for your defiance, girl! You can tell all the tall tales you like! Honestly, could you not come up with something better than that! Stories about spirits resurrecting from the grave and voices through the corridor will get you nowhere in this world other than a nice padded cell on Nightengale Isle. You were warned about wandering into that wing and you deliberately disobeyed me. That is all there is to it!"

"You know I am not a liar!" Mia said breathlessly.

She felt the spawn of hatred in her and it was mocking her, taunting her. She wanted the magic to flow now, yet at the time when she wanted it most, it abandoned her. For a brief second, she willed it to fill her with a power to set him aflame were he stood. It hurt her that she knew he couldn't have ever cared for her the way that she cared for him. But her love for him was damaged one too many times.

"What I know is that you are disturbed," he said maliciously.

"You never had any use for me as a child and now you cannot bear to see me as an adult. This game you play is over despite your desire to have it go on forever!" Mia said dangerously.

"Do you honestly think anyone would believe your outlandish claim?" he barked rough laughter.

"And are you going to tell me that my real mother burning before me was just my mind playing tricks on me. How dare you hide something like that from me? What gave you the right?" Mia cried.

"I am not going to deny what you saw in the mirror. Keeping it from you wasn't my intention. I was going to tell you the truth when you were more mature simply because I knew you were not ready for it. Clearly your reaction proved me right."

"I now know why Arabella left. I am leaving too," Mia tossed her hands outward.

"You will go nowhere. You will be confined to your chambers until I say otherwise. I trusted you not to take advantage of me in *my* castle. But you disrespected me. Now you must be taught a lesson. Perhaps next time you will have a little more respect toward my rules!" he spat through grit teeth.

"I am not a prisoner. You cannot lock me up because it's unnatural!"

He was punishing her for discovering his secret, for discovering the true him and the root of this vile castle. He looked at her severely. She was beyond caring.

"I don't think I like your tone with me girl!"

"I don't like it either," Merle's cold voice snapped.

Mia spun on her. Merle wore a half amused expression on her face, but her black eyes revealed nothing of her thoughts.

"Mother," Mia spat it like a curse, "I will not be contained here for the lies of you and him." Mia stabbed a finger in Aiden's direction.

"You still call me mother, even after you have discovered the truth," Merle cocked her head.

"Perhaps I should call you deceiver!" Mia reproached, "I don't know what else would be more fitting."

"You have become fresh with your words lately. I'd watch my step if I were you," Merle warned.

"Why did you lie to me?" Mia questioned as her entire insides pinched with the realization. She was all alone.

"Your mother loved you selfishly. It was I who protected you from the Elders. Had they known you to be the child of Ahriman, your life would've been much different," Merle said lightly extending her fingers for inspection.

"That answer isn't good enough," Mia retorted.

Merle laughed and shook her head as if she enjoyed the desperation and anger. Her cackle silenced abruptly and her expression hardened into steel.

"You will not say another word about this in my dwelling. I will not have my name questioned," Merle's frown was growing.

"What if I do? You deserve no less than to be recognized for your true self."

"If you say a word, it isn't I whom you will answer too." Merle curved her lips into a wicked smile, "The daughter of Ahriman Maladinto would be the perfect scapegoat to any dark wizardry the Elders have discovered."

"You are so cold to me. You always hated me and now I finally know why," Mia shot back and ran from them.

Mia was breathless in her going, a nail shredded her heart. She was always alone. Always.

She hated Merle. She hated Aiden. She hated Vastadon. The world was a pyre, and so Mia too would burn as her true mother did.

Aiden stared down at his mother with narrowed eyes. He could see that she was enjoying this and he was beginning to think the woman *wanted* things to come out. The vines of guilt twined its way around his mind, but he quickly disposed of them with a shake of his head. Cassiandra DeBurke Maladinto was a fair woman, but she was strong willed and openly disgusted with her new life in Falias, ideal for the blame of Ahriman's downfall among his loyal followers.

Soon after Ahriman's banishment, Cassiandra fled from Falias and took the children. By the time Merle discovered her disappearance, Cassiandra was already dead. Merle hated her. However, he couldn't believe his mother would command the death of her own son's wife.

"I don't see how we can release her to the Barbarians now, Mother," Aiden threw his arms up in the air.

"We are not releasing her to the Barbarians, she is marrying one. The High Prince to be exact," Merle flared.

"She knows too much. If she happens to slip…?" Aiden left the question hang in the air. He became worried of the consequences to such fraud.

"She won't," Merle promised with finality. "And even if she did, it would be waved off by her Barbarian Lover."

"I'll not allow her to go," Aiden leaped from his throne.

"You will," Merle met eyes with him, and it made him shrink. "Let her go! It is abnormal, this obsession you have with her!"

"Just like you to turn the subject into something perverse," Aiden scowled.

"Try, if you must, Son, to prevent her from going. I promise not to stop you, but you will be setting yourself up for disappointment."

Aiden sunk down in his throne into the shadow of his mother's presence. He would try, and he wouldn't be the one who was disappointed.

CHAPTER FIFTEEN

Choices

From the high window of the corridor, Mia watched the rise of dawn, thick layers of purple and grey fog, above the jagged teeth of the ice covered mountains. The market stirred with the beginning of a new day, but Mia paid no mind to it. She hadn't slept the whole night, nor did she attempt to find solitude in her room. She evaded Jacob like the plague and shut herself away from any distraction.

The world no longer held her awareness and the discovery of new lands didn't stir her with anticipation as it once had. The air was sucked from her along with her will to move from the very spot she stood the entire night since she fled from Merle's cold gaze. Truth had slapped her hard leaving a red blotch on her numbing heart.

Mia would no longer speak of her unearthing, but it would remain a tiny seed in her mind that she would nurture every time she remembered the cursed truth. Her true mother, Cassiandra, loved her beyond life, her own life ripped from her by the flame of Ahriman's brood.

Curse you, true father, curse you for your weakness!

Mia's thoughts were scattered among the whirlwind of hatred and blame, sorrow and regrets, and decisions. The only person in the world, who was ever truthful, was the very man who loathed her. All of the desolate night she thought of Jacob and how she would manage if she *was* to marry him.

"There you are, my lady!" Lynn bellowed. "His majesty was worried!"

Mia snorted contemptuously at the idea of Aiden going mad. She doubted he worried for her safety. He was apprehensive about the unearthing of the great secret he and Merle harbored.

"I'm sure he was worried," Mia spat refusing to look in Lynn's direction.

Lynn was one of the last people she wanted to see. Mia was careful to keep her frame of mind from betraying her presence, her mask of stone.

"The Barbarian Emperor and his son have arrived. We are their final stop before he returns to his lands. King Aiden wants you present during the final partings," Lynn said.

Vastadon, that traitor, the man who I still cannot forgive. The man I still cannot forget…

Bitterness swelled in her mouth and settled at the base of her tongue. She scowled deeply and turned her angry eyes on Lynn.

"So take my place among the table, Lynn. Sit by my brother's side as his mistress. It is, after all, what you want! Is it not?" Mia snapped at her. Sshe gasped at her own words.

They were spoken ill, rude, and for a minute she sounded just like Merle. She wasn't Merle, nor would she ever be. She wouldn't be around long enough to absorb that poison of contempt.

"If I were to be welcomed, I'd take that place," Lynn shot back as equally vile, "Now come, Eve awaits you in your chamber. Freshen yourself up for the company of our lords."

Mia strode past her, paying no mind to the wench's words, "I have no need to dote on myself. I shall invade their little party with a surprise of my own."

Mia fled down the hall as fast as the rage pumped through her veins and then descended the stairs to the hall. She burst through the doors in an explosion of venom. The very poison dripped from her lips, when she caught sight of Jacob.

"If I am to be your wife, do you vow complete honesty?" Mia rushed up behind Jacob, with Lynn at her heels.

Aiden and Aldrich jolted from the abruptness of her voice. Aiden frowned, but the Barbarian Emperor looked as if he were about to laugh. She had an audience of lords, ladies, servants and last but not least, Merle gaped at her. Jacob froze first before wheeling around to meet her head on.

Aiden darted to his feet intercepting a response. "Dismissed," He hissed and stomped his foot on the floor sending the court, save Merle, from the hall.

Aiden was at Mia's side within seconds, clinging to her arm like a child clung to its mother's waist. Mia ripped from his clutch, and moved in on Jacob. She stood so close to the Barbarian that she could feel the heat of his skin spread to her face.

"Let her speak, Aiden!" the voice of Merle cracked like a whip.

The facade of Merle's defense made Mia jump. But she was no fool. The woman, she called mother her entire life, was a phony, a witch who wore a different disguise for each person's liking.

Mia swallowed hard and looked deep into the eyes of a man she grew to dislike so she could see the truth of his answer, "Would you always be honest with me?"

Jacob's jaw shifted, but he returned her gaze with straight and cool eyes just long enough to enforce his honesty.

"I do not play games, and I think you know by now that I'm not a liar. I could make that promise," He declared.

"And if I agreed to marry you, then where would we live?" she asked to be certain of an answer she already knew.

"In Vansant Summits, the northeastern part of the Barbarian Nations." Aldrich interceded with haste. "I know that it is far, but you may find comfort in knowing that Vansant Summit is very close to Vhladic and you will be protected by the east wall from the Tribes."

Mia nodded slowly and looked across the room from her mother to Aiden before her eyes came to a rest on Vastadon. The sight of him made her ill, not only from his betrayal, but from the ghost of a love she felt in her heart whenever she was near him.

You could've stopped all of this before it reached this far, she bitterly thought, *had your love been true. I loved you!*

"Then I will be your wife," Her lips split into a satisfied smile.

Vastadon grimaced and the jealously ignited a fire beneath the surface of his skin. It pleased Mia to see him this way. He deserved no less. Aldrich was smiling from ear to ear, Merle maintained her composure, but Aiden blanched.

Coward!

"Mia, perhaps we should discuss this privately before you make a hurried decision! You loathe the man and you'd be so far from home..." Aiden interceded nervously.

"Good!" Mia turned on him, "The farther from here the better. I grow tired of your political games and your lies! I'm not a little pawn for you to poke and shove around as you wish to make things better for you!"

"Mia..." Aiden weakly pleaded.

"It isn't going to be the way you want it this time! I've made my decision!" Mia bellowed.

"Unbelievable," Vastadon muttered from the corner of his mouth.

Mia took deliberate steps toward Vastadon, her eyes as narrow as two crescent moons, but her words were directed toward Jacob.

"Jacob, I know that we harbor no warmth toward one another, but I believe that your desires to return home for the well being of your people are noble. I shall respect you as your wife and honor your opinion above all from this point on. You have also done one thing to me, which no other man has ever done. You told me the truth. It's a quality in which I am willing to sacrifice."

Vastadon's breath quickened and the flesh on his cheeks redden. The meaning underneath her words sunk in. She would be happy if she never had to look upon his face again.

"Come," Merle took hold of Jacob and Mia's arms and guided them onto the hall balcony.

The village was now alive and full of the hustle and bustle of people. The snow was falling gently and the sky was white with the purity of dove's wing. Below the balcony, the villagers stopped immediately with the sight of Merle and eagerly waited for an announcement.

Merle strode forward and waved to the populous graciously. Her eyes glittered with a new light that Mia couldn't remember seeing before. Could it be that Merle was happy for her and trying in her own way to make things right again? Or could it be that she was happy to be rid of her? Something strange gnawed at Mia's gut. Did she make a big mistake?

Merle cleared her throat. Her soft hands still clung to their hands and all below quieted down. "My fellow people of Winter Falias, I have wondrous news I wish to share with you! My daughter, the fair princess of Falias, Miarosa Maladinto, is to be married to the High Prince of the Barbarian Nations, Jacobane Hilliard!" She thundered and placed Mia's hand in Jacob's rough palm holding them high for all to see, "Let this be a symbol of unity and peace between our kinds!"

Priestess Janella pushed her way through the crowd within the depths of a haze. She couldn't believe her ears. Just before she reached the threshold of Falias, just before she was about to inquire permission to take the princess back to the Brosia Caves to learn of Danu, this was announced. She could hardly hear the reaction of the crowd over her own panicked thoughts.

"Lady?" Sierra whispered with great concern, "Are you alright?"

"Nay, my child, none of us are," Janella looked to her and then to Darius, "They just started the second war."

Darius Percival wasn't one to show his emotions, but as Janella met his eyes, they were alight with concerns. And they were justified, for now the princess would be alone, far away from the eyes of the Goddess' Circle and the High Priestess.

Just then, Aunyia rejoined them and laid a hand on the Priestess' shoulder. Her face was pinched with the subtle signs of anger.

Janella glanced up to the balcony where malicious Merle stood content between her pawns, her daughter and the Barbarian prince who despised all Thaumaturi. Then, as if the sight couldn't get any worse, the curtains stirred behind them and Janella felt a pain like no other.

Aldrich, the man she loved and trusted, stood side by side with them, beaming with glory.

How could you betray me?

"I shall have a word with my father," Aunyia hissed through clenched teeth.

"I do not wish for you to quarrel with your father," She replied sadly, "Our plans have changed."

Darius's strong arm encircled her. "Let us go and inform the Elders of this. Perhaps they can put a halt to such a marriage."

"Not yet, Darius. I must do what I can to salvage this without involving *them*," she said and took hold of the Sierra's hand, "I know that you have endured so much, Sierra. But I must ask one last thing of you."

Sierra nodded without any questions and, as fast as she could, Janella made her way through the crowd to the main gates of the palace.

"Welcome Lady of the Caves, to my home! I am sure you have heard the good news today. My daughter and the Barbarian High Prince will be married immediately!" Merle regarded Janella with mock hospitality. "Have you foreseen such a joyous occasion? Is that why you have come here today?"

Merle stood on the threshold of the throne steps with her arms outstretched and her face loose with artificial warmth. The dark woman made a mockery out of Danu and Her priestesses with every front she put on before the weaker minded people.

Aldrich…

"I haven't come for such reasons," Janella shoved her thoughts aside, "although I bless the princess in her marriage. I did however, come to invite Miarosa to return with me to the ministry so that she may learn more of Danu and how to serve her. A good princess should deepen her bond with the Goddess and bestow her knowledge on those who honor her."

"Oh, my, Lady Priestess, I am truly sorry you've wasted your time. My sister marries in three days, and the dawn of their first day as man and wife, she will return with the High Prince to his land," Aiden said sourly and plucked a grape in his mouth, "I fear such followers will show little interest in the ways of the Goddess."

"If the princess wishes, she could still take advantage of my knowledge. There are no laws saying a married woman cannot gain the deepened awareness of the Goddess," Janella retorted and looked at the princess.

The young girl stood beside her future husband dressed in a simple gown of pink and a red tunic. Her eyes were blank and she had lost some of the color she noticed during their last meeting. Sadness came upon Janella.

"It wouldn't be fair to rip the Prince's wife from his side as soon as they marry," Merle interceded smoothly.

"I see," Janella replied, "Well, what is meant to be is meant to be. Goddess be with you all."

"Stay, Lady, and sit at table with me," Merle offered sadistically.

I'd rather not sit at any table with you, heretic! Janella thought but kept them from invading her voice.

"I am afraid there is much for me to do. But to show my gratitude, I offer your daughter a wedding gift," Janella said as her veiled priestess stepped forward.

Janella waved a hand to Mia and the girl immediately obeyed. Merle's eyes betrayed little of what Janella knew she felt.

"Will your women take leave with you, Princess?" Janella asked the girl, gently cupping her chin.

"Not necessary," The Barbarian Prince spoke for the girl, "I have plenty of women that will attend to her in Vansant Summit."

Janella studied him for a minute. Although they met briefly once before, she didn't have the chance to really see him. The prince towered above the princess, though she wasn't a short woman at all, his long fair hair fell well past his shoulders in scattered braids. He was dressed in a sweeping muddy brown robe, fur nestled at his neck. And his body was noticeably well formed beneath his breeches. He was ruggedly handsome as his brother, but he had wildness in his eyes, and fear. He feared change and he wasn't pleased about this marriage in the least. Yet he agreed, for surely the princess had very little choice in the matter. The young man could scarcely hold her gaze.

"I will that the priestess, Sierra, go with you to the Nations, so that you have accessible guidance in Danu's way," Janella offered and placed a hand on Sierra's shoulder.

"There will be no magic in my dwelling. I forbid it," Jacob cut in sharply.

Janella turned on him and smiled as pleasantly as she could.

"Do you expect the princess to relinquish her beliefs and devotion to the Goddess? You cannot, for she would never turn her back on the Great Mother. And it would be cruel to bully her into submission and I perceive you as someone who wouldn't think himself cruel. It will be as you wish, but the Priestess will go," Janella enforced.

"It is done," Aldrich interceded from behind her.

Janella wouldn't meet his eyes. She felt the heat of his stare on the back of her head.

"I cannot guarantee the safety of this woman. She isn't mine to protect," Jacob growled and fixed his eyes on Aldrich.

"Goddess will protect her," Janella replied in a commanding voice.

"I will protect her!" Mia jumped forward, "I would guard the priestess with my life, for she is a messenger of the Great Goddess."

Janella concealed a smile and kept her eyes from wandering into the direction of Merle to see her reaction. It was a good sign to see such conviction and love toward the Great Mother. Perhaps it wouldn't be as bad as she thought. Jacob opened his mouth to argue, but he was silenced from the mere touch of the girl's hand to his arm.

"High Priestess," Mia bowed and kissed her palms, "I vow to you the safety of your priestess. The High Prince will protect her too."

"You speak for me..." Jacob hissed through clenched teeth.

"You are angry with me now, but I know you wouldn't allow such terrible things to happen to a woman," Mia replied without even looking at her future husband. "Priestess Sierra, come and sit with me so that we may get to know one another better."

Sierra bowed to Janella and allowed Mia to guide her from the hall. An instant later, Jacob stomped off in an entirely separate direction. Aldrich was behind her, she could feel his presence as she always did. The brush of his arm against her sent her heart pounding. He stood now, before her looking into her eyes. She turned from him and his betrayal and she excused herself from the hall.

He would follow she knew, but what was the point? Done is done, and there could be no tolerable plea or excuse to validate what he had just agreed to. She stood in between two pillars decorated with blue silk adorned with the banners of the Maladintos. A wolf, with its gleaming white fangs watched her from behind the banner through its laden silk eyes. The symbol of the wolf, although its nature was often confused with trickery, had seen horrible things within its house. The wind set the emblem banner adrift and it sent the wolf aimless.

"I know you are angry," Aldrich's calm voice invaded her, "You don't understand why."

Janella didn't reply, nor did she acknowledge his presence behind her, luring her into his ultimate seduction. She inched forward just as she felt the warmth of his hand on her shoulder. She wouldn't let him see her vulnerable.

"Please, Janella, don't ignore me. I've done what I have done for you," Aldrich said softly.

Laughter escaped her lips, "You have started a war. That is what you have done. How could you betray me so? I trusted you."

"I didn't betray you. They would've betrothed her to Vastidrich. You know that our son has been lost to his own hunger. I trust my brother to—"

"Your brother hates her as he hates all Thaumaturi! If he knew what he truly had, he would be enraged," Janella interrupted.

"Jacobane can be trusted," Aldrich said, "Unity will prevail."

"You are as power hungry as the Elders and as deceptive as those who oppose us! I now understand where Vastadon gets it from. I never want to look upon your face again Aldrich!" Janella bellowed and shoved a tear from her cheek, "Never!"

She left him alone beneath the bitter sky and the coldness he deserved. It was time to disregard the rules. Many are those who feel the wrath of a scorned priestess.

CHAPTER SIXTEEN

The Thorn

Three days had gone by fast and now Mia was a married woman. She looked across the courtyard and spotted Jacob drinking deeply from a goblet. Aldrich and Viscount Birch stood near him laughing. Twilight came in brilliant auras of purple and yellow, an oddity for Falias.

Her heart skipped a beat when Jacob glanced up at her. He was frowning, and he was much more beautiful than she would like to admit underneath the lustrous light of the sky. They were to mate as all husbands and wives did on their wedding night. She knew nothing of a man's intimate touch, nor what a man looked like naked. How could she do this with him?

The wedding had been a small and private affair. The gown Arabella chose for Mia was quite contradictory, however. It was a high waist flurry of silk and meshes, the hemlines were embroidered with silver lace, and the shoulders were round with red roses cascading along the sleeves. She wore a diamond diadem that was pinned inside a nest of curls. The affair before the vows kept Mia's mind from wandering back on the past week. The lies were too much to bear and it hurt to feel so aimlessly bound. Arabella had lied too, after all. She said nothing of the ordeal to her sister, who was too young at the time to have any influence on Merle and Aiden's clandestine.

Soon I will be gone from this *place anyhow.*

Jacob looked his royal status. He was garbed in a black tunic, white breeches and a black cape designed with gold stitch panthers and thorns encircled his large form. A matching onyx and gold torque encircled his shoulders and a circlet that accented the smoothness of his braid-less hair.

The ceremony was blessed by the Barbarian Emperor and Priestess Sierra in Aiden's throne room, and it was over within five minutes. Mia had caught glimpses of approval in all eyes when she glided into the hall in her gown. But their admiration wasn't matched with the man she was marrying and she was surprised to find she was disappointed that he seemed so uninterested.

Jacob grazed her lips awkwardly to seal the vows. Yet in that subtle gesture, a fire spread throughout her body. He was unaffected. The man of stone and ice could feel nothing, she was sure.

Mia didn't go directly to the bonfire reception in the white garden. Her nerves frayed even then. She smirked when she remembered the sage words of her sister. Arabella helped prepare her bath with scented oils and she chattered pointers and encouragement in her ear all the while.

"You don't have to like a man to enjoy his company in bed," Arabella said, "It will hurt for only a moment, but thereafter, if he knows what he is doing, it's a whole different matter," She giggled.

Mia didn't find humor in the advice, yet her sister's excitement eased the tension a little. Not entirely. She dragged herself from the scene and paced within the chambers she would soon lose her maidenhead.

"Aren't you cold?" A drawing voice came from behind her.

She spun to see Vastadon leaning against the door, his eyes wandered slowly over her body. She swallowed hard. Something strange flashed behind his icy blue eyes when he took the sight of her in and his arrogant smile that alarmed her. She drew the wrap tighter around her naked form and shuddered.

"How did you get in here?" Mia asked shifting her eyes.

"I have my ways," he approached her slow.

"You should go," she said and turned her back on him.

"I will in time," he taunted. The hairs on the back of her neck rose when he ran a cold hand over her arm.

"It is inappropriate," She whispered.

He betrayed you...

Mia shoved his hand from her and turned on him. "You betrayed me, Vastadon."

"Not my heart," He traced her face with a feather light finger.

Mia withdrew from his touch, but she couldn't pull away from his hypnotic eyes.

"Why are you here?" Mia breathed. He crowded her against the wall, and awe gave way to anxiety.

"You're going to have my son," he hissed and grabbed her by the back of the neck.

He pressed his lips against her mouth, smothering her response and forced her lips apart with his tongue. She couldn't breathe anything in but the smell of whiskey on his breath. She tasted the potency of it in his mouth. She kicked him and he let out a howl. He responded with a blow to her face that snapped her head back hard. She was dizzy enough for him to toss her on the bed.

"You are mine, not his," he growled between his kisses, "I will have you first."

He pried her legs open with his knees and tore the sheet from her body. This wasn't the way it should be!

"Get off of me Vastadon!" Mia cried violently, "You are hurting me!"

He ignored her mercilessly, but she didn't give in. She struggled until her body became too weak. Tears streaked her face as he impaled himself inside of her, slaying the layer of her maidenhead. He tore at her back with his violent grip, carelessly ripping her hair. The weight of his body crashed down on her over and over again until her body became limp.

Her hand tingled with fire, and she prayed to Danu for the magic she possessed. He halted, his manhood still buried between her legs, and drew his head back to look at her. A wicked smile spread across his face and his eyes twinkled with amusement.

"My beautiful Mia," he tilted his head mockingly, "Are you foolish enough to think you can attempt magic with me?"

The amusement melted from his face and was replaced with fury. He rolled his eyes back into his head and hissed a foreign incantation. The burn from her fingers dissolved and an icy sheet moved beneath her skin making her immobile. It was his spell, and the power of it left her defenseless. All that Mia could do was pretend she wasn't there. Her mind went blank, and she lifted above the repulsion. And below she saw herself as a small frightened animal devoured and shredded within the jaws of a predator. He quivered as he spilled his seed inside of her and lifted his body from her. He fixed his eyes on her joyously, as if he had done nothing wrong.

"You will never be free of me. No matter where you run, I will find you," he said and adjusted his breeches. He planted a kiss on her forehead and left the room a content man.

Vastadon stepped into the corridor and ran a tongue across his lips. He arched his brows. And with a shrug of his shoulders, he trotted passed a wide-eyed servant.

Mia lay there for what seemed like hours. She feared Vastadon's return and had it in her mind not to move lest he was drawn back to her. Her heart pounded against her ribs, and her breath was caught up in panic and weakness.

Goddess, help me forget…

It was as if someone pushed her off of the bed. She tumbled to the floor in a heap of sheets at the foot of Merle.

The woman peered down coldly at her.

"Mother…help me," Mia whispered and reached a shaken hand to her.

"I am not mother to you, remember?" Merle stepped over her and tore the sheet from the bed. She inspected it carefully and sighed with relief when she saw the bloodstain from her shattered maidenhead.

"You have brought this on yourself, Mia," Merle regarded her unemotionally. "It is no ones fault but your own."

The pain of Merle's words hurt almost as badly as being raped. Merle walked out on her just as Arabella came through the door, Aldrich at her heels.

"Mia!" Arabella cried and fell to her knees beside her, "Oh my Goddess, Mia who has done this to you?"

Mia could barely part her lips to speak. They were swollen and dry, and her tongue was heavy. She looked into her sister's tear filled face and whispered, "Vastadon will never let me go."

Jacob stormed into the room and rested his eyes on his wife. She was alive, beaten, but alive and wrapped in a tattered sheet.

"Was she raped?" he demanded. He already knew the answer.

Aldrich was beside her, while Arabella cradled Mia's head in her lap cleaning her face. They didn't answer him. Jacob rushed to his brother and yanked him up. With fierce eyes, he refused to let his brother turn from his question.

"Was she *raped?*" Jacob thundered and Aldrich nodded. Jacob let go of his brother and spun his back.

"Who did this?" Jacob asked already suspecting who it would be.

"Vastadon," Arabella answered bitterly.

His nephew drank heavily all night and sunk deep into the shadows of solitude. An unusual type of behavior for the half-blood. He watched Mia like a dragon and simmered throughout the whole ordeal.

Jacob shot for the door, rage and heat, death and blood jumbled up in his head. Aldrich leaped at him and tackled him to the floor before he could leave. Jacob wrestled with him, but Aldrich had already pinned him beneath his weight.

"You side with your half-blood son in this? *This?*" Jacob spat, his face contorted with anger.

"Instead of leaving her to satisfy your blood thirst, you should soothe her from such a shock so that she will not fear *all* men from *his* actions," Aldrich bellowed. "Let me handle Vastidrich."

"Please," Mia whispered, "I am shamed to have people know what happened. Not yet..."

Arabella hugged her close and snapped, "He raped you, Sister. He must pay."

"No," Mia cried hoarsely, "Vow it that no one will ever know."

Arabella remained silent as Jacob did.

"Vow it!" Mia repeated desperately, "Sister…"

Arabella's face went taut and red, but she nodded, "I vow it that no other will know without your consent."

Jacob shoved his brother aside and lifted Mia in his arms. He carried her to the chaise in the sitting room and laid her down gently. He covered her with a wool blanket and look at her with a blank expression, but behind his mask, the seed of hatred rooted. Vastadon would pay for his disrespect, and as much as he would never openly admit it, his nephew would suffer for the pain and torture he put this woman through. Rape was a vicious crime, unacceptable in Jacob's eyes no matter who the woman was.

My wife…

Jacob bit his lip hard drawing his own blood against the murderous tide that swept through him. He reached into his pocket and pulled out a delicate gold chain with a simple thorn charm dangling from it. The necklace belonged to his mother, Cordelia. She left it to him to give to his bride when he married. The women of his mother's descent all wore the emblem of their family. Sasha wore one similar to this that once belonged to their grandmother. He ran his pinky finger across the delicate pendant before he put it around Mia's neck. He hadn't expected the gift to be given warmly to her, but he certainly didn't want things to turn out the way they did.

Mia's eyes fluttered open, and she smiled softly up at him. Her left eye was swelling and purple touched its corner. Jacob wrenched.

"Now I can sleep," She whispered and placed a hand on his cheek.

Normally he would've shrunk from her touch, but he couldn't do so now. A few moments later she was sleeping. Guilt consumed him. He accepted this arrangement and now it was his responsibility to look after her no matter his personal conflicts. He left her wide open.

Jacob returned stopping short at the adjoining door. Aldrich and Arabella were deep in conversation, so he listened.

"Tell me Aldrich, I must know," Arabella ordered softly.

"If you do not know, then it isn't my place to tell you, my lady," Aldrich replied.

"You remembered me when you saw me the day of my father's death. Was it she?" Arabella pressed.

"Why must you know? What does it have to do with anything?" Aldrich questioned skeptically.

"Trust me. It has everything to do with it," Arabella waved a hand impatiently, "You know what, Aldrich, keep your silence. I will just dispose of the child that might have begun to grow in her womb."

She stomped off and brushed passed Jacob. After a glare, she hurried to her sister's side.

"What did she want to know?" Jacob asked.

Aldrich shook his head, "She asked me who Vastidrich's mother was. Her suspicions were right, but it isn't for me to reveal her secret."

"One day, Brother, I hope that you'll stop protecting the Thaumaturi and return yourself to our kind loyally," Jacob said still sour with his brother's quick defense of Vastadon. "Now, would the two of you leave me be with my wife on our wedding night." Jacob's voice rose loud enough for Arabella to hear.

Arabella stomped back into the room, her eyes were narrow, "You do not plan on bedding her tonight, after all this has happened?"

"I am no monster, *magician*," Jacob growled his insult and Arabella struck him.

He hardly flinched, and she shrank, a little surprised with her own actions, when he turned his angered expression on her.

"She might wake up frightened without me here!" Arabella argued taking a retreating step, "I haven't spent enough time with her before she leaves."

"She will be safe, and you will have the entire day to spend with her tomorrow. She isn't well enough to travel yet," Jacob snapped, "And never raise your hand to me again for I cannot promise you that I will hold tight to my hand."

Aldrich held out his arm and she lifted her chin allowing him to guide her out of the room.

After they were gone, he carried Mia back to the bed and arranged pillows and blankets on the floor beside the bed. He gazed out the balcony doors and froze midway down to his hand made pallet. A glowing white owl, nearly three feet high, perched on the balcony balustrades. Jacob grounded his fists in his eyes, and when he looked again, the great creature was gone. He had once before saw something of that nature. He hardly slept the rest of the night, and he made certain to hold tight to his sword beneath the covers.

CHAPTER SEVENTEEN

Sacrifices

The room was alive. The sound of a heartbeat echoed throughout the crimson vapor cavern. Veins curved along the wall pulsing and pounding. In the center of the room, a round altar erected, and upon its surface, two gold jagged pieces of amber pointed to the black ceilings. A pale stone smothered with flames was placed between the shards.

Any who discovered this place would've fled with fear and possession. And those who stood still within this place would emerge with soulless eyes.

Only one man could dare enter without invite. The Stone of Destiny stroked Hector with fingers of seduction. He could only look at it, but not touch. Its Power was too strong for the hands of a mere mortal.

Hector inhaled the power of this temple within a temple. His eyes danced wickedly when they fell on the golden shards and the crimson veins lightened his face to demonic pleasure. When he was so close to Him, it was orgasmic. No such pleasure could arouse him more. The room smelled of coal and sulfur, and static threads filled with the presence of the Darkgod, Bile, forced Hector to his knees. He lowered his head and stretched his arms out beside him, waiting.

The earth beneath his knees boomed. The walls began to bleed, cracking in two, and a red glow blinded Hector. The swiftness of Bile's approach was a sign of restlessness and disturbance, but Hector knew that He would never harm His most useful servant. Once Hector adjusted his eyes to the awesome sight, he lowered his head further, kissing the rock between two metal boots. He then lifted his eyes to the Darkgod before him.

The Darkgod peered down at his servant through a veil of black hair. His piercing red eyes danced with fire and death from the chasm of his face. He was covered in black iron and silver chains hung loosely from His muscular arms and legs. He circled his head and the popping sound made Hector jump a little. The Darkgod howled with a wraithlike anger and fanned out his black wings. Hector shrank, placing his lips to the stone floor once again until the Darkgod's shadow no longer darkened him.

Hector searched the room and saw Bile unsheathe His double edged sword. The huge figure breathed heavily, red and purple mist shot from His trembling nostrils, as He attacked the cavern wall with heavy deadly lashes. The clank of steel upon rock echoed in between the Darkgod's horrendous growls. A fountain of sparks rained on Him having no effect on His already flaming form. Bile wasn't used to restriction and had been sleeping for the better half of the decade, but when Hector first Awakened Him, Bile was less powerful than He was now. For five years, Hector nurtured the Darkgod's form with the blood of Danu's people, the Thaumaturi. He grew more impatient with each ritual.

Once Bile simmered down, Hector pulled a key from his pocket and lifted to his feet. He unlocked a panel along the wall and pulled forth a screaming woman by her brown hair. She was a thin woman, of about thirty or so, and Thaumaturi. The Darkgod wheeled about and His scowl melted into a look of hunger. He approached the screaming girl in slow controlled steps and caressed her cheek with a massive hand. Soon He soothed her into silence.

"I can give you what your heart desires, woman," He whispered and tilted her pointed chin to the right. The woman's eyes lit up with whatever she saw. Hector knew nothing of what any of them saw, because whatever it was, it was meant only for the prey's eyes. She smiled, holding her arms out to embrace something. The Darkgod released her and watched with a strange and amusing expression. The woman lowered her body to the ground and embraced the air weeping.

"You can have your child back." He promised, "I can give him too you. All you need to do is vow your loyalty and profess your love for me."

She stood tall and ran into the open arms of the Darkgod, "I pledge my life to you, my lord, if you can bring him back."

Bile guided her over to the shards and whispered something in her ear. He laid his fist on the flaming Stone, and with His touch, the pale flames devoured His hand into a ball of fire. His eyes rolled into his head, and His strokes against the woman's hair became rough and encouraging. The woman placed her hands on the shard, and it lit beneath her fingers in colors of purple, green and blue. She lifted it from its altar and pierced the nape of her neck with the jagged edge. Blood ran across her throat and spilled in between her little breasts. The Darkgod snatched her by the back of her head and drank from her like a beast overwhelmed with the thirst of thousand years. The girl's face paled and her eyes rolled back into her head as He lifted her fully into the air. He finished and wiped his mouth dropping her to the ground, carelessly.

Smoke rose from her trembling form and she convulsed like a fish out of water. Hector curled his lips at the pathetic sight. Although it was part of the process of Turning, Hector could never quite get used to it. When she opened her eyes, they were black and inexpressive. She slithered to her feet and over to Bile, who paid no attention to her, with her lips parted in a malevolent smile. Hector grasped her arm and tossed her out of the room. The prey reacted with passion after the first breath of the Power. Sometimes Bile welcomed them lustfully, and he would care not if Hector was in the temple. Thankfully, Bile was in no such mood this night. The woman could be trusted now, so he couldn't wait to remove her from his sight. When he turned his attention back to Bile, He was pacing restlessly.

"How long must I wait, servant, before I can discard these chains that bind me?" His voice was deep and distorted as He commanded.

"It will be done soon, My Master," Hector said humbly.

"Have you no more Thaumaturi blood for me?" Bile whipped the full of his awesome form toward Hector.

"It will be soon, my—"

"I am tired of waiting!" Bile thundered dashing at Hector.

Hector lowered his eyes from Bile's glare and trembled beneath Him. The blood of the Thaumaturi was sacred and through it the Darkgod could take form in the world, though He was a prisoner to the confinements of the deep earth until a Solar Eclipse is summoned.

"The season for Thaumaturi voyage breaches. You will be well satisfied soon, My Master. Once You take their blood, they will be Your army. And as Your army grows, the easier it will be for Your return." Hector replied.

"The world should be Mine as we speak!" He thundered.

"The Emperor is too strong, Master. I need some time to gain his court's favor."

"Kill him," the Darkgod ordered impatiently

"In due time," Hector promised and bowed lowly.

"I have seen what they have done to My pawn. I watch her when she sleeps. She comes to My domain soon in the arms of her Barbarian husband." Darkgod hissed.

"What? I know nothing of this," Hector turned his body away and pounded his fists against the hard wall.

"I make it a point to know everything about her for it is she who must bring Me the rest of Danu's weapons. I feel her emotions and I do not like what I have felt. She has married the Emperor's brother and it displeases Me that she is no longer a virgin."

"Merle!" Hector growled knowing full well she was behind such a thing.

"Ah," the Darkgod sneered, "The lovely queen of the Winter Thaumaturi. I have tasted her blood before. My first drop of Thaumaturi blood it was. Nothing tastes sweeter than such a gracious offering. It isn't the bitterness of one who is forced. I am a master of manipulation and it has won Me the taste of such blood freely."

"That witch!" Hector growled still trapped in his anger with Merle.

"It is she who has brought the Bearer to My domain, not you." the Darkgod laughed wickedly.

"I do what I can, My Master." Hector bit his lip against the rush of his poisonous fit.

"Don't be envious. You both have your separate uses. Now," He spun to face the shards and the pale flamed Stone, "I want the Mageborns. They are most powerful and their blood will make me stronger. Then I can leave this prison I am forced to live in."

"That is impossible, My Master. There is only one left," Hector murmured.

"You are wrong. There are eight others." Bile grinned baring all His jagged teeth, "Not counting a young priestess."

"If that is true, they will never turn freely," Hector shook his head slightly.

"They will turn one way or another," Bile stroked the Stone gently, "because without every last piece of the puzzle, the gates to My world will cease to open. Bring them to Me." Bile hissed and retreated into the crimson crevice of the wall.

"What has become of these lands?" *Enchantra* Corbin spun his back on the Elders. "A Thaumaturi princess marries a Barbarian blasphemer! You have no idea what this means!"

"Agreed," Valance leaned back in his seat, "But I'm afraid her fate lies in the hands of Danu."

Corbin set his jaw and slowly turned his body back to the Order. He was so enraged it seemed that columns of steam spiraled from his red face. Valance remained calm and poised, but shivers of trepidation rippled through the room. They feared the loss of their prize.

"Your secrecy burdens you, *Enchantra*," Valance pointed out using the proper title of an Elder deliberately. "If you chose to avoid seeking the aid of the House and the Ministry, you will become weak from such burdens."

"Some things are better left unsaid, Valance," *Enchantra* Rhea interceded.

"There are consequences to silence as well," *Enchantra* Dragan countered.

"The consequences of silence could never amount to the consequences of sharing knowledge with the House!" Karenna interceded.

Valance heard enough of the distress. It was time they were put straight.

"In my opinion, all of you fear the loss of control," Valance said blatantly. "And you fail to see that we were never to control of anything that was Blessed. It's in Danu's hands," He repeated.

The girl would be far from Thaumatur and from them. They offered no trust in her. Valance knew she would make the right choices when the time came. He felt it.

"How can you sit there so calmly?" Corbin's eyes narrowed. "The Bearer will be of no use to us if she is tainted or worse yet, dead! Curse the High Priestess for springing this on us now!"

"Is that what she is to you?" Valance darted from his seat. His voice hardened and it took most of them by surprise. "Another weapon?"

He scanned them intently. Their expressions were stony with the control of their highest training. They were so different from the days of the beginning.

"You know what I mean, Valance!" Corbin broke the silence.

"We must trust in the girl. After all, she wasn't the one responsible for the disappearance of *three* of the weapons," Their faces paled, "Yes, I know about the missing Sword. I have kept the information quiet from the Ministry, but I implore you to tell the High Priestess. It's not right to keep such things from her. After all, is it not she who you will all go to when things collapse."

"She knows already," Karenna leaped to her feet and scowled. "How else would you know of this."

Valance smiled and he was sure his eyes twinkled mischievously.

"Never try to best a High Priestess blessed with the Goddess' insight," His voice chirped.

"Gamesmanship," Karenna hissed, "That is your ambition, Valance. It leaves me wondering whose side you are really on."

Valance let out a drawn sigh, "I'm on the same side as the Ministry. I'm on the same side as you. I'm on Danu's side. Is it not the same with you?"

Karenna scowled, "Foolish question."

"Then, let us start acting like it," Valance snapped his fingers and his globe-crowned staff flew to his hands, "Trust in Danu and by Her name, trust in the redeemer She has sent us."

"And what of the High Priestess's secrets? She has many I am sure," Karenna retorted.

"She tells you what Danu wills her to. No one should question that."

Karenna left out a haughty laugh. The others shifted in their seats and muttered derisive comments.

"You are more loyal to her than you are to your own Order, Llewellyn!" *Enchantra* Yerodin growled and his eyes grew cruel, "You put her up above us all just as you worshipped her half-sister, Cassiandra *Maladinto*. You never supported us when it came to *her!*"

Valance grimaced and his blood rushed with a rage he hadn't felt for a long time. He drove his staff into the ground and the room rumbled forcefully. He threw his hands out sending a burst of lightning toward the rostrum beyond the table. A portion of a marble pilaster burst and sent fragments of wreckage spewing into the chamber. The members of the Order took cover beneath the table and shielded their faces with flailing arms and hands.

Valance was a ball of white static. His eyes had gone completely misted and his hair crackled beneath the rage of his magic.

"Never patronize me again or I will walk out of here and never return," He warned.

He inclined his head and left them alone in their shock. He knew they valued him as the strongest. But, by Danu's name, he meant what he said. Another ill word to taint Cassiandra's name and he would leave them to their pitiful squabbling forever.

BOOK TWO

The Barbarian Nations

CHAPTER EIGHTEEN

Farewell to Home

Jacob was firm on delaying their leave not only because he saw Mia unfit to travel. A great glacier blocked the land connection between Thaumatur and the Nations and it was his hope to wait it out. His impatience got the better of him and when he checked on her the prior evening, he declared leave at dawn.

The first half of the journey would be through the Celse Forest, the very forest that Mia heard so many legends about. She couldn't meet such a dream eagerly. The shadows she lived in for the past two weeks wouldn't let her. Vastadon haunted her every night and Demons had visited her dreaming mind. She wouldn't fear them, she would only live silently among them. Pretending the reality of such things was only in her head.

The Demons that swam around in her dreams were dark and grey masses of robes and they surrounded the same potent winged-figure she first saw on the night she discovered the mirror. She couldn't see his face. It was only a shadow beneath a shroud of ebony. He was familiar, if she could call him a he, but she didn't know why. He promised her life eternally, power of the entire world and vengeance for her pain. She shivered and shunned the seduction. Each time she awoke tangled inside sweat soaked sheets, it was as if dark blemished her spirit. And it was growing inside of her, grasping for its life like a parasite leeching off of her memories.

Mia swung her head to the right and took in the sight of the Winter Palace. Arabella stood at the edge of the draw bridge amidst the twirling snow. Fresh tears nearly froze to her cheeks and she craned her head low with sorrow. The two sisters had gained a better understanding toward one another since Arabella's return for Father's funeral. Mia didn't ignore the fact that her beloved sister, true birth aunt, knew the dark secrets of her family. Yet she couldn't bear to shred the last thing left of her family to a quarrel. Arabella was the best of them. She took herself from that castle as soon as she could and didn't look back. Mia would never look back either.

Mia wrapped the wool blanket around her body and caught a glimpse of herself in the ice covered glass reflection of the carriage litter. Her eyes were sunk in, her cheeks pale of all life and the circles beneath her eyes were purple and puffy. The hair that she so delicately cared for fell in a mass of untamed gold. There would've been a time not so long ago that such an image would've appalled her. On this day, she desired the ugly homely appearance she saw.

It would be less desirable for the beasts called men to see me this way.

The young priestess, Sierra placed a cold hand on Mia's cheek, yet she hardly was aware of her entrance into the litter. The touch stimulated her, attacking her with the bitter bite of tears. It was as if it wanted her to feel again. It wouldn't be so. Not soon anyhow. Mia's head rolled to one shoulder, shaking from the touch of life and she raised her eyes to Sierra veiled in springtime green. The woman's eyes were warm and concerned, but not angry from being shunned. Instead, she placed a palm over Mia's numb fingers.

"In time, the wounds he inflicted on you will heal, inside and out. He will one day suffer the pain and shame he bequeathed upon you," Sierra whispered with a gypsy's accent.

The words meant something. They rang true through Mia's ears, and she felt the corner of her mouth tremble. The carriage jingled, and then moved out, sending the two women's bodies into a slight nudge. The sound of the horses' hooves clopped down the road and gruff voices bellowed orders she couldn't make out. Mia nodded her understanding to the priestess, and returned her gaze out the window.

Two Barbarian warriors galloped past her window followed by her husband. He spared her no look into the sheet in which she hopelessly gaped out. He never came that night, as he should have, until it was too late. He hated her, and she was punished for accepting such a betrothal. She couldn't deny the fire that darkened her husband's blue orbs the very night she lay beaten beneath his gaze. She shivered and lightly touched the gold thorn at her throat she vaguely remembered her husband giving her.

"Not all men are evil, my lady," Sierra commented.

Mia felt as if the priestess spoke the talk of another, far more superior than any mere mortal, Mageborn or not, could begin to know. She spoke to her as if she were inside of her head.

"Forgive me, Sierra, but I have yet to come across a man worthy of such a compliment," Mia replied bitterly. "They take what they want and what they cannot have. They twist truths into their own ugly reality. For what, I ask? Just so they can claim power and lands and women as if they have the right to. This is the Goddess' land. The Great Mother lives in every tree, every drop of water, and every birdsong. She is all that is beautiful and man has done everything they can to destroy it with their greed and their personal wars."

Mia brought her knees to her chest and rested her head upon them. She sounded cold and cruel. But she had spoken the truth of her heart. She couldn't meet the eyes of the priestess.

"Many have tried to destroy Danu. They didn't succeed, for without Her, we wouldn't exist. And as long as there are those who honor Her name, She will never fade from our world. She has tried to protect us always," Sierra answered leaning forward with conviction.

Mia snorted, and a black haze encircled her. It was as if Vastadon was everywhere. Her head shot up, and the haze faded to the heat of her pain.

"Where was Danu on my wedding night?" Mia clenched her teeth. "If it is She who is our protector, then were was She when I lay there beneath *his* weight, beneath his whiskey stench, when he shredded my body and took from me what no man has any right to take!" Tears fell silently from her cold eyes and her voice became uncontrolled, "Where was the Great Mother, who I have always loved, when he ripped from me what I can no longer give my husband!"

Where was She when my mother burned in agony above the sneering vicious crowd of my father's followers?

Mia almost dared to scream all of it.

Sierra went to embrace her, but she snatched herself away and flung the tears from her cheeks. The priestess eased back from her.

Never will I cry again. Never will he have that from me again.

"The Goddess is always with you. Sometimes things happen that cannot be controlled. Too many have turned against Danu, and have made other Gods stronger. They are dark, and they will stop at nothing to take what they can from us. You mustn't let it take you, my lady. Be strong," Sierra said softly.

"Darkness will never have me!"

The Priestess remained silent for awhile, and Mia couldn't sleep. She felt evil and bitter although it wasn't the way she wanted things. The magic had abandoned her since that night. It was almost as if a big black chasm sucked away all things from her that were good. Secrets and shame bound her to this.

Guilt suddenly filled her when she looked at Sierra. The woman was pure and strong with the presence of the Goddess. She shouldn't have been so cold to such a kind woman. Her manner was blasphemy against Danu.

"I am sorry, Priestess, for speaking so poorly to you," Mia whispered and the woman shined her eyes on her. "It is so difficult to be what you are supposed to be, when all works against you."

"I am your priestess, my lady. What ever burden you bear is mine to share with you. You can reveal anything to me and it will remain as sacred as if you were speaking with the Goddess Herself. I want to be your crutch, your teacher, your guidance, and above all, your friend."

"Then I must tell you something. Something that devours me as fiercely as my wedding night," Mia whispered.

"Anything, Princess," Sierra nodded and placed a hand over hers.

"I am the daughter of Ahriman Maladinto," Mia said and studied the priestess' eyes for her reaction.

The Priestess reacted as if she already knew, but said nothing. Mia spoke to her of everything she saw in the mirror, Merle's warnings and the Powers she held of Earth and Fire. When she was through, silence enveloped them. Sierra squeezed her hand and shifted her eyes away.

"I now understand why you have chosen this path. The decision to marry the Barbarian prince was solely yours," she said as if she answered a long awaiting question.

Mia nodded, "Yes."

Sierra drew in a deep breath, "Then the choice you have made was the right one. You couldn't remain in such clutches. The High Priestess had not thought you wished for this."

Mia arched her brows, "The High Priestess has inquired about me?"

Sierra focused her piercing eyes on her, "She fears for you."

"I don't understand," Mia questioned not grasping why a woman so consumed with the will of the Goddess would give her a second thought.

High Priestess Janella *DeBurke's* words invaded her mind from their first meeting.

She is Lady Cassiandra DeBurke, Eldest Princess from Murias, sister to the Spring King. My sister... She was murdered... Do not let the darkness sweep over you.

She knew that her sister was murdered! Did she know that Cassiandra had a daughter all along? Did the High Priestess know she had a niece? Is that why she cared?

"You are a Mageborn, but much more as well," Sierra said in mysterious awe, "You are chosen."

"How could that be?" Mia asked

"You have much more to learn, and so do I. I will teach you the ways of the Goddess and show you how to control and summon your magic. As long as you stay close to me, we will find out all of the answers," Sierra whispered. "Rest, my lady, for the journey will be long."

Mia nodded and rested her head back against the pillow. It was as if a weight was lifted off of her chest. The burden of her bottled up knowledge was shared between them now.

Ten men in blue and silver armor halted before the brigade, their hands resting on their weapons and their faces pinched and weary. The banner of the Winter King and the flag of the Barbarian Empire whipped through the winds. Three Barbarians trotted forward until they placed themselves before the guards. Aunyia strode to one of the towering Barbarians and smiled up at him. His mouth twitched into the tiniest smile until his gaze fell upon Cole, Horace, and Darius, who now stood directly behind her.

"My Lord Hilliard," Horace greeted the Barbarian with a proud smile, "we meet again."

He nodded and said, "Have you come to bid me farewell niece, since you were unable to attend my wedding?"

"We are your escorts," Darius approached flatly, his dark eyes shone daringly.

"Escorts!" Jacob snapped incredulously, "For what?"

Darius shifted his eyes to Aunyia, "He wasn't informed?"

"Jacobane," Aunyia began swallowing hard, "It would be unwise to take the forest route without the protection of skilled Sun Knights. We will guide you to the Murias Harbors. I will bid you farewell there."

"We need no protection," Jacob said shortly, his eyes narrowed, "We have the skills needed to travel through a Barbarian war, and you tell me we should worry about a mere acre of woods."

"The forest is vast," Cole finally spoke up. "We are ordered on behalf of the Thaumaturi princess. We must accompany you."

Jacob sneered, but Aunyia diverted his attention away with a touch of her hand.

"Uncle, let us guide you and once we reach the harbors, you will be rid of us."

He didn't disagree. He said nothing and dismounted with a grace that couldn't be common for a man his size. He strode to the carriage behind the brigade and swung open a door. Cole gave his companions a confused look and watched as a blonde woman emerged from the carriage. She held tight to Jacob's hand like a fearful child as he guided her back towards them. She was travel worn and her hair a mass of unruly gold, her body was wrapped in a muddy colored blanket giving her the look of a commoner.

The very woman, who was the center of their Circle's power, looked directly into Cole's eyes. Her face was drawn, but her blue-violet eyes varnished with an untamed Power. He froze, and almost inched a way when she smiled.

"My husband has told me that you were ordered to guide us through the forest on my behalf. I myself wouldn't mind your company, but it will be unnecessary for you to waste your time when you could be useful elsewhere," The Princess said softly.

So, the Barbarian is clever to think his princess could discourage such a precaution, Cole thought beneath a stifled scoff. "It would be our pleasure to escort you, my lady."

He swept her hand in his and placed his lips to her knuckles. A feeling even more potent than one of the Circle surged through his veins with the simple gesture. Her face retained color and her lips trembled when he touched her. She felt it too.

Cole laughed to himself from the giddiness of his state. He released the girl's hand when he sensed her Barbarian husband's irritation, although it secretly amused him. When he looked to his side, Darius was stomping away.

Darius wasn't a people's person and he tended to be a loner. He could be trusted, but to be liked was another thing. He was a critical man, meticulous and extremely self punishing. And he didn't stop the punishment at himself either.

The Princess smiled widely when she noticed Aunyia and Horace and embraced them each.

"I suppose I can call you *Aunt* now!" Aunyia laughed.

"Please, Mia is fine," she inclined her head.

"Mia," Jacob hissed through tight lips, "Come."

She nodded to the knights and followed him back to the litter like a puppy. The Barbarian's witty plan backfired.

Cole snorted and met eyes with Aunyia, "He has *her* under control."

"Remember, my valiant friend, that man is still my kin," Aunyia playfully warned, "He is stiff, but I assure you that he is decent inside the rugged shell."

"So he is," Cole smirked, but his eyes remained fixed on Mia. "When I touched her, a strange feeling came over me. It was like fire and rain pumped through my veins."

"Horace and I felt it too," Aunyia nodded.

"Darius didn't stick around long enough," Cole said and jerked his head to the left.

Darius was crouched down like a wild animal, his face blank, but something bizarre glittered in his eyes.

"Sometimes I wonder if he *is* a part of this Circle," Aunyia rolled her eyes and headed in the direction of Jacob.

Cole kept his eyes on Darius. The dark Mind Mage twined his hands angrily around his black cape, though his face showed no sign of his emotion. Inside Darius' head, no one would ever get close enough to know. Cole was around long enough to sense vibes within his companions. There was a strange energy emanating from him, and it wasn't pretty.

It had taken no more than two nights to reach the forest edge, but it was uncomfortably cold most of the way. Mia could feel the icy bite of the wind warming with each league they took, and the white surface of the ground dissipated into muddy sludge. The men of Aiden's army rode quietly alongside the litter carriage in which held Mia and Sierra, each soldier resting one hand on the hilts of their weapons. Their faces were pinched with trepidation and they rode their steeds in a stiff manner. Jacob traveled at the head of the line in between two of his Barbarian warriors, as far away from her as he possibly could be. Mia's husband was very displeased with the change of plans and even unhappier with the new companions that escorted them east. It was his hope she would discourage them from their orders to escort her.

The four Sun Knights took up the rear, traveling more assuage. It seemed to Mia, when she glanced back, that they carried themselves with self assurance more so than the provision she had seen in the eyes of her brother's men. They were cloaked in black hooded robes, that revealed nothing of their expressions, but the skill and confidence flowed with the movement of their bodies and their steeds. Mia was surprised at her sudden replenishment and delight with the new addition to the caravan. The knight called Cole sent verve into her dismal form with a mere touch.

It gave Mia a sudden peace, and a sense of security under their care. It was the same feeling she had when she touched Aunyia and Horace. They were like her, Mageborn, and it made her feel less diverse. Strange, though, Nan had said the Mageborn a forgotten people. Perhaps it was fate that brought them all together. The intensity left no room for doubting her current ease. Not even this odd comfort could find her sleep.

The secret, the very seed of Merle's twisted dealings, tore at the edges of Mia's mind once again. The truth of her parentage hurt and comforted her at the same time. To be loved and cherished by a mother she would only know through gossip, pictures, and a horrible image of death seen within the shards of an old enchanted mirror left a whole inside of her. And to be labeled as the daughter of a man so vile that he killed his own kind without mercy brought nothing but fears and doubts in her already fragile mind. Even if the blood of Ahriman propelled through her veins, she would never hate as he did. Is that what Merle wanted? For hatred to nestle itself comfortably around her heart? Her eyes wandered about the litter until they rested on the woman who sat with her.

The Priestess rested her head against the pillows that were provided from Arabella for the journey. At once Mia was envious that she had the courage to sleep at all.

A fragrant wind swirled into the litter. Mia couldn't place the smell, but it was a lovely and familiar smell. And the wind itself didn't seem real to her as it should. Instead, it was a gentle finger caressing her soul and her cheeks in the delicate way of a mother to a child.

I am with you now. All will be well, now. The Great Mother will protect you.

The Whisper was one of love and comfort. She had almost forgotten the musical sound of the Great Owl. It was as if she convinced herself that she dreamt of the beautiful form, but as the potent presence swallowed her, she knew the entity was near and real. A simple smile drifted across her face. She embraced herself and the warmth of such comfort. Her eyes began to lower and at last, the sparkled horizon of sleep settled in. Danu would protect her, and to Her she would give her very spirit to do what She willed. There will be no pause for evil to take hold.

Cole Alexander cast his eyes to what little of the sky that could be seen through the combs of branches and the fog. The Prince pushed the journey to the forest through the night and was hardly ready to slow the pace. Twilight was breaching and soon it would be too dark to travel any further. They were not very far from the Spring Kingdom's edge, but it would be too risky to travel in such large numbers when the cloak of night fell. It was a feeling that nagged him since their departure from the crown of the Celse Forest. Cole gave his companions a swift nod before charging to the front of the caravan.

"My Lord," Cole said in low voice to Jacob, "twilight has come. We must make camp until morning. You have pushed this journey with restless means."

Jacob didn't slow his pace. Instead Cole needed to hasten his stallion's canter to keep up with him. The Prince's features were pinched with annoyance that matched the rigidity of his massive form. After a moment, Jacob guided his steed to a halt. There was an air of reluctance about him. He still didn't grace Cole with acknowledgement. However, judging from what Cole saw, the Barbarian silently agreed despite the grimace he displayed. He dismounted and strode away from Cole without so much as a glance. The heat of Cole's temper rose into his cheeks. He gaited after him.

"What is it with you?" Cole said to his back, "We are here to aid you, yet you treat us as if we are parasites."

"I never asked for your aid, Thaumaturi," Jacob said without facing him.

He was staring into the forest, his hands on his hips, and one finger tapping on the hilt of his weapon.

"Regardless if you asked or not, you know nothing about these woods. The passes through here haven't been used in ages. You would've never made it this far," Cole ran a hand through his black curls with frustration.

Jacob faced Cole with hard eyes. The corner of his mouth curved up into a half amused smile. "My men and I are highly trained and most efficient in urgent situations. So do not swell your pride at my expense."

Cole was about to reply when he heard Aunyia call his name. She was approaching them with great pace. Once she saw the scene before her, she halted. Her eyes bounced from Jacob to Cole and the smile on her face melted with what she saw.

"Uncle, Cole?" she asked taking hold of each of their arms. "Is there something wrong?"

"No, Niece," Jacob answered sardonically, "All is well."

For a moment, the silence was penetrating. Aunyia drew her breath in with concern or possibly exasperation. Despite Jacob's ignorance to the Thaumaturi in his niece, Cole knew Aunyia was no fool. She could feel the same tension Cole was feeling. It was like that with all of them.

"I have found what looks to be the remains of some ancient fort when I scouted the area," Aunyia began, "It is into the forest a little, but it will provide us with good shelter for the night and little use for the tents."

Jacob didn't remove his eyes from Cole and said, "Well done, Niece. Why don't you have your fellow knights lead the brigade there and have them prepare for the night? Then go to my wife and provide her with a woman's company. I am quite certain she will need it being that she isn't accustomed to such surroundings," he sneered.

"She has Sierra to provide her with companionship," Aunyia pointed out. "I wish to remain on guard with my knights."

"And I asked *you* to sit with my wife. I haven't the patience to deal with her on this night."

Cole watched as Aunyia, the stubborn knight he had known her to be, walked away with a simple nod. And once he returned his sights on Jacob, he was gone. Cole grunted and stomped off.

When Cole caught up with Horace and Darius, they were standing before the ruined foundation Aunyia spoke about. The stone pillars that circled the entire premises were cracked and bending beneath the gravity of the air. Thick unmanaged vines climbed the rounded stone columns, and the path leading to the entrance was barely visible beneath years of rocks and dirt. The first half of the fort was hollow and roofless yet the further they entered, Cole noticed there were several alcoves which at one time could've served as cells. The place smelled of age old death, the rotting stench of remains and that wasn't all. The gnarled hand of something unknown, churned within the knights.

"Something does not seem right about this place," Cole said to them quirking a brow.

"You feel it too?" Horace crouched down to look closer at the withered stones.

"Evil stirs within this place," Darius said flatly and strode to one of the alcoves.

They followed him with the same morbid curiosity. Darius removed his leather glove sliding his fingers along the rocky wall, his expression unreadable.

"Sacrifices," Darius muttered and turned his dark eyes to his companions, "It is a place of the Old Legion's Necromancers. A temple in which they practiced ritualistic sacrifices."

Bewilderment held Cole's tongue, but Horace said, "Clearly the sacrifices were not made in the name of the Goddess. It isn't Her way."

"Nay, it's not," Darius confirmed and shifted his eyes to the north of them at the group of Falian soldiers.

Through the folds of men, Mia stepped through, with Aunyia by her side. Cole didn't remember seeing the girl smile since their first meeting, and she still looked to him so pale. A part of him wanted to reach out and embrace her and protect her from the sadness that settled into little discolored balls beneath her eyes. Cole met eyes with Horace and then they both looked at Darius. Strangely, his ominous empty face twitched with what appeared to be distaste and his eyes flared daringly when he looked at the girl. Cole concluded that his eccentric companion wasn't one to share territory with any brigade.

After a moment, Darius brought his attention back to them, "Say nothing of what we feel to *them*."

He pulled his hood over his head, brushed by them, his robe billowing behind him, and disappeared in between the shadows.

CHAPTER NINETEEN

The Mind Mage

"All will be well, Mia." Aunyia draped an arm over her shoulder, "You are well guarded."

Mia nodded, a feeling of uncertainty crept over her from her surroundings. Oddly, she didn't feel fear for herself. Only for those who traveled with her. She walked by Aunyia's side and her eyes rested on the old fortress. Chills prickled beneath her skin when she breathed the air. It was stagnant and stale. Unusual.

"Have you ever been here before?" Mia asked Aunyia pulling her cloak more snugly around her.

"No," Aunyia replied.

She was crouching beside a newly sparked fire, unfolding the sack she carried. She spread several thick coverlets on the ground and nodded for Mia to sit beside her.

She found the simplicity of Aunyia's answer unnerving. She decided to speak nothing more about the matter.

"So, you will be visiting your father?" Mia attempted to conjure up small talk.

"Aye, and my brother, well you know him. Everyone in Thaumatur knows Vastadon," Aunyia commented a bit scornfully.

"Yes, I do know him," Mia replied and prayed to the Goddess that the bitterness she felt couldn't be found in her voice as she spoke about this woman's brother, "I thought him to marry soon. He is in Vhladic?"

"Aye. He has postponed his marriage and escorted my father home a week ago," Aunyia replied. "Apparently my father has ordered a Senate meeting. Vastadon, as always, wants to place himself in the center of things."

Aunyia didn't know what her brother did, surely. Mia was certain that she was the type of woman who wouldn't condone such actions.

"It seems that everyone knows him well." Aunyia laughed, "Except me."

Mia bowed her head, stretching the muscles in her aching neck. It was soothing and a good excuse to change the subject of conversation. When she lifted her head up, she noticed the other knights standing against the back wall of the ruins. They were looking down at her, but their eyes appeared to see something beyond their mere vision. Onyx eyes bore into her filling her with awkwardness. The third man, the one who she hadn't met, was watching her. He spun from her sight and fled into the trees after saying something to his companions. Mia leaned into Aunyia.

"The third knight, not Cole or Horace."

"Darius," Aunyia replied before she finished the question. "His name is Darius Percival. He is what you would call a recluse. He can be trusted despite his ill manners, Lady."

Mia nodded instictively and held out her hands above the campfire to warm them. There was something more to this Darius Percival, as if he knew something more than the others. Rising from Aunyia's side, she smiled down at the knight.

"I'll be right back. I find myself quite curious about this place and wish to explore a little."

Aunyia stood.

"No need," Mia told her, "Rest and I shall return soon. I promise to remain in the sight of the brigade."

"Alright, but please, stay near to the men. There are predators in the forest," Aunyia eased back down by the fire.

"I promise," she said and strolled to the main foundation.

It wasn't the foundation that drew her in, but the curiosity of following Darius. She shifted her eyes once she crept behind the rear pillar to make certain no one was looking. Then she melted away into the shadows and slinked in the direction that she knew Darius went.

It was dark indeed, so she pressed a palm from tree to tree as she went deeper to maintain the balance of her footing. The moonlight was only a sliver in the sky, and with the looming arms of the tree branches, it provided little aid to her sight. Yet fear didn't seize her, and the sense of foreboding faded with the distance she placed between herself and the camp.

Crickets sang in an uneven chorus and the howl of a wolf crying to the moon sliced through the air. What caught her attention was the sound of rustling leaves. Without hesitation, she hastened her pace in the direction of the noise. The sound came to an abrupt stop, and the hairs on the back of her neck began to rise with a sudden knowledge that someone was behind her. She wheeled around, but in mid spin, a gloved hand clamped over her mouth and around her waist. The captor drug her backward and then released her with a twirl. She saw his face, a narrow outline pale as her own, and onyx eyes that remained blank when they fell on her.

"Why have you wandered off from camp?" Darius asked in a deep irritated manner.

For a moment, Mia couldn't find her tongue. She stared at him torn between wonderment and caution. He was different from those he traveled with, almost as if he were a shadow. She didn't feel from his touch the quickened pulse of fire as she did with the others. Then she took notice that he wore leather gloves. He wasn't as willing as the others to connect.

"I wanted to stretch my legs," Mia replied casting her eyes down to her feet that were now covered by the blur of darkness.

He took a deep breath and removed his grasp from her arm. He spun on his heels and snapped, "Come. I am bringing you back."

"What of you?" she asked quickly. "Why are you so far away from camp?"

He returned his attention to her and sneered. Perhaps her words came off a little more challenging than she intended.

THE MARRIAGE OF THE SWORD

"I watch."

"For what?"

"Anything that is *suspicious*," He said stabbing his meaning into her.

When he looked at her, his eyes were accusing and unexplainably cold. He reeked with the smell of sulfur she had assumed to be magic at work, but it didn't feel evil. It oozed with caution and protection. She felt the tiny embers of her temper simmering in her blood. "What you are implying?"

"I am no fool. You are hiding something," he accused. "I only pray that your secret does not betray those who have come to trust you."

"I hide nothing that could possibly harm anyone," Mia shot back, but inside her heart flutter with panic.

He couldn't know the truth, could he…?

"Yes, I do," He answered her thoughts with an arrogant tilt of his head.

"What?" Mia stammered. "How?"

"I am a Mind Mage. I know what you are thinking by the expression on your face," he scowled. "Do not fret. I will not reveal your secrets. But rest assure that I will be watching."

"You know nothing of me or my thoughts. Your threats are meaningless," she replied pulling her eyes away from the accusation, the knowing, and the truth in his face.

"I see her in you," he whispered, "And I see *him*, Daughter of Ahriman."

He was taunting her, pushing her into admission. She had no choice. He knew.

"I am not like him, my lord," she whispered over her shoulder. "The truth was hidden from me too."

"We shall see," he grunted and tugged at her robe, "Let us go back to camp, before your Barbarian decides to blame the Thaumaturi for your irresponsibility."

Mia followed him and told herself to make certain she avoided Darius at all causes.

When they returned to the camp, it was as if no one noticed her absence. Three small fires burned brightly as everyone huddled around the warmth in groups. She searched the scene for Jacob, but Darius gave her an impatient tug forward in the direction of Aunyia and the Priestess. Mia threw him an annoyed glance and dropped on the blanket in between the women.

"You were gone for far too long," Aunyia gently chastised and stirred the stew inside of the cauldron.

"I am here now," Mia replied.

"She wandered off into the forest," Darius said from above them shooting Aunyia a look of reprimand. "I wouldn't let her out of your sight unless you wish to have him," he pointed, "on your back."

Darius was pointing at Jacob, who was pacing restlessly by the steeds. Mia's heart skipped a beat when she took the sight of him in. As much as they were at odds, she couldn't shake the feeling of need inside of her. It was as if the sight of him made her strong and assured that no harm would come to her.

Not like that night...Mia shook the thoughts from her head.

The supper was quick and soon all had drifted to sleep. It took much time for Mia to welcome the sleep she had often denied herself since the beginning of the voyage. Too many things haunted her, even within the grasp of dreams.

Mia...

Mia jolted upright. All were deep in slumber within bundles of wool and cloaks. A Whisper called to her, beckoning her name in a way she had never heard before. It wasn't the capricious chime of the Great Owl. It was the sound of urgency that willed her to rise from her warm spot in between Aunyia and the Priestess. She wrapped herself in her cloak and stepped gently over the bodies of her traveling companions. Invisible fingers caressed her body, brushing her back and gently grasped her wrists, guiding her. Contentment and confidence lifted her from herself, leaving her no cares at all in where she was being taken. *Mia...*

Exhilaration and mystery flowed through her pumping blood. Power beyond any mortal. The faint outline of a pale flamed stone caught her curiosity. It was before her set deep within the shadows of the trees. The flame waved fingers of warmth to her.

Lia Fáil...The Stone of Destiny. Become one with me....

In a sudden flash, Mia was blinded and her body went limp within the invisible arms that held her. The majestic stone was gone. Then, as if another set of hands took hold of her, she felt like a piece of rope in a tug of war.

A screeching noise echoed through the dark night, slowly escalating into a chorus of hissing. She tried to raise her arms to cover her ears, but she was restrained by the invisible war of hands. A fly in a web.

Through the mist of her vision, two red piercing eyes became more vivid until they fell behind the darkness of a hood. The eyes looked down at her with uncontrolled hatred. Something evil filled her.

Mia gasped when she pulled her eyes away from her tormentor. Standing in a blazing circle, six hooded figures stared at her with the same crimson eyes. The large battle axes and spiked scepters sputtered in their grips. Fear seized Mia in a panic. The hissing sound grew louder in her ears to the point of deafness.

They were invading her mind with their threatening words.

You will do our bidding and the bidding of our Darkgod. We will haunt you, torture you…make you remember us until you free him….

Mia's head was scorching with pain. She stumbled back against a large robed shadow. She bounced back from the impact, and looked up to see another set of crimson eyes; a jagged scar ran down the left side of his ghostly face. He reached his hand out to her, inviting her up. But she turned away slamming her eyes shut to the terrorizing scene.

A song of gentle wind filled her ears, dying out the horrible hissing noise. She opened her eyes. She was no longer beneath the shadow of evil. Instead she was surrounded by flourishing green shrubs, crystal blue streams and roses of every color. It was daylight and beautiful. The hand still reached down for her, and her heart sailed when she met the gaze of Lady Cassiandra, her true mother, glowing in flowing white. She placed her hand in Cassiandra's and got to her feet. Mia smiled widely and embraced her tightly.

"You live, Mother, You live…" Mia murmured over and over again.

CHAPTER TWENTY

The Demons

Darius dreamt of white things, beating wings and whispered murmurs, but it was the shrieking hoot of an owl that startled him awake. He jerked to his feet, and glanced over the camp. Mia was gone.

"Stir yourselves," Darius ordered nudging Horace and Cole from sleep with his foot. "The girl is gone."

The men darted upright and armed themselves with their weapons. Faint hissing swirled about the air and the night songs of animals were silent. Cole inhaled the air.

"The fires are out," Horace's breath coiled in mist from his mouth. "And it is entirely too cold for the Cusp between Fall and Spring."

Cole agreed quaking beneath his cloak. He snatched his cowl over his head and sniffed.

"The sound. Let us follow it," Cole said and dashed into the twisted maze of trees.

The others followed closely behind. With each step they made, the sound of hissing grew louder. Somehow Darius ended up in the front of them, blending in with the shadows of the night. Cole hastened his speed to keep up with the outline of the Mind Mage. Abruptly Darius halted before him almost causing a collision, and when Cole saw what he was looking at, he nearly dropped his sword.

A band of Demons surrounded Mia and she was embracing one of them. The Demon's pale hands pulled her close, stroking its claws through her disheveled hair with jagged movements. The Demon's mouth hovered over her lips and it was drawing a white gauzy cloud of life from her. She, however, had a faint smile on her face. Cole blinked, allowing the scene to soak in. The magic was unfamiliar to him, but he knew for sure that the enchantment was a trap.

"Horace," Cole whispered over his shoulder. "Return to camp and wake the brigade. Bring them here at once, *armed*."

Horace lightly patted his back in understanding and leaves rustled behind him sounding Horace's retreat.

Darius crouched and tilted his head to the side, watching. Cole poked his back with the tip of his sword and when Darius looked over his shoulder, memorization covered his face.

"We have to do something," Cole growled.

"She is in the arms of a Demon!" Darius snapped. "I warned you not to trust her!"

Cole charged forward with his sword unsheathed. Beneath his breath he muttered a command that responded instantly with an eruption of flames around his blade. He moved with such agility, weaving between the hooded figures with great insight on his opponent's movements. He swung his inferno blade cutting anything in his path. He had in his mind one goal; to reach the Demon that held Mia at his mercy. As he spun to the right he sliced through one, while ducking a blow from the second one. His blade sizzled out from the blood of the fallen, but there was no time for surprise and no time to conjure the command again. He flipped up and drove his sword straight through the third one's heart. With no moment to spare, the second tormentor jumped on his back clawing his neck.

The features of the figure sent a crawling chill down his back. The Demon's eyes burned with the fury of crimson and his face was so translucent, he could almost see his skull rupture through the thin surface of flesh. His square jaw hung open.

These are no ordinary Demons!

The relieving sounds of swords unsheathing came from behind him. The brigade was joined in battle. One of the brigands must've aided Cole, for the grip was completely released from his neck. His eyes fell to the ground where the wounded lay. They were still alive, squirming to get to their feet from a puddle of their own blood. The first of the fallen snapped its head up. Cole jumped back and screwed up his face.

"You will never save her... We will see to the death of all of you before that happens."

There was a loud popping sound as the two wounded disappeared into thin air.

When Mia opened her eyes again, she was on the soggy ground covered with dead leaves and mud beneath a joined battle. She crawled low to the ground until she found the knight, Cole. He quickly gathered her into his arms and attempted to move her to safety, but a Demon leaped at them. She went tumbling to the ground.

Once she regained her bearings, she searched the ground until her hand found the smooth handle of a sword. She lunged at the creature. In one swift movement she drove it into flesh, but lack of battle skill and the tangle of movements landed her the wrong target. The blade was ripped from her sweaty palms, and for a heartbeat she feared she hit Cole by mistake.

The blade was protruding out of the shoulder of the creature as he spun on her and released Cole with a thud. Enraged, the creature ripped the sword from his skin with a cracking, threw it aside, and went straight for her throat. She struggled against the creature's inhuman strength relentlessly. She was gripping, scratching, and squeezing the clammy flesh that entrapped her to no avail. This thing could kill her with its physical strength. A flick of the wrists and it would be over. But it wanted her to die slowly, painfully, mercilessly.

Dear Goddess, where is my magic?

Her eyesight began to fade as the breath was squeezed from her body. The creature jolted, and the struggle to breath was gone. She fell from its claws, onto the ground coughing, trying to regain control of her jolting body. When she looked up, the Demon was felled by Cole. The creature dropped beside her in a thumping mass, but it was still living, staring directly in her eye. She scrambled away from it, bouncing her eyes from Cole back to it.

"Why won't it die?" Mia screamed.

Cole was stationed above it, his sword at his side, bewildered as well. Then a recognizable voice yelled from behind them, *"Enivid Nus!"*

Darius aimed his wand directly at Mia and it exploded with silvery and white threads of light. The hissing escalated into agonizing howls, and once the blinding light subsided, the creatures were gone.

The power of the spell lifted the dark curtains of Darius's hair. He was heaving, his wand still frozen in the direction of Mia. Time seemed to stop for a moment and all that Mia thought was that Darius wanted to send her sailing along with the creatures with his spell. The Mind Mage whipped his head away and lowered the wand.

"They are powerless in the light," he said flatly before he strode back into the darkness.

Cole lifted Mia to her feet. She swayed for an instant, but he held tight to her supporting her against his chest.

"You should've shared your knowledge before it got this far!" Cole bellowed after him.

Darius ignored him and melted away from the scene. Mia learned quickly that he had an annoying habit of doing so.

"Jacob!" alarm filled her, "Where is my husband!"

She scanned the darkness for some sign of him. Horace was to the left, his hands tight around his sword standing protectively before Sierra. Aunyia was kneeling down probing green fingers at one of the fallen. A part of Mia was thankful to see her new friends safe, but she didn't ease entirely. Jacob's Barbarian companions hovered nearby what was left of the brigade, but she couldn't find her husband.

"Jacob!" she bellowed again.

Jacob lifted himself like a rising spirit into the shaft of moonlight. His face distorted with confusion. Relief released the constriction of her chest.

"This place is cursed!" Jacob shot Cole an accusing look, "Your presence attracts them!"

"*We* disposed of them!" Cole growled through grit teeth.

"More than half of the brigade lay dead now!" Jacob scanned the grounds, "Kennik!"

"Yes, Majesty," Kennik called back.

"How many live aside from the new addition we have so *luckily* acquired?" Jacob asked and took a firm hold on Mia's trembling hands.

"Four of the brigade, myself, and Euan, but he has a bad wound in his shoulder, my lord!" Kennik replied grimly. "We should prepare to leave. This place has made itself clear. We are unwanted." His laugh was deep and scornful.

Jacob guided Mia away from Cole and took hold of her chin, inspecting her intently, "Are you hurt, wife?"

"I am okay. A little shaken up…" Mia's grip tightened on his hand.

"I cannot wait to leave this blasted place!" Jacob sneered and tugged his hand away.

But Mia clung to it. She felt safe with his touch. "Don't leave my side, Jacob," Mia whispered. "Whatever evil that was, it has gone from this place. Let us wait 'til morn before we leave."

"I don't think it wise to linger here," Jacob replied sharply.

"It isn't safe to wander," Mia pleaded and for ten heartbeats it was silent.

Jacob nodded his agreement and called Kennik to come forth, "We shall remain here until morn. If we travel now, we could invite more danger. In the morning, we bury the dead and move out. Have the priestess woman tend to Euan and let it be done without the ridiculous display of magic!"

"Very well, my lord," Kennik bowed. Sierra rose from behind Horace and went to Euan's side.

"What were they?" Mia shifted her eyes to Cole. He frowned, shot a considering look at Jacob, and shook his head.

"Demons, they were Demons of some sort." Cole ran a hand through his black curls, "It should not be so, but it is."

"How?" Mia exclaimed, "Where did they come from?"

"*Someone* unleashed them," Darius interceded. "Perhaps there is something you wish to tell us?"

Mia jerked her head up. The Mind Mage was standing on a higher level of ground, a rock perhaps, looking down his nose at her. His accusing eyes hone and dance with mysterious thought. Suddenly she felt the heaviness of all of their eyes on her.

"I know nothing of these things!" she spread a look between all of them.

"You *do* know the history of your bloodline?" Darius sneered. "And we all know that her *brother*, the traitor he was, had the Power to summon such things."

Mia drew her breath in sharply. Silence settled among them and it made Mia want to shrink from their questioning gazes. Darius leapt down and circled her.

"Enough, Darius," Horace murmured.

"Enough?" the corner of Darius' mouth twitched into a smile. "The kin of this woman was a traitor. He stole what didn't belong to him, defiled the Season Temple, massacred our lands with his Demons and charged onward to foreign lands. Not so far from the mark now, is it?"

"You speak in riddles!" Mia snapped, but she felt her own mind spin into a blur. What if he was right?

"You make your place in our world just when these things surface and then you claim your position among the Barbarians by marrying one," Darius accused. "Perhaps to unleash your Demons there as well?"

"Enough!" Cole placed himself between Mia and Darius. "We don't have time for your paranoid imagination!"

"Did you not see what I saw when we first came onto the scene?" Darius lifted his chin and scanned the group. "You all missed it!"

"You are being ridiculous, Darius," Cole simmered.

Darius ignored Cole and stabbed a finger in Mia's direction, "She was in the embrace of one of those foul creatures and it looked like she rather enjoyed it!"

"You lie," Mia hissed, a slow fire building in her chilled blood.

She would never give herself over to such things! But her mind squirmed to find memory of how she came to the floor of a joined battle. She couldn't be sure. The memory of a beautiful warm place and her mother was all that she recalled. She embraced Cassiandra. Perhaps it was only an image and that the true thing she held close was indeed a Demon. She shivered.

"It was killing her! Come on man, you know best out of all of us what you saw. The magic that was used, it was sucking the life right out of her!" Cole growled.

"You wish to quarrel with me, one of your own, over that lying traitor you just met!" Darius let out an incredulous snort.

"Mind your tongue, *magician*!" Jacob growled and lunged for Darius.

Darius spun with ease away from Jacob's attack, allowing enough time for the Barbarians and the remaining guards to collect him back. In one graceful move, Darius drew out his wand and aimed it directly at Jacob. Mia leapt in front of her husband extending her hands. Aunyia swung Darius's wand away from his target.

"Cool off, Darius! We are in no mood!" Aunyia commanded.

Darius gave one long challenging look at Jacob before he stomped off in a direction away from camp. Mia watched him go. She didn't despise him. Instead she pitied him because she knew how it felt to lack trust.

"Never embarrass me again by placing yourself before me!" Jacob thundered.

"No man or woman's blood will spill because of me. I will not have that on my conscience," Mia snapped back at him. "Now come. Show me to your camp."

Jacob's camp was set apart from the others in a clearing east of the main camp near a rushing stream. He shared his fire with no one. Just like him to separate himself from everyone. Mia washed up in the stream, thankful she didn't freeze to death from the night chill wind. She glanced over her shoulder to see if her husband at all watched her. He didn't even turn his body her way. Maybe she was hideous to him, but sooner or later she knew he would be forced to perform intimately with her. That is if he wanted a true legitimate heir to his position.

Mia dressed herself in a loose-fitted white tunic that fell as long as a dress would on her. She fastened her cloak at her throat with a sapphire knotted broach. She didn't bother with the circlet Arabella insisted she wore at all times to show her caste. Beneath the slit-sided tunic, she wore scarlet leather breeches. She pulled the Sword Nan had given to her from her bag. The warmth and humming instantly filled her with one touch. After the earlier events, she would make certain to keep the Sword close to her. She secured it within the outer robes she would wear in the morn and headed back to Jacob's camp to find him rummaging through one of his sacks.

Without saying a word to her, he unraveled a bundle of thick woolen blankets and arranged it close to the flames. He lowered himself onto the arrangement and poked at the fire, turning branches until fiery tongues danced into the air. When he was satisfied with the bonfire, he grabbed a skin that was nearby and drank deeply from it. Mia sat beside him and held her hand out for the skin. Jacob thrust the skin at her, tore off his vest, and drifted down on his back, his eyes fixed on the swaying tree branches. Quickly, she gulped the ale, set it aside, and fell back alongside of him. Then she did the most peculiar thing.

She nestled her cheek against his chest. She felt him stiffen, but he didn't shrink away. This was the man who would save her from her past. He would take her far away from this cursed country. Soon she wouldn't have to fear Demons at all. She found sleep that night. Dreamless peaceful sleep.

"The Mageborns plan to cross the sea with My pawn," Bile grumbled. "Let them come to Me then. I will not stop them."

"Your pawn, Master, isn't on course for Vhladic. She will reside in Vansant Summit with her husband." Hector sneered.

"So be it. She will come to Me in due time to fulfill her fate. We are intertwined like the woven bands of the Barbarian's deities. I have touched her dreams with My presence. She has yet to reject me."

"You have reached her?" Hector asked.

"Aye," Bile growled and opened his closed fist releasing an orb of fire.

"The particular Demons I have summoned from the Stone hunts her as we speak. Soon she will be unable to resist her true destiny. It is the influence of the Imperia that concerns me now."

The sphere blazed and floated to the circle of the altar and hovered above the Lia Fáil. The tiny orb expanded into the size of two fists and churned with vitality, overlapping its fiery surface with the Stone's pale tongues.

"Show me The Imperial Family!" Bile commanded.

The ball reacted instantly stretching its surface into a Barbarian man of about forty garbed in long onyx robes and a silver torque handmade with thorns. His hair was smooth flaxen, braided only at the temples. His jaw was strong, his eyes a narrow blue, and his beard was neatly kempt with two micro-braids on both sides of his chin, a gleaming silver stud beneath his lower lip.

Hector smiled wickedly at the image and approached it making certain to keep a safe distance between himself and the Stone. He imagined himself striking the man before him.

"The foremost member of the Imperial Family that stands before us," Hector took on an educating tone, "is the Emperor Aldrich Luthros Hilliard. He prides himself on being called the Mage Lover and strides for peace between the Barbarian Nations and Thaumatur. His people, despite their disagreements with his ideas, revere him as the man who protected the land from the Tribes. Disputes amongst the Imperial Senate are usually solved quickly and efficiently beneath his rule."

"Weaknesses!" Bile ordered impatiently.

"Where shall I start?" Hector jested but quickly continued when Bile flashed him a threatening scowl. "The one thing that held the council together was the fact that the Emperor's younger brother is true to their father, the late Emperor's ways. With that in mind, as first successor to the throne, he'd most certainly pick up where Luthros left off. However, the ever-so-clever Emperor marries his brother off to a Thaumaturi shattering the Senates hopes," Hector smirked. "Which means they will come to rely on me more. Another weakness, perhaps the most vulnerable of weaknesses, is his undying love for the mother of his children. The female deity's High Priestess, Janella DeBurke."

Hector paused for a moment watching his Darkgod in awe. Although Bile was forced to live in a prison of flesh and bone, He radiated the power of His wraithlike force. But the body and mind of a shell was limiting Him to His full knowledge. Desires of the mortals taunted Him as it would any other man. He depended on Hector to nurture His form until it was strong enough to be released into the world.

"Onward!" Bile sliced the pulsing air of the temple.

The orb engulfed into flames and stretched into another Barbarian with great resemblance to Aldrich. He was garbed in chain mail, a waist length vest and iron armor from the waist down. He held in his right hand a sword and nestled beneath his left elbow was an armor crown. His blonde hair was tied loosely behind him and his blue eyes stared fiercely ahead.

"High Prince Jacobane Hilliard," Hector began walking around the image. "A man of honor and respect, and one the Nations have come to rely heavily on. He's known for his unyielding courage and strength, and is responsible for the wellbeing of the Tribes. He provides the Tribes with the necessities to live and in return the Tribes have remained content and peaceful. There hasn't been a raid on the west side of the wall for nearly six years. His passionate beliefs regarding the Thaumaturi have gained him an advantage over the Senate," Hector paused and shook his head. "His weaknesses, however, have placed him in a fragile position. He sacrificed his own person for the love and loyalty of the Emperor by agreeing to marry a Thaumaturi. The Tribes hatred of the Thaumaturi will drive them into attack against Vansant Summits."

"It'll not be hard to get rid of that one," Bile grunted. "He would be useless to me."

Bile flicked a finger at Jacob's image and it shrank into a slightly smaller form. The man before them now was clearly the product of the two prominent races. Liquid platinum hair spilled past his shoulders framing a cleanly shaven face. His nose was sharp and his lips curved up into an arrogant grin. But his ice-blue eyes sputtered with dark Power. His poise was languidly in the dazzling silver trimmed ebony robe of a Thaumaturi politician and he carried a viper headed javelin crafted out of silver and diamonds.

Bile leaned forward a little more interested and commented, "This one here proudly carries the symbol of the Legion, yet others do not look upon him suspiciously?"

"Vastadon DeLucible, birth name Vastidrich Hilliard, Prince Regent," Hector chuckled. "This man could walk side by side with You in the middle of Thaumatur and still the people wouldn't look upon him with suspicion. He has centered himself in the Barbarian Senate and is respected in the House of the Thaumaturi politicians. Alluring, manipulating, and deceiving are qualities he is proud to have. He reminds me of Ahriman in his prime."

"We may have use for him," Bile considered narrowing his eyes. "He could be very useful if he has evolved the Power."

"His weaknesses are desires; one being his uncle's new wife."

Bile nodded, "If we must. Leave this one be for now. Next!"

The image of Vastadon faded into the voluptuous woman who Hector recognized to be Sasha. Oh, how she was entertaining to toy with. Hector thought. With any luck, she would be spared the fate of her two brothers.

"Sasha, sister to the Emperor," Hector slid a tongue over his lips. "She is a *fun* woman, a selfish manipulative woman who was responsible for her husband's murder. She is open with her animosity towards Aldrich's children and the Thaumaturi. I do see a use for her. She believes I can convince Aldrich into naming her his successor as *sole empress*." Hector nearly lost his breath trying to stop himself from laughing, "I, of course, knowingly fed into her petty delusions. Her father raised her to believe she could get whatever she wants no matter how it's done. That is a weakness."

"She'd be more of an annoyance to Me than a useful servant. Do what you must with her, but if she fails to prove her use to Me, then I'll give her to you for your keeping."

"Thank you. You are good to me." Hector humbly inclined his head. "I believe that to be all—" Hector was cut of by the zipping sound of Sasha's image.

The image faded but was replaced by another female. Her hair cascaded fiery red curls passed her strong shoulders down to her slender waist. The girl's eyes were an odd green with hints of blue, and her face was smooth and oval. She was garbed in a yellow and jade wrap cut on an angle from her waist. Beneath the wrap, golden armor gleamed. A torque of leaves was attached to the purple flamed cape of the Sun Knighthood.

"Well, this must be Anne Hilliard, Aldrich's daughter, but I haven't seen her since she was seven years old," Hector stopped when he glanced at Bile.

The huge man-Demon stood above the image with a dumbstruck look on his face. He raised His clawed hands to the image and lightly stroked the air where her hair would've been. Hector's bewilderment froze his tongue. He had never seen this massive force so mesmerized by one thing. Of course there was the occasional lust fest after the Turnings, but this wasn't such a thing. The Darkgod was awestruck. Hector saw nothing special about the girl.

"Tell me more about her, for she is one of the Mageborns," Bile said in a low voice.

"There isn't much more I can say about her. She has been in Thaumatur for twelve years."

"Bring that Mageborn to me!" Bile thundered, "Have the Pariahs retrieve her and bring her to me at once!"

Hector shrank beneath the Darkgod's temper. Perhaps she would be *His* weakness. But Hector wouldn't think on that now.

"Master, You mustn't let Your desires misguide You. If You attempt to taste the blood of a Mageborn by force, it'll do You no good. Their Powers would only die along with their bodies and leave You much hungrier than before," Hector stuttered bowing before him.

"I wouldn't force *her!*" He pointed at the image, but it faded from the room. Bile growled.

"You will have her, Master. But be cautious for she is our enemy and daughter to the Emperor."

"Do not concern yourself with *this* girl. Her fate lies with Me!" Bile thundered and slammed through the red crack in the wall.

Hector released his breath and took himself from the temple. So the Darkgod will have His woman. That left His pawn free game. Hector's plan was most definitely heading in the right direction.

Sweet concubine, your fate will lie with me.

CHAPTER TWENTY-ONE

The Undry

It took the entire day to reach Murias, just in time to see the sunset twirl the sky with purple and pink ribbons. It was a breathtaking sight. The first sight Mia could actually enjoy.

The day was devoured quickly as they made their way out of the Celse Forest passed the rolling hills of Rose Hill Gardens. In spite of the fact that Nan remained silent about Mia's true birth parents, she was tempted to flee this whole damned fate straight away to the Hill in search for the warmth of Nan's comfort. But she bit her lip and sunk deeper into the blankets.

Mia knew when they neared the harbors because the warm winds carried a strange scent of salt and fish. Sierra noticed Mia crinkle her nose to the scent and explained to her that it was the breeze from the Lunar Sea. Mia had only seen the ice crackled part of the sea in Falias and it carried no such scents.

Jacob and Darius didn't settle their differences from the prior night but thankfully they kept their distance from one another. Jacob rode with his Barbarian companions at the head of the caravan and Darius well behind even his own companions.

Aunyia arranged a group of knights to take charge of the horses while they unloaded the litter with all of Mia's belongings onto a medium sized vessel. Jacob was angry to see the Sun Knights climb aboard as well. Gathering from the conversation between them, the knights were not supposed to voyage over water.

Mia smiled to herself. She was again pleased that she would be among her new friends a little while longer. Unfortunately Darius accompanied them as well. For the entire day, despite his distance from her, she could feel his convictions bore into the back of her head. It would take a great amount of time to gain his trust. But then, she thought, why should it bother her at all? He was, after all, going to part ways with her once they arrive on Barbarian soil.

A crowd of colorful garbed people waved from the dock as the mighty vessel at full mast parted the cerulean sea. Mia perched on the deck and gazed across the parting blue waters. She stretched her arms out and closed her eyes as the wind blasted through her hair and her clothing. It felt as if she was flying.

A circle of crying seagulls retreated from the endless horizon. It seemed to Mia that the brilliant flock of white fled to the safety of Thaumatur, away from the place she would call home.

"My lady?"

Mia turned her attention from the receding harbor to a slender man with a pointed nose, a long face, and an uncommonly short hair style dressed in a hoodless dark blue robe with a tawny embroidering. His smile was wide and warm when he reached out his hand to her. She returned the smile and allowed him to kiss her knuckle.

"I am Nikoli Oliver, my lady, and a Watcher from the Scholar Islands," he said in a nasal voice.

Mia remembered Nan's enlightenment of a Watcher's talents. She was careful not to show her discomfort with him because of it.

"My name is Miarosa Mal—" she corrected herself before she used her maiden name, "Miarosa Hilliard, wife to the Barbarian High Prince."

It was the first time she had cause to use her married name. It felt good to drop the cursed name of Maladinto into a well within her mind. She learned rather quickly the contempt that followed her lineage.

219

Darius made it quite clear last night.

"High Princess, then?" Nikoli asked.

"What…. Oh yes," she said feeling a little foolish with the title. "Just call me Mia if you please, my lord."

Nikoli chuckled, "My Lord is a term I am not used too! You can call me what I am. And I am Nikoli, the superior scholar and the wittiest Watcher Thaumatur has ever seen." Nikoli swept into a haughty bow.

Mia laughed at him and some of the tension left her shoulders. He was comfortable to be around.

"The Scholar Islands are near Nightingale Isle?" Mia asked.

Aiden often used the idea of that Isle and its prison to scare her into behaving the way he deemed appropriate. He said that the most dangerous of criminals were incapacitated there.

"Thank Goddess, no," a shiver visibly affected him. "That place gives me the creeps and for a Watcher to go there it's even worse. Imagine being surrounded by the lights of dark magic. It's invisible to you Mageborns, but not to us."

"You call me a Mageborn," Mia smirked.

"Of course, you have the most beautiful aura of magic around you. It's what drew me up on the deck. You see, if you knew me, you would know that I become sea sick. I need a Healer to give me something for it, but on my way, I saw the softest purples and pinks. Just like the twilight above us now," Nikoli grinned widely.

"Thank you, I think," Mia arched her eyebrows. "I've yet to meet the crew of this ship. Have you?"

"I have known the two of them for a very long time. If you will, a few of us are gathering in the captain's cabin for fish sandwiches, wine, and cheese soon. Why not join us. If the High Prince doesn't object, that is." His cheeks reddened a little, "I mean he's more than welcome to accompany you."

"I'd think he'd decline," Mia laughed and noticed Nikoli's face loosen. "But I will join you and the captain's crew."

"It's a date, then," Nikoli stuttered a little. "I mean, well you know dinner."

He shook his head and looked around nervously. She sensed he feared

Jacob would hurdle out of the shadows and attack him because of his innocent invitation.

"I know what you mean," Mia laughed. "Do not fear, for my husband will not misunderstand your kindness."

"Ah," Nikoli said and shoved his hands into his pocket.

"You sail to your islands?" Mia asked interrupting the uneasy silence.

"I am," he replied quickly, "but I'll wait until the returning trip to get off the boat. Now, about the Healer." Nikoli clutched his stomach. "Excuse me, my lady."

He stumbled halfway up the deck, before he heaved over the side of the boat. He indeed wasn't lying about being sea sick and she was certain his anxiety didn't help. Once he was done, he gave her a lop-sided smile and a lethargic wave before taking off. Such a nervous fellow he was.

Mia was grateful not to suffer from such sickness, especially since it was her first time on a ship. Her legs were wobbly, but aside from that she enjoyed the feel of the warm Spring wind zipping past her face and the sound of water rushing beneath the boat. She looked to the sky where the sun dipped into the vast sea. It was so big and fascinating with the shades of fire and gold. She longed to stretch her arms out to touch its vibrant surface. It was much different than the Winter Sun. How strange it was that the four kingdoms in Thaumatur cold be so different.

Her days at Falias seemed distant. It was her belonging for many years. Yet she often wondered these days if she could ever belong anywhere.

You are a part of the Goddess' Circle, the whimsical voice of the Great Owl Whispered. *By now you know that much.*

Mia shifted her gaze to the balustrade directly right of her and gasped. The Great Owl perched lazily before her inspecting its large talons as a noble would inspect their polished nails.

You truly thought me a part of your imagination?

The owl blinked huge gold-green eyes looking truly hurt.

"I am sorry. Many things seem unreal to me," Mia moved closer to the owl. "Please, I must know who you are? Why do you come to only me?" Mia inched her hand toward the owl's wings.

The Great Owl extended its wing inviting her. Mia ran a finger along the feathers and caught her breath. It was plush, almost silky beneath her fingers.

You are not the only one I go to. I've gone to your husband, although he probably didn't notice. And it was I who sent the Mind Mage to save you in the forest last night.

"You went to Jacob? And Darius? Darius didn't save me. He spat venom at me like a dragon who breaths fire!" Mia huffed.

Darius isn't what he seems and he is part of the Circle whether you like it or not. He saw much in his life to justify his paranoia. But I am not here for him. I am only for you to call upon for strength and guidance. Yet I am not of such great use in this form.

The owl mimicked a little frown. Mia shook her head.

"You aren't an owl? What are you?" Mia questioned.

The owl puffed out its chest and lowered it with the intake of breath.

I am a Shape-Changer caught inside of a dreadful curse! I once walked the world as you did when Shape-Changing was looked upon with honor. No longer...

The Great Owl paused and craned its head with wide eyes in the direction behind her. Mia spun to see nothing. She looked back and the owl was gone.

"Why do you keep doing that?" Mia threw her hands up in the air and huffed.

"Who are you talking to?"

Mia wheeled about just in time to see Darius walk from the darkness. His hair and cape whipped about him in the sea blast.

"No one," Mia eyed him.

Darius leaned his body against the railing beside her.

"I would've thought you inside with the others," Darius said locking his blank eyes onto her.

Underneath his stare, she suddenly felt vulnerable. She tore her eyes away. An invisible hand gripped her chin, forcing her to look at him. He was using magic, but in an invading way.

"I wanted some air. I wanted to see the sea," Mia felt like a child learning how to talk for the first time. "I've never seen the sea like this before."

He scrutinized her silently, feeding his curiosity with a forced hand. The spark of anger stirred her free. She could play this game too. She remembered his caution when he touched her. Like lightening, she cupped his face between her hands.

A current swept through her stronger than the touch of the other knights. She could feel his futile attempts to pull away, but the Power overtook him too. His onyx eyes changed to molten silver. His breath caught in his lungs in sync with her constraint. She pulled him close as the world fell from beneath her.

Waves collapsed. Nothing but water surrounded her. But her lungs didn't burn from its cold flood. Darius vanished behind the walls of water. Within the palms of her hands, she no longer felt the smooth face of Darius. Instead she cupped a silver cauldron. She lowered the cauldron to eye level and saw inside the surface of the liquid rupture into bubbles of blue and green. It beckoned her to indulge.

The Undry...Drink from me

She lowered her lips to the sparking rim of the Undry and tipped her head back.

Darius broke the link and shoved her hard from him. Mia's back connected with the surface of the deck. The ache that spread across her bottom and lower back resurrected her from the whirlpool of his Power. Or was it her Power? Her heart thudded and her body shuttered with the feeling of Earth she hadn't felt since the Outlanders' attack near Gorias. Could this cold accusing man give her replenishment to the Powers within her?

"It cannot be," Darius murmured from his hunching position.

Mia leaned her weight on her hands trying to catch her breath and looked at him with confusion. His head shot up.

"How dare you!" he hissed. "What right have you?"

Mia pushed herself up and gripped onto the deck's banister to steady her body.

"How dare *you?*" she scowled, "You were picking at my brain as if it were yours to do so!"

"I do what I must for the safety of my companions!" he growled lifting to his feet.

The chiming of anger and frustration renewed Mia's strength and her skin rippled with Fire. She stomped toward Darius, and he shrank away. This man wasn't likely to fear much, yet he cringed before her.

"You fear me!" Mia laughed. "Yet I've done nothing to encourage this fear! I am not Ahriman Maladinto and I never will be! His name falls like poison from my lips!"

She spat on the ground the sourness that her birth father's name left in her mouth.

"I fear nothing. I simply don't trust you," Darius replied regaining his cool composure. He folded his arms encircling his robe around his body and quirked an eyebrow. "You're using magic, aren't you?"

Mia almost forgot the surge of Fire through her veins and the rhythmic pound of her heart. It was still there, all of it. Mia lifted her hands before her and spanned out her fingers. Threads webbed in between her fingers. Green leapt from her thumb to forefinger. A bright blue thread circled her middle finger. Little fiery forks replaced her fingernails and smooth purple orbits encircled the whole of her hand.

Mia swallowed hard. She didn't like Darius, but she didn't want to hurt him with her feral magic.

"Darius, step away from me," She commanded.

He didn't move and stared unflinchingly at her hand.

"Darius please, move! I don't know how to control this Power!"

He jerked his head and cracked a satisfied smile to her admission. He closed in on her slowly. "Slow your breathing, girl!"

Mia looked at him with bafflement as he approached her. He lifted his chin impatiently. "Do it!"

"I am fearful—!"

"Of what?" he cut her off, "I'm able to handle anything you might *accidentally* do to me. Now do as I say if you wish to gain control. Slow your breathing and consume your panic. The wildness of a Mageborn's magic will feed on anxiety and work against you."

Mia drew her breath in deeply and slowly exhaled. She repeated the steps until she felt the panic's seize on her loosen.

"Now, drop the hand your magic is flowing from to your side," He nodded as she did what he instructed. "Let the magic-flow circulate through your arm, and once you feel the surge reach your shoulder, join your hands together."

Her blood felt dissolved pumping rapidly against the invading static that worked its way up her wrist to her elbow. The sensation was making her arm slowly fall asleep. She went to jerk, but Darius hindered her with a wave of his finger. "You mustn't move until it reaches your shoulder!"

The feeling finally peaked at her shoulder. She joined her hands together just as Darius told her and an explosive sphere fanned out around her intertwined fists before it diminished completely. The magic re-entered her body and simmered down until it was entirely gone.

Mia's jaw dropped. She stared at her hands with amazement and then looked back at Darius. Laughter flew from her lips and without thinking she embraced him. He stiffened until she let him go.

"Wife!" Jacob eyed Darius. "What are you doing out here?"

"Nothing, Jacob," Mia replied quickly. If he knew that she was playing with magic he would be enraged. "We were just headed down to the captain's cabin for some dinner. Care to join me, Husband?" she asked sweetly, but he grunted something that sounded like "No" and walked away.

The captain's cabin was tiny. Aunyia and Horace sat on one side of the table across from Nikoli and a big dark-skinned bald man. A man who reminded Mia of a male version of Aunyia sat on a bunk with his legs dangling playfully over a woman with tightly braided hair.

"You have come, my lady!" Nikoli rose and bowed before her. "Lady Mia, High Princess of the Barbarians, and Mageborn, might I add, I would like for you to meet the ship's very talented mariners!"

Mia laughed at Nikoli's light nature and inclined her head gracefully.

"I told you, Nikoli, just Mia is fine." She blushed.

"I know. I like the dramatic sound of my voice though. I cannot help myself." He grinned.

"I'm your capt'n, Diamond, at your service," the woman said with a devilish twinkle in her honey eyes.

Beneath the lantern light, hints of blue sparked from her brunette braids. She tossed a sandwich to Mia. She fumbled with the sandwich until she finally maintained a grip on it."Thanks."

"Let us not jest now, Diamond Dear," the red headed man jumped down from his perch onto the table before Diamond. "It is I who is the true master of this beauty!" He swept down and caught Mia's hand in his, "My name is Phoenix."

He winked releasing her. The sensation of his touch left a mark in her veins, like the others. But it couldn't erase the whirlpool of Power that flowed between Darius and herself moments ago. She cast a glance over her shoulder and noticed he hadn't followed her. He didn't trust her, yet he instructed her in a small way to control the feral magic within her.

The walls of water and the bubbling goblet flashed through her mind.

"What is the Undry?" Mia hadn't realized she spoken the question out loud until she found herself faced with abrupt silence and gaping faces.

"Did you say 'Undry'?" Diamond leaned forward. Her face was stony, but the curiosity sparked in her eyes.

"I think she did!" Nikoli approached Mia with a wide smile and drew from a tent-like bag the biggest book she had ever seen before He thumbed through it and slammed the book on the table with excitement.

"The Undry," he began in a pleasurable voice. "The Cauldron of Plenty was a gift from the Great Goddess Danu to the Lord of Water, Uiscias. And from Uiscias came the great cauldron, the Undry which gave all sustenance based on ones need and worth. It was given as a peace offering to Murias." Nikoli read from the book and slammed it shut.

"One of the four treasures." Aunyia confirmed, "But it was said that the treasures were destroyed twenty years ago at the end of the tyranny."

"Not destroyed," Darius said flatly from the cabin's entrance. "Three missing and one in the hands of the House Mysteries Sector."

"The weapons cannot be destroyed by any mortal hands," Horace added and glanced at Mia. "Only the Bearer has that Power."

"Ah," Diamond swung her legs up on the table and leaned back in her seat lazily, "I remember now. The treasures were the gifts to be used scarcely and for peaceful purposes. However the original Elders misused them leaving them vulnerable to darkness, hence turning them into weapons."

"What is said in these riddles only crack the surface of the weapons' Powers." Nikoli pulled from his robe several pieces of parchment. "According to the Vestibule of Watchers, the Undry's gift brought forth wisdom and foresight, until of course one or more of the Mageborns used the wisdom for selfish reasons. The dark side of wisdom is corruption. The Spear of Healing was used to injure, the

Stone of Destiny was used to control, and the Sword of Light was used to murder selfishly."

Mia squirmed, *The Sword of Light!*

She said nothing to them, but she remembered Nan's words before she left for the Hills. She fluffed her skirts to better conceal the Sword strapped to her.

How could such a treasure Call to someone like me who knows nothing of the ancient legends?

How did Nan manage to get this treasure? She averted her eyes from Darius recalling his tactics and his Power to unearth the secret of her parentage. She would say nothing now. But once she landed her feet on solid ground, she would make sure she spoke to Sierra on the matter.

Mia nibbled on the sandwich and was relieved that the conversation took on a lighter tone. Diamond spoke of Horace's run in with an old drunk who pretended he was blind and then proceeded to *rob* Horace blind. And Phoenix picked on Diamond about her fear of spiders and flying beetles. Mia was also quickly introduced to Alabaster, the big bald man, and Phoenix explained that he couldn't speak but his magical ability made up for it. He was a Locator Mage. They were all apart of her and this Circle. Their fates were intertwined.

The hour became late and Mia politely bid them all goodnight and went to her cabin.

The howling screech of a woman jolted Jacob to his feet. He armed himself and followed the sound before he was fully awake. It was coming from the captain's cabin. The last place he knew Mia to be. He flung open the door to the cabin and froze.

The horrible sounds were coming from the female captain. The girl was lashing out, sweating profusely, and kicking beneath the firm grasp of her shipmate. To Jacob the girl looked ill with hysteria.

He felt his wife brush by. He didn't see her because her movements were rapid and sloppy. He recognized the sweet scent of ginger that he vividly remembered from the night she nestled against his chest.

Mia tore Phoenix from the girl with a strength that surprised Jacob and spun on him. Her eyes lit up with deadly rage. She seized upon him like a cat and began beating him with closed fists. Before Jacob knew it, his niece was restraining Diamond and the rest of the blasted knights piled into the whirlwind. Jacob ripped his wife from Phoenix and pulled her tight against his body. She struggled.

"You disgusting creature!" she screamed, "You vile rapist!"

Phoenix's eyes widened, "I'm her *brother!*"

"Some foul knaves don't stop for that reason!" Mia bellowed sounding much like a wounded animal.

Jacob at once knew how bitter she was and how the scene must've looked to a victim to such horrendous things.

"Mia!" Aunyia cried, "He wasn't hurting her."

Mia slowed her struggle and whipped her head in Aunyia's direction. His niece loosened her face into a plea as she clung tight to the calming Diamond. His wife trembled within his arms and he felt a force like no other urge him to pull her closer. But she wiggled free from his hold before he could act and flew up onto the deck. Jacob shifted his eyes from the awe of the group and followed her. They had no idea what happened to her.

She was sitting against the banister hugging her knees tight against her chest. Jacob couldn't move. He simply watched her rock comfort into her shaken form. He bit his lip against the wrenching feeling in his stomach. It hurt *him* to see her suffer. She lowered her head in between her knees and wept.

Jacob took a step forward, but someone passed him by. Horace ran to Mia and cradled her in his embrace. Jacob turned and walked away.

"It's complicated to explain, Mia," Horace whispered stroking her cheek. "Diamond's body sometimes convulses into the Change. Phoenix was simply soothing her pain."

"A Shape-Changer?" Mia asked. "I hadn't known."

"It's illegal to use such magic, but it's such a strong force in Diamond, that it's difficult for her to fight alone." Horace pulled her close to him.

The interlocking of their vibes rocked Mia soothingly along with the swaggering movements of the vessel. He smelled of apples and it reminded her of the orchard in Gorias.

"Diamond and her brother had no easy time of it, Mia. When Diamond was but a child, she was severely beaten by a man twice her size. It did some damage to her abdomen and that particular charka is a focal point for control in Shape-Changing," Horace continued.

"Why would a man hurt a child?"

"I'm not certain of the entire story," Horace sighed. "Their mother died when she gave birth to Diamond. Their father was a gambler and he wasn't beyond using his children to get him what he wanted. A fisherman who imagined he was born with a golden spoon in his mouth. Then one day, when gambling got the best of him, he sold his own children to a noble who ran a vineyard in the Hills. The noble went too far with Diamond one day, and Phoenix took her and ran away. Currency Slavery is illegal so there was nothing the noble could do about it once they had left his land. When they returned to their father's dock, they were told how their father drank himself into a stupor and fell into the sea. The bastard got himself drowned. And that is how they got this beauty of a vessel. It was their father's only possession."

"She was raped," her words were no louder than the gentle sea wind.

"I don't know. She hasn't spoken openly about it. You wouldn't guess it behind the bravery she fronts." Horace gave her one last squeeze, "But whatever it was that happened to her then has physically and permanently damaged her."

"Poor Diamond," Mia pulled Horace back to her. He was warm and she was chilled and full of dark sorrow.

The world was too wicked. It was as wicked in Falias as it was anywhere else. She wouldn't escape these things so she would have to learn to toughen her skin.

"Please tell Phoenix I'm sorry," Mia whispered and looked into Horace's eyes.

She could fall into those hazel eyes. He looked upon her not with lust and not with loath, but with the true intensity of his concern. She wanted to kiss him, but instead she pressed her cheek to his shoulder and held him. His body melted around hers and the static of his magic lifted her into elation. She was flooded with desires to be loved, to be cherished, to be protected. She had desired him from the first moment they touched back in Gorias. She was a married woman. She couldn't fall in love with another.

She pulled herself from his magical embrace putting out a fire that should lay dead and cold. Her breathing was heavy and he was calm and controlled as if he hadn't known how he affected her.

"Goodnight Horace," Mia said and returned to the cabin where she would lay wide awake in for the duration of the night.

Four days later, they were docking in a great port in Vhladic. Huge masts of black snapped in the wind and ships twice the size of the vessel were cluttered in the bay. Swarms of people jumbled at the gates, some happy, some crying, some angry. But they were all Barbarian. The sky was brilliantly blue with little clouds and the smell of salt air and body odor mingled in the mist.

Jacob gave strict instructions to his Barbarians and tossed three sacks on the ground in the cabin.

"We must conceal ourselves completely. I don't want to rouse anyone with our arrival." Jacob commanded and wrapped his whole body tightly in a brown travelers robe. "My First Warrior will meet us."

Everyone did as instructed, including the knights. Mia suspected her husband didn't wish to deal with a royal procession upon his return and she also sensed he wasn't up for explaining his Thaumaturi consort either.

Jacob held tight to Mia's hand, giving her no time to say goodbye to her new friends, and guided her swiftly through a small wooden gate vacant from any bystanders. They followed a thin dirt path around a two story building with a flat roof and red columns. He didn't pause in his flight until they reached an open field behind a farmstead facing the mountains. His companions somehow managed to get horses and the luggage from the boat. They accumulated another three Barbarians, one bald with a rusty colored beard, another which surpassed Jacob in width and height, and the third was an older man with grey hair.

Jacob looked down on Mia from atop his horse.

"I can present you a smaller litter, if you feel you cannot ride alone," He offered.

He avoided the option of riding with her, but she shook the jab off and told him she would ride alone. He nodded and the procession started onward to the mountains.

Mia mounted her horse, but a helping hand gave her a boost. When she looked down, Horace smiled up at her charmingly. "Could not part with you, my lady." He laughed and jerked his head, "Neither could she."

Aunyia galloped right for her with a bright smile. "To Vansant Summit!"

CHAPTER TWENTY-TWO

Vansant Summit

The streets became less traveled when the caravan departed from the great imperial city. Mia watched as her husband loosened with each pace they took en route for Vansant Summit. He and his Barbarian companions bantered sporadically though she couldn't make out the jests. It was quite pleasing to hear the chorus of husky laughter coming from within the triangle of her husband.

It was sad to part ways with Cole and the others, because she grew rather fond of their company over the past several days. Aunyia and Horace however didn't separate themselves from her so easily and decided to ride on to Vansant Summit. If it disturbed Jacob, he didn't reveal it. Mia supposed he was too eager to see his dwelling and his people to care at this point. After all, he had been gone for nearly two years. Mia wondered if she would yearn for Falias after two years absence. Despite the coldness and the lies, it was her home for all her life. Until now.

The tales Nan had told Mia when she was a child about the Outlanders and the experience she herself had on the way to Gorias itched at her sides. Mia felt shock and shame gripping at her, and clenched her fists against the enveloping fear. This would be her home for the duration of her life. She needed to be brave.

She looked at Aunyia, who rode tall and composed, much like the knights. Although Aunyia was a knight herself, she was still a woman. It wasn't common for a woman to enlist into the Sun Knighthood back at Thaumatur unless they were born into a military family. Aunyia, however, wasn't born in Thaumatur at all. She had explained how her father wanted her to learn of her mother's heritage. Mia imagined Aldrich loved his Thaumatur concubine very much to go against his people's obvious disagreement. Mia didn't pry, but she often wondered who Aunyia's mother truly was.

Who Vastadon's mother was.

Mia swallowed the sourness of the thought and shook her head. Aunyia was nothing like him. Even before Mia learned what kind of man Vastadon truly was, she had felt a connection when he touched her. But that connection was lustful, almost blinding to important cares. She had confused the feelings for love. He was a dark veil of hate.

Mia studied her new friend. No. She definitely wasn't like her brother. She could be trusted. When Mia had first met her, she seemed at ease. Now on the edges of Vansant Summit, so close to the wall, she looked stern and disciplined, with no trace of the terror Mia felt. How could she be so calm?

"Aren't you fearful?" Mia ventured. "Being so close to-."

"Nay, Mia. These lands are the lands of my early childhood," Aunyia said with a small smile. "It is unlikely that the Tribes will crawl over such a massive wall for a mere procession. Especially one that carries the High Prince."

Mia nodded and Aunyia reached out and took her hand, smoothing her palm.

"I have forgotten you have never traveled so far from your home. You needn't fear. We will protect you if need be."

The heat was smoldering, although she enjoyed the way the sunlight fell on her face. The golden beams threaded through the thin line of white wooded ash trees and over the rolling green hills brilliantly. The sky was azure with feathery like clouds and the air was clean and fresh, carrying fragrances of pollen and flora.

In the distance, something monstrous gleamed beneath the sunlight. It was a solid sheet of shiny brick that towered over the largest of trees and stretched well out of view toward the eastern hills. The great wall. The Tribes cell. Mia shrank, feeling knots in her stomach.

"I'm truly pleased you decided to ride in the open. The fresh air will do you some good, and the color you lost from the sea voyage and the litter has returned to you," Horace commented diverting Mia's attention from the sight of it.

Mia inclined her head and didn't look again at the wall.

They arrived at Vansant Summit shortly before sunset. The crest of the dwelling protruded above a cluster of small wooden shelters and a market not too different from the one she looked over for so many years from her balcony. From what she did see of the crest, it looked to be made of stone, surrounded by high parapets, its architecture quite simple. A simple, uncomplicated home. Mia welcomed the idea with a small chuckle.

"You will soon see that not all castles are as elaborate as the ones you are accustomed too," Jacob's cool voice invaded her ears and for a moment Mia thought he may have mistook her chuckle for mocking.

"It doesn't matter to me the appearance of our new home. I am not that shallow," Mia snorted. "I'd rather not be reminded of such things in Thaumatur."

She didn't lie. Yet she couldn't bring herself to tell him how thrilled she was at the sight of her new dwelling and city. It would be a new beginning for her.

"We will see," He shot back and squeezed his steed into a gallop leaving her behind.

Pure frustration drove her to his side in full gallop. But as he neared the gate, he slowed his pace and grimaced. Mia removed herself from the cloud of irritation and saw why Jacob was angered.

The surrounding fields were empty from cattle, dotted with brown waste, and overgrown with weeds. Ahead, the gates to the inner city were flung open carelessly and, from what Mia could see, no villagers or guards were visible. Jacob grunted making eye contact with his Barbarian companions and charged his horse in full speed through the gates.

Sasha snuggled against the royal blue blankets and pillows and sighed heavily. She was becoming bored of late, for it didn't take her long to tire of Vhladic. Lucia, her handmaiden, spun quietly in the corner of the room by the window. The room wasn't extravagant, a little waste of a stone paneled space. It left Sasha wondering why she always ended up returning. To see her children, maybe? Or to be in quiet solitude. That must be it. Why else would a great lady, sister to the Emperor retreat to such a pathetic place deep in the country. Jacobane was so simple. Sasha frowned and then lifted herself from the little bit of comfort she brought with her and stretched her arms above her head.

"Momma, Lucia! Come quickly!" Sasha's oldest daughter, Maire cried from the hallway. "Uncle Jacobane has returned and he brings with him *magician* folk!"

Sasha leapt to attention and met eyes with Lucia who reflected the same confusion as she.

Why in the Gods' names would Jacobane bring Thaumaturi to Vansant Summit?

Sasha's scowl deepened and she fled to the window near Lucia, spread the cotton drapes and peered out.

"My lady, it's true. Look!" Lucia cried pointing to a golden haired maiden. "There is a man *magician* too, my lady. He walked off with the Prince's warriors with the horses."

The girl's skin was too ivory and her hair too golden to be her niece, Anne. She rode alongside Jacobane, as if she were his equal. Then, as if it couldn't get worse, a *magician* veiled in the robes of a priestess rode behind her. A circus it was!

"A witch of the female deity dares set foot on our lands!" Sasha snorted and flung the drape back down. "I shall see an end to this!"

Sasha flew down the stairs, and just before she opened the doors of the keep, she composed herself and put on a very forced smile.

Jacob exploded through the door snarling before she could greet him. His fists were clenched and his jaw was tight.

"Where is he?" Jacob howled.

"Greetings to you too, Brother!" Sasha huffed.

Jacob turned on her and she could see he was extremely angered as she knew he would be upon his return. Sasha cared not, for she knew he wouldn't place the blame on her.

"Uncle!" Maire ran into his embrace. "I have missed you so!"

Jacob's scowl immediately left his face when he pulled from his niece's embrace to look at her.

"Maire? My goodness, you've grown!"

"Aye, Uncle, I have. And not only that, I have been practicing all of the combat skills you have shown me!" Maire exclaimed.

Sasha frowned. Maire could be a pretty girl, if she kept herself clean. She swore that her daughter thought she was born a boy with her breeches and over sized blouses.

"Maire, you are in no condition to greet your Uncle!" Sasha scolded. "Wash up and put on a lady's gown for the Gods' sake! And see to it that Ethane and Midian are proper before they come to meet their uncle!"

Maire huffed defiantly, but with one sharp gaze from her mother, she obeyed and went stomping up the stairs.

"You have become harsh, Sister," Jacob lifted his eyebrows.

"She is out of control, Jacobane," Sasha waved a hand in the air. "Now, come and rest. Surely the journey has been long."

"We will indeed rest soon enough," Jacob replied flatly, "Now, where's the man who is responsible for the mess out there."

Jacob jabbed his finger to the door nearly poking the blonde Thaumaturi in the eye. His gaze met the *magician's* briefly and then he returned his attention back to Sasha. A hint of something strange clouded his eyes. Sasha cocked her head to the side and craned her neck around her massive brother to get a better look.

The foreigner wore upon her head a circlet of fine braided silver centered with a sapphire rose indicating that she was of high caste. She was taller than Sasha expected, but her slender hands and petite features were *magician* for sure. Sasha's stomach turned and she made no effort to hide her disgust. The witch who stood meekly behind the golden hair *magician* was the size of a Barbarian child. Her green eyes were the only thing visible within the folds of dark burgundy robes and they stared back at her unflinchingly. Sasha cringed and looked hastily to her brother.

"I haven't all day," Jacob growled ignoring Sasha's questioning gaze and pushed by her.

Sasha was at his heels when he shoved through the receiving hall doors. Fershius, in all his roundness, looked up and his face paled beneath his grey beard. He was lounging comfortably upon Jacob's high chair, women scattered at his feet. The servants nearly dropped their trays and the bard, who was playing his harp, disappeared from sight. Jacob closed his eyes tightly to gain control and his lower lip twitched with suppressed rage. The hall was a mess. The lower tables were scattered throughout the room, some turned on its heads, and the hearth was filled with broken jugs, goblets, dinner bones and soot from the winter burnings.

"You have two nights to get out of my dwelling, slob!" Jacob bellowed.

The women scattered like field mice into the shadowed corners of the hall at the sound of the Prince's voice. Fershius swallowed hard.

"My Lord, I haven't received news of your return," Fershius' voice curved arrogantly.

"No notice, no matter how early, could give you enough time to clean this mess up! Where are my warriors? My field workers?" Jacob ordered.

"Your warriors were sent to Vhladic to service the Emperor. And sadly, a fever has touched Vansant Summit earlier this year. It wiped most of your field men away," Fershius said smoothly. "I wouldn't dare call for more workers without your consent."

"Earlier this year?" Jacob growled, "It looks as if the grounds haven't been touched since I've left! And who are you to send my warriors away!"

"I am a peaceful man. There was no need for the warriors to stay in your leave. I even think they welcomed the idea of going to Vhladic. They only remained here for the sake of—" his voice cracked when he looked beyond Jacob at the gold haired *magician*, "the sake of you." He finished and floated by Jacob.

He stood so close to the girl, it made Sasha shiver.

"A Thaumaturi, High Prince?" Fershius asked incredulously. "The

Great High Prince has brought home one of the *magicians*, or two?" He lifted his chin to meet the sight of the priestess witch.

"Mind your manners, Brother Fershius," A red headed knight, who Sasha immediately recognized as her niece, strode through the doors.

"Anne!" Sasha exclaimed falsely. "You have finally returned after all of these years! You have grown lovely, Child!"

"Aunt," she greeted kissing her cheeks respectfully, "I am called Aunyia, now. You look as lovely as I remember you."

Sasha flashed a genuine smile, for she wasn't one to criticize another's flattery when it pertained to her. Aunyia frowned at Fershius.

"Princess Anne," he bowed imperial style—fluttering hands, right leg extended before him—and took her hand in his.

She snatched it away.

"Apologize to the women at once for your rudeness!" Aunyia ordered sharply.

Fershius sighed, "If I said anything to offend you, I must say it wasn't my intent, *Ladies*."

The golden hair witch nodded gracefully, but the priestess didn't respond.

"Good, Brother Fershius," Aunyia grinned, "It will do you a great justice to hold your tongue in the future before your new High Princess."

A jug crashed in the background. Sasha nearly fainted and Fershius drew his head back in shock. Sasha turned her sharp gaze on Jacob. He looked at her sideways. She didn't need to ask. The truth was there in his eyes. She bounced her head back to the blonde bitch and noticed she wore around her neck the thorn.

Her mother's thorn.

She spun on her heels and stormed off.

"Sasha," Jacob called from behind, but she lengthened her strides.

He called her name two more times before she stopped in the upper stairwell far enough away from the heretics.

Jacobane, my fair brother, my foster son, the only thing I have left in this world of Father and not of Mother. How could it come to this?

"Are you mad, Jacobane? You take a Thaumaturi child as a wife and dare call her the Barbarian High Princess?" She spun on him.

238

"I did," He said flatly.

"You hate them! Your people hate them! The Tribes utterly despise them!" Sasha cried and tossed her hands in the air. "Have you no thought on the consequences if the Tribes catch wind of this?"

"Done is done, Sister," He replied emotionlessly.

"Is that all you have to say for yourself? No explanation? Do you have any idea what you have done?" Sasha gripped his arms tightly, "And dare you give that bitch our mother's heirloom!"

"Mother wanted it around the neck of my bride. No matter who," Jacob pointed out.

"She is turning in her grave, I'd imagine. I'm quite certain she thought you'd marry a noble *Barbarian* woman," Sasha hissed releasing him.

"Mother's views were much like Aldrich's," Jacob mumbled.

"That is it then!" realization dawned on her. "Aldrich has forced his will on you! I should've known! Look what he did to you. You are stuck with a Thaumaturi wife, and after all you have done to serve him. You loved him most, even beyond Mother."

"Do not dare speak of Mother to me. You never loved her," Jacob growled.

"You were but a child," Sasha replied hurtfully. "How could you know enough about it to say such cruel things to me? Oh, my poor brother, I don't want to quarrel with you! This mess isn't your fault! We can fix it." Sasha's eyes glittered anew. "All we need to do is appeal to Chaplain Hector! He would surely fix it for you."

"I think it too late, Sister," Jacob murmured.

Sasha pursed her lips sourly. "You didn't bed her, did you?"

"No," Jacob answered quickly and turned his head away. "But she's no longer a virgin."

"Whore! You are stuck with a *magician* whore!" She spat.

"No, she was raped on our wedding night," he paused and drew his breath in, "by Vastidrich."

The sound of her nephew's name made her sick. She loathed him so, even more than her half-blooded niece. At least Anne—or Aunyia, whatever the hell she called herself—kept her distance and modesty. Vastidrich's actions were deliberate for he always was jealous of his uncle.

239

Everything Jacob achieved, the half-blood either attempted to steal the glory or outdo him. Little did it work.

"Damn him! And damn Aldrich! He should've married his precious half-blood son to her then," Sasha put her fist in her mouth and stomped her foot.

Jacob was too damned loyal to back out of his predicament now. She would have to practice her theatre skills from this point on. Then she remembered a conversation she held with Chaplain Hector. *Sole Empress.* Sasha rather liked the sound of it and if the High Chaplain was able to convince Aldrich to choose her as his successor, she would give the reverent chaplain what he desired most.

Sasha studied her brother. Something was different about him. Could he, who has a strong reputation for despising the Thaumaturi, actually *care* for the *magician?* Inconceivable, but still.

Sasha loved Jacob perhaps the most of her kin. She would take whatever measures needed to protect him from the wench. Even if she needed to become the mastermind she once was. Perhaps a word with Fershius would remedy the situation. Sasha spun and smiled widely.

"Jacobane," she caressed his bearded chin with a motherly hand, "You know I love you. I will try my best to be civil with her, if it's your will. I just feel so hurt for you. How cruel of Aldrich to place such a burden on you. But, as you said, done is done."

Sasha embraced him tightly and headed for her little dismal chamber where she could openly vent before Lucia. And she was sure Lucia would be devastated, being that she was always *fond* of Jacob.

CHAPTER TWENTY-THREE

Horace

"They hate me!" Mia cried. "I will never fit in here."

Mia followed Aunyia down a long narrow hall to the north side of the dwelling and through double oak doors. The sitting room was furnished with a white blossoms chaise, a large polished metal mirror and a bare credenza. Another set of doors opened up to a larger sleeping chamber. The bed was covered in pink and brown blankets beneath a ring of sheer fabric.

Aunyia spun and flashed Mia a smile. "This is your personal chambers. It's the best here. And do not focus so much on fitting in. *You* are the High Princess. It's for them to adjust, not you."

"I suppose you are right. It seems so unfair." Mia shook her head and studied the room. "It is perfect, Aunyia! I love it."

"Of course you do," Aunyia arched her eyebrows. "There is a balcony from the sitting room. You can see the forest from there."

"Am I to, um, share this—" Mia tripped over her tongue.

"Only if you want to," Aunyia winked. "The High Prince has a chamber of his own." Aunyia grew serious, "Do not be wary of my uncle, Mia. I know that the situation isn't what the two of you would choose for yourselves, but Jacobane will not mistreat you."

For a moment Mia wished she could be honest with her about the Sword of Light, about her true parentage, and about the rape. Mia wanted Aunyia to understand her better. Yet she couldn't tell this woman how the man she called brother violated her.

"Thank you, Aunyia."

"I will return to Vhladic tomorrow to see my father. I just wanted to see you settled in first. I know it must be hard to leave all that you know behind. Horace has decided to *vacation* here for a few Moon Cycles before he visits Vhladic," Aunyia sniggered. "I am sure he could use the company if you feel lonely."

"Well, that is very encouraging!" Mia laughed and embraced Aunyia.

She would call Aunyia friend for a long time, even if this would be the last time they saw each other. But Mia knew they would cross paths again.

Aunyia left Mia to her unpacking for the rest of the evening. She was undisturbed for most of the night, all except a servant named Lucia. The woman was rude when she came to call her to dinner, but Mia politely declined. She wasn't hungry and she didn't want to face anymore of the scowling members of Jacob's court. An hour or so after Lucia left, Sierra brought her up some tea brewed with Hawthorne. It was to calm her nerves. She stepped onto the balcony.

The moonlight spilled in a pool before the forest. In its center stood Horace bathed in the glittering silver. He was looking to the east, his long hair and cape whipped through the wind and his profile shimmered with a blue-silver luster. Mia caught her breath. It looked as if the light from the moon longed only to share its circle of luminosity with him.

Mia turned her head from his direction and felt her cheeks set fire. She was attracted to him She had been from the moment she met him, but she couldn't allow it to influence her this way. She was a married woman, for the love of Danu.

Against her own scolding, she shifted her eyes back, and this time was met with the full of his soft face. A smile spread on his lips and a glint of silver flickered in his hazel pools. Even in the shroud of night, he shined like a spirit from heaven. He lifted a hand and waved her down. She shook her head in protest. He began jumping up and down vigorously waving. She sighed heavily and submitted.

She was greeted at the door by Lucia—more like sneered at.

"If my husband calls on me, tell him I've gone for a walk with my guard." Mia nodded and fled around the dwelling passed three gardens, a pavilion, and a small lake. As she did so, she made a mental note to explore the yard more once daylight came.

"Come, Lady!" Horace called to her. "Let us walk beneath the cascade of stars and the forest veil!"

She felt like a little girl. Impulsive and fearless. She went to him and laced her fingers through his. Her heart pounded and a spell of dizziness swept through her when he gazed at her. He let out a laugh and sprinted into the forest, dragging her with him.

He was like a Forest-Dweller in an old child's tale. He took hold of her free hand and spun her around in a whimsical dance. Mia giggled and leaned her head back to catch the whirl of the wind on her face. She opened her eyes and watched the spinning leaves glow in a frenzy with the diamonds of the sky. It was like a dream, wordless and filled with joyous laughter. An experience she should've had when she was a young girl, but she never had children friends to do so. They both fell onto the ground in a giggling heap and he embraced her nestling against an old gnarled oak tree. She rested her head on his shoulder.

"It is wondrous here in the forest! Like a fairytale!" Mia cried through her laughter.

"I have always loved the forest. I grew up in a cottage outside of Murias in the Celse Forest. I used to run and play with Sidhe, but my mother called me crazy to make up such things. I often thought I was a Sidhe King and my Faerie folk waited patiently for me to grow and return to them." Horace grinned and pinched her cheek.

"If I didn't know any better, I would believe you are the Sidhe King, beautiful and courteous!" Mia whispered with a giddy smile.

The heat of embarrassment set in. Her tongue was too loose before him.

"And if it were true, I would believe you to be the fair haired maiden in waiting. The sleeping beauty!" He laughed and pulled her closer.

He was childlike, yet in his innocence she felt the power of seduction stroke her. If something were to happen, the blame would lie on her alone. The thought of him against her was intoxicating. The smell of him was inviting. The fear of sex melted away into a puddle of new cravings. She lifted from his arms and turned to face him.

"So why have you decided to stay here?" Mia asked him curiously. "It is so far from Thaumatur."

A conversation diversion.

"I have stayed on behalf of the Goddess," Horace replied as if the answer would ease Mia's wonderment.

"The Goddess?" Mia asked incredulously, "I don't understand. These lands do not honor Danu. They respect Gods of war and prosperity, so my governess told me."

"It matters not what Gods the Barbarians worship. Danu is Mother to all, even to the Barbarians *and* their Gods. She looks to them as petulant children who are either misled or unruly. But they are still Her children." Horace carved a large red apple he pulled from his tunic sleeve.

Mia studied him as he curved the knife with nimble hands and plucked a juicy wedge into his mouth.

"It reminds me of home," Mia said distantly.

"What?" He queried while he chewed.

"The apple," Mia said and pointed to the fruit. "It reminds me of my visit to Gorias. It was the most amazing thing that happened to me, and one of the most painful. If that makes any sense."

"Sometimes things don't make sense," Horace replied.

"I am going to ask Jacob for his permission to visit Vhladic before the Agustu Moon Cycle ends," Mia began dreading Horace's leave already. "I want to visit the imperial city and I am afraid he didn't allow me enough time there today. Perhaps we could travel together since you will be going there as well."

"No!" Horace almost choked on the apple when he spoke. "That wouldn't be wise."

"Goddess, why not?" Mia responded breathlessly.

"You are a Thaumaturi, and although the Emperor opposes the bigotry of his father, there are many in Vhladic that hold firm to their views on our kind. Princess or not, it wouldn't be safe to go there without your husband," Horace warned.

"I think you are being a little over zealous about this—"

"Promise me you will not go without your husband!"

"But why?" Mia asked.

"Promise me and I will tell you why!" He stared at her firmly.

"I promise alright!" Mia exclaimed. "Now tell me why."

His shoulders slumped. He set the apple aside and fixed his complete attention on her.

"The Emperor's Chaplain has ill-concealed his disagreements with Emperor Aldrich on religious matters. He does not respect our free will and believes that in order for a Thaumaturi—for *anyone*—to be welcomed is by means of religious conversion. Those who have resisted, well, they are no longer around to tell the tale."

"How can men of the holy robes brutalize people just because they are different? Our priestesses only teach by love, not by fear!" Mia replied hotly.

"Fear is a weapon within the Barbarian Brotherhood. And it's my belief that the Chaplain serves a foreign God much different from the Gods of your husband." Horace shook his head and scowled. "Many have seen the High Chaplain's Brotherhood shudder with horror at the sight of how the rejecters of their faith are punished. After suffering the most agonizing tortures that could be devised, the prisoners are destroyed by the most terrible deaths, beheaded, pressed to death by spiked walls, brains dashed out with objects twisted of metal," Horace said dismally. "I have seen it with my own eyes."

"How could the Emperor allow such things to happen?" Mia gasped.

"He doesn't know its happening," Horace answered and cast his eyes downward. "The Elders, however, choose to ignore it although they would be the only Order powerful enough to raise questions."

"What!" Mia cried. "What keeps them from doing so?"

Horace took hold of her hands. A chill swept through her.

"I don't wish to speak ill of the Sun Order, but they have become obsessed with their own dealings. They will come to you one day, Mia, and expect you to follow their will. You mustn't let them influence you. Your heart will guide you."

"My heart speaks to me now," she whispered impulsively and placed a hand on his cheek.

His eyes went wide and his face reddened, but her desires ignored his surprise. He gently took her hand from his face and looked into her eyes.

"You are special, Mia," he paused. "You cannot go to Vhladic without your husband. It isn't safe. You wouldn't make it to the Emperor."

"If these horrific acts are not openly done, then how is it that you witnessed them?" Mia snapped with irritation from his obvious rejection.

He fumbled with his cape, wrapping it tighter around him and got to his feet.

"We should be getting back before the Prince grows concerned," he answered deliberately ignoring her question.

"Wait, Horace," Mia halted him, "Is it a game you play? Luring me in only telling me half truths whenever you feel the need for fun?"

"There are no games when it comes to matters of dark religions," he said in his most stern voice. "I am afraid that sometimes we must observe before we can become the redeemers."

Mia instantly regretted her words. What did she know about the dangers and pains of a knight? His eyes were the darkest she ever saw and his face was distorted with memories and sacrifices.

"I'm sorry, Horace," Mia covered his hand. "I didn't mean to hurt you."

His smile half returned, but Mia was satisfied to see even the tiniest fraction of his normal warmth return.

"I know that. It's why I fear for you in this conflict-ridden land," he said and squeezed her hand. "I promise you one thing. I will inform you what I can, but only what I am permitted to."

"I'll never take offense again," Mia laughed and then turned serious. "I am quite timid when it comes to politics and wars. Teach me of it! Teach me to fight with a sword!"

"We will see," He winked and they walked hand in hand back through the gardens.

CHAPTER TWENTY-FOUR

Shrouded Desires

Mia ran up the pathway to the door and headed straight for the kitchens. She was happy to find no one about. She missed the dinner feast, so she rummaged through the cupboards and settled for some cheese and bread.

While she nibbled on a piece of bread, Horace's revelation invaded her mind with images of cruelty. Her stomach churned with such hideous acts and suddenly she lost her appetite. Surely Jacob knew nothing of this Chaplain's tactics. He was a man firm in his one-sided beliefs, but he'd never condone such merciless acts. If he did, he would've killed her before now.

"You were out late," Lucia snapped. "The kitchen fires have burned out already."

Mia turned and fixed her eyes on the woman's face. Her posture was tall and straight and she wore a green fur cuffed gown that gave her a shapely appearance. It wasn't the garb of a servant.

"I lost track of time," Mia began to slice the wedge of cheese.

She needed something to do to avoid looking at her husband's servant. Lucia watched her with stabbing eyes. The woman knew not her place.

"It is inappropriate."

"I don't know what you mean," Mia answered innocently.

Lucia flew to the front of Mia and ripped the knife out her hand. She peered down at her darkly.

"You know what I mean, *magician*! The foreigner I saw you run off with. I would hate for rumors to emerge that you're being disloyal to my Prince," Lucia threatened.

"What is a rumor that has no truth in it? He is my knight and protector. I wanted to take a walk and he came to guard me. I wouldn't dishonor Jacob. I'm not so sure my husband can say the same," Mia replied losing her grip on her temper.

"You dare!" Lucia said and sprung her open hand back to strike her.

"Do it, servant," she said with an iniquitous grin. "Go on, I will you too. But I must warn you. You should strike knowing the consequences of reactions."

The strike didn't come, as Mia expected, but she continued with her own warning. "Do it. I shall not strike you back with my *hands*! A curse on the other hand would be my only defense against a woman with your strength."

"You heretic!" Lucia retreated.

"To your people, I may be. But it's you, a lowly servant, who has resorted to aggressiveness first."

"Lady Sasha shall hear of this!" she tightened her jaw and lifted her chin. "And I am no servant! I am a daughter of a chieftain and I ran this house long before you were even a whisper in the Prince's ear."

"I am here now. And be sure that my husband will hear of this as well," Mia replied airily.

"What is going on here?" Jacob growled.

For a moment, Mia didn't realize he was there. Jacob shoved himself between them and grimaced. "I will ask you one more time."

"Do not bother, Husband," Mia cut him off, "There shall be no more of it now. I am retiring for the night."

Mia gaited away from the kitchen and ascended the stairs. She could feel the cold silhouette of her husband chill her back. She continued down the hall, ignoring him at her heels and flung open the door to her chamber. Jacob grabbed the swinging door firmly, but remained halfway outside of the chamber.

"Tell me where you have been all night," he commanded.

"Oh, you mean your servant didn't tell you?" Mia snorted. "Of course she wouldn't."

"Where were you?" Jacob repeated ignoring her remarks.

"I was in the mood to take a walk. So I did with my knight, Horace. But she tried to turn it around into something much more," Mia sneered.

"And what is it?" Jacob commanded. "Since when did *he* become your personal knight?"

"He is from Thaumatur, a knight who was sent to guard me," Mia shot back.

"Only through the forest," Jacob countered. "Not to Vansant Summit where one of my warriors could guard you."

"One of your warriors?" Mia laughed. "I would be found in a trench somewhere with a sword in my back."

"You insult my warriors now?" Jacob growled and stomped through the door.

"I am by no means insulting anyone. It's obvious that I'm unwelcome here. The servant woman has even dared to step out of her place. If she acted so in Falias, Merle would've put her out."

"We are in the Nations now!" Jacob's face was red. "My warriors will protect you."

"I want Horace. I trust him," Mia retorted.

"I *don't* trust him! Damn him!" Jacob hissed and pushed by her.

"What's the matter husband? Are you jealous?" Mia hissed and followed him deeper into her chambers.

She circled him methodically, scornfully, with the entirety of her rage. She wanted to pretend he was Vastadon and rip his throat out. The dark veil draped over her, Vastadon's hungry eyes flashed before her. She cringed and exploded with red fury.

"Is that what it is?" she spat, bafflement covered his face. "Are you afraid that another *magician* might take the body of your whore?" she screamed, "Or is it that you wish for me to be shredded, my womb murdered because it's unworthy to carry your Barbarian heir!"

Mia shoved him. He didn't strike her back. She deserved it if he did. He towered over her like a mountain and she drowned in his black shadow. Guilt slammed into her when she thought she saw hurt in his eyes. He wasn't the monster who raped her.

"I am sorry," she whispered and took hold of his hand.

It felt limp beneath her fingers, but warm. She drew his palm to her face and closed her eyes.

"Just once, Husband, draw me into your arms," Mia whispered. "Just once so that I can feel safe again."

For a long moment he didn't move. He neither embraced her, nor left her. Probably because he thought her to be crazy. Perhaps she *was* crazy. She was so confused. The pain, the fear, the desire, jumbled itself into a mangled ball replacing her good sense.

Then Mia felt the heat of his form beside her. She laid her head against his chest, closed her eyes, and opened herself to the feeling of warmth and protection that instantly circled around her. She wanted to lose herself within him and his strength, she wanted for him to desire her. She knew it was within her grasp to desire him, but she didn't despise his kind as he did hers. She needed to trust *him* to overcome the razor that tore at her heart.

Mia bit back the shaken feelings within her and slowly traced a finger down his chest beneath his loose-fitted chemise, spinning it over the fine curls that covered his skin. She could've sworn she felt his arms shutter beneath her head. She continued down and traced a line over his naval. If she were to ever heal, she needed to give herself to him completely. His skin was warm and muscled, but it was soft where she caressed. He made a slight move, cupping her hand with his, but ceased to stop her. The thumping of his heart echoed in her ears and his chest rose and fell more swiftly.

She continued her path sliding her shaking fingers to his stirring manhood. She worked the snaps of his pants and pulled his erection free. She gasped, as she explored his hardness, and an aching throb spread from her inner thighs, the birth of her wet heat, down to her curling toes. She rubbed his growing spear more vigorously. He lifted his hips against her strokes.

He snatched her above him. With deft hands, he lifted her skirt and shifted her under garment aside. He dipped the throbbing tip within her moistness and sheathed himself. Her body constricted around him, but soon comfort escalated into the desire she often dreamed of experiencing. She rocked her body and he matched her movements with rhythmic thrusts. She collapsed to his chest, clinging to him and closed her eyes tightly, feeling the tension of their bodies build. He roared with pleasure and shifted his large form above her, increasing the tempo of his plunge.

When she opened her eyes, she froze. Jacob's face twisted into a grin when he looked down at her. His scattered braids unwound, spilling platinum down his shoulders. Vastadon was above her, rutting and sneering.

You are mine, not his.

Vastadon's cruel voice invaded the bliss she was scarcely reaching. Mia wanted to scream, but her tongue was numb, and it was as if her body became a sheet of ice.

You will never be free of me, Mia. No matter where you run to, I will find you.

He shuddered violently above her releasing himself within her. He lifted himself from her, and in that instant, she curled into a fetal position and cradled her head.

No, Goddess, this cannot be real! Not again! Mia's mind screamed in defiance.

Acid fluid flooded her mouth. Her ears and face were on fire. She attempted to force the vile down, but her gut churned and hot fluid spewed from her mouth onto the floor. A hand clamped down on her shoulder. She ripped her body from the hold.

"Stay away!" she ordered hoarsely, "Stay away, Vastadon!"

For a long moment, the silence taunted her, reminding her that she had just mistaken her husband for the cruel man who hurt her. She heard the door open and shut. He was gone. Once Mia caught her breath, she fled to the wash room in her chambers and soaked her body. What a fool she was. A fearful child who needed to heal, yet she rejected it. Would it always be this way? Could she never know passion? Could she never forget the beast that ravaged her?

Sierra appeared in the white doorway, her face unveiled for the first time before her. The beautiful olive smile was comforting, but her strong eyes caved in with concern.

"He didn't deserve that," Mia whispered. "I cannot even give him my body. I am nothing he wants!"

"He will understand, Mia." Sierra drew closer to her. "Things will be better soon. I promise you that time and prayer will heal you."

Sierra placed a hand over Mia's. She was a fool to believe a new beginning would be easy. Falias was only the start of it.

Jacob had never made love before. He had sex many times and with numerous women. He had even felt affection for some of them. But he had never before made love.

His expectations for such a thing faded from his mind many years ago. He had never *loved* a woman. She was frightened, scarred beneath that soft pale skin, hidden beneath the maddened pools of blue-violet.

She was beautiful. He couldn't deny it to himself, although he tried. He always thought her beautiful. From the moment they first met, she mesmerized him with one look, and from that moment on, he pulled the visor of ice over his eyes.

His body reacted with a mind of its own. He held no control when he was so close to her. Anger was his only defense, but he could not find that rage any longer. His normal tension, even the tension he managed to grip during sex, melted inside of her over and over again. He hadn't even noticed her wide eyes of fear until he released himself within her.

He went to his chamber after he sent for the priestess to care for his wife. Lucia awaited him there. He'd slept with the tribe-girl often before his leave to the *magicians'* lands, but he didn't love her. He didn't believe Lucia loved him any more than one could love their liege. She was a good and loyal woman, but overbearingly stifling.

She was sitting on the wooden chair beside the terrace doors nearly asleep. A sheer pale night gown clung to her well muscled body. Her long light red hair was wound loosely at the crown of her head. She was an attractive woman and he thought her appeal made it easy for a warrior to quickly become infatuated with her. He couldn't begin to count the times one of his warriors inquired about her. She showed no interest beyond him. But he hadn't deceived her. She knew fully well he wasn't ready to marry. He still wasn't.

Jacob knew what Lucia eagerly waited for in his chambers. It was the same thing she waited for every night before. He had yet to give in being that he was married, but his resistance was wearing down. He needed normalcy and familiarity that came with Lucia's company. Not this dominating enchantment that continued to revisit his throbbing loins. He would stay clear of Mia. He didn't want to fall spellbound to her again.

"My Lord," Lucia cried and darted to her feet. "You look awful? Are you well?"

"I am well," He nodded. "But I wish to be alone tonight."

She frowned, but was obedient to his will. Once she was gone, Jacob took comfort in his bed and shoved his desires for his wife far from his mind.

CHAPTER TWENTY-FIVE

Clandestine Vhladic

"My sister is gone!" Phoenix stormed into the cabin.

Dawn was barely stretching across the bay and the light spilled a tiny illuminated blotch on the sea. Nikoli, Cole, and Alabaster were already stirring.

"You don't think she attempted to find the inn on her own, do you?" Cole offered and Alabaster shook his head in agreement to the question.

"I doubt it. Not that I think she wouldn't brave it on her own. Look at this," Phoenix said thrusting his medallion in Cole's face.

The circle of stars that surrounded the owl and the lion lit up in a rainbow of colors. The amethyst was darkened where Phoenix pointed.

"That is her gem. Somehow she has been snipped from the Circle. How do you suppose this happened?" Phoenix scowled.

Cole clamped a hand on Phoenix's shoulder. "We will find her," He promised. "First we must find the inn the High Priestess spoke of. Perhaps we'll find her along the way. I know your sister, friend. She wouldn't be put down easily."

Phoenix scowled, "You go to the inn. I'll go find my sister." He slammed the cabin door, and when Cole went to follow, Nikoli called him back.

"Let him be." Nikoli replied, "He will come around."

"Someone should stay behind on the boat in case she returns." Darius called from the rear.

Vhladic was alive the entire day and with no sign of Diamond anywhere. It took Cole some time to convince Phoenix to remain behind on the boat with the provision of her return. Phoenix wouldn't be clear headed enough to control himself in the mist of a situation if one occurred. Alabaster agreed to remain with him and the Watcher, but it was only because of Darius' insistence. Darius of course couldn't stay still long enough to wait on a boat.

Cole pulled his medallion from beneath his tunic and studied it. The colors of the star ring were vibrant, but the amethyst gem was dim. Diamond's gem.

Cole swallowed hard, but he held fast to the hope that the light wasn't entirely distinguished. And that meant she still lived.

The conversation between Cole and Darius was absent. But it didn't disturb him that much because the trip through the thickly crowded streets went much swifter. A Barbarian parade marched through the town and fire blazed along the streets in huge panther sconces. The city was like nothing Cole seen before, but Horace, who habitually visited Vhladic, often described the architecture.

The main buildings were close together and high with pillar supported vaulted roofs. There were no fields and farms. No rivers and lakes aside from the elaborate fountains and the sea.

Soon the buildings began to scale down their appearance and insulae apartments became more common in the lower class areas. The torch lights were burning low in rusty metal sconces. People littered the streets near shabby troughs and outside a few rugged pubs, apparently homeless. The inn was at the end of the block and it looked more like a poorhouse barn.

A round woman with missing teeth and a peach fuss chin made a snide remark from behind a metal slab that was supposed to serve as a service counter. Piles of disheveled papers cluttered the surface and over-boiling cauldrons hung on uneven hooks above the cooking fires. The sound of a well frequented tavern rumbled from behind a set of wooden shutters to the rear of the woman. An inn with a shabby bar and a she-man keeper, Cole thought cynically. The place was dusty and untidy, and smelled of sex and rotten mead, causing Cole to suddenly lose the hunger he worked up during the day.

"Separate rooms or *one*?" the husky woman laughed at her own insinuations.

"One room, two beds," Cole tossed a coin at her.

"I've one room. Take it or leave it boys," She shoved the coin in her pocket.

"We will take it," Darius swatted Cole's clenched fists away.

The woman's face went pale when she saw Darius. He removed his hood and his pale face was pinched with little patience.

It dawned on Cole that she was fearful of their kind and he too yanked his hood back. The loose skin on the woman's face jiggled as she tossed the keys on the counter.

"Great Pariah!" The woman whined and covered her head. "I meant no harm."

Cole stared at her for a moment. It was as if he saw two different people emerge from this very woman. Darius grimaced and snatched the keys from the counter and sauntered up the stairs.

"We can find our own way," he snorted and Cole followed him.

Two dingy cots and a small round table with two rusting chairs furnished the room. Cole raised his eyebrows.

"I'll be up all night."

"I don't plan to stay here longer than needed," Darius growled and crouched in a shadowy corner.

"What was that Pariah stuff all about?" Cole asked.

"Pariah is a term used for those cast out from their own lands into exile," Darius paused and for a terse moment his onyx eyes flashed in the darkness. "'The' Pariah is an old horror tale told to young children to scare them into obedience. The tale indicates how runaway children are abducted and taken to a lair deep beneath the earth They are never heard from again because this great shadow would rip out their throats so they couldn't scream and would drink all of their blood. But the children wouldn't die. Instead they were transformed into soulless

256

shells that suffered madness for eternity. The children were called the Pariah."

"What a tale!" Cole unsheathed his sword for inspection.

"It might not be such an imprudent tale," Darius grunted and no more words were spoken.

Three hours went by before a gentle knock came. Cole gripped his weapon and crept to the door.

"Open the door, I have been sent. Quickly!" A woman's voice came from between the cracks of the doorway.

Cole pulled open the door and a robed figure squeezed through.

"Shut the door!" she waved a frantic hand, "Shut it!"

Once the woman was content she was safe, she removed her cowl. Dark and gold spirals fell in one long tail from the crown of her head to the right side of her brown cheeks. She wore a gold torque at her throat and a pearl circlet at her forehead. Her big eyes were a flurry of gold and ebony specks. She was a plump woman, but her body was curved with appeal, and Cole found it hard not to stare at her beauty. She spread her frosted lips into a sweet smile. Cole shifted his eyes to Darius and noticed a hint of approval in the Mind Mage's eyes as well.

"I have very little time. My name is Mina," she spoke with an unusual accent and extended a delicate hand to Darius first then to Cole.

"You are not Barbarian," Cole mused.

"Neither are you," she paused and took a seat in the rusty chair without a care to its condition. "I come from an island called Sihoma. Until two years ago we were a free and simple people. The Barbarians discovered that great wealth was buried beneath our soil. So they invaded us and claimed our lands and enslaved the people of Sihoma to dig the island's riches. Several of us came to Vhladic to beg the Emperor for our freedom. Sadly, we were intercepted by the temple soldiers and most of my people are now held in captivity."

"I've never heard of Sihoma," Darius rose to his feet and turned his back away from her.

"That is because the invasion wasn't orchestrated by the Emperor. As a matter of fact, the Emperor has no knowledge of my island. We were attacked by a band of the Brotherhood soldiers. We were no match to them. We dance and sing the magic of healing and have no knowledge of weapons or their uses. We save lives, not take them." Her brilliant eyes began to water.

"They swept through us as if we were animals being hunted. The highest point of our island, where the great spirits of life blessed, is called the Peak of Virya. The soldiers stand before the mountain as we speak, guarding it with the greatest urgency. They summon *Dementias*. Demons." She folded her hands in her lap and lifted her shoulders with a sigh.

"Demons have been sited in our lands as well. Horace has mentioned something of a mountain. But he didn't mention its location or Sihoma," Cole said

"I have met on many occasions with your companion, Horace Ebonis," she nodded.

"Funny, he never mentioned you," Cole grinned charmingly.

"Why would he?" she smiled. "He is your Emissary, no?"

"What can you tell us of the Pariah?" Darius interceded impatiently.

"It is a tale, Darius," Cole snorted.

"Sometimes a tale is a shroud for many truths," the woman replied. "The Pariah is the name of the temple soldiers. The eyes of these soldiers are black and soulless. Most of them are of your kind, although there are those who are Barbarian." She stood and replaced her cloak.

"Wait Lady," Darius said flatly. "How is it that you are free from captivity?"

"I was noticed by a member of the Emperor's Senate. He knows nothing of my true intentions. He lets me go as I please," She whispered.

"So you are a slave with privileges?" Cole grunted trying to hide his anger.

"I am whatever he wants me to be. But it's a little price to pay for the freedom of my people. It's why I make haste to leave you. I would like to keep the freedom I have," she paused and studied Cole's angry expression. "The Senator is kind to me. I've been lucky."

"I have a friend who is missing," Cole began and handed Mina the medallion around his neck.

She studied it and smoothed the glittering star circle. She closed her eyes and swayed her head to some unseen melody.

"She lives, but she has been taken," She tilted her head. "She is special to you, isn't she?"

Cole nodded and her smile widened. From the instant he met Diamond, he felt immediately drawn to her. His heart always attached itself to the stubborn and tough mariner. He could almost call it love. But it was a secret he shared with no one, not even with Aunyia, who he considered his best friend. At that moment any doubts regarding Mina dissipated.

"The temple has the answers we both search for. My people plan to make a move at Lugh Celebration and it's my suggestion that you wait as well. During that week, the worship and devotion to the God of battle weakens the evil hidden in this city. Your lover will not be harmed. Her captors will use her to bait a certain woman," Mina whispered and cupped his cheek. "I am sorry I cannot see her location."

"What are we to do in the meantime?" Darius growled.

"Retreat and pull yourselves together. Seek advice from your High Priestess. I will meet you here with plans when I sense your return." She strode to the door.

"What of you? Will you be safe?" Darius snorted in attempt to sound casual.

Cole nearly laughed aloud at the soft side of Darius. The grump was truly enchanted by her.

"I stay close to my consort. I am safe, my lord," Mina inclined her head and bid them goodnight.

"How soft she made you!" Cole laughed once she was gone and Darius shot him a dirty look.

"How soft of you to have a crush and not share the information with anyone else. I am quite sure Phoenix would love to hear how the womanizer has an eye on his sister." Darius lifted his chin. "Let us go back to the boat. We will not leave so hastily, however."

Cole cursed under his breath. The Mind Mage was good at what he did.

Diamond awoke to darkness. Concrete was beneath her cheek and she was weighted down by metal bondage. She lifted her head and clenched her teeth against the sharp pain that pierced the inside of her skull. Her memory was shattered and anger drove her to her feet. She lifted her arms into a stretch and shuffled her feet to circulate the blood flow. Thankfully—or foolishly on her captors' part—her wrists were not bound. Her hands roamed her body to her waist. She let out a hiss when she found herself unarmed. Her captors were not *that* foolish. Well, at least she still had her clothes.

She took slow counted steps forward. Once she counted five steps, a chain clanked and her legs could no longer move forward. The bud of fear began to open, but she swallowed hard against it with the fire of her temper. Fear would be useless now.

So would a bad temper, she thought bitterly.

She closed her eyes and inhaled the musty air. She needed to be calm in order to take the next step. Figuring out where she was. Once she felt calmer, she summoned the Air magic within her so that she could reach out to any beast willing to communicate with her outside of this dark prison. The flow of Air didn't come. She focused and tried again after saying a short prayer to Danu. Nothing.

"Damn!" Diamond cursed and the echo of her voice filled her ears. She was somewhere hollow.

She paced in the darkness as far as the chains would let her and scoured her brain.

The last thing she recalled was saying farewell to Aunyia and Horace at the harbor. A short conversation took place with Darius and Phoenix about sleeping on the boat and setting out for the inn first thing at dawn. Then she awoke here. Who had taken her with such ease? Who had the balls to sneak onto a vessel guarded by Mageborns, of the Circle no less, and run off with her? And, Goddess, why?

"Where the hell am I?" she mused aloud.

"A wondrous place isn't it?" A joyous voice sliced through the air.

Diamond jerked back and gathered herself beneath the concealment of her robe. Flint struck against something rough and birthed a flame in the darkness. Diamond kept her eyes unmasked from her cloak and watched as the flame streaked across the dark. With a click of a lantern door, a wider globe of light revealed rock wall.

"Reveal yourself to me!" Diamond commanded with no fear.

"But of course, Lady," the joyous voice sang.

The flickering circumference lifted from the wall and fell on a sharp faced man with a clean chin and thick eyebrows. The glow of the lamp made his eyes look like empty pits and the shadows beneath his cheeks blended with the darkness around them.

"Why am I here?" Diamond commanded.

His lips twisted into a menacing grin. The noise that came from his mouth was almost eerie. Diamond bit her lip to keep from shivering.

"To meet what fate has chosen for you," he laughed and clapped his hands.

Before Diamond could reply, a crack of light blinded her and several rough hands seized her. She heard keys jingle and felt the freedom of her ankles. She had to try magic again. She closed her eyes tightly and focused one more time.

"It is useless to attempt your magic. You have been warded with the blood of a Thaumaturi," the joyous voice whispered in her ear.

She opened her eyes again and desperately tried to readjust her vision against the blinding light. She inhaled the air. It was no longer musty, but thick with the smell of heavy incense. She was being dragged somewhere and she was pissed at not knowing, or seeing where. Another swift sound of unlatching and she was tossed into a room dim with a red hue. The thudding of a beating heart and humid heat swirled about her. Her eyes came to a focus and she drew her breath in sharply.

Before her, placed on a circular altar, she saw the two missing shards. In between them, with its pale combustion, sat the Lai Fáil.

Goddess, no! The wrong hands indeed!

The ground trembled beneath her feet and the wall split spewing out crimson light. Two sets of hands gripped her shoulders and forced her to her knees. When she shifted her eyes to her captors, she could see orbs of black staring sightlessly at the crack in the wall as it expanded into a blood-red chasm.

Booming footsteps drew closer until they came to a rumbling halt. When Diamond looked up again, her heart nearly fell into her stomach. A towering form garbed in black and steel with large bat-like wings smiled down at her with a razor-toothed grin. His eyes changed from green to red to black as he stared at her. A curtain of black hair hung across his strong face.

"Get her to her feet and leave us!" the thunderous voice sent the sightless captors in a frenzy of obedience. "Not you. You stay." He pointed to the man in which Diamond first saw since her kidnapping.

It was most definitely a kidnapping.

He walked to her, his movements predatory. He looked like some mangled nightmare with the aspects of Demon, Barbarian, and Thaumaturi. His magnetism paralyzed her rebellious tongue. She felt his hungry stare tear through her soul and her skin tingled with repulsion of his intentions. Evil.

"I have dreamt of this moment from the first time I saw you," His voice attempted a softer tone. It failed. "Remove your cloak. I must look upon you."

Diamond cringed from His outstretched hand. They were like claws of a tiger upon a man's hand. He frowned.

"You needn't fear me," He grinned, the sharp teeth protruded. "You are the only one."

Diamond shivered and this time she couldn't hide it. What the hell was this thing talking about? She wrapped the cloak around her tighter and took a retreating step.

"Allow me, My Darkgod." The joyous man strode forward his cleric green robes swirled about his ankles.

Darkgod!

The cleric gripped her cloak and yanked it, but Diamond didn't release it. The struggle finally gave way and she was before him unconcealed.

The smile immediately evaporated from the Darkgod's face. In its place, the most venomous and frightening scowl surfaced. He howled and lunged for the wide-eyed cleric."What is this!"

The cleric's face lost all color when the massive form gripped him up against the wall with one claw.

"The fault isn't mine! I gave detailed instructions!" the cleric whimpered.

He dropped the cleric with a thud and spun on Diamond. Her instincts kicked in and she scrambled for the door. He grasped a handful of hair and yanked her back against His burning torso.

"Wait!" the cleric cried, "She cannot be forced! She is a Mageborn!"

The Darkgod snapped his head to the side, "I want *her*!"

"And you shall have *her*," the cleric promised. "They will come looking for this one."

Diamond thought it sounded as if the cleric was speaking to a child. With a growl, He spun her out of His grasp and into the cleric. Firm hands gripped her as well as the fear she felt with the knowledge of a trap being set for her friends.

"Anne will be mine or you will pay!" He hissed and ran through the crack in the wall.

He wants Aunyia!

The thought of her closest female companion falling into the grips of this creature tore at the edges of her mind. Diamond tightened her jaw and watched as the wall swallowed the Darkgod and sealed itself. She needed to find a way out of this place.

Priestess Janella was right about her worst fears. But she had no idea how close they were to emerging.

CHAPTER TWENTY-SIX

Reunited

Falias advisor, Sermino, always knew something wasn't right with the Maladintos, but it seemed they were the slightest of the Sihoman's tribulations. Word reached him that his younger sister Mina needed counsel and finances for the refugees to strengthen their campaign against the Brotherhood that massacred their island.

Mina took on the more dangerous duty as a spy in the Barbarian Nations. Her exquisiteness won her a more comfortable fate than the other Sihoman, but she took risks everyday for their sake. She mastered the languages of the Barbarians and Thaumaturi as well as Sermino himself had. The two races spoke nearly the same tongue, with little enough differences to speak either. It was another skill won from her consort.

Queen Merle granted Sermino permission to leave, despite Aiden's weak wiles, to observe one of the Barbarian sessions of Senate. He knew Merle would be disappointed with his report because only the basic topics were discussed. The city halls reconstruction, the Lugh Celebration security, the rise and fall of tax, the overcrowded harbors, but nothing was mentioned of the High Prince's marriage. Perhaps its ignorance was due to the attendance of a Thaumaturi envoy.

Sermino at all times met Mina in the temple. Everyday she paid her dues to the Barbarian Gods at the same time so it wasn't difficult for them to maintain contact. On this day, many gathered before the three shrines of the Gods, so Mina snuck him into the side door past the altar to Ogma. The domed ceiling curved above them and the scent of incense reminded him of Merle's desolate tower in the Winter Palace, a place he often avoided. The inky-black passageway was a rift that spiraled down into the earth. Sermino dug into his pocket and fingered the sealed plans with prudence. He couldn't risk either one of their capture. He longed to speak with his sister, to embrace her, but there never was time for such leisure during their concise meetings.

Just as he decided to pull the sealed plans and sachet of gold from his robe, the sound of a door opening from behind drove them deeper into the dim cavern.

"Come," Mina tugged his arm. "I know another way out but we must make haste."

Their flight led them into a jade hued vestibule. Chaplains in deep green eddying robes pushed through a set of groaning wooden doors followed by two fleece clad Brothers. Mina stretched her plump form along the shade of the walls until they passed.

"The sliver of a flap straight to the fore," Mina whispered in their native tongue wrenching her head toward a skinny metal transom. "That is where we go now."

Mina darted across the main corridor Sermino at her heels, but the sound or what seemed to be the hum of woman's voice pleaded to him for help. Sermino stilled Mina with his right arm when he caught a glimpse of one of the Brothers in a passing room.

"What are you doing? We must hurry—" Mina disagreed.

Sermino ignored her, dragging her back against a wall deep in the shadows of the passage. A sensation, more like a silent calling compelled him to peer around the corner of the room.

The Brother was no longer in sight, but in a small ball of tattered robe, he saw a woman beaten and wavering. Her head jolted up as if she sensed him examining her. For a split second she locked her eyes on him. They were warm honey filled with perplexity and defiance, her face was

265

battered, yet he still found enormous strength within her. Her engorged lip twitched into a smile of reprieve, her eyes widened with recognition, a recognition that Sermino too felt. He knew her not, of that he was positive, but somehow their spirits were kindred.

"Come on, we must move on before the sentinels find us."

Realization of Mina's words sunk in, but he couldn't leave the woman behind to be defiled, mutilated at the hands of such evil.

"I must rescue her. I don't know why, but I have a strong feeling," he called back to her and moved forward before she could reproach.

He hurried to the girl's side and was grateful that she was knotted by rope. In one swift movement, he unsheathed his ceremonial dagger and cut her free. She tumbled into his arms."You must warn my friends. A trap has been set and I'm the decoy."

She was just a child-woman. It was then that he realized what was familiar about her. She reminded him of Miarosa. He cradled her protectively and followed Mina until they reached the salvation of the open city air.

It was a flash, a blur, and distortion. Diamond knew she was in danger no longer, but how it all came about she wasn't certain. She remembered gold kissed eyes of gentle wisdom and an embrace that made her feel safe.

"I am Mina. You are Diamond," Mina whispered as she massaged salve on her wounds.

"How do you know my name?" Diamond rebutted skeptically.

They were in a room that resembled a scruffy stable converted into a servant's sleeping quarters. As her eyes adjusted, bits and pieces of her memory came back. Diamond remembered the kind lined face of a dark man smiling down on her within the mists of her nightmare. She shuddered. Her liberator came at a paramount time, for she was sure the revolting clerics would've returned to force their will upon her. At that point they toyed with her mind, grabbed her with their filthy hands and tortured for amusement. Thank Danu they hadn't taken her body. She didn't know how long she was separated from her companions.

"I have met with your lover and his escort," Mina said.

Diamond glowered, "Lover?"

The strange woman giggled. Her striking gold-black eyes danced with enchantment. Her face was a soft brown rounded with great beauty when she smiled. She could tell she was a foreigner noble by the fragrant jasmine that lifted from her.

"I'm your priestess' contact. I met two men of your brigade here one week ago. They have returned to your vessel, but Sermino, the man who freed you, went to the harbors to inform them you are safe," Mina replied.

"I must go and warn them." Diamond shot her body up, but Mina's smooth hand eased her back down.

"They will come to us," She soothed her with a sing-song voice. "He will come to you."

"What is all this?" Diamond scowled. "This lover stuff and he will come to me."

"You know in your obstinate heart," Mina replied gleefully.

Diamond grunted and swatted the woman's hand away from her forehead. Mina was rather amused at the notion and strolled over to the tarnished chair before the busted windowpane. She hummed quietly.

Diamond refused to confess her heart raced whenever she was near Cole. It would never work because he was too charming. Charming made Diamond sick. Yet he was tall, fine-looking and bronzed to an almost golden sheen. Every time she looked into his grey eyes, a violent stream of feelings poured between them. She was drawn to him automatically, and she had the overpowering longing to be taken up in his powerful golden arms.

Diamond shook the sappy thoughts from her head and bit down on her lip firmly. She was sure that every woman who looked into Cole's eyes felt that line of attack. He was beyond beauty, as if his image was painted by the Goddess' perfect hands. A man who one day deserved children...

Damn! Stop thinking so childishly!

Diamond closed her eyes and Mina's humming came to a halt. Silence fell on the room until one hour later when the man who saved her stepped through the door. Phoenix flew in from behind him to Diamond's side. Cole, Nikoli, and Alabaster followed his lead and she was once again surrounded by the warmth of their link. Darius poked his head around. Then his gaze found Mina and a half smile touched the corners of his mouth.

"Thank Danu!" Cole breathed. "What has happened to you?"

"I woke up in the middle of a nightmare," Diamond hissed.

Cole touched her bruised cheek and snarled. "I want to know who! I want their heads!"

"I can only tell you that the Darkgod lives where I came from. I saw him," Diamond said. "And he must be stopped."

"Darkgod!" Nikoli exclaimed in a high voice.

"How, where?" Phoenix stuttered.

"Beneath the temple is where I found her." Sermino said from the corner.

"Who are *you*?" Darius questioned skeptically.

"It is alright, my lord. He is my brother," Mina touched Darius' arm.

"There were other people down there!" Diamond snapped. "I am going to the Emperor!"

"You will never get that far," Mina replied. "If it was possible, my people would've gone to him before this. It seems that the Brotherhood's sentries control the city beneath the palace. Surely whoever held you will be looking for you again."

"Aunyia is the Emperor's daughter. She would get us to him," Cole said and took hold of Diamond's hand firmly. "I want justice served for what has happened to her."

"No!" Diamond bellowed clinging to Cole's hand, "Aunyia cannot come anywhere near here!"

Cole arched his brows. Her companions glanced down at her with confusion.

"It would be safer for Aunyia than any of us," Phoenix replied.

"When they kidnapped me, they thought I *was* Aunyia. The Darkgod demands he has her. He has the whole underground hunting her with his obsession. His army is strange. Their eyes are completely black."

"The Pariah," Mina whispered.

268

"We were wrong, then. We thought they were after Mia. Why would this Darkgod want Aunyia?" Cole mused.

"I don't know. He seemed infatuated," Diamond shook the image of the Darkgod's hungry eyes from her head.

"A Darkgod, infatuated with a woman?" Darius asked incredulously.

"It was as if he was a mortal shell with Demon wings and he was as big as a Barbarian…bigger." Diamond narrowed her eyes to remember, "But his eyes…they were so strange and evil!"

Diamond told them how the Darkgod worked closely with a cleric. But she couldn't begin to remember the face of the cleric. It was as if something was eating her memory away. She also mentioned what was said about the Thaumaturi blood.

"The boundaries of the dimensions cannot be crossed over unless it's Solar Eclipse. It's impossible." Nikoli stepped into the circle of light and clung to his book with a bemused look. "This dark entity Diamond speaks of must be somewhat mortal. The sacrifice of Thaumaturi blood provides this Darkgod the power to exist."

"It is why Thaumaturi go missing during the seasons of voyage," Sermino interceded.

"How do you know of the disappearances?" Phoenix questioned.

"I'm an advisor to one of the four kings," Sermino replied. "The king of Falias."

"Then surely you must know much more than us. The Queen Mother there has a hand in this!" Darius retorted.

"If she is involved with what is happening here, I would know of it. She is clean of this matter."

"There must be a way to reach the Emperor," Darius spoke low into the silence.

"Let us think on it," Diamond interceded. "In the morning, our heads will be much clearer."

They nodded their agreements and decided to stay at the inn for the night. Diamond embraced Sermino and thanked him for saving her life before he left, followed by his sister. Darius escorted them downstairs. When he returned, he lowered himself in the shadows. Phoenix and Nikoli slept on the floor, Alabaster slept on the second cot, and Cole sat at the edge of Diamond's cot. While he thought she was sleeping, she felt him stroke her face and hair.

"I couldn't live if something fatal befell you, Love," He whispered.

She, the fearless knight, wasn't brave enough to open her eyes.

Dawn had long past and the shabby streets below were alive with the daily city life. They remained at the inn for two days trying to decide the best way to gain entrance into the palace or the temple. Cole also wanted to make certain Diamond was well enough to fight.

"It is important that I return to the Scholar Islands!" Nikoli exclaimed. "I need to research this information!"

"Take ease, Nikoli!" Phoenix silenced Nikoli for the time being.

Alabaster and Darius departed early to find something for them to eat and Diamond secretly hoped they would bring back some wine. The warmth of it would definitely fill her with the strength needed to move onward. Throbbing pain and soreness pinned her down to the cot. What had they done to her? She wasn't recovering and it was unlike her body to heal so slowly.

"I'm certain the Sihomans are being held where I was," Diamond murmured to Cole.

"I wouldn't be surprised." He went to her side promptly and scooped her hand into his.

"We must help them," Diamond thought of Sermino. "He could've left me for dead, Cole. But he saved me and I couldn't be more grateful."

"We'll band together." Cole squeezed her hand. "I think we should bring you home to the priestess so that you can better recover. And we can bring Nikoli home so he will stop complaining."

"No way, Cole. I'm staying right here." Diamond shot up but grit her teeth against the pain. "I am the only one who has any idea where prisoners are being held."

"He is right," Phoenix agreed looking down on her with concern in his eyes. "You should go. Besides, you heard what the foreigner said. Nothing can be done until the Celebration."

"Who will stay here?" Diamond asked urgently. "Aunyia is to return to the city if she isn't already back. Someone needs to stay here to warn her!"

"I will stay," Cole said and soothed her cheek. "It will be much easier for one of us to roam around this city than a whole mass of us."

Diamond despised the idea, but she was growing more concerned with her condition. She knew she would only hinder Cole in his duties.

Three hours past and they made haste to the port. Cole remained behind at the inn, but his farewell embrace left her aching for the nearness of him. She would fear for his safety despite the fact that she knew he was supreme in his talents.

From the vessel deck, Diamond could see the place she was held captive not so long ago. The temple dwarfed even the imperial palace, embodying the conception of their Gods—diminishing, unreachable, and unknowable. Its towering spires could be seen from miles away, Diamond was certain. The deceptively jeweled pergolas and a cavalcade of flying ramparts displayed the boundaries against intruders, yet welcomed those who sought peace. She shuddered. The house of a religious deity should not be feared. But it was feared by so many.

Alabaster draped a cloak over her shoulders and pulled her into a comforting embrace. His smile was warm and she could almost hear his thoughts as if they were words from his mute tongue. He was telling her that all would be well. *He* would be well.

The big man came into his magic nicely since the first day he found her in Findias. Diamond reached up and squeezed his hand. He guided her into the warmth of her cabin.

CHAPTER TWENTY-SEVEN

The Great Owl

Each passing week, Mia spent most of her time with Sierra and Horace. She was disappointed that Aunyia left before she could say goodbye. However, she knew she would see her again. The people of Vansant Summit had yet to warm up to her.

Mia attempted to push the night spent with her husband from her mind, but it seemed to follow her like a dark cloud. Not even the magical feelings she felt for Horace were able to chase the gloom away.

Horace taught her the basics on swordsmanship as he promised in the later hours of the day. She found that, aside from the clumsiness of a typical novice, she felt comfortable holding a sword. The true test of swordsmanship was upon a horse's back. He also prepped her on archery, a skill he was exceedingly proficient. Mia decided that the skill was much more difficult than it appeared. The graceful flow of the arrow didn't come easily to her.

Sierra schooled Mia on the ancient scribes of the Tuatha Dé Danann and the fundamentals in elemental magic in the earlier hours of the day. Mia's magic strengthened, although it wasn't entirely controlled. It felt natural to her.

Lucia stayed out of her way most of the time, but the wench made it a point to tend to Jacob's every desire. Mia didn't think he minded and she certainly didn't think he wanted *her* to tend to him after the way she behaved their first night in bed.

Sasha couldn't decide where she wanted to live. She constantly traveled back and forth between Vansant Summit and Vhladic. When she *was* at Vansant Summit, she spent most of her days napping in her chambers. When they crossed paths, Lucia was usually at her heels. Sasha wasn't cold, nor was she warm. It was as if she ignored her entirely. Mia rather liked it that way.

Sasha had implored Jacob to forgive Fershius for his mistreatment of the land throwing any excuse she could think of at him. In the end he chose to ignore the cleric's presence. Fershius was stuck to Sasha like a second head and whenever she left, he went with her. Mia felt awkward near the cleric so she made it a point to avoid him at all times.

Jacob was gone for most of the day to hunt or sport with his warriors. When he returned each day, he made his rounds through the market and the fields making certain all was in order. He even helped with some of the labor. The people revered him and Mia understood why.

He is a prince who isn't afraid to get his hands dirty. Aiden could only dream to have such respect.

She watched Jacob one day from the shadows of the stable. He had just returned from his hunt. His hair was an unruly mass and his bare chest and arms were painted with blue lines—the ritual hunting paint for the warriors. He knelt down before his kill and inclined his head. She watched him gently stroked the dead animal before he lifted it and took it off to be prepared for consummation. It was strange to Mia, but it reached the deepest parts of her heart. He didn't like to kill, even what he needed to kill for means of survival.

The wind fluttered the drapes of her windows with warning of an oncoming storm. The humidity thickened, but a rainfall would be welcomed. It hadn't rained since she came to Vansant Summit and judging by the looks of the fields, it hadn't come for some time before she settled here.

Mia stepped out onto the balcony. The sun was beginning to slope below the horizon emanating a twilight hue of golden lace. The sky to the west was grey and cloudy, pressing on with the speed of the whipping wind. She was slow and spellbound in her going, like one who was sleep-walking, moved by some impulse profounder. She inhaled deeply the scent of the forest and cast her eyes to the skies. It smelled of water, but not the fishy aroma of the sea. Mia didn't know how she could distinguish such a smell, but to her she thought it just water.

"My lady," A small voice called from the corridor.

Mia smiled when she saw the tiny face of Jacob's youngest niece, Ethane, peek into her room.

"Come in, little one." Mia outstretched her arms. "Come and watch the sunset with me."

The little girl giggled and bounced over to her nearly tripping over her plum colored dress. She was adorable with her rosy cheeks and her chestnut braided pigtails. Mia didn't see the coloring of this child's hair elsewhere in the Nations, but it was unique and beautiful against her rose-kissed skin.

Ethane raised her arms and Mia scooped her up, spinning her around playfully.

"You've married my Uncle, Lady. Shall I call you Aunt?" Ethane giggled.

"You can, if you wish, but only if I can call you little angel?" Mia squeezed the girl and stroked her nose teasingly.

"My Uncle, the Lord Emperor calls me that, but Momma says I'm more like a sprite that never stops getting into trouble." Ethane's eyes were wide with animation.

"Little sprites can be angels too!" Mia laughed at her funny face.

Ethane tilted her head and placed one of her little hands on Mia's cheek. She was staring intently into her eyes. "You have purple in your eyes. Momma says that they're ugly, but I think they're pretty."

Mia ignored the hurtful words the child said and smiled. It wasn't the child's intentions to be cruel. "Thank you."

"I know why my Uncle married you." The girl shook her head from side to side with an impish grin.

Mia wasn't sure she wanted to hear the answer. "You do?"

Ethane nodded vigorously, "Because you're beautiful, Aunt. Maybe that is why Momma doesn't like you. You are prettier than she."

"Your mother is very beautiful, little one. I wouldn't say that. It might hurt her feelings," Mia chided gently.

"But she says mean things about people all the time. She tells Maire that she's ugly because she wears boys clothing."

Mia was speechless. To hear those words come from a child made her sick. Sasha was indeed cruel.

"Well I think you and your sister are very lovely girls. Midian is handsome." Mia tried to change the subject.

"Midi is a boy!" Ethane scrunched up her nose.

"I suppose he is!" Mia cried and spun the girl around in a circle. It was nice to hear the child's giggles. It was like a sweet song on this gloomy day.

Rain spilled from the skies and a static wind picked up speed setting Mia and Ethane's hair whipping. Quickly, Mia lifted her skirt and carried the child back into the chamber. She set Ethane on her bed and fetched a towel from the washroom. She placed the towel on Ethane's tiny shoulders after drying her pigtails.

"It never rains!" Ethane cried. "You have brought rain with your magic to nourish our land!"

"I'm sorry to disappoint you, but it wasn't I." Mia couldn't help but laugh at the child's excitement. "It's a blessing from the Great Mother."

Mia gasped at her own words and wished she didn't say anything about Danu. She didn't want to confuse Ethane about religious beliefs. She was sure the child was raised to worship the Trinity of Gods.

"Who is the Great Mother?" she asked curiously. What child would not?

"Mother Nature. It's merely a saying," Mia quickly recovered. "It's getting late, little one. Have you taken supper yet?"

"Nay, Aunt," she replied properly.

"Surely your mother awaits you. You must take your supper now. But you may visit with me anytime."

"I guess so." Ethane pouted, but a little beam replaced it. "Will you come with us tomorrow morning to pick berries? Lugh Celebration is coming, but we like to start early."

Ethane had a hopeful expression, but Mia didn't want to promise her something she might not be able to fulfill.

"We shall see, Ethane," Mia replied and gathered the child to her.

"I like you," she said curtly.

Mia drew her head back and looked down at her. "I like you too. But now you must go."

"There you are, little girl!" Jacob exclaimed from the door. "Your mother searched everywhere for you."

Ethane's face lit up when she saw Jacob and in an instant she leapt onto him. She was swallowed by his rippling arms when he cradled her. He lowered her swiftly. She bid Mia good eve with a proper curtsey and fled from sight. Mia stared at Jacob who lingered in the doorway. Her cheeks flushed and she shifted her eyes from him. They had not been alone since that night.

"My Lord," she inclined her head. "Welcome back this eve."

"Thank you," He replied. "As you can tell, there would be no more time spent out doors. The rain has finally come."

"Yes," she replied quickly. Perhaps too quickly and too hopeful to converse with him.

"Will you take supper in the hall?" he asked.

"I plan to dine here this eve."

"Are you ill?" he said urgently.

"I will be fine," she answered.

The sight of him quickened her pulse. She wanted him to stay with her, but she hadn't the courage to ask. She couldn't put him through that ordeal again.

"I'll see to it that your priestess brings you something. Good eve," he said.

"Thank you, Husband," Mia replied flatly. "I would like some Hawthorne tea as well."

He nodded and ebbed from the pale doorway.

Cold, Mia thought, *I sound so cold.*

It isn't his fault, you know!

Mia spun to see the Great Owl perched on her bed frame. If it had been a human, the face she saw before her was reproachful. The owl spread her silver speck wings out in a languid stretch.

"You have finally come back to visit with me." Mia arched her brow.

But of course. Yet I am astonished with your attitude lately. The child has been the first person you were kind too since that night!

"You know about—"

I am your guardian and make it my business to know what happens to you. I must say that I feel like I am in Falias when I observe you lately. It seems that everything around you freezes.

"I don't know what you are talking about!" Mia darted up and turned her back from the owl's green eyes of reprimand. Her temper was ill-handled of late and she, despite her annoyance, didn't wish to birth a conflict with her.

What did the owl know about anything, anyway? She came into her life whenever she wanted and disappeared when she needed her most. Needed her? Why on earth would she need an owl who gave her no answers anyhow! Mia spun back to her and frowned.

"What gives you the right to question my behavior when you haven't the nerve to tell me who you are?" Mia snapped.

The Great Owl puffed her breast out, let out a shriek, and flapped her white wings about with irritation.

I didn't say I wouldn't tell you who I am. If you recall on our last meeting we were interrupted by a certain Mind Mage who, by the way, cannot stand you! I couldn't stay and explain such things with him watching! Besides, I cannot be surrounded by adversity. It makes me sick!

The owl pouted, so it seemed to Mia, and for one silly moment she felt guilty for reacting so snappishly. Was she truly becoming an ice queen? She couldn't become Merle. She wouldn't let it happen. She drifted over to the owl and stroked her feathers.

"I didn't mean to be snide," Mia whispered. "It's just that sometimes I feel strange these days. I suppose I'm trying to hide my weaknesses."

I know, Beauty. But you cannot trade one weakness for another. You are much stronger than you give yourself recognition for. There is darkness in all of us. Even those who perceive themselves as virtuous. Even Danu is haunted by darkness. Do you think there would be a Great Mother without a Great Father?

"A Great Father? Our kind doesn't believe in such a thing."

I know this, but it's something that not even I know for certain. If you truly think about it, it could be a conceivable concept. It's said in the great scribes of the Tuatha Dé Danann that the Great Mother has created mankind in the image of the Dwellers of Heaven. That would explain to us that all Dwellers would be man and woman. Could a Great Father be so unbelievable? It's something that we should all think on.

"It seems a bit silly, but I'm the last person to judge religious matters. I pray to Danu Who has given me the magic of two Elements." Mia smiled widely. "But I suppose you knew that too."

The owl swiveled its head and bounced from foot to foot anxiously.

I do, Beauty, but I know even more about you! Did you not see the rain? Did you not feel the wind? The tears you will not let yourself shed has fallen from the sky with your sadness and the strange winds have come from your happiness to share company with your young niece. It has been brought forth by you for you are daughter to all the Elements! It's why your fate is so special! The blood of all Tuatha Dé Danann runs through your veins.

"How is that possible?" Mia sat her face paled.

Sierra tutored her on the Lords of Elements and their origin. It was they who had brought forth the four treasures in peace and they who had guided the first of all Mageborns. It wasn't known that they had kin. At least it wasn't mentioned to her.

The first sins to taint our land, it was. The Lord of Earth had fallen beneath the spell of desire, and in his weakness, his brothers also fell from their vows to Danu. They each took liberties with the queens of the four kingdoms. The queens bore children and if you trace the bloodline, you will see that you are the first of their kin to be born with all blood in you. That is why you have the ability to summon all of the Elemental Rights and that is also why you are the Bearer of the four weapons. In your hands shall fall these weapons when the time is right. One already has. When the day comes, you will know in your heart what must be done. You and only you control the destiny of this world.

Inconceivable. The first word to enter her mind. Could the Goddess not make a better choice, Mia thought. She was nowhere near ready to except such rubbish. But her heart sang with the ancient wisdom. As sure as the blood flowed through her veins, she felt the truth in the Great Owl's words.

In time you will understand more of what I have revealed to you. You must practice strength and patience. The rest shall come to you. In the meantime, I shall do my own research on the matters at hand.

"I truly hope so, because I have no clue as to what you speak of," Mia whispered.

She was wrapped in her blanket, suddenly drained, and her head rested upon a pillow. She didn't noticed when or how she came to lie down.

I must go. I am never far, Beauty. Sleep and when you wake, remember my words. Take full advantage of your trainings with the priestess and the handsome Horace. It will one day prove to be wise of you.

"Goodnight..." Mia said with twilight in her voice. It almost seemed as if the revelation derived her to the horizon of dreams. She heard the thump of the Great Owls wings prepare to take flight.

Oh, my name is Blodeuwedd, by the way. I will save my tale for another day, Beauty, the Great Owl sang before taking flight into the dark crystal sky.

The faint sound of the owl's name sparked a tiny memory of an old tale but was rapidly stomped out with the weight of her eyelids. If Sierra brought up the dinner and tea, Mia didn't notice. She was deep within the arms of a dreamless slumber.

Mia jerked from her sleep and got to her feet when she sensed she wasn't alone. She turned up her lamp and frowned. Fershius Cornict leaned his round body against the door frame.

"It's the middle of the night and I *was* sleeping." Mia inclined her head and drew her sleep gown closer to her body.

Fershius didn't move. He folded his arms close to him and lifted his chin attempting to appear more important than he truly was. He moved in on her and crowded her. She felt trapped and flashes of Vastadon made her shiver.

"I didn't know that the *magicians* came with gold hair. However, you are still hideous," he sneered cruelly. "I can hardly stand here and look at you." He turned his cheek and made a sour face. Mia gasped at his vile and blatant approach.

"Leave me to my slumber, cleric," Mia commanded.

"You don't belong here, heretic. I don't understand how this marriage has happened, but I'll do my High Prince a great justice!" he hissed and clamped his mammoth hands around her throat.

His eyes bulged with insanity and pressure increased with each passing moment. Mia clawed at his hands and tried to pry them open ceaselessly. Her vision blurred and panic set it. She was dying. He was killing her right beneath Jacob's nose. Her knees buckled, but before she went down, she kicked the rotund man with all her might. The grip around her throat was gone. She fell to the floor gasping and crawling around him.

"You witch!" he howled.

Mia looked up at him. He was clinging to his shin and lunged at her as quickly as his fat body would move.

The chamber door slam shut and it snatched Fershius around in shock. A strong thread of magic strummed inside of her with a familiar presence.

"Step away from the princess, Brother," the soft accented voice of Sierra commanded.

Fershius laughed, drew out some sort of blade and said, "So I must end the life of yet another evil heretic!"

Fershius palmed the blade and yanked Mia up by her hair, but before the cold steel of the blade could slice her throat, Sierra flung her robes.

Sulfur filled Mia's lungs and an unseen heat exploded in the room. It raced through Mia's entire body, jerking her into a sudden arc. Fershius' blade flung from his hand and onto the floor. Sierra charged him in a whirlwind of kicks and fists. Fershius was on his back beneath Sierra's boot in a matter of seconds. She leaned down close to Fershius' face and lifted her eyebrows. She was glowing in flames, her eyes sparkled yellow, and her body clad in formfitting yellow battle attire.

"Do you beseech forgiveness for your evil attempts?" Sierra whispered softly as she caressed the pale faced cleric.

He made a gurgling sound and scowled. His hands twisted into huge fists and he wretched to free himself from beneath her hold. Sierra closed her eyes and traced a circle upon his brow, followed by his lips and over his heart. She removed her foot from him and retrieved the blade from the ground.

"Witch!" Fershius cried rolling around on the floor until he managed to lift his obese body from the ground. "Heretic! The High Prince will know of this use of evil magic!"

Sierra turned her sweet smile on him while she dressed herself back into the robes. "And he will be informed about your attempt on the princess' life. I will give you two minutes head start."

Fershius drew his breath in so deeply, it echoed in Mia's ears. After a long silent moment, the cleric was running through the door. Mia got to her feet and fled into the priestess' embrace. She had to stoop to hug the little woman. However, her actions spoke otherwise. Sierra guided her to the edge of the bed and lowered herself beside her. Mia could only dream of fighting as Sierra had just fought. She was gentle yet powerful and full of courage. Mia was so fearful.

"I couldn't believe my eyes!" Mia exclaimed, "I didn't know you were so powerful!"

Sierra laughed and squeezed her shoulder. "I only use my skills when necessary, my lady. He would've killed you had I not acted."

"You saved my life. *Goddess,*" Mia swore, "I felt magic all around me, in me!"

Sierra snapped to attention, "You felt my magic!"

"Is that bad?" Mia questioned.

"Nay! It's really good, Mia!" Sierra exclaimed. "I didn't actually form the magic. I only called forth my element to make the cleric aware of it in my appearance. That I wasn't afraid to use it if necessary! Imagine the connection if I had actually formed it!"

Mia didn't understand what kind of break through this was or why it was so important, but she was swept away with Sierra's enthusiasm. And she was pleased that the priestess used her name as opposed to 'My lady' or 'Princess'.

"What does this mean?" Mia asked with exhilaration.

"It means that you are truly part of the Goddess' Circle. You have accepted the Call. We could sense emotions and vibes, but never before could any of us actually *feel* each others magic. You are our link!"

Mia didn't ask anymore questions. She had too many and there would be time for her to ask them later. She was just happy to know that she was a part of something magnificent. It lifted some of the rain clouds from her mind and once Sierra was gone, she found wonderful Demon-free slumber for the rest of the night.

CHAPTER TWENTY-EIGHT

High Chaplain

Cole had seen the others off with a heavy heart. It was for the better that they left. He was concerned for Diamond's health and he didn't want to take the risk on hopes that she would recover on her own.

He wasn't entirely alone during his lengthy weeks in Vhladic. Mina stopped by a couple of times during the week to bring him food and clothing. She informed him that Aunyia had returned three weeks prior. She couldn't get close enough to the imperial palace to alert her of his whereabouts. Her Senator said nothing and she didn't press him with questions.

Mina briefed Cole some more on her race's rituals and beliefs. She also described the streets and the important locations within the city of Vhladic by drawing up a map.

The door busted open and Cole leaped to his feet with a firm grip on his sword. He released his breath and smiled widely when he saw the face of his lovely friend. Aunyia no longer dressed in the tunic of her knighthood but was garbed in a glittering chiton fitted for the Emperor's daughter. She gathered her pastel pink skirt and leaped into Cole's waiting arms. He squeezed his dearest and closest friend tightly.

"I have missed you so!" Aunyia cried. "I have heard that Diamond departed ill! I hope she is well!"

"I hope so too," Cole said and nodded to Mina who stood behind Aunyia. "Have you heard of her capture and what she has discovered?"

"Yes." Aunyia frowned. "Mina has told me everything. I understand that I'm being hunted by some sort of monster. It isn't such bad news. Better our enemies focus on one of us than Mia. I am more capable of defending myself."

"I still don't like it and I wouldn't get too cocky with the idea. The Senate will not protect you. Most of them oppose Thaumaturi and would most likely ignore dangers that surround you. You could be harmed, Aunyia." Cole squeezed her elbows.

"Well, we'll see about that, won't we?" Aunyia lifted the left side of her skirt and unsheathed the short sword strapped to her thigh. Cole laughed at her humor, but in truth he was concerned. Even Diamond was more adept with combat skills and he saw what her captivity did to her. Although it was a necessity for all of them to learn beneath Valance's combat guidance, Aunyia was a Healer beyond anything as Phoenix was. The two of them wouldn't be on the front lines of a battle. Those privileges were strictly for Darius, Diamond, and he.

"The temple is well guarded," Cole huffed and Mina nodded her agreement.

"I know, but I believe there is a cave south of the city's main port. Although Diamond was rescued from within the confines of the temple, I doubt the Brotherhood would solidify the clandestine so close to his domain. Mina was correct in instructing us to wait until Lugh Celebration."

"The Sihoman people must be freed," Mina quietly added. "It will give us a greater number in a revolt as I am told that your Order hasn't extended their hand in your affairs to uncover the heinous activities of the Brotherhood."

"That's precisely why we will not tell the Elders of our discovery of the Stone and the shards." Cole added, "But the other weapons, have you an idea where they are?"

"Nay, friend, but it was brought to my attention the activities of the temple guards in Sihoma. Something must be there, perhaps a weapon in which we seek." Aunyia replied nibbling on her nails.

"What exactly is your plan for Lugh Celebration?" Cole lifted his eyebrows.

"I am not certain yet. For now I want to focus on freeing what we can of the Sihomans and see what they have learned during their captivity before we jump into seize. We know of this entity, but we know nothing of where he came from and who he truly is. Thaumaturi blood is involved, but can we honestly rely on an old fable to guide us?" Aunyia sighed and answered her own question. "No, we must find out for ourselves."

"I want to stay here with you until Horace arrives. I just feel that I should and I won't take no for an answer. Horace has his circles here and would have no trouble traveling closely with you in the upper caste, but he isn't here yet and I will not take the risk of something happening to you. I already almost lost Diamond." Cole shook his head, "Goddess forbid if that creature took you. The look on Diamond's face when she described this obsession…"

"Very well, Cole. If you must. Remember it isn't any less risky for you to roam these streets alone." Aunyia waved a finger at him.

"Me? I am the finest defender you'll ever meet!" Cole exclaimed.

Aunyia hugged him again, "I know my friend. Every day at noon I am at the Spa for bathing, lunch, and I watch the sportsmanship. It's called the Hakinal Springs on the main street that runs between the palace and the temple. Meet me there and I will find a way every day to converse."

Cole nodded and saw Mina mark the spot on the map as to where to go. Aunyia then tossed a sachet of gold at him.

"You must pay for admission. It's the highest quality Spa in Vhladic. Once your face becomes familiar and that'll happen more rapidly with good tipping, you will be more accepted into the higher castes." Aunyia smiled and followed Mina out of the scruffy room.

Cole opened the sachet and nearly swallowed his tongue. The gold inside of the bag could support him for the rest of his life.

Nothing was mentioned to Jacob about Fershius' attempts. He would no longer bother Mia after his confrontation with Sierra. Who would? Fershius simply disappeared and Mia was all the more interested in magic study because of it. She wanted to be able to protect herself and not have to flee behind a massive man or in this case a tiny priestess, whenever she was in peril.

The Elemental Rites calmed her and allowed her more insight to understand the words of Blodeuwedd. The Great Owl hadn't come to her since that night. Mia could call to her, but she wasn't sure she wanted to hear what the owl had to say.

For four nights straight, Mia dreamt of cities being swept away by floods, swallowed into crackling grounds, shredded apart by some unseen force and burning. Burning. The most horrific memory she had was of burning. Her soul spoke to her and told her that the dreams will come to pass if something wasn't done. Thaumatur would die. How could she help if she didn't even know how?

The forest was brilliant beneath the golden circle of the sun. Huge birch trees cradled the bank of the brook. Their white wood looked pale silver beneath the light. Flowers bloomed from the forest floor and dotted the shrubs. Sierra blended beautifully with the natural surroundings. It was as if she was a part of the grove.

There were no secrets between Mia and her priestess. She knew all of it, the truth of her birthright, the rape, the Sword of Light—which pleased Sierra beyond belief—and even her strange feelings whenever she came in contact with Horace. Yett she couldn't bring herself to tell Sierra of Blodeuwedd's visits and revelations. Perhaps it was too overwhelming for even her to accept. Mia needed a little more time to think on it before she brought it to her priestess's attention.

"Remember to notice the deep green shadows on the grass, the gentle flurry of the leaves, rustling softly." Sierra's soft voice brought her back from her thoughts. "Close your eyes and feel the profusion of life all around you." Sierra displayed in her hand a bright green leaf.

Mia closed her eyes as she was told. At first, she could only notice the common sounds of the woods. The chirping of blue birds weaved in and out of the trees and the stream beneath the bridge rolled peacefully. She heard the bustle of the trees and a buzzing of a bee near her ear. Mia took a deep breath in of the fresh forest air.

"Fire energy from the sun sparks life," Sierra touched the palms of Mia's hand with gentleness as she spoke. "Water from the heavens nourishes each leaf. Air from the wind is abundant. Earth cradles the roots with the bones and blood of its rocks and soil."

Sierra's words were no more than a murmur to Mia, faint and mingling with the drumming of the Earth and the caress of the Air. The fingers of Sierra's wisdom massaged the tendons in her feet and traveled to the crown of her hair lifting it ever so lightly. An overwhelming feeling of love and respect swarmed her body. The warmth was familiar and intoxicating, coaxing Mia to let go of the world around her.

In her trance, she could see something glitter within the twirl of the white mists. As she focused on the silver glitter, a strange warrior with eyes that blazed through a savage mask galloped forth with a gleaming staff in hand. What appeared to be the handle was braided with four strands of gold and silver. As she focused even more, the object began to churn and pulse with violet and jade lights until the horseman was completely blotted out. The wind that whistled carried a song message.

Gáe Assail…bring it to life…accept immortality.

"This is the ultimate power of the elements in pure flow," Sierra whispered. "The power to bring forth life."

"And to bring forth death," Mia interceded and the vision of the beautiful object exploded leaving her with the darkness of her closed eyelids.

Silence befell them, and Mia opened her eyes. Sierra was before her, her emerald eyes wide. For a moment, Mia was confused and not exactly sure what startled her until she followed her line of sight.

Mia gasped and a panic seized her still. Six pairs of crimson eyes peeked through shadowed hoods. No hissing sound erupted as before and their forms didn't tremble with their rage. Instead they were looking upon Mia with alertness. And she somehow knew that they wanted something from her.

Mia placed herself before Sierra protectively and slammed her eyes shut. "Be gone!" She thundered. "Be gone at once!"

When she opened her eyes, they were gone.

"Why didn't they attack us?" Mia turned on Sierra who was composed as she was before the presence of the Demons.

"They awaited your command, Mia," Sierra said calmly.

"I don't understand?' Mia turned her back with forcefulness.

Sierra placed a hand on her shoulder, "Somehow you summoned them into the light of the day. Light is their death, yet here they stood."

How could this be? Mia thought grimly. Had Darius spoken truthfully about her involvement with the Demon slaughter in the Celse Forest? Had innocent blood been spilt by her hands? The Sun Knights refused to give Darius the recognitions.

Somehow she needed to find Darius and ask him some questions. After all, was it not he who helped her gain control over the Power she held? She needed to know exactly what and how she could bring forth such things. If there wasn't a way to control such things, Mia would see herself dead before she unleashed such beasts. The palm of her hand burned and for the first time she realized that she held the pommel of the Sword in her concealed hand. The Sword summoned the Demons?

The sound of hoof beats drummed in her ears. The noise resounded strangely leaving her uncertain whether she was hearing it through her ears, or by some other means. She saw by Sierra's expression that she must've heard the same thing.

"Your husband comes," Sierra whispered. "He will not be pleased to see us with no warrior."

"Hide, Sierra. He will blame you," Mia said pushing her away from the road without pausing to hear Sierra's disagreement.

Mia turned her back to the galloping and awaited his coming. He would be angry, but at least he wouldn't have Sierra as his scapegoat. A shadow loomed over her, and she turned to see Jacob high above her on his steed. Next to him, an unfamiliar man who wore the dark green robes of a Barbarian cleric looked down at her with an unwelcoming expression. Of course the clerics of this nation wouldn't give her a *warm* welcome. He resembled a Barbarian, but his sharp chin was cleanly shaven. It was difficult to pull her gaze from the man's demanding presence.

"You have defied me yet again, Wife," Jacob's angered voice brought her attention to him.

"It wasn't my purpose to defy you, Husband. I lost myself in the splendor of the day," Mia recovered quickly.

"Untamed and outspoken," the cleric said joyously. "Such a combination."

Mia arched her brows and opened her mouth but shut it quickly with one piercing gaze from the stranger. Something moved inside of her with his dark eyes, but it wasn't the same sweet feeling of tenderness she knew. The man handed Jacob his reigns and dismounted gracefully. He approached her in a manner that reminded Mia of a snake. Every part of her screamed at her to run away from him, but she didn't act upon it. The man outstretched his arm to touch her. Her skin crawled with the thought of it, but her body leaned forward to receive his gesture.

"Forgive me, my lord, but it was my idea to walk on this fine day," Sierra's soft voice jerked the man's attention away from Mia before he touched her.

It was as if a hand was released from around Mia's throat when the man stepped away from her. Once the feeling of suffocation ceased, Mia became irritated with Sierra's admittance.

"I should've known you were responsible, Woman," Jacob growled.

"You will not punish my priestess for my actions," Mia demanded.

Jacob's cool eyes turned to her. He cocked his head and lifted the corner's of his mouth slowly. "You will not tell me how to run my dwelling." Jacob reached a massive arm down dragging Mia up onto his steed.

"Find your own way home," he said callously to Sierra.

"You cannot leave her here, Jacob!" Mia protested.

"She found her way here. She can find her way back," Jacob snapped.

"Fear not, Lady," said the stranger, "I will see to the safety of your companion."

Sierra nodded calmly despite the uncomfortable vibe Mia felt from her. Mia didn't forget Horace's accounts on what he witnessed at the hands of the Barbarian Brotherhood. Mia leaned back against her husband's torso and tilted her head to his ear. "My priestess is ill-eased, Jacob. I don't trust this stranger."

Jacob responded with a grunt and squeezed the sides of his horse into a speedy cantor. Mia stared behind them as her priestess' form ebbed from her vision.

Chaplain Hector set his mind on visiting Vansant Summit and it wouldn't be a long one. He needed to see Merle's Mageborn for himself. He nearly lost his composure with the site of Merle's kin. The girl was attractive enough, but it was the pools of deep blue violet that drew him to touch her. He didn't, however, expect the priestess Mageborn to interfere. Had Sasha intentionally left such an important detail out of the message? She was probably too engulfed in her loathe for her younger brother's new wife to think clearly. For many years Sasha's brothers went wifeless, and Hector thought she liked it that way. She wasn't one to share attention with another woman in her family. Especially a *Thaumaturi* woman. Hector enjoyed such petty jealousy and bigotry. Such diversions made his life much more interesting and his duties with little impediments.

The Darkgod had plans for the imperial family. He didn't mercifully exclude Sasha from that list. Jacob and Aldrich would both fall to death. Sasha would be Turned and Anne, well that was another story. The Darkgod's horrendous outburst when he learned that his Pariah retrieved the wrong female only confirmed Hector's suspicion. The Darkgod intended on using the feisty female as bait for his true prize. Unfortunately the blue-haired bitch managed escape. Death wasn't a good enough punishment for those responsible for the watch that day.

The Priestess before him was a tousled bundle of jade robes leaving her form entirely concealed but her eyes. She showed no fear, although he knew she sensed something bizarre in him. Only the penetrating emerald gaze left him a little unnerved. He wasn't used to such scrutiny. Even the dark orbs of Merle didn't affect him so. He inclined his head to her after a long uncomfortable stretch of silence.

"Shall we walk together, Lady?" he asked specifically avoiding the option of riding with this woman.

"There is no need for you to escort me, Chaplain. I can find my own way," she said with an accented twitter, not so rudely as commanding.

"You are insightful to assume I am a Chaplain."

"Perhaps," she chirped. "I believe your garb could be a great clue to your identity. It isn't often one could be seen in Vansant Summit with such fine woven robes. And the Trinity is clearly embroidered at the base of your cowl." She pointed at the knotted triangle of the Trinity just above his chest.

Hector tilted his head and smiled widely, "Why I suppose you are right. I am the High Chaplain Hector Altorius. I know that you are capable of finding your way home, but I insist. Walk with me."

The woman nodded gracefully. Hector took hold of the horse's reigns and they began to walk the route in which the High Prince galloped off with his wife.

"Why do you cover your face and body in such heat?" Hector asked abruptly.

"It is a vow I made to the Goddess, Danu. Surely you have heard of our deity and worship."

"I have. Do you not think such sufferance should be left to those who have defied your female deity?" He pressed on.

"It is an honor, not penance, to bond with Danu through a sacred vow," she replied quickly and plucked a leaf from a passing bush. "Do you not vow to your Gods?"

"In ways much different than yours," Hector replied. "Celibacy and devout rituals."

"And you do not consider it an honor?" Sierra questioned handing the leaf to Hector. The witch was trying to trap him into a religious bout. He was no fool. He took the leaf from her, careful not to touch her. As he closed his hand around the frail flower of the bush, she slid a finger across his knuckle. He shivered within his skin.

"It is sufferance to us. The sufferances of all mortals fall onto the Brotherhood's shoulders. An honor it is too."

"The Gods you serve, do they will sacrifices of innocents?" she turned her eyes on him.

He dropped the leaf and it fluttered to his feet. He silently cursed inside because he allowed himself to be placed in a state of vulnerability.

"The Barbarian Gods do not encourage such savage things," he said in a controlled tone. He hastened his gait and was pleased to hear her struggle to keep up with him. "Dagda is the God of new life and plenty who wills to be honored in the spring with great bonfire feasts and freely flowing ale. Much like your Spring Daughter, Stara." Hector continued displaying his knowledge of the female deity and demi-goddesses, "Lugh is the God of war and hunting. He wills to be honored through sport. In summer, bonfires are also lit and mutton is cooked over them with wine. It is said that He blesses loyal men with the conception of sons during the Celebrations. Ogma is the God of wisdom. He is honored throughout the year with things such as theatre, scribes, art, and Halls of Records in his name. I am sure you have heard that Vhladic is known to have the most elaborate Hall of Records, Ogma Columns. It is said to be as grand as the Scholar Islands."

"Yes I have heard of the Ogma Columns and I have also heard much about your great temple," Sierra replied not allowing her voice to reveal her implications.

"I cannot begin to describe the beauty of our Gods' temple. You should *pay a visit* sometime and see the splendor for yourself, Lady," Chaplain Hector replied loosing some of his temper. He could strike this woman and drag her ever pious person straight into her worst nightmare. She would squirm like a little fawn in the clutches of Bile. Yet Hector swallowed his urges to act, for it would do no good in such a precarious time.

They continued their walk silently until they reached the side gates of the market. He was pleased to remove himself from this woman's penetrating presence.

Jacob didn't ride directly home. Instead he took a long route so that he could inspect the grounds. Mia said nothing to him of her thoughts and she was too angry to notice his duty. It was when they finally returned to the stables she let loose.

"You left her there alone with *that* stranger!" Mia snapped when he lifted her off of the horse.

He ignored her and called to a skinny boy with colicky light brown hair and a muddy face to care for the horse. Jacob stomped off to the stable doors. Mia was on his tail.

"Must you ignore me always, Jacob?" she cried trying to move her smaller legs to keep up with his stride.

"I ignore the foolish things you say because I don't see the use of wasting my breath with an answer," Jacob grumbled and continued onward through the market. The villagers bowed as he passed.

"They have been gone too long!" Mia swallowed when the vivid memory of Brother Fershius' attack came back to her. He, like the stranger, was a Brother of these so called Gods. Panic rose into her throat choking her. Mia knew above all that Sierra was capable of defending herself but something was different with the cleric. Power surrounded him like an omnipotent cloak. Mia grabbed Jacob's arm so tight she could feel her nails pierce his tough skin. After a few steps of dragging her along, he finally stopped.

"I assure you that the Chaplain of *my* Gods will see to your priestess' safety!" he growled ripping his arm from her and pointed. "Do you not see what I see?"

Mia relaxed her shoulders with the exhalation of her breath. Sierra followed the Chaplain at an arms length distance and from what Mia could see the woman looked to be fine. "Thank Goddess!"

Jacob shook his head impatiently and frowned, "Aldrich is coming. You must prepare to receive him properly instead of concerning yourself with imagined threats!"

The Chaplain's eyes found Mia's and for a moment he paused in his flight. A shudder went through her as he smiled slowly. She jerked her head up to her husband and nodded. "Very well, Husband. I shall seek out Lady Sasha and ask her what she needs of me. I am most certain I will have plenty of time to help being that you have Lucia to serve you as you see fit with little use of your wife's hands." Mia spat a little more irritable than she cared to.

Jealousy was the last thing she thought she would feel in regards to her husband.

CHAPTER TWENTY-NINE

Bittersweet

The smell of body odor and cooking fires tickled Vastadon's nose. The place was a putrid sight, half naked Barbarian women ran about under the light blue sky. Several Graven Barbarians wrestled and drank around the roaring bonfire.

In summer these parts of the Barbarian Nations suffered the worst of the season. The grass cracked beneath Vastadon's boot with each step he took. The fields and valleys were brown with death. Quite contrary to his uncle's well tended land. The air was thick and humid, making him sweat beneath his concealment. The slip past the east wall was no easy task for a normal man in the middle of the afternoon. For Vastadon it was swift and stealthy. And he had the use of magic. He considered himself lucky to be born with the Powers of a Mageborn as his sister Anne was, but he intended to use his ability for more useful things.

The air and stench was even worse within the largest tent among the camp. He was careful to keep his thoughts to himself. He didn't come here to fight.

The man before him was tall and massive. He was hardly clothed, which disgusted Vastadon, wearing only a beige drape over his loin, and strange symbols were painted on his chest in blue circular patterns. Around his left eye, what appeared to be a wing was tattooed in the same inky blue. His hair was a fair scarlet untamed with two small braids that hung languorously across his shoulder. Spiked piercings decorated his chin, ears, and nipples proudly representing his bravery. Vastadon sneered at such tedious rituals. The knave before him was the Graven Clan leader, who went by the name of Hawk.

"What are your reasons for betraying your own uncle? Why should I trust you? After all, part of you is Thaumaturi." Hawk wiped the sweat from his face.

"The girl," Vastadon leaned forward, his eyes blazing with an insane fire. "I believe his wife might carry my bastard."

Hawk paused for a moment and stared at Vastadon with a bewildered expression. His lips curved, or so it looked it beneath the thick red mustache, before he abruptly jerked his head back in laughter.

"You find something amusing." Vastadon gripped the snake head of his staff as his temper rose. He reminded himself the true purpose of this most undesirable visit.

"Let me get this straight, half-blood," Hawk laughed. "You want me to align the Graven Clan with the Tuskans, the tribe we are barely civil with, to declare war on a man that has been fair to us over a *girl?* It sounds to me that this manner of infidelity is between you, your uncle, and his whore."

Hawk plopped down on a thick pile of wool and furs and nestled between two bare breasted women. He was laughing so hard, he nearly toppled over the tankard of ale beside him.

"The girl is a Thaumaturi." Vastadon smiled maliciously when Hawk's laughter came to a halt.

For a second, Hawk lost all of the well obtained coloring he gained from drink. Then anger formed lines around his eyes and he sat straight up, shoving the half naked women away from him. "Out!" he bellowed and the women scurried to their feet and darted through the flap of the tent.

The Chieftain's nostrils flared when he bore his heat into Vastadon."I pray you do not lie, half-blood, for I will rip out your heart with my teeth if I learn otherwise."

295

"I can assure you that I speak truth. You see, my uncle has one weakness, as hard to believe as it may be. It is his loyalty to my father. He has sacrificed his very strong-willed beliefs to please the Emperor without even a care for the consequences."

"I should kill you now, where you stand, son of the Emperor or not. Be sure I would have, if you had not justified your intrusion," Hawk growled. "The High Prince has betrayed us with this union. There will be no mercy once the other tribes catch wind of this. It was the common knowledge of the Prince's contempt toward the Thaumaturi that allowed us to keep the others at bay. And my tribe will not suffer for it. I have no choice but to join with them as you suggested." He met eyes with Vastadon and scowled, "I cannot speak for the Clawclan. Their Chieftain's Wiseman, Erikrates, has a certain bond with Hilliard. You might've been cleverer to seek their support in this first."

"I have made my choice wisely. The mighty Gravens are the highest respected tribe in this imprisoned land."

And they serve my purpose well enough now, Vastadon thought wickedly.

"I cannot promise you the girl and your unborn bastard unharmed if she would happen to cross paths with a tribe warrior. You will have to see to that."

"I shall. And if you need my aid, I will heed you. My uncle has been ignored for far too long. Vansant Summit is yours." Vastadon stood and strode for the flap of the tent. He paused and looked over his shoulder, "I'll deny any involvement with your actions, so why not call it an even trade. I have provided you with what you need and in return, you say nothing of my visit."

"It is done, half-blood," Hawk growled.

"Oh, and remember that it was I who will give you your freedom back when I become Emperor." He studied his varnished fingers, "And lose the little nickname you have given me," He added and strode away from the camp. Trailing behind him, he could hear the cries of war ensue. His smile widened with the sound. Now to the nest of the High Prince. Surely his visit would be quite interesting.

Mia was in search for her husband's sister. She expected Sasha to be involved with the preparations of the feast even if it was to bark orders. She could not be found in the hall or the kitchens. When she asked the servants of it, they either totally ignored her or shrugged their shoulders.

Mia gave up and headed for her chambers when she caught a glimpse of Sasha before her mirror through the open door of her chamber.

"Mia, come and braid my hair," Sasha called to her.

"I've searched everywhere for you," Mia said and grabbed one of Sasha's jeweled combs. She began to work the comb through her wavy hair, careful not to rip at the little snags. "Where's Lucia? I'd think her envious to see me pamper you," Mia snorted.

"Lucia has been buzzing around all day after the children," Sasha said haughtily. "And I'm afraid her time will be well occupied once the High Prince is ready for his grooming and bath." There was a hint of satisfaction masked behind Sasha's languid tone.

Mia suppressed her frown. She seethed with the idea of Jacob calling Lucia. Why should she give a damn? Let him have his fun.

"Are you not anxious to welcome the Lord Emperor?" Mia swerved the topic.

"I'm afraid that I no longer find visits from my brother pleasurable. All that he and Jacobane talk about is that damned wall and its occupants. If I yearn to enjoy his company, it's better done in Vhladic. I think I will soon return to Vhladic. I long to see Aldrich's decorated city. It can become rather lonesome here in the country," Sasha replied. "My children, of course, favor Vansant Summit. Especially Maire. I think I shall make Maire take the return trip with me. She needs to learn her place as a lady. To me, she looks more like a warrior than the niece of the Emperor."

"Perhaps she is happy as she is," Mia replied mindlessly.

Sasha reached up and stilled Mia's hands from weaving the second braid. "Sometimes happiness does not come with the duty sworn to the Emperor."

Mia stared into the mirrored reflection of Sasha's taunting eyes. In that very instant, she knew that Sasha was pretending before Jacob her desires to be civil. Sasha released her hand and inspected her face and hair. Mia couldn't deny she was attractive. She looked more like a maiden than the mother she was.

"I think I like it the way it is. One braid tonight it shall be, then." She snatched a long jeweled box from the drawer of her dressing table and flung it open.

Inside there was a gold latticed circlet accented with a thorn shaped onyx. She fumbled with it and set it delicately on her head. Mia assisted her with its adjustment and forced a smile on her face. Could this woman ever accept her as a sister? How Mia longed for acceptance, but sadly she already knew the answer to her own question.

"My lady." Lucia approached them. Her smile melted off of her face with one gander at the scene.

"Ah, Lucia, come," Sasha invited her with the extension of her hand. "How do I look? Mia has prepared me."

In a swirl of pastel blue skirts, Lucia was at her mistress' side fumbling with the circlet. "You always look lovely, my lady," Lucia replied. "But I think it would suit the great sister of the Emperor better if she wore two braids."

"Of course," Sasha replied and Lucia undid the circlet and began braiding Sasha's hair with skillful hands. Irritation swept through Mia.

"I am sorry I wasn't here sooner to serve you, my lady," Lucia began. "Had you a little patience you would've seen that I always make time for you. Once I am done, the High Prince will be ready for his bath."

A fire sparked in Mia's gut. Were they deliberately taunting her?

"You have all the time you need to pamper your lady, servant," Mia remarked sternly. "I will see to the care of my husband."

Lucia dropped the comb and tightened her jaw. Sasha's expression was of awe, but quickly devoured by a glint of amusement.

"I always see to the High Prince," Lucia began to protest, but with one wave of Sasha's hand she was silenced.

"Let her do what she will, Lucia. For when my brother sends her fleeing from his chambers in tears, to us she will not come for comfort.

We have done all we could to spare her shame and embarrassment," Sasha replied airily.

"If indeed I need comfort, it will not be your arms I seek," Mia snapped.

"That's right." Sasha let out a derisive laugh. "I've almost forgotten about your priestess. Or that lusty stable warrior you cling too. He could fill the *void* my brother doesn't." She was referring to Horace.

"How dare you imply such things?" Mia challenged.

"Whatever do you mean?" Sasha rose from her seat and slithered over to her. Her face was pinched with false confusion, "I was merely stating the truth. I pity you and truly understand your need for intimate feelings. The fact still remains. You are married to my brother. He who cannot stomach you."

"Do not waste your pity on me, woman!" Mia balled her fists up.

"Angry are you?" Sasha laughed. "You have no reason to be. Honesty doesn't call for such measures."

Jacob swung open the door and stormed into the room. He bounced his head from Mia to his sister. Lucia swept into a curtsy.

"What is the bickering about?" he commanded. "The servants grow nervous."

"We weren't bickering, Brother," Sasha said sweetly. "We were just bantering, getting to know one another. Has the High Chaplain agreed to stay for the bonfires?" She quickly shifted the subject.

"Nay. He is gone—"

Ethane pushed by Jacob, her cheeks bright red, and went straight for the window. "Mamma, there's a carriage and large men outside our gates dressed in long black capes. The squire called on Uncle Jacobane and said that Prince Vastidrich wishes to be received!"

Mia's heart dropped and she found her hand clinging to the bed frame beside her. When her eyes met Sasha, the woman smiled with wicked pleasure.

"Bastard!" Jacob howled. "The nerve—"

"Jacobane, he is our nephew. It wouldn't look good to the people if we turn Aldrich's son away," Sasha encouraged him. "And do not speak so foully around the child. You might frighten her."

"Sister, I ask of you this one thing," Jacob whispered. "Receive him, for I will not be able to control myself before him. Find out what he wants and then send him on his way."

Sasha took hold of his hand, "We both know what he wants."

"I will prepare you for this eve's feast, my lord," Lucia offered obliviously.

"I have already told you, Lucia. I will tend to my husband and that is final!" Mia firmly took hold of Jacob's hand and guided him toward his personal chamber.

The chamber was oval with thick fur rugs and tapestries along the walls. The hearth was made from white granite that coordinated with the woolen blankets and curtains of his large bed. Mia took deep breaths before she plopped on the bed. She was terrified.

"You are my wife. I will not let him near you so swallow your fear." Jacob stood calmly before her, his head bent with irritation. Instantly, Mia darted into his arms not caring about his reaction. She squeezed him to her tightly and inhaled the musky scent of him into her gasping lungs. She absorbed his strength with each moment she clung to him. If there couldn't be love between them, Mia would be content enough to know that he would protect her. His big hands flailed at his sides before she felt them lightly encircle her. He stroked her hair and his breath was hot against her ear. His body vividly reacted from her before he placed distance between them.

"I will prepare you a bath," Mia said and he nodded his agreement.

"Then you must prepare yourself one as well. I will be fine on my own," he said. Mia looked to her feet with disappointment and rose to prepare his bath. She couldn't help but wish that they could one day try to be intimate again.

CHAPTER THIRTY

Secret

Vastadon strode with an arrogant lift of his chin into the hall bordered by a band of guards. He curled his lips as he took in the surroundings of the receiving hall. Sasha couldn't deny her half-blooded nephew's resplendence and exotic beauty, with flowing platinum hair and a smooth flawless face. He had the influence of seduction that made her question his need to rape her brother's wife. Perhaps the wench willed his body onto hers only to frantically claim rape later.

"Aunt, where is Jacobane?" he commanded removing his gloves.

"He and his wife are preparing to receive the Lord Emperor, nephew." Sasha smiled when he sneered.

"I see." He embraced her, placing a kiss on both sides of her cheek, "A pity, for they waste their time. My father cannot come but he has extended an invitation to Jacobane to come to Vhladic for Lugh Celebration."

"He was never to come, was he Vastidrich?" Sasha replied with a cynical smile.

"Senate has been called early because of the celebration. With only one week left until then, he has no other choice," He responded and took her hand in his. "Will you settle for my company instead?"

Sasha knew instantly that the spiteful boy had deliberately set it up. She allowed only a faint smile to cross her face. She wanted Mia in ruins, but she wished for nothing to disturb her brother. She eyed the guards and cast a glance over her shoulder to the gathering group including her wide-eyed children. Maire was the only one old enough to remember the face of her cousin. She gazed at him with a flattering eye.

So there is hope for my young daughter to act as a woman after all.

"Leave us!" She cut the air with a dismissing wave and then suggested. "Send your guards to the courtyard. Ale flows freely there and I'm sure that your men would enjoy some leisure before your leave."

Vastadon flicked two fingers and the guards were gone on command. He followed Sasha into the sitting area of the hall. He sat in a chair nearest to her seating and stretched his arms languidly above his head.

"I gather that you are satisfied with my company, then?"

"Of course not, nephew. Trouble follows you and it's usually directed towards Jacobane," Sasha grinned.

"Call him to me. I have come to see him, not you." He leaned forward smiling equally as wide.

"He has asked me to see exactly what you want. He does not welcome you here," Sasha paused. "Dare you lay with his wife!"

Vastadon laughed coldly, his eyes a pyre of blue madness. He darted to his feet and looked down his sharp nose at her.

"Did my uncle tell you that, until my vindictive father arranged this mock marriage, we were *involved?*" he said flatly, drinking in the look of surprise on his aunt's face. "Yes, Aunt, it's true. I took what rightfully belonged to me first."

"Had it been any other man, I wouldn't care. You stuck your uncle with damaged goods! Can you not stop this jealous gamesmanship with Jacobane? You always were in competition with him!" Sasha retorted darting to her feet.

"Father has always loved him best. Mia should've been my wife, but she will serve just as well as my mistress when I become Emperor."

"You have become very confidant, Vastidrich. If you believe your father loves Jacobane more, then who is to say he will not name *him* his successor." Sasha finally lost her frigid smile.

"Stranger things have happened," he said forebodingly.

"I hate that woman for the rift she has created! If there's a way you could take her from here and give Jacobane the freedom to marry a good Barbarian woman, I'd be pleased with you for once."

"Truly?" he scooped her hand up in his and tilted his head innocently—insanely.

"Of course!" she snapped and narrowed her eyes, "You are insane nephew. The Thaumaturi in you has eaten your brain."

"I believe her to carry my bastard," Vastadon smirked. "And I truly doubt my uncle could lust after her enough to bed her since *my* night. If she's with child, it's mine."

Sasha dropped into her seat, a hand fluttered to her neck. The realization of his words sunk in. If he did get Mia with child, it'd be much easier convincing Jacob to dissolve the marriage. He is loyal, but not foolish. A scandal could be avoided; a scandal that would surely shatter the private world Jacob had built around him.

"Call him, Aunt, and make sure she comes with him." Vastadon chucked her under the chin and strolled aimlessly away.

She went swiftly to retrieve her brother.

Jacob stormed down the stairs and flew into the hall. He held his breath and his spitting rage beneath the sneer on his face with the sight of the malicious man. Vastadon smiled and stretched his arms with mock warmth. "Uncle!"

"Your business!" Jacob thundered.

"Mia," he spat back at him craning his neck to see if Mia was present. "Where is she?"

"She has no desire to see you after what you've done to her," Jacob retorted. "State your business."

"Desire?" Vastadon smirked and fumbled with his flopping gloves. "What would you know about her desires? I gave her what she wanted. She was so delicious—"

Before Vastadon could speak another word, Jacob had the point of his sword aimed at his throat. "She is my wife regardless. I will not have you speak so of her!"

"Funny you've become protective of a woman you loathe," Vastadon snickered and with the same swiftness as his uncle, he unsheathed his own sword.

There was a clank of swords and they were both frozen, their weapons crossed in mid combat for endless minutes. Vastadon withdrew his weapon. He summoned a servant with the snap of his fingers and ordered her to retrieve his guards. "Farewell, Uncle. We shall meet again soon enough. Please give Mia my regards." He spun on his heels in a flurry of royal blue and disappeared behind a mass of guards.

Jacob sneered. He promised himself that the time to settle this feud would come. He hurled his sword on the floor and sauntered out of the hall passed all of his wide-eyed servants.

Janella felt a twinge when she dipped the tip of her finger into the well's water. Apprehension and discovery. She ran another finger across the circle of stones at her throat. They were warm beneath her touch, even Mia's opal that was embedded into the center of her medallion. Even the *emerald* was warm. The magic of the Goddess' Circle was at work. Relief and fear ebbed constantly everyday since their parting.

Danu had Whispered to her throughout her solitude in the caves about the capture of Diamond and the rescue at the hands of a foreigner who wore the crest of Falias. Danu allowed her a glimpse of his face. He had a likeness to the female contact she aligned herself with many moons ago.

Mina came one time, nearly a year before the Prophecy was determined to be flawed, concealed in dark robes. She was of no race Janella recognized, but she didn't question her. The woman had mentioned corruption in the heart of Vhladic and that when the time came she requested permission to call upon Janella's aid. She offered her services without any further explanation and Janella immediately accepted her alliance.

The Goddess willed it so. The woman had gifts, and for a moment Janella thought she could've been a stray Mageborn, but she quickly reminded herself of Danu's Whisper. Ten would be born, the last of Her Mageborn. Two would turn to the Power. Janella knew all of the Mageborn and to her knowledge, only one had rejected the Call to the Circle leaving one traitor to be determined. Her son. She gently glided a finger across her son's emerald gem again. Sadness flooded her. What would become of him?

Janella left out a weighing sigh and disrobed before the well. In order to see the world as she needed to see it, she would have to do this. Janella was no Mageborn, but she was blessed with great vision and was touched with the ability to hear the Goddess' Whispers. The elemental magic would come painful to her once she stepped into the Waters of the Wysteria Well. She was fearful, for it would take days to recover her strength after such a thing, but she grew impatient.

She lowered her head and placed her palms firmly together in the form of a steeple. She maneuvered her fingers into swift signs, drawing strength from the brightly lit sun. A hand snatched her around to face the vacant yard, interrupting the advanced spell. She quickly pulled her robe on and stepped away from the well. The wind whistled a small tune and the forest air was fragrant with a soft citrine scent.

They approach!

Danu's ethereal voice alerted her to attention. She quickly flew down into the sole cave entrance—the only means to reach her garden for sacred and cautious reasons—through the corridors of spitting torchlight.

Alabaster stepped in her path, his gentle face solemn. In his arms he carried Diamond in a bundle of wool. Janella gasped and sorrow swept through her.

"Follow me," she ordered.

She brought him to her quarters and motioned for him to place the girl gently on the chaise. She looked down upon the girl's face and frowned. Diamond was pale, her lips blue, and her eyes were nearly swollen shut.

Her chest rose and fell swiftly with labored breaths. She hadn't realized that she was so brutalized during her capture until this moment. She met eyes with Alabaster.

He raised his hand to his head and pointed to his temple.

"Her head?" Janella tried to understand, "She has been having pain in her head?"

He nodded vigorously. Janella went to her small round dresser and pulled out a sachet and emptied the *Rosmarinus* in a charcoal basin. She ignited a flame and said a silent prayer. She had hoped that the woody healing scent would penetrate Diamond enough to stir her from her disorientation.

Phoenix rushed in with Darius at his heels. Janella embraced them and craned her head. "Where is Cole?"

"He stayed behind to meet with Aunyia," Phoenix said quickly and crouched near his sister. "She's gotten worse since we reached land and we cannot understand why."

Janella placed a palm on her head. She had no fever. "It is in her brain, this sickness. Have you attempted Reading Magic on her, Phoenix?"

"This day, but I can't break through her mind. She rebels against me."

"She must rest. I will have my young apprentice see her to a warm herb sponge bath and nurse her some chamomile tea. In the morning, if she isn't well, I'll have no other choice but to seek out the Elders for their aid. It isn't something I will look forward to, but nothing matters more than my Diamond," Janella declared.

"They would do nothing but mock us!" Darius hissed.

"I will have no choice, Darius," Janella explained. "Now come and let's give her rest. We'll assemble into the dining quarter. I'm sure you're all very tired and hungry from your journey."

They followed her into the vacant cavern and explained the details of their discoveries while they ate.

"Sacrifices..." Janella repeated the word softly. "This entity is trying to violate the boundaries of the plains before the Solar Eclipse!"

"You mean it can be done?" Darius questioned and took a long swig of wine.

"I imagine so, Darius. Demons have been sighted and this entity is clearly not of our plain, a god of some sort. What could this have to do with the foreign island of Sihoma? Gold is desired, but I do not think the Brotherhood would waste much time on it. There is something more there. But what?" Janella conversed with herself and paced the floor.

"Mina said the refugees will wait to attempt the freedom of her people until Barbarian Celebration of their Lugh God," Phoenix added.

"Yes, I think she is right. When will Cole return?" Janella asked them.

"He told us once he has informed Aunyia he will return here. He worries for Diamond," Phoenix answered and when he saw a small spark of interest flair in the High Priestess' eyes he added, "He also said he would bring back a report from Aunyia on how the Lady Mia is fairing."

"Very Good," Janella said appraisingly. "Then here is my plan." She clapped her hands together, "Upon Cole's return, in which I estimate to be about the start of Agustu Moon, and once he has rested from his journey, we will part into two separate missions. Alabaster your locating skills will be most needed to find this Sihoma. With Cole and Phoenix you are to go there and find out what the Brotherhood is desperately trying to conceal from their own Emperor," She paused.

The mention of Aldrich's title sent her dizzy with pain and longing. She had tried to shove him from her mind with her solitude and prayer, but Danu wouldn't grant her the ability to forget him. She loved him so much. Could he truly have known what he did? How, in his actions, he betrayed her?

"Very well," Phoenix brought her back from her thoughts.

"I don't think it wise to send Diamond back to Vhladic. Once she recuperates, she will remain here with me," Janella recovered. "Darius go to Miarosa at once."

The Mind Mage sneered and spun his back in swirl of ebony robes, "Priestess, is Horace not with her?"

Janella turned to the others and gave them a dismissing nod. This would be a conversation restricted between the two of them. Phoenix and Alabaster left swiftly, almost too easily. She could understand why.

"Horace will be leaving her soon to reunite with Aunyia. Miarosa will be left alone without a knight," Janella began.

"She has Sierra—who is *also* Mageborn—and do you not think she has become comfortable with her husband by now. He wouldn't welcome a Thaumaturi intruder, especially me. We had words," Darius spoke low.

"Have you caressed her magic? Linked to it as the others have?" Janella questioned.

"Not by choice," he grunted.

"What happened?" Janella pressed. "Hasn't it softened you to her?"

"No!" He spun, his face snarling. "It has hardened me to her. I work alone."

"I think there is more to it than that, Darius. I have been honest with you," Janella told him softly.

"There is nothing." He dismissed her with a wave of his hand.

"There is," she strode to him.

"There isn't," he impressed through clenched teeth.

"Stop hiding yourself behind this cold ward, Darius!" Janella snapped with command.

"It's better unsaid!"

"Tell me, I'm the only mother you have known! I want to comfort you, not grow angry," Janella pleaded

"You wanna know so damned badly?" Darius gripped her arms, "I saw your sister burn to death and I wasn't the only one. Your precious Miarosa stood among them, a child mesmerized and cold, uncaring to the death of *my mother!*"

Janella gasped and nearly crumbled to the ground. She would have had Darius not supported her by her elbow.

"My sister, burned..." tears stung her eyes, "Cassiandra."

"I didn't want you to hurt," he said breathlessly. "I couldn't hurt you so."

"She was your mother? I hadn't known she gave birth to a child," Janella cried and turned her teary eyes to Darius. "Why did you bear the burden of this all on your own. You could've told me anything."

"She tried to save me and got herself killed by doing so. She tried to save *her* too," He paused and clenched his fists. "*She* has lied to us from the beginning, Priestess. She isn't who she says she is."

"What are you saying?" Janella's eyes went wide.

"I'm saying that she is the daughter of your sister!" Darius hissed.

"*Your* sister?" Janella exclaimed. "My niece?"

"Yes! She was nearly five when our mother was murdered before her eyes. There's no way she could forget something like that!"

Janella wrapped her arms around him and held him close. She needed to comfort him to ease her own pain. She always knew that her sister was murdered. It was instinctive knowledge. But she did not, *couldn not* imagine her dying such a cruel and brutal death. To be burned alive, no escape, slowly...Janella slammed her eyes shut and pain and grief slammed into her.

"I am so sorry," she cooed in her own silent tears, "Oh, my foster son, my nephew..."

"She told me of the Fall King with love in her eyes and he was the first man I went to. She told me how he was wondrous and loving. She loved him truly and she was ripped away from him to marry that monster." he whispered.

"Valance," his name drifted from her lips like a floating rain cloud.

"Aye. And he's everything she said he was. I couldn't tell him. I couldn't hurt him with word of her murder."

"We *must* tell him." Janella spoke urgently. "He would never shut you out! He would love you still!"

"He has loved me as a son and he doesn't even know the truth," Darius said sadly. "I'm not ready to pain him so. Not yet. I must figure things out first."

"I understand," Janella replied reluctantly.

Darius was much more advanced than she already gave him credit for. The magic of his Mind shut even Valance away from the truth. Valance who could swim within any mind and snatch whatever information he wanted couldn't penetrate this Mind Mage's wards.

"It's possible that Mia didn't know the truth. Merle is wicked and manipulating. You must give her a chance to explain. She is your sister. If only my own sister still lived, by Danu, I would give her that chance," Janella pleaded. "You must lower your walls."

After several heartbeats he nodded, "I shall try. I'll travel as you have asked me, but allow me to meet up with Aunyia and Cole in Vhladic before I go to her. I need to know what I am walking into there."

"Very well," Janella replied and was satisfied that he agreed to go at all.

Janella knew it wouldn't be easy for him, but at least the weight of such a mystery was lifted from both of their shoulders. Janella wouldn't let Cassiandra's murder go in vain.

Mia wandered into the lily garden through the twilight. She felt drawn to the water of the river. She was disappointed that Aldrich didn't come because she missed his smiling face and she secretly hoped that Aunyia would've accompanied him.

"My lady."

Mia jumped and spun on her heals to the deep voice that haunted her dreams for the past two Moons.

Vastadon.

She had thought him to be gone as Sasha had said. Yet he was there, staring at her with his amused ice-blue eyes, his waxen face loose with eccentric calm. He was gathered within the folds of a royal blue cowl that sloped down into an imperial adorned cape. A deceptively modest torque garnished beneath the pale moonlight. Even from within a circle of five feet she could smell the musky scent of him. And it mingled with the sulfur stench of his magic. She couldn't forget the sweet and poisonous smell of him. At one time she welcomed it, but now it sent chills adrift beneath her skin.

She took a withdrawing step ignorant to the river bank behind her. She would sooner face the white rifts of the rushing river than to fall prey to this man again. He tilted his head and lifted the corners of his mouth into a grin.

"It has been too long. I have missed you so." He spoke as if he was trapped in a memory prior to his actions when they had once found love between them.

"Dare you speak so to me!" Mia snapped. "Do not come any closer!"

Her whipping words halted his approach and his childlike expression faded into a painful sneer.

"You don't mean what you say," He hissed. "My uncle has poisoned you against me. But he will no longer be able to come between us. I'm here now and have come to take you away. We'll go to Vhladic where it will be safe for the two of us."

She felt the fingers of his magic brush her cheeks and slink into her ears. It spiraled up into her mind. Sensations too varied, too contradictory to assimilate, flashed through her muscles, across her skin.

Mia closed her eyes tightly and focused on energy. The river behind her rumbled and splashed against her back as she drew her magic from its waters. A fresh liquid devoured her form, weaving threw her veins and into her mind washing his spell away. She opened her eyes again. Her spanned out hands radiated a soft sapphire aura. She jerked her head back up and met eyes with her enemy triumphantly.

"Don't try to brain wash me with your dark incantations. I am much stronger than the victim you last violated. Now leave my dwelling at once," She said proudly.

Vastadon didn't look alarmed or even the least bit surprised by her actions. He laughed lowly and clapped his hands with mock appreciation. "You have come into your own. I knew that you would one day. You cannot blame a man for trying to rekindle the pure pleasure he once held within the arms of a whore!"

Mia darted toward him, and grasped his throat with all of her strength. He clamped a hand down on her grip and weaved symbols with his fingers. She gasped all of the air into her lungs when her hand burned. She held on as long as she could before coiling her hand back. She inspected her fingers and noticed they were undamaged from whatever inflicted pain on her.

He snatched her around the back of her neck and pulled her hard against him.

"Don't worry, if you wish to remain a useless puppet to my uncle, so be it. But I want my child, wench! That is what I've come for," he snarled.

A blast of light exploded from within her as she called upon the waters again. She tossed her hands outward flinging him from her.

"Your pitiful seed didn't have enough time to get me with child. I killed the rampant demon before it had a chance to grow!" she bellowed the lie down into his furious face.

"You lie!" he hissed.

"I would sooner die than conceive a child with you!" she spat and walked away. She knew she was taking a big risk turning her back on him, but she could no longer stand the sight of him. She felt heat on her back and red threads of light laced into the darkness beyond her.

She looked over her shoulder and saw that Vastadon was no longer there.

CHAPTER THIRTY-ONE

The Bond

"We have enough problems," Sasha hissed beneath the crackling flames of the bonfire.

Jacob consumed much ale and his mind was swimming with thoughts he'd rather ignore. Vastadon's deliberate appearance ignited something so fearsome within in him that it took all of his highly skilled control to keep him from beheading the bastard. And Vastadon *knew* it. His nephew wouldn't stop this jealous rampage. Competition. Vastadon constantly competed with him. Though it became tedious at times, Jacob could overlook it. That was until Vastadon violated Mia. She who was his wife innocent to the choices Aldrich made.

Sasha poked him impatiently drawing him back to the serenity of the night and the quiet leisure he and his sister shared by their lonesome away from the festivities. The villagers and the servants surrounded the pavilions and the blazing fires far enough away.

"Did you hear anything I said?" Sasha frowned.

Jacob hardly did but he nodded and said, "Go on."

"Vastidrich will not stop this time, Jacobane. I saw it in his eyes." Sasha shook her head, "Is there no other way to dissolve this marriage?"

"Aldrich will not have it. And I told you, she is no longer a maiden." Jacob rubbed his eyes and pushed forward. "I cannot change that now."

"That's absolutely fabulous of you except you weren't the one who relieved her maidenhead!" Sasha tossed her hands in the air and let them fall onto her legs with a smack. "Besides, I see her with the *magician* quite often *sparring*. Perhaps he would have her regardless, although I don't see what is so appealing about her. She is fragile, her witchy eyes are so ugly, and that hair…a *magician* with hair so gold, you would think it was a trick of light. And don't you find it odd that she has taken an interest in sword fighting?"

"Perhaps she wishes to know how to defend herself," Jacob replied gruffly. "How am I to know?"

"I don't trust her and I don't like her. She should've been married to Vastidrich. Maybe his marriage vows could also be dissolved and then yours. You know he wouldn't mind," Sasha rambled on.

"I would see her home to her eccentric family, a spinster for all time, before I'd allow her to be taken up by that man. I actually feel sorry for the arrogant aristocrat he married," Jacob responded quickly.

Sasha frowned and fluttered to Jacob's side. She placed a gentle hand on his broad shoulder and whispered, "You cannot let her go because you don't *want* to let her go. She has bewitched you and it's my duty as your sister to protect you from her wily ways."

"I assure you that I need no one's protection." Jacob laughed at his sister's over paranoid way of thinking. Could she be right? How could he even dare to care about what would happen to Mia if by some chance the marriage was annulled? Sasha kissed his cheek in the way his mother used to when he was a child. Memories and rage turned his skin into knots. He darted to his feet with aggravation.

"Did you have sex with her?" Sasha asked.

"Sex isn't something I wish to speak with my sister about," he retorted, but in his response, his clever sister would have the answer she sought.

"You did!" she snapped. "That explains it. You are repulsed by her, yet you fornicated with her. She has cursed you!"

Before Jacob could reply, Mia flew across the garden and jump into Sasha's face. His sister took a retreating step away and scowled.

"I've done nothing to you, Sasha! Yet you insult me constantly!" Mia spat.

"You are a witch. You best stay away from me and my children!" Sasha cringed.

"And you are a whore, but I don't constantly call you one!" Mia snapped.

Sasha gasped and shoved her hard. Mia faltered but didn't lose her balance. She tightened her jaw and lunged at her. They tumbled to the ground in a tangled mess of hair pulling, scratching and kicking. Jacob snatched them apart and glowered at Mia.

It was the last straw and despite Mia's self-satisfaction with the Power she conjured on her own to fight against Vastadon, her good mood was shredded with Sasha's incite to Jacob. Mia tore herself away from her husband's clutch and strode into the garden. She couldn't be so near to Sasha. She was afraid she might attack her again. Oh, how she longed to see the look on Sasha's face had she unleashed a small amount of the magic that was flowing profusely through her. Mia scowled when she saw Jacob embracing her in supportive arms while she spilled her tears of poison.

Damn her.

The woman had the nerve to insinuate infidelity and now she bent Jacob's ear to ridiculous accusations of curses. Soon Sasha left him alone and fled to her comforts and scheming. He turned on her and sneered. He was going to take his sister's side. Mia could see it in his eyes.

"How dare you speak cruelly to my sister!" Jacob stormed over to her. Mia nearly laughed aloud at the irony of his words.

"And what about the things she calls me? You allow her to treat me as if I'm nothing. Yet you blame me when I am quick for the first time to defend myself!" Mia cried.

"She has tried. You must remember that your—our marriage has been a shock to my people including my sister!" Jacob grabbed her by her elbows.

She nearly went limp and she caught a gasp before it escaped. It wasn't a reaction of fear, or pain. He scarcely touched her since the night of their lovemaking. The sensation was quickly erased when she thought of how his sister deceived him so well.

"She has never tried, Jacob. And she never will. She finds pleasure in goading me especially with Lucia," Mia grimaced.

"Lucia has nothing to do with this little display!" He spun his back on her, "You always put her into this."

Jealousy sharpened her tongue and bitterness consumed her. He always defended Lucia too, *always!*

"Just because she is your lover, it doesn't place her above me. I'm your wife and High Princess here." Mia's words of ice slowly spun him around.

His eyes were alight with mystery and he didn't allow them to connect with hers long enough for her to decipher his thoughts. "You speak of things you know nothing about."

"I know plenty about it," Mia controlled her voice. "The servants talk and it is she who comforts you in your private chamber every single night."

Anger came because she willed it. Anger would destroy the threatening tears and mask pain from invading her face. He was made of stone and it showed in his posture and on his face. Could nothing hurt this man?

"You resort to gossiping with the servants now?" He raised an eyebrow.

"Have your lover! I have said it before and I don't care, but it is all going to change! I'll not allow your sister to bully me anymore and I will not stand for a servant treating me as if I am knave."

It killed her, but what good would it do to allow him a glance at her weakness. He devoured her weaknesses and enjoyed them. He always did and she was foolish to think that would change now.

"Watch your attitude with me. This is my land and my people. Not yours," he replied coldly.

"Goddess forbid if I threaten your *poor* woman," Mia lifted her chin. "Perhaps it was she you imagined when we slept together. Perhaps it is why you could even bear to touch me."

"What of you? You cannot seem to forget your old lover. I am beginning to wonder if you welcomed him on our wedding night!" He spat bitterly.

She drew in her breath painfully. Better he had struck her than that. "You are a bitter man."

She could mask her face with a sneer but she couldn't hide the pain in her eyes that he inflicted with his brutal remark. She spun on her heels and left him alone. His drunkenness was no justification although she tried pitifully to grasp it as an excuse. She hated him and she was a fool to have come here. It was too painful.

The bonfires blazed and the people sang and danced maniacally to the flutes and drums. The night was enchanting yet she didn't want to be part of the celebration. She had no plans to return to the dwelling just yet. She went in flight to the place where she knew she would find someone who cared for her.

Horace crouched low beneath an oak tree before the river bank, his head bent in trance or prayer. Mia couldn't tell. He looked up and with the sight of her, he lifted to his feet urgently. Wordlessly, she approached him. His hazel eyes spit a concern so deep, it made Mia gasp. Without even a touch, she felt his hands on her body. Her desire to be in his arms burned too deeply for such contact. She placed a hand on his cheek and stroked it as if her fingers were a feather. He would be going in two days. Leaving her alone in this cold place. Could he not see how he made her feel?

"Mia—" He began to protest in a breathless whisper.

She silenced him with a sliding finger across his lips. She tilted her head up and studied every spot she stroked; her body was on fire with yearning. He made her pain and sorrow go away. All of it gone in a gusty wind.

She worked her fingers around to the nape of his neck and pulled his kiss deep into her mouth. She drank from his sweet soft lips caring about nothing else in the world and he returned it equally passionate. His hands flew up to her waist, pressing his form against her.

Something was wrong about it. It was so wrong, yet so powerful.

He broke the kiss and when she opened her eyes. The magic of her desires was gone.

"What is happening between us, Horace?" Mia cried.

"Magic." He took hold of her hand and guided her to the bank. "Magic to desire. Even the most hopeless can desire around me. Of course, being that I am an Emissary, it can be very useful." He embraced her shoulder, "You see, Mia, you were so sad. I wanted to help you so I let my ward down before you. I wanted to give you hope, and a happiness you never knew as a child. Instead it went beyond a child's affection. We love each other, but it's much different than passion between lovers. I needed to show you the truth of your heart."

"Something terrible happened before I came here," Mia whispered.

"I know now," Horace said. "But you love *him*. You need his love to heal."

"That is absurd!" Mia scowled. "He is cruel."

"How do you know of whom I speak?" Horace smirked leaving her speechless. "Although we are not the Bond, I feel so close to you. You cannot lie to me."

"The Bond?" Mia sniffed in hopes to change the subject. "What is that nonsense?"

"The Bond is a ribbon of Power shared between two Mageborns. It's a force that is undeniably strong and it connects the two for life, in all our lives. Aunyia is my Bond," Horace said.

"You love her?" Mia questioned. A day ago the news would've disappointed her, but on this night it sparked her curiosity. She was relieved that she didn't feel the temptation any longer.

"Very much. It was so even before the Bond was recognized. You don't have to even like each other to be Bonded."

Mia remembered someone who she didn't like, but the feel of his magic swept across her like no other. Darius.

"Your husband is guarded, not cold. He is confused because, for his entire life, he believed in his father's counsel to loathe our kind. In order to protect himself he becomes cold. You must break through to him. He is for you," Horace whispered.

"You are fond of him, aren't you?" Mia jested. "Despite the animosity."

"It is only because I know where it's coming from," he laughed.

They remained for a little while longer talking aimlessly, but Horace was growing sleepy. Mia knew he stayed to be with her, yet she wasn't tired. She bid him goodnight anyhow so that he may find his bed.

The fires were low and people were winding down from the nights festivities. The music slowed into a drunken hum. The hills and courtyard were nearly empty. The weight of fatigue finally reached her so she decided to turn in. Before she retired to her chamber, she glanced at Jacob's door. For a moment she contemplated entering, but decided to let the truth of her heart settle before she braved to tell him how she felt, or how she didn't feel. It was all too confusing. How could one hate and love someone at the same time? Mia didn't think it was possible and she wouldn't leave herself open to more heartache.

She sighed heavily and went to her chamber.

Their aspect was terrifying…Men, very tall, with swelling muscles under lucid white skin gathered in a motionless mass. Cacophonous horns were sounded, deep and harsh voices rumbled from the hills. They beat their swords steadily against their shields.

They charged bathed in blood.

Mia leaped from a pool of sweat soaked sheets. Her heart pounded beneath her breast so hard that she clutched her chest.

The prophecies have come to pass.

She shivered within her blanket. She tried to shake the haziness and clamminess from her form, but it wouldn't cease.

The seed of battle has been planted. You must remain vigilant now.

Something came to pass, for sure, and it wasn't of good.

"Come," Lucia called from behind the door. "We have a messenger."

Many of Jacob's men had already gathered in the hall by the time she arrived. A young boy, about ten years old, stood before Jacob, his face ashen and his eyes wide. Jacob studied him with intensity, or maybe concern. As Mia walked further into the receiving room, she noticed something red and jagged held within the trembling fist of the child.

"What has happened?" Mia asked nervously.

The boy bowed lowly before her, and nearly burst into tears. She ran to the child's side and embraced him.

"A man, I couldn't see his face. He gave this to me and said that I should give it to the Prince," The boy stuttered. "He told me he was an Elder. He said the Lady must leave and that the High Prince must go to the imperial city for protection."

"An Elder, here?" Mia scoffed.

Jacob fixed his cold gaze on her and stepped down from his throne. He took hold of the red object and tossed it at her feet. She looked down to see a thorn made from wood drenched with blood, the letter "G" carved on its side.

Mia jumped back from it and looked up at Jacob worriedly. He could scarcely look at her before he stormed off.

Just as he reached the door he turned and said, "The Gravens have declared war on us. No longer will the wall be sustained on their behalf."

He then wheeled and exploded through the doors. Mia gasped. She was no fool and knew the cause of such a war. She lunged after him with the force of her regrets, but a hand grabbed her arm and spun her about.

"You are the last thing he wants to see right now. Let him go," Sasha said coldly.

"I will see to my husband," Mia ripped her arm from the wicked woman's grip and followed his path.

"You have done this," Sasha called after her. "You have destroyed everything he worked so hard for."

Mia ignored Sasha in her flight, but she knew that the wench wasn't entirely wrong. She ran through the kitchens and out the back door toward the courtyard.

Jacob was leaning against the stone portico wall. Pain swelled within her and regret. She needed to make him see that she was sorry. He was so unreachable and ignorant to…. To what? It mattered not, because she would do what she could to salvage the situation.

The Tribes had reason to declare battle. Jacob had silenced them with his treaties of trade and hunting weapons, but to them, he knew that they felt somehow betrayed when he brought a Thaumaturi home as his wife. It was only a matter of time before they found out. And how could he not weigh out the consequences. He did such an outlandish thing for his brother, his emperor, who he protected from the very tribes beyond the wall. Jacob wouldn't leave Vansant Summit for dead. If they were to endure such a battle, he would stand right along with them and lead them as a prince should do for his people.

Damn you, Aldrich, what have you done?

Jacob slammed his fist into the stone wall. The pain didn't come as he wished. He was numb, hardened into a man who was made from rock. Nothing could penetrate the man he molded himself to be. Only the nearness of her...the girl would have to go. He should not release her, for this damned war started because of his union with her, but he knew he would send her as far away from this place as he could. She had reached a part within him so well hidden that he wasn't sure it existed. How foolish of him to let a woman affect him so, a Thaumaturi no less.

"I do not wish to see you troubled, my lord."

Jacob glanced over his shoulder at his wife. He was so engrossed in his thoughts that he had not heard her approach.

"What wouldn't trouble me with such news? Thaumaturi are unwelcome here and beyond the wall alike."

"I know that I have been the cause of all this, please. Tell me what I can do to prevent this battle," her voice cracked.

He sneered at her, "You've done enough."

She snapped her head back as if he had struck her, though she didn't fight back with her own cold words. Her eyes welled up, a sight he seldom saw lately, but she fought each teardrop back behind the shield of her eyelids.

"I deserved that," she replied softly.

In his mind he knew that he was just as much at fault, if not more than she. It wouldn't be right to place the entire burden of blame on her, yet he didn't speak of it.

"You've been hurt or betrayed perhaps," Mia asked abruptly, her eyes painfully honest.

He could never meet her gaze. It singed him to do so. He turned his back to her, and prayed to the Gods she wouldn't see through him.

"You've mistaken me for one who would allow such a thing to happen," he replied.

"Was it a woman or a Thaumaturi?" Mia continued as if she ignored his answer.

"Girl, the seer isn't strong with you, so do not assume," he retorted with annoyance.

"I'm not claiming to have such gifts. I just—I want to—" she broke off.

"Do not," Jacob held his hand up.

For a moment, he glimpsed at her profile. Her golden hair was bound in a ringlet of curls that fell languidly across her face. He could see the smooth curve of her neck. She was hurt by his coldness, and he somehow wished she wasn't. Desire for her welled inside of him and it was as commanding as his duty to protect his people. It couldn't be so. A distraction such as this would weaken him and his weakness could bring forth a certain loss to the hands of the rebellious war party headed in this direction. If the Senate has their way, the city of Vhladic would most likely abandon him to his own demise. He wouldn't run to hide beneath his brother's robe while his land was ravaged and burned to the ground.

She must've felt the heat of his gaze, because she spun to face him. Her wide perfectly shaped eyes bore into him. He was steadied a moment, returning her gander with a bewildered look of his own.

"I fear for you." She plucked a yellow blossom from the tree beside her. He had a sudden urge to take her into his embrace. He restrained himself.

"Don't fear for me. I can take care of myself," he joined his hands behind his back to assure his restraint, "You must leave now that the Elders have inquired about your safety. I will arrange for transport immediately. I promised your people on the day I married you, that no harm would come to you."

"You would hold true to your vow with such people, the people you loathe?" Mia asked incredulously.

"I'm a man of my word."

"I will not go. I would be no safer in their hands," Mia scowled. "I'd rather die here in the most brutal way than submit myself to them."

"You speak ill of your holy ones?" Jacob strode ahead of her and looked to the sky. It was the color of crimson and gold. It was a sign and a promise to the fate of his dwelling.

"They aren't holy. They are no more than greedy animals. I honor the

322

Goddess, yes, and respect the Brosia Ministry, but the Elders have no right to hold themselves above us," Mia said bitterly.

The words she spoke stirred him. How confusing this woman was. Everything he despised, yet he couldn't ignore the alluring force that drew him to her. She spoke openly about her anger towards her own people, yet he understood nothing of her reasons. The only thing he knew for sure was that he didn't want harm to come to her. Even in the days of his confinement in her world, where he guarded her from the dangers all around. It would've been so easy to allow her harm. Her family wouldn't have cared in spite of how possessive and concerned they appeared to be.

"If war is upon us, you'll go home to your country with the proper escort," Jacob said with finality.

The sound of rustling reached his ears and he could feel her breath upon his back. The smell of her was everywhere, taunting him. She was too near...

"How certain is this attack? You don't know for sure. Maintain communication with them," Mia cried desperately. "Don't let them take me. Vow to *me*, your wife, that you will not let them take me."

Her palm pressed against his back along with the tickle of her hair and the softness of her cheek. A shudder passed through him and he stepped away from her clutch. She quickly placed herself before him, her face alight with fear. He looked down upon her face with cold shifting eyes, a mask of definiteness until she frowned and stomped off.

Jacob let all of the air out of lungs once she was gone. Perhaps she had a point when she mentioned communication. He retreated into his dwelling and called to his first warrior Jovich once he reached the entrance hall. Moments later the husky man was greeting him with a small bow. He signaled for his warrior to follow him out to the stables.

"What is it?" Jovich asked more casually when they were alone.

"Ride with me out to the wall. I'm sure Erikrates is on the look out for us now that the Gravens have made their point clear."

Jovich nodded and after the horses were prepared, the two men charged through the gates and over the hills along the forest edge. The moment they reached the gathering spot, Erikrates, buried beneath a mass of silver braided hair, came to greet them urgently. Jacob dismounted while Jovich remained a good distance to give Jacob privacy.

Jacob grasped his old friend's hand tightly and pulled him into a warriors embrace. He had known Erikrates since he was an adolescent. It was because of his quick attachment to the Clawclan Wise Man that gained him some of the Tribes favor. The man was as close as kin to Jacob and he respected him unyieldingly.

"It wasn't I who exposed your person, my friend," Erikrates said in a hoarse voice.

"I know, friend. The thought never crossed my mind. Tell me. Is there any way to salvage this?" Jacob rubbed his chin vigorously.

"I don't know. The Clawclan wasn't happy about your choices, but they don't want part in the attack," Erikrates replied. "But they will not interfere either."

"So there will be an attack, then?" Jacob folded his arms across his chest flexing his tense muscles.

"There has been talk about an attack but I haven't heard definite details," Erikrates drew a raspy breath in and lowered himself on a nearby rock. "The only way to satisfy the aligned Tribes is to give the girl up. Perhaps they will better aid the wall against the Tuskans once again if you implore your brother to annul the marriage."

Jacob growled and turned his back. "There is no other way?"

"I can attempt to reason with them, but it is unlikely they will accept a Thaumaturi as High Princess," Erikrates paused for a moment. "You seem disappointed with your option. I would think you eager to use these threats to an advantage with your brother."

"It isn't that," Jacob replied quickly and faced the man. "To annul the marriage would give her no chance in her country. She would never again be matched."

"So it's about an attachment to her." The old man smiled and his blue eyes glittered with knowing.

"It is about honor. Nothing more," Jacob grimaced.

"Ah," he said in his wise tone, "Then if it is about honor, an annulment would save your people from bloodshed. If that act alone does not display honor then I couldn't know what would."

Jacob didn't respond. Erikrates was right. So why didn't he just do it? How could he not? He felt strange inside with either decision. Why did he cling to her when he should not even give a damn? The Thaumaturi were not his problem including her. Set her free already. She is a princess in her country. Of course she could be matched again.

"Your advice is wise," Jacob responded.

"I hear a 'but' coming." Erikrates smiled again as if he knew some big secret no one else in the world knew.

"No 'but'. I am agreeing with you," Jacob answered dryly.

"It is alright you know, my friend. Love is confusing and sometimes you do not even know you have it until a moment comes along where it could be ripped from you." Erikrates placed a hand on Jacob's shoulder.

"Nothing like that!" Jacob snapped. "I love my people and she is part of my people now. She, like all of the others, depends on me to protect her. I cannot turn my back."

"I understand." Erikrates clapped his hands together. "I'll see what I can do for you. I'd say you have at least until the end of Septembre Moon before they would assemble an attack. In the meantime, go see your brother. See what he has to say on the matter. Think on your decision."

"The Tuskans," Jacob questioned quickly to change the subject. "Have they learned of my marriage?"

"I'm not certain. The Tusk Tribe has been withdrawn from the other Tribes. There is something strange going on in their parts. Some say they have come into magic ironically, but you and I both know that is ridiculous gossip. They are up to something nonetheless."

"Okay, friend," Jacob nodded, "Do what you can."

"I will and meet me here in two days so that I can inform you of what I accomplished." Erikrates embraced Jacob.

They parted ways. Although it wasn't completely settled, Jacob was pleased with the hopes of resolve. His wife was clever and with her clear minded advice, he had just bought them some time.

CHAPTER THIRTY-TWO

Vision of Death

Twilight fell swiftly. Mia sat beyond the dwelling within the lake tent deep in thought. She wasn't ignorant to the Elders' intentions, and she owed her knowledge to Horace. She would never go with them.

Jacob wanted to rid himself of her, and how could she blame him. She would leave, if indeed that was what he truly wanted, but she would go on her own terms. Arabella would be eager to take her in, and that would be the first place she went *if* she left.

"My lady."

Mia didn't need to turn around to know who had called on her. It was the voice of the driving force in her home, in her life, in her marriage.

"What is it, Lucia?" Mia replied with strained patience.

Lucia made a small breathing noise between a growl and a sigh. Her skirts ruffled and she was before Mia. She was hooded, but her face wasn't veiled as all servant women were in Falias upon leaving the palace. Her almond eyes flashed underneath the moonlight and her smile was straight and frozen. She drew back her hood.

"If I may have a moment of your time, I would like to speak with you about some concerns. You see," Lucia continued without any care to hear

Mia's response in defiance of her true status in Vansant Summit, "I am concerned about the High Prince. He needs an heir, only he has yet to get you with child."

Mia turned her eyes on Lucia aghast at the way this woman spoke so freely about things servants had no business meddling in.

"What gives you the right?" Mia asked coldly.

Lucia flinched, "Whatever do you mean, my lady?"

Mia sighed and stood, turning away so that she couldn't see the gleaming hatred Lucia tried so hard to conceal. She poked her head between the drapes of the tent and stared up at the waning moon. Twilight was dying into the chasm of a new hour and it sent a refreshing breeze in between the crease of the trees. What could she say to this lecherous woman?

That my husband hasn't even the stomach to bed me? That he cannot even look into my eyes for even a moment's time?

"I have no answer for you, Lucia." Mia replied to the warm night's wind.

"I know that it isn't your fault," Lucia said quickly and laid a gentle hand upon Mia's shoulder. The skin in which Lucia touched tensed. There was something more than console in her tone of voice. It was traced with pity. Mia's lip curled bitterly at the notion

"For some women, it takes years to conceive. If they conceive at all," Lucia began in that soft voice, "And, Gods forbid, you could've been damaged from the rape…"

Mia wheeled about and looked at Lucia viciously. Lucia stepped back quickly.

"How did you know about that?"

"I haven't told anyone else about it!" Lucia drew her head back defensively.

Mia snatched Lucia's sleeve and pulled her closer. "Who told you?"

The feel of his body crushing down onto hers, the power of his hold and the pounding fist against her face seized her again when Lucia said those words. The memory of the pain he inflicted on her countenance and the flesh he tore as he impaled her ached in her heart.

I will find you, Mia. No matter the case. You were mine first.

His promises and threats were spoken as if he were a Demon. And he did come as he promised, in a ball of insane fire. Yet her triumphant display of Power against him didn't change the nightmares. He would come again. Mia shook her head free of the memories and then focused her eyes on Lucia. The woman was pale and her eyes lost the arrogance they held only moments ago.

"Who told you?" Mia asked again forcing the trembling from her voice.

"The High Prince confides many of his secrets in me," Lucia replied flatly.

"He did?" Mia asked in a whisper.

Lucia nodded slowly. Mia released her hold on her and returned to the chaise, slowly drifting down into it as if she were a dove's feather fluttering to the green brush of the forest. She was angry and sad and hurt all at once. The feelings were so overwhelming that she didn't know which emotion affected her the most.

Only those of the royal family were informed of that rape. Now, of all, people, he has decided to tell her, *her*!

Lucia took a seat beside her, and for several moments, they remained silent.

Mia was certain Jacob took Lucia to his bed while he was bound to their marriage, although he didn't speak on it with her. After all, he was a man, and men needed the feel of a woman. And the betrothal was something neither of them wanted.

The spawn of war.

"Perhaps I come off worse than what I intend, my lady," Lucia interrupted the silence. "I know you are so unhappy here. You have no one here, and a husband who is resentful to the fact that he was ordered into this union. He doesn't hide his loathe for your kind well. He cannot even bear the thought of weakening his Barbarian blood by getting you with child. It must make you feel like an outcast."

"You love him," Mia said distantly and when no answer came, Mia shifted her glance to Lucia. "Before I came, that is."

"Everyone loves him," Lucia replied edgily.

"Did he love you too?" Mia asked suddenly feeling a trickle of guilt.

Had this marriage taken away their chance for a loving life together? But even still, how could such a marriage between a High Prince and a servant sanctioned by the royals and the Barbarian Gods' Chaplains? Perhaps it was the reason Jacob didn't marry in the first place. No, she chooses to serve Jacob, for she is a Chieftain's daughter...

Mia was working her lower lip and wringing her hands unconsciously waiting for her answer. Lucia let out a short shrill laugh.

"I'm afraid that our High Prince is incapable of loving one person with the full of his heart," Lucia huffed with a sort of bitter madness. "I thought you would've figured that out by now!"

Mia nodded, but she was washed over with a relief that went deeper than the guilt of two broken lovers. Lucia darted from her seat and drifted to the wavering drapes.

"He is good to his people," Mia agreed.

"I've come to plead for your consent. You and I both know that the prince wants a full-blooded barbarian heir. I can give him that. You can't. Perhaps he would fancy the idea if you permitted it," Lucia said quickly.

Mia's heart sank. Suddenly a feeling of unworthiness came upon her. She was sure that Jacob would agree, but jealousy was spreading through her veins like poison. Lucia was right. A child from their union would never be. How could she deny him this chance. She owed him that much.

"You may ask him only once, Lucia. If he refuses, I want nothing more said on the matter," Mia ordered.

"And if he consents?" Lucia asked ill-concealing her excitement.

"If he consents, let it be done tonight. And I shall leave your mothering to you and leave this place the moment it's done," Mia answered frigidly and undid the clasp of her necklace. She stared at it for a moment, remembering the day Jacob had given it to her. The tiny jagged object felt heavy in the palm of her hand.

A thorn shared between two. The thorn in their sides.

Mia reached her hand behind her and dropped the necklace in Lucia's open palm. "So that he knows I consent."

Lucia nodded, quickly kissing Mia's hand showing the first sign of respect since she arrived at Vansant Summit, and sprinted to the main house.

When Mia was sure she was alone, she lowered her head and wept.

An hour past when Lucia finally returned. She was smiling, nestled inside of a silk sheet. The servant nodded hastily and left as swiftly as she came. Mia rose a few minutes after, and prepared to leave Vansant Summit for a long time.

A cold hand clutched Jacob, waking him from his sleep. His eyes darted about the room as he grabbed the hilt of his sword. Nothing was there. The shadows of the dancing drapes formed haunting images on the wall before him, and the wind whistled. He smirked and eased his grip on his weapon.

"Blasted wind."

Save her...

The voice was soft and distant, almost convincing him that he had not heard it all. But he knew he did. Suddenly Mia's face entered his mind. He swung himself out of bed when he saw something gleaming from the corner of his eye on the small table beside him. He reached out and grabbed the object. It was the necklace he had given to his wife on their wedding day. His mother's necklace before her, the prickly gold thorn.

The doors flung open and the veiled woman, Sierra, look at him with green eyes of utter terror.

"She is gone," she cried. "She has taken with her my Earth Crystal."

"I know," he surprised even himself when he darted up and followed her out of his chamber. "I have a feeling I know just the person to tell us were she has gone."

Jacob strode past Sierra and sprint down the stairs out the front door into the bite of the stormy wind. He circled the back of the main dwelling into the stables. Just as Jacob suspected, Horace, the *magician* who refused to leave Vansant Summit, slept peacefully in the hay. With great force, Jacob grabbed the neck of his robe and pulled him to his feet. The Thaumaturi awoke with a shudder and instinctively reached for any weapon he could retrieve.

"Do not bother!" Jacob bellowed.

The little priestess clung to Jacob's massive arm pleading, for him to release the Thaumaturi. But his anger was too great, and possibly something else inside of him awaited the moment he would have cause to confront the man who spent too much time with his wife.

"Where is she?" he growled.

"What are you talking about?" Horace asked with annoyance.

"Do not play with me," Jacob threatened.

"I have no idea what you are talking about." Horace replied his own voice angered.

"I'll kill you!" Jacob hissed and reached for his sword.

Sierra stilled Jacob's hand and said, "If you kill him, you will start another war, my lord! He is one with the Goddess' Circle!"

Jacob's scowl didn't leave his face, but he released Horace and his hilt quickly. He knew how the Thaumaturi valued their superstitions and he knew a war would indeed be started with the death of one like him. Another war was something Vansant Summit didn't need now, although he wanted so much to rid himself of this interfering *magician*.

"Mia has gone, Horace!" Sierra exclaimed clutching at Horace's robe. "You must go with the prince and help him find her."

Jacob couldn't ever remember seeing the priestess so fearful and shaken.

Horace nodded. "Then we must go now, for rain is coming soon. She will get ill if we do not find her."

The two men gathered a few weapons, men, and horses. Then they flew into the night like phantoms to find the princess.

It was inky-dark and a gentle mist of rain blurred Mia's vision. The looming oak trees obscured the little bit of light the moon offered, so Mia ripped a branch from a passing tree limb and whispered a simple incantation she vaguely remembered to light the wood on fire. It wasn't the strongest magic she held, but it was a simple and helpful spell Sierra had taught her on their first voyage to Vansant Summit. She opened the rectangular door of the lantern she snagged from the pantry on her way out and lit it to provide some illumination.

A bird cried in the distance resounding above the normal nocturnal chorus that accompanied nightfall and it made the hairs on the back of her neck rise. She knew she was foolish to leave so hastily and without a guard, but she couldn't face Jacob in the morn after he lay with Lucia. She didn't want him to see the hurt in her eyes and risk the mock amusement he would surely have because of it. She hated him. She didn't want to marry him. So why did her insides betray her with such prevailing dread about leaving him.

An icy breeze crawled up her back, and her mare halted and shifted its legs back restlessly. Something was near, and it was watching her. Her breath became heavy and coils of smoke rose from her mouth and nose. In the humid heat of the summer rain, she was freezing, chattering teeth drummed behind her ears. Quickly, she tugged on the reigns and dropped a comforting hand to the mare's side.

"It is okay, girl. Just a few more steps before we can use the Earth Crystal and be gone from this cursed place." Mia whispered to the anxious beast as much as she whispered to herself. She had also snagged the Earth Crystal from Sierra and she had learned of it's power to teleport. She was not quite sure how to use it. She simply prayed that it would come to her.

The mare didn't calm, nor did the icy wind cease. Mia squeezed the horse's side, but instead of moving forward, it lifted its front legs in a panic, knocking Mia completely off its backside. The back of her head cracked against the craggy rocks at the foot of a tree.

For a second, she was groggy, but she quickly regained enough senses to see the horse's behind galloping back out of the forest. She fumbled with the leather strap around her thigh with her thumb unfastening the Sword of Light from its sheath. She held the blade in front of her protectively, allowing the humming sensations to take hold of her, and pushed herself up from the ground. The Sword didn't Call to her so she prayed she didn't have to use it. Planting her back against the solidity of a tree, she scanned the area with wide eyes. The lantern was on its side by her feet in pieces, the flames completely smothered out. Even if she was focused enough to do another incantation, she couldn't summon fire into a broken lantern.

An eerie embrace held Mia, and the chill was getting colder, but there was something else. The nocturnal sounds of the creatures were silenced. Not even the sound of the raindrops could be heard. And then a sudden eruption of hissing sliced through the air like a sword of death.

No, it cannot be!

She hastened her pace, but the faster she went, the louder the sound became. She was full blown running.

Mia gasped remembering her first encounter with the creatures responsible for that horrible noise. Her heart raced like a caged animal and despite the chilly wind and rain, she was sweating with fear. She kept running as fast as her legs could take her, and when she cast a glance behind her, she saw nothing.

Suddenly, Mia ran right into something so solid that she thought it was the trunk of a tree. She fell into the mud and lost her grip on the Sword. When she regained her bearings, she looked deep into a set of crimson eyes. She saw nothing but a torturous fire in them.

Mia froze, almost hypnotized, by the sight of this hooded tyrant. She could see him struggle with such rage, as if he were fighting himself from ripping her apart. His hissing formed into words of some language that was foreign to her. It was at that moment she regained control of her body. She slid herself back away from him as fast as she could. He reached his clawed hands out to her in attempt to grab her. She swung her foot at him out of desperation. He didn't yield.

He crept closer, his robes swaying about him. His movements were so swift and smooth that she swore he was only an apparition. She pulled her gaze away from him in hopes for an escape. She let out a scream to what she saw. She was completely surrounded by shadows with gleaming teeth and red eyes. Two of them held torches, while the others sat high upon horse like beasts. She was alone this time.

The beasts had eyes to match their masters and their heads resembled oversized wolves. She got to her feet certain she wouldn't escape. Their ring was too tight around her. A cold hand clutched her upper arm and lunged her outward. She struggled with all of her might when she was snatched up by two more hands. They played with her, bouncing her from one shadow to another until one of them gripped her tightly. The one who grabbed her raised a gleaming blade above his head. She closed her eyes tightly bracing herself for the searing flesh and the tearing pains of an axe. One of the others deflected his blow from her. They loosened their circle around her, leaving her utterly bewildered.

They hissed to one another and although Mia didn't understand what they were saying, it was obvious their intentions were to keep her alive. The very one that saved her from a fatal blow, turned on her. He twisted his head to the side and shoved her to the ground. He hissed to her in a native tongue.

"With you, our freedom is inevitable. Let the skies open up to the Father of Darkness…" he thundered triumphantly.

"Who are you?" she demanded in her bravest voice.

A mangled smile conquered his face. He slithered to the ground so that he was eye level with her and took hold of her cheek with his clammy hand. She resisted with disgust and cringed with his touch.

"We are the dark corners of the night, the shadows that speak. We are the future of this dying realm. We are of the Necromancers of the Old Legion and the true Emperor, soon to return and dominate the entire plane of existence…Ahriman…"

"My father?" she whispered. "My father is gone. You are living in a world of delusions! All of you!"

He grabbed a handful of her hair and yanked her up. *"Look, girl, deep into the eyes of hate and tell me what you see."*

His red eyes formed into a pit of fire.

A phoenix rose from the inferno and transformed into a chaotic figure of the man she saw in the paintings within the sacred wing. He was laughing as he sat upon a silver and sapphire throne. The chair spun, revealing the Winter crest upon its back. The crest transformed into three vipers. The vipers encroached upon her and just as they nearly reached her, they snapped their heads to the right and plunged into a crimson pool, slithering up a human form that emerged from the bloody surface. Mia gasped when the blood poured from the figure's face.

"Aldrich!" she was filled with such horror that she pulled away from his vision.

"Aldrich will not fall to you!" she sneered.

Laughter such as no other reverberated through the forest.

"Now, who is living in a world of delusions?" he hissed through laughter, *"Visions do not lie!"*

"I will not aid you in your plots! So if you are going to kill me, then get it over with already. Or do you like to play with your food before you eat it?" she said angrily.

"We are going to do much more than play with our food, girl. Let's say, you will be accompanying us for a very long time." he said waving to the others to collect her.

When they reached for her, something changed. Power enveloped her as she fought them, a familiar burn that surged through her body with the force of a volcano, the rumble of her heart slammed with every bit of fight she delivered. Her skin was alive with Air and Water. The gleam of the Sword caught her eye and she lunged for it as it sang in her grip. She raised the Sword and an explosion of blue shielded her. She punched and kicked them and cut them down as they wailed from her attacks. The remainder of them scattered backwards fleeing from her. They were gone. The evil was gone.

She fell to her knees, weakened from the magic, and when she looked up, all she could see were the wearisome eyes of her husband staring down at her. She was safe.

"What were you thinking?" Jacob lifted her up to her feet.

Horace was standing behind him drawn with anxiety, sweat dripping down his face, and his hand a pulsing blue. Horace must've aided her without her realizing it. She had thought she felt the Power of a second defender.

Mia was dizzy and a fatigued hand ripped all senses from her. She shook her head and balanced her body against Jacob's strong arm.

"Aldrich is in danger," she gasped. "He is in grave danger."

"You don't know what you are saying, girl. Aldrich is well and safe behind the many men who devote their life protecting him."

"You don't understand," Mia tried to force some urgency in her voice. "Those creatures showed me what they plan to do."

Jacob shook his head and looked over his shoulder at Horace. Belief danced across Horace's troubled face. Mia was content in knowing he understood. Jacob waved Horace away, and with one last encouraging look, Horace retreated from them.

Mia turned her head from Jacob's angry gaze to hide the tears that burned trails down her cheeks. She was thankful for the rainfall to help camouflage some of the tears.

"What in the hell did you think you were doing?" he repeated angrily.

"I don't belong here! You are right, but I'm not about to submit myself to the Elders!" she spat.

The rain was falling strong against the treetops and the ground, raising a clamor that drowned out any words below shouting.

"A wife belongs with her husband! Nowhere else until I say otherwise! So let us go now!" Jacob commanded.

He reached for her sleeve, but she yanked it from him nearly collapsing on him. His long blonde hair was dark and slick from being wet and his cheeks were dripping endlessly into his neatly kempt beard. He was soaked, as she, but he didn't shiver like she was. She stared at him fiercely, locking her eyes with his. Only a moment passed before he tore his gaze from hers. This angered her, giving her some of the strength she had lost back. She took hold of his chin and jerked his face back to her.

"You cannot even look at me! Me, your wife, as if you are afraid of what you might see in my eyes!" she shouted. "What are you afraid of!"

Jacob wrenched his head from her and took hold of her wrist dragging her away. "Stop resisting, wife! We are both soaked to the bone! We can talk about this when we reach the keep!"

"Let me go, you coward!" she screamed. "I'll not go back there and watch a servant mother a child that should be born to me!"

Jacob stopped abruptly and grimaced, "What are you talking about?"

Mia covered her face with her hands. "I don't understand what is happening to me. I see you differently now. You aren't the man I assumed you were in our days at Falias. I was a spoilt girl, who didn't know any better!" She shook her head violently. "And it kills me inside when I know that you could never look at me without disgust!"

He was silent, frozen, and his eyes were empty. She fell into him and met his lips with a hungry kiss. He stiffened. And when she felt him loosen, the use of magic and the weight of the Earth Crystal brought her down. Jacob's face darkened and the sound of the plummeting rain faded to blackness.

CHAPTER THIRTY-THREE

Unity

Mia stirred when the heat of sunlight played upon her face. Her head was heavy and her mouth felt like cotton. She opened her eyes and focused on Sierra drawing the drapes. The priestess hurried to her side and stroked her hair.

"You are ill," the priestess whispered. "You must rest."

"What happened?" Mia strained to pull herself up. Sierra pressed her palm against her.

"We found you in the woods," Sierra replied and stirred the contents in an earthenware goblet. "You fled in the middle of the night and you took with you the Earth Crystal. I'm afraid that you were not quite ready to carry such a burden of magic. You were foolish to leave," she chastised and handed Mia the goblet, "Drink."

Mia took the goblet with both hands and drank deeply. The fluid was warm and as tasteless as water. She remembered the small details of that night, the sound of the rain, and the horrible hissing noise of the red-eyed-Demons. She remembered a vision of something strange and threatening, yet she couldn't piece the flashes together. Then she remembered *him*. Her husband found her a raving mess. She kissed him!

Dear Goddess, what have I done?

Mia's stomach knotted in fear of facing him now. She scanned her surroundings and noticed that she wasn't in her own chamber.

"Where are we, Sierra?" Mia questioned.

Sierra patted a wet cloth against her head, "The Prince wished for you to recover in his chamber. It's by far the most peaceful in the dwelling. You have been sleeping for three days. The Prince asked to be called upon if you woke."

Mia instantly reached out to grab hold of the priestess' arm and pleaded, "Do not send for him yet, priestess."

Sierra studied her for a moment, and even though the priestess wore a white veil over her face, Mia could feel the soft smile behind the concealment.

"I must, Mia, because he is your husband and this is his home. Do not fret, for he has been more concerned than angry," Sierra whispered and caressed Mia's cheek.

The priestess turned, her white robe swirling about her ankles, and disappeared behind the door.

Mia had no time to pull together her thoughts when the big form of her husband stumbled through the entry. He was well dressed with a white cotton tunic that hung loosely over brown open sided breeches. His hair was plaited and his beard was neatly trimmed, but his eyes betrayed his strong appearance. The pools of blue were clouded with exhaustion. He strode to her side darting his eyes from her face to her form.

"How do you fair?" His voice was rich and edgeless as he regarded her.

"I am well," she answered and attempted to pull her gaze from him. She could not. He took her breath away.

"I didn't concede with your request," he snapped and reached deep into his pocket pulling out the thorn necklace. He tossed it on the bed at her feet. It gleamed beneath the morning light.

"I didn't mean to offend anyone I was just…"

"You insulted me!" Jacob said sharply. "You labeled me as something that I am not. I am loyal to my people's laws and the law says that one of royal decent cannot take another woman as concubine unless it's obvious that one's wife cannot bear."

"I was ill advised, I suppose. I was trying to give you what you desire, my lord. An heir to your name. You have no interest in giving *me* a child. So I did what I thought was right and left. I wouldn't have dishonored you. I only wished to go to my sister!"

"And what happened, girl? You would've been done for if we hadn't arrived when we did. You would've never made it to Arabella!"

"You love another, and I cannot bear to live around it!" Mia blurted out.

"You have lost your mind!" he planted his hands on his waist.

"No I haven't!" she paused breathlessly and looked away from him. "I hear the women talk and I see Lucia in your room every night tending to you, doing the things meant for a wife to do."

"I am no monster despite what you think of me. I have sworn to protect all of those beneath my roof and that includes you." He banged his fist on the table beside her. "I wouldn't force you into anything you didn't want to do, especially after that night!"

"So that is it then! You are disgusted with me not only because I am a Thaumaturi, but because *he* had his way with me first!" Her face showed no anguish, but her voice cracked to betray her.

"Let us not argue now, girl. You need your rest." He ignored her outburst.

"Something happened between us that night didn't it?" Mia whispered.

"You were delirious." He turned from her.

And then the invading thought forced a hasty answer from her. How she wished his words were false. But they weren't.

Forget him. Forget your desperation!

"Maybe I was," she knew it was a lie the moment it fell from her lips.

He inclined his head, "If you need anything, Sierra will be near to you. Rest, Wife, for we will be going to Vhladic in two days. If you are not well before then, I am afraid that you will have to remain behind."

"The Tribes?" Mia questioned.

"I have taken your advice and called a meeting with Ark, the Clawclan Chieftain, his first warriors and Erikrates. They promised me enough time to go to Vhladic and speak with Aldrich on the matter. They also believe they can salvage the situation without resorting to battle."

"That is wonderful, Jacob," Mia whispered with great joy that he had actually listened to something she said. "Perhaps things will turn around for the better."

"We are not clear, yet. Jovich will be in command of Vansant Summit and the wall. He will send word if things turn to peril during my absence," he replied and gaited toward the door.

"Has Horace departed or will he be riding with us?" Mia questioned remembering the vision the creatures showed her of Aldrich.

Mia saw in Horace's eyes that he had believed her words, unlike Jacob, and she desperately hoped that the Emissary made haste to investigate Aldrich's wellbeing.

Jacob returned his attention to her, his eyes cold and narrow, and said, "He left the moment he knew you were secure in your home. I am certain you will see him again." He left the room.

His attitude and eyes spoke in volumes. He thought her in love with Horace. A tiny charge sputtered within her, battling anger and satisfaction. She didn't like his accusations, but it seemed to her that he did care about their relationship enough to grow angry with his own conclusions.

She inhaled deeply and rested as much as she could throughout the day. She wanted to be well enough to visit Vhladic to do some snooping herself. Things Horace had told her and the visions she was having, first of the strange stone, then of a cauldron, a spear of healing, and finally the vision of Aldrich seemed to point her in the direction of Vhladic. It was her destiny to go there and retrieve whatever answers she could so that she could understand better what her duty to mankind was.

She rested so well during the first part of the day that she found herself restless in the later part of the afternoon and decided to sneak out for a stroll in the forest to clear her mind.

She didn't stray too far into the forest because her movements took much more effort due to her three day sleep. She found a portion of the river and lowered herself on the bank. She dipped a finger into the cool waters and allowed the element to soothe her blood and fill her body with some of the energy she had lost during her walk. Water was an element she had yet to master in her magic. She knew enough that she could draw energy from it. She had done it once before.

Her thoughts gathered around Blodeuwedd. It seemed so long ago since the Great Owl had last visited. And she made no effort to call her. In truth, Mia rather missed her. She closed her eyes and smiled as the wind lifted her hair. A stir from behind her attracted her attention.

"Blodeuwedd?" Mia whispered hopefully.

No answer came. She got to her feet and turn toward the direction in which she heard the disturbance. She gasped and nearly fell back into the river. The wall rose directly behind her. How could she not have noticed how far she wandered away from the keep? An outlander came before her and to her surprise, the old man ran to support her from falling.

"Do not fear me," his voice was raspy. "I am Erikrates and a good friend of your husband."

Mia could hardly find her voice, "You're a—from behind the—"

He laughed at her panic joyously and lowered himself on the river bank by her feet. His countenance reminded her of an over-sized King Valance, but he wore the garb of a Barbarian. Did he come for her to end the fighting? How did he even know that she was Jacob's wife? Then again there are not many Thaumaturi in these parts. How hard would it be to figure such a thing out? Mia's mind went spinning with so many thoughts.

"I am from the Clawclan." He pointed to a tattoo of blue talons as if she would understand what that meant. "Even if there is to be a battle, the Clawclan wouldn't take part in it. As I said, you needn't fear me."

Mia swallowed and remembered her husband mention the help of the Clawclan. "You mean the Clawclan has accepted me?"

"I didn't say that. However, they wouldn't allow it to bend their loyalty to the High Prince were as the other clans would. As for me, I would accept you and anything else that Jacobane does. He is a good man." Erikrates looked up at her.

"I see," Mia said and eased up with his presence. "You speak so warmly of him."

The old man chuckled and then grew serious with her. "In his presence, we are better than ourselves. We began to respect the value of life and the beauty of the land. Even as a boy he taught us these things." Erikrates folded his old scarred hands on his lap and smiled kindly at her.

Despite his Clawclan markings and his warrior garb, Mia was no longer fearful before him. His sage eyes and words drew her to sit across from him. The wall towered over them in a massive heap of shining iron. Its shadow swallowed them into the coolness of the fragrant breezes.

"My husband is a teacher to the Tribes, then?" Mia whispered.

The old man tapped his staff on the ground and smiled widely.

"Yes, Thaumaturi, he is. And our protector. It was Jacobane that united the Tribes beyond the wall and gave them satisfaction enough to quench their lusts for savagery. A brave warrior with the compassion of a good leader. He has loved," he replied hoarsely.

"My husband is a warrior with no room in his heart for love," Mia mused and looked at her feet.

"There is much more that you wouldn't know, my lady." His gnarled hands brushed over top of hers. "He loves nothing, not himself, nor one maiden, nor one child, nor one man, more than he loves his people as a whole. A prince that fights his own battles, he is."

"You have a special friendship with the High Prince. I can tell." Mia smiled and covered his hand with hers.

"And I can see that you are enchanted by the man you never truly knew. It's in us all to love Jacobane that way." The old man's laugh whistled like a raspy wind.

"I—I have, I suppose," she paused. "The Tribes will not view me as an ally. And all of the good he has done will mean nothing. I'd rather leave him a widower before blood could be shed in my name."

"And despite what you think you know of him, he would protect you to his own death. He would do it for even the lowliest peasant who lives under his protection. It seems it has finally caught up with him." The old man sighed.

"I will surrender. Take me to the Tribes were I can plead for the safety of Vansant Summit." Mia trembled, but she wouldn't allow a war to touch the children of the village and her home.

"I will not send anyone to such a fate. My Tribe, the Clawclan has done everything they could to spare Jacobane and still do." Erikrates eyes became watery as he paused for a moment. "In two Moons, the land that you know as your home now, could be covered in blood. It could be a burning abyss, and by the Gods, he would burn with them. The Holy Ones of your land will not let you meet the same fate that your husband has chosen for himself."

"You are wise enough to know the ways of the Elders. But you have much to learn about me. I would never submit to them," Mia said sharply. "Come back to my dwelling. I will have my women feed you and bathe you."

Erikrates laughed. His big body and his round bearded face jiggled with delight. "I cannot." He held a hand up.

Mia rose to her feet and frowned. She gripped the old man's hand and tugged him up.

"I didn't ask you. I ordered you," she jested. "Now don't make me hold you my first prisoner."

"Very well," he sighed. "I'm so old and have come to exercise my brain more than this feeble old body. I will be a poor match to you."

There was no more talk of war and Jacob as they walked back to the village. Only the idle bantering occurred between them. Mia found she really like Erikrates. He was very wise and very respectful toward her. His attitude gave her hope in finding more like him among the Tribes.

The sun was setting, warming the colors of the sky tawny gold. The fires for the first night of Lugh Celebration were being lit over the hills and by the lake as the two of them drew near to the gates of her dwelling.

Two of Jacob's warriors stood post laughing with one another, gripping their swords in one hand, holding a jug of ale in the other. Upon her approach, they instinctively went to draw the iron gates. Once they caught sight of her companion, they stilled. Mia smiled up into the hard face of Jacob's General Warrior, Kennick. He frowned and thrust her behind him. He aimed the sword directly at Erikrates throat. "Your business, outlander!"

Erikrates didn't cringe before the massive form's aggression. His old face remained peaceful. Mia darted to his side and forced the blade away from his throat.

"He is my guest, General," Mia told the big guy. When he didn't ease, Mia swallowed hard. "It is okay. He is Erikrates."

Kennick immediately lowered his defenses, gave a stiff nod and stepped aside to let them through.

Mia placed a hand through the old man's arm and allowed him to walk with her up the steps to the dwelling's portico where Lucia awaited her return. Her hand was planted upon her hip and her face was in repose arrogance.

She hadn't seen Lucia since the night she came upon her with her selfish wishes. But who could blame her. Jacob was a man who many loved and that didn't exclude this woman. Jealousy brought the demon out in both of them. He had rejected Lucia. Mia knew that now and if she felt the need to defend herself against Lucia again, she wouldn't be afraid to remind her of it.

"I thought you still in bed recovering. Jacobane will be angry," she spat.

"Lucia, I have brought a guest with me," Mia replied and Erikrates stepped forward.

"Erikrates!" Lucia's eyes lit up in a childish joy. She threw her arms around him and smiled brightly. The man smoothed her heavy coils with tenderness.

"Lucia, you've grow lovlier each time we meet. If only your father could see you," Erikrates laughed.

"It is such a surprise! I didn't think you would ever come across the wall to see me."

"The High Princess," Erikrates nodded at Mia, "insisted that I take supper and a bath here tonight. Perhaps the sight of me plucked one of her heartstrings."

Lucia stared at Mia. Some of the contempt gave way to warmth.

"It was quite nice of you to invite him, my lady." She inclined her head. "The High Prince will be pleased."

"I'm glad it pleases you. Erikrates is a remarkable man," Mia replied. "Come, let us dine."

Mia strode past them into the dining hall. The tables were set up with wheels of hard cheese, finely cut breads and honey milk sauces. Mia nearly forgot that the mutton would be cooked over the fires in the courtyard. She spun and smiled widely.

"If you wish to nibble before your bath, please come." Mia invited Erikrates to the tables.

"I will bathe first, my lady. Then I'll fill my belly with mead and mutton once I'm through!" He laughed.

"I will attend you, Erikrates," Lucia replied curtly and slipped her hand through the old man's arm. She briefly looked over her shoulder and bowed her head in approval before she led Erikrates away.

Mia floated into the courtyard and looked to the garden fires where Jacob always ate his meal on bonfire nights. His spot was empty. She ascended the stairs inside and stopped before the door to her room. After a moment of contemplation, she bypassed the urge to see if her husband was there and headed for the chamber she recovered in. She lied down. Despite her tired body, she couldn't find sleep.

Courage and loneliness pulled her from the bed again. She drifted to the terrace and cast her eyes to the lake dotted with blazing flames and Barbarian folk. The late Agustu moon danced upon the lake's rippling surface, taunting her and encouraging her all in one stroke. Jacob invaded her mind and she became breathless with confusion. She knew how to find him, but what to say to him was a different matter. She turned on her heels and made her way back to her chamber door.

Damn fear!

When she entered, he cast a cold glare at her. "You should be in bed."

"I'm okay," Mia replied and slipped through.

"You've been ill for three days. Do not push it."

"Sometimes things need to be pushed in order for them to become better," She whispered.

"I'm glad to see you haven't lost your rebel tongue," he said and strode onto the curtained terrace. Away from her.

"Why are you here instead of enjoying the festivities?" Mia questioned him.

"I was down earlier," he grunted.

His chest and back were bare. Several long scars glistened on the surface of his skin beneath the moonlight. Mia hadn't seen such scars before. She followed him, drawn to him by an invisible rope. She studied each scar on his back with awe. She shivered and he must've sensed it.

346

A Prince who fights his own battles…

"Are you cold?" he asked lowly.

"No," she answered softly.

She didn't lie, because the night was only vague with the signs of autumn. It was thoughts of him.

She traced a finger along the longest scar down his back. His skin tensed beneath her strokes until he finally moved forward from her. It hurt her, the way he shunned her, while she shed her childish animosity like a serpent sheds its skin. She needed to face the fact that he would never accept her for what she was, and that he'd never try. She brought her hand back and stared at him. His body was beautiful, even the scars appeared so to her. Everything. If she valued her heart, she'd leave.

Stop being so afraid. You mustn't deceive yourself or him.

The Whisper of Blodeuwedd tugged at her ear like a scolding from a mother. "What happened that night—" Mia drew closer to him.

"I paid no mind to it. I told you that you were delirious," he cut her off.

"Look at me," Mia commanded. She had to see the eyes he always hid from her.

He shook his head. She ran her hand down the length of his arm until her hand intertwined in his large fingers. He didn't snatch his hand away as she expected him to. He glanced over his shoulder at her. She couldn't see anything in his face.

"I know that you are set in your beliefs about my kind and I'll not try to change your mind, but there is something I must say to you," Mia whispered.

"Don't," he said softly. Was that fear in his voice?

"I must," Mia said desperately, "Because I cannot lie any longer."

"It isn't necessary," he breathed.

She felt his attempt to untangle his hand from hers. She reinforced her own strong grip.

"I feel something, so strong and deep, when I'm near you. I cannot explain it. It hurts in my stomach and in my heart." Her voice cracked with the fresh tears that stung beneath her eyelids. "I've not felt this way before. I know now that my sacrifice wasn't ever about knowing true love. My sacrifice is to love a man who could never love me back."

Mia turned from him with shame and darted away, but Jacob held firm to her hand. He pulled her back to him and looked into her eyes unflinchingly for the first time. For a lifetime, it seemed, their gazes locked. She fell victim to the jeweled pools of his eyes. Heat rushed to her head. The world stopped. She wanted to pull his mouth to hers and embrace his large and protecting form. But she held back and gave him whatever time he needed to see that she didn't lie. She loved him.

"My mother would've loved you, Princess." His smile was distant.

"You loved your mother very much," she whispered catching a strand of his hair between her fingers.

"Aye," he said, "She had a good heart and never looked down on another. There's much of her in Aldrich. It was everything my father hated in him." His face shadowed with the memories held captive inside of his head.

"I see that in you." She placed a hand on his cheek, trying so desperately to ignore the throbbing desire she had for him.

"No," he half laughed, "I could never compare."

Mia said nothing and smiled softly encouraging him to speak more. At least he was talking. It was a magical start.

"I hated the Thaumaturi. They wanted too much and while my father's men were out battling this foreign magic, a few of the Thaumaturi invaded the Empire's palace, killing all who stood in their way including my mother." Jacob turned from her, clenching his fists, "I saw the whole thing. They used their chants and one of them held a gold shard. They incinerated her before my very eyes with it. When I tried to run to save her, it was as if an invisible hand restrained me."

Mia's heart broke and she embraced his back with overwhelming sympathy. He was hurting and the feelings surged through her body as well. He trembled in her arms, like a child that couldn't cry.

"It isn't your fault! You were but a child!" she cried. "Stop blaming yourself!"

He spun his body and took hold of her arms with a solid grip. His eyes were narrow and it almost seemed as if he trapped tears behind his fierce stare.

"I blamed myself! I blamed the Thaumaturi! I blamed my father for leaving us! Gods help me, I even blamed you!" Jacob growled. "I blamed you for forcing me to see the truth! I blamed you for showing me that I cannot hate you as I so desperately willed!'"

Mia's lips quivered. He stared at her, his face hungry and fierce.

"I hadn't known such a feeling before you," he said and pressed his mouth against her lips. He withdrew from her and his features were twisted with pain and desire.

In an instant, Mia flung her arms around his neck and fell into his arms. He grabbed hold of her waist and wound a hand tightly in her hair. Her mouth was on his, and he opened to her, drowning her with his taste.

It was a long and hungry kiss, attaching their souls. A hot wave washed over her body with his touch and lips. It wasn't the same as it was with Vastadon. She was so afraid with him, but in the arms of this man, her husband, the man she had cursed, the man she didn't want to marry, she felt sheltered and safe. Jacob scooped her up with ease and carried her to the bed, never removing his mouth from hers. He lowered her gently and lay down beside her. She grasped his neck and pulled his lips down to yield to him again.

He slid his hand along the length of her back. She arched ever so lightly with his strokes. He was so close to her, closer than she ever dreamed. The musky smell of his hair and his skin was intoxicating. He lowered his body on her, pulling her upward, absorbing her body with his hot muscled embrace. His cheek pressed against her hair and he moved his mouth down the smooth curve of her neck, slowly following the path that lead to the valley of her heaving breasts. She stroked his hair, pulling him closer to her. Her shaken legs cradled his waist, adding more power to her leverage. She could feel his body hard against her thigh, and in between her legs.

No fear this time, no panic, and no immobility consumed her. Only the desires that now moistened the hidden place between her legs. She could sense his gentleness, his anxiety and his need to slow the pace in which he ravaged her. Her light fingers roamed down to his firm buttocks and squeezed with great vigor impatiently thrusting him inside of her. She drew her breath in sharply as his erection slid into her, stretching her with the pleasure that summoned her body into hot passion. He met eyes with her nervously, perhaps in fear that she might become panicked. She smiled quickly encouraging him onward.

They rocked slowly within the tide of savoring pleasure, until the tension built. The world around her became an ocean of blur and she clung to him and felt her body peak into a vortex of heat she had never before felt. They trembled while the explosion of their wet heat collided.

Their bodies lay in a sweating heap joined with hunger, lust and love, and a final peace between two tormented races.

Unity will protect all...

The Whisper only tickled the edge of her mind as she fell asleep in her husband's arms.

The Stone exploded into angry green, blue, and tawny flames beneath Bile's clawed grip. He ripped His hand away and howled monstrously.

"What is happening?" he growled and turned a livid eye on Hector.

Before the Chaplain could answer, the Darkgod slammed His palm onto the surface of the Stone once again, and quickly recoiled.

It was the first time since Bile's awakening that the Lia Fáil rejected His touch. Hector couldn't begin to explain this turn around and he swallowed hard when the Darkgod glared at him. Bile always looked to him for the answers His mortal aspect couldn't understand.

"I—I don't know, My Master," Hector stuttered and lowered his head. "I don't understand."

Something changed and Hector couldn't begin to explain an answer.

"How can it be that the Stone rejects me? *Me!*" Bile howled and spread His wings to its full width. His face began to ripple giving Hector a glimpse of the evil force trapped within the mortal shell.

Hector did the only thing he could think of. He unlocked the panel wall and tossed Bile a Thaumaturi male he had managed to come across in the night at the harbors.

Bile ravaged the man, forced him without an attempt to seduce him and once He was done, His form was calmer.

"I will see what I can learn, My Master." Hector promised and slid from the red pulsing temple before Bile grew enraged again.

CHAPTER THIRTY-FOUR

Lugh Celebration

The city of Vhladic chimed with harvest bliss as a great procession was arranged for the return of the High Prince and his new wife. Several women garbed in autumn vibrancy fluttered about Mia and wedged themselves in between her childishly tight grip on Jacob's hand. Mia couldn't help but beam with excitement when she fell into the hands of such vigorous women. She flashed Jacob a smile, who nodded in return, and stifled a laugh when a round grey haired woman fussed with re-braiding his hair.

Once the women satisfied themselves with their grooming and straightening, they shoved Mia and Jacob into a fine litter canopied in tasseled lavender silk. The Senate, shining in silks and ceremonial chain mail, gleaming in charms and jewels, rode upon stallions on either side of the canopied litter. By their insignia they were known as the Emperor's High Court. The women of the Senate wore cerise while the men wore copper. Pennants fluttered from formal lances and were fastened to their sides with the ensign of their importance. Satins drifted the fragranced air and an array of autumn oranges and gold fluttered in the manes of their tall stallions.

Grand Chaplain Hector, a man who Mia felt most uneasy around, rode to the head of the litter surrounded by guards in silver and jade, whom she presumed to be the temple guards. He sat upon his steed in his deep green regalia resplendent with his regal arrogance, but not to the point were it wouldn't seem graceful. The Chaplain wore upon his russet head a garland of gold leaves.

Mia let out a sigh once she was comfortably secured in the litter with her husband. She held out her hand and he placed his palm against hers. Slowly their fingers entwined. They gazed into one another's eyes. She hadn't seen him smile so much, but it was as if the sun shone from his eyes when he did. Mia never knew that love could be so warming and magical.

During their day journey to the imperial city, the two of them opened up to one another, joking and laughing together, holding each other and speaking of dreams and plans. The night they had shared together passionately had opened new doors to Mia's heart.

The words of Blodeuwedd and the memories of her past dimmed beneath the brilliance of their deep bonding. She found herself yearning to forget all that she had learned and everything she didn't learn about her fate. Could life not be less complicated?

"I am pleased to see you so happy," Mia whispered.

"I enjoy watching your face as you discover the splendor of my childhood home," Jacob replied with a laugh and then lifted her fingers to his lips.

He spread the silk drapes and encircled an arm around her. Mia leaned over his lap, nestled close to his chest and peered out at the passing city.

Men, women, and children, servants and merchants, went laughing from the bakery to the pubs, from foreign weavers to antique stands and merchant stands. They gathered around the barrels of apples and baskets of nuts. Wineries and Alehouses had stands set on every corner. Even farmers from the country fields brought the best of their harvest to gain profit.

The Barbarian's loved beauty and it showed with each passing building. Columns of gold and lattice terraces and verandas decorated each dwelling. Although the buildings didn't seem to have windows facing the front, Mia could make out the stained glass that was embedded into the siding. Each causeway that wound behind the streets was lined with gardens and tiny fountains. The Emperor's signet and the sign of Jacob's three Gods—a braided triangle with the Gods' jewels set at each point—marked banners that wavered in the late summer breeze.

Mia leaned a little forward to see a group of satin clad dancers. Musicians, harpers and drummers rounded about a dazzlingly jeweled pavilion, and within the circle, dancers spiraled hypnotically around the courtyard in a flurry of gold, browns, reds, and oranges. Mia gasped at the sight of them and fell back on a fond memory from when she was in Gorias. It was the day she met Horace and Aunyia. Her heart fluttered anew. She was anxious to reunite with Horace, and even more so with the thought of reuniting with Aunyia. They were both here in the imperial city.

Suddenly, Mia jumped and drew her husband's attention back to her.

"Sierra, I hope she is okay!" Mia exclaimed.

Jacob smirked and squeezed her hand. He then pulled her onto his lap. She gasped delightfully with his swift control. Jacob threw his head back in laughter when he saw the wide eyed look of his wife.

"I wouldn't want to risk another man's eyes on my wife," he said impishly reading her mind, "I wanted you to get a better look so that you can see your priestess rides safely within the regal circle of the Senators and guards."

"Oh," Mia blushed and craned her neck around to see Sierra veiled in her priestess robes riding two rows behind them, "I suppose they will show her to the Ogma Columns where she intends to spend her mornings during our time in the city."

"Yes. My estate here in Vhladic is near to the Imperial Palace. She would find her way easily. But I have, for the sake of your frame of mind, assigned Kennick to guard and guide her," Jacob said.

"You are a wondrously remarkable man. Thank you so much." She embraced him, still perched on his lap.

She felt her pulse quicken with arousal, and he too stirred beneath her buttocks. She quickly slid from his lap so she didn't lose control before the eyes of the populace.

A good two hours had passed since they began the march to the palace. The procession was relaxing and exciting, but Mia soon felt the lids of her eyes grow heavy.

Jacob leaned his head out between the curtains and called for a halt in the march.

"We will stop at the Spa. I want you to experience the grandiose of our baths here in Vhladic. Although we cannot publicly bathe together, I'm sure you will find it comforting nonetheless." Jacob told her and leaped from the litter.

He reached a hand up to her and secured it around her waist, spinning her down to the ground in a graceful dance.

The common folk fell to their knees with the sight of Jacob and they didn't lift to their feet until he walked past them. He indicated that the procession continue onward. Mia asked Sierra if she would join her, but she politely declined. Hector sneered down at Jacob, but once his eyes fell on Mia, he softened and inclined his head. Mia nodded slightly with intent not to be rude.

"Take royal care of my wife." Mia heard Jacob tell the man at the service area. Jacob kissed her quickly on her cheek and set off.

A young dark-skinned woman with a thick accent led her to the apodyterium where she was able to remove her gown and garments. The changing room was a wide comfortable stall and little bronze rings held three thick bath sheets. Once she removed her gown, she wrapped a white bath sheet around her form and followed the servant to the Spa.

Luxurious. There was no better word to describe what she looked at. Polished mirrors covered the walls. The ceilings were buried in yellow and clear glass. The waters of a stone-like fountain spilled into the rich marble pools. Complicated colorful mosaics covered the floors and it felt smooth beneath her bare feet.

The extravagance of the Spa surpassed the cavern pools beneath the Winter Palace. Mia shifted her attention to the servant. Although she was accustomed to the aid of her women in Falias, she grew rather used to bathing alone in her husband's dwelling.

"*Gratsie.*" Mia inclined her head graciously.

The servant swept into a curtsy, "Do you wish for milk, my lady?"

"Milk?" Mia cocked her head to the side.

"Aye," she replied, "For bath?"

"No, it's quite fit how it is." Mia thought it strange but reacted politely.

"If you need anything, please ring." She indicated a tiny bell to the right of her and scurried from the room.

Finally alone. Since her arrival to Vhladic, she found it impossible to get a moment alone. Women from all directions and all castes eagerly encircled her in chat and gossip. She supposed she should be grateful. After all, she half expected the reception in Vhladic to be no different from the one she received in Vansant Summit. It seemed that the imperial city was full of diversity. Aldrich had done a great justice with the Empire.

The clear waters were adorned with roses and herbs. It was arranged in a fashion that reminded Mia of a paradise pond that shouldn't be disturbed. She dipped her toes into the pool anyway and watched the gentle ripple spiral outward. The bath was pleasantly warm and soft with petal oils against her skin. She exhaled delightfully and tossed the sheet away from her. Eagerly, she submerged her entire body beneath the steaming water and let out a dreamy sigh. She could get used to this. She chuckled and thought of how Arabella would be envious if she could see her now.

"Princess Miarosa." A voice snatched her attention around.

In his reverent green robes and his garland headdress, High Chaplain Hector Altorius looked down his nose at her. She curled into a ball and crossed her arms over her bosoms. His lips spread into an uneven smile at her reaction.

"No need to be modest, my lady," his voice was deep and his eyes spit a strange fire, "I am a man of the Gods true to my vows."

He lowered himself to the pool's edge and reeked of strange incense and deep spices. She drew away from the nearness of him. Despite his words, she felt his gaze linger on her.

"Your Reverence, could this not wait until I'm through with my bathing," Mia breathed.

"Actually I'm taking leave from the temple for the day. I know you and your husband will pay your respects this eve, but sadly I'll not be there to welcome you. I merely wanted to bid you farewell before I go," Hector replied haughtily.

"Where are you to go?" Mia huffed.

"I'm to take up solitude," He said quickly. "Such a lovely face." He caught his hand before he touched her cheek, "I often wondered what kind of woman could win the heart of a man so famous for his bigotry against your kind. I look at you now and know exactly what has driven a barrier between two kinsmen."

A shiver visibly affected him with his words. She splashed further away from him. And she grew angry with his implications. She wouldn't feed into small talk about her private life.

"I bid you farewell then."

He rose to his feet slowly, yet the sluggish movements managed to demand attention. His face was straight, but Mia felt the anger of her rejection rise off of him. He spun inside the silk circle of robes and strode out of her sight. She released all of the air from her lungs and sunk deeper into the warm waters. Her heart beat ceaselessly against her ribs.

The chaplain wanted her to know that he could effortlessly gain control at her most vulnerable moments. He dappled in magic despite the Barbarian's discrimination against it. She could smell it on him and feel its clammy hands grope at her.

"My lady," the servant called causing Mia to nearly jump out of her skin, "Are you okay?" The servant rushed to her side urgently.

"I'm alright," Mia sighed, "I'm ready to emerge."

"Would you like to watch the warriors' sport in the palaestra?"

"I would meet with my husband, if he is through in the Spa." Mia smiled.

"The High Prince asked me to provide you comfort while he is in council with the Emperor and his Senate," the servant said nervously.

"I hadn't known about this," Mia replied.

"It was short noticed, my lady. The Prince didn't wish to alarm or disturb you from your first visit to the imperial Spa," the woman answered quickly, "I—the High Chaplain…"

"It is quite alright." Mia exhaled, the icy hand stroked her briefly again. "I can tell that he is a man who walks where he wants and answers to no one. I highly doubt you would've been able to stop him if you tried."

"I would've done my best, my lady," she replied sweetly and it caught Mia's attention.

Mia looked at her closely for the first time. She was beautiful and too well poised to be a servant. Her gold-black eyes were wide and warm when they looked upon her. A tiny thought nagged her mind.

"Tell me your name. For I know you are of a much higher caste than to pass for a Spa servant," Mia said compassionately. "I know that times can be hard. You may speak freely before me. It's safe."

"What is said about you is true." The servant's faced brightened and shifted her eyes to make certain they were alone. "You are a Prophetess. A redeemer to some. My name is Mina." She extended her hand discretely.

They were smooth and Mia could see the bands of lighter skin around her fingers where jewels were most likely worn. A vision flashed through her mind of this woman garbed in concealing robes watching her and Jacob's arrival from afar. This woman buried herself deep inside of an unbreakable shell. Fear was hidden in there somewhere.

"I'm flattered, but I would disappoint your high expectations. You've been following me, Mina." Mia lifted her brows, "Whatever for?"

"Dress. We will go to the palaestra." She went to retrieve the bath sheet.

"I have a feeling that you are shunning my question," Mia said shortly.

The woman clucked and unfolded the bath sheet to accommodate her emerge.

"You'll soon see. Trust me, my lady," She implored.

Mia sighed and lifted herself into the cool air. Mina wrapped the sheet around her and escorted her back to the apodyterium. An imperial-style mauve gown with a gold laced bodice and a diamond circlet was hung on a circle in the stall.

"The stola is a gift from your husband. The color of an imperial princess," Mina called to her as if she could hear her awestruck thoughts. "I'll attend to your circlet, my lady."

A warm flood of emotion swept her away from her husband's gesture. She embraced the gown as if it were her beautiful Barbarian man. How she loved him and how blind she was to his brilliant soul.

She dressed and allowed Mina to style her hair and to fuss with her circlet. Then she followed the woman out onto a portico balcony that was supported by silver pillars. Beneath them she saw a vast green and brown field where several groups of Barbarians battled with javelins and swords, wrestled on the ground like animals, and some were even battling fist to fist. Three story tiers full of cheering spectators surrounded the action.

"Mia!" Mia craned her head around just as she was gathered into a mauve and green silk embrace.

"Aunyia! It has been too long since we've seen one another!" Mia smiled at her friend.

Aunyia was suitably garbed as the Emperor's daughter. Her scarlet hair was loosely gathered within a leaf latticed headdress, a jeweled circlet at her brow. She wore a jade and mauve stola that swept gracefully to her feet. Quickly, she lowered herself into the cushioned seat beside Mia and placed her smooth jeweled hand over hers.

"I want you to pretend you are enjoying yourself while I speak to you," Aunyia said through the side of her mouth while waving to the crowd who bowed respectfully before them.

Mia nodded and mimicked Aunyia's gestures. She listened intently as her friend explained what she knew of Mina's people and how they were being held in captivity.

"There are illegal activities going on beneath the temple and tunnels that run below the city and I believe that it's all being done with the High Chaplain's approval. Diamond was held captive there for several days. What little she was able to remember she told us. But the most fearsome information she discovered was that some supernatural creature called the Darkgod is hidden their."

"Oh, my Goddess! Is Diamond well?" Mia exclaimed fearfully, "As if she had not endured enough!"

"She is safe and most likely with the High Priestess back in Thaumatur. Her rescue is owed to Mina's brother, a man you might know. Sermino says he is an advisor in Falias," Aunyia replied.

Mia couldn't contain her smile. She had known something was special about Sermino.

"I know him! I am very fond of him. I find it hard to believe that Aiden

THE MARRIAGE OF THE SWORD

allowed him to wander so much as five feet away from his side. My brother is extremely dependant on Sermino," Mia smirked. The darkness of betrayal flooded her with the fleeting thought of Aiden. She quickly stomped it down.

"I know nothing of that. He has indeed been a good ally, so I've been told." Aunyia nodded to a group of people paying respects below.

"Have you told your father what you've learned?"

"The Senate won't let me anywhere near my father alone long enough to share this with him. I'm having second thoughts now about telling him, anyhow. I fear for his safety. The High Chaplain is too influential among the Empire. I need you to convince my uncle to lengthen his stay here until we can sort out a plan. It will be much easier for me to contact you here through Mina."

"How can we put an end to this if we are not entirely sure what it is they're doing?" Mia questioned.

"I have spies and I have a fleet. We must locate the remaining weapons," Aunyia whispered.

"There is a connection with this island. I have a feeling," Mia answered.

"If there is a connection, then it's apparent to me that the chaplain *wants* legions of Demons to conquer our lands."

"Not the Nations," Mia whispered through the fake smile. "Thaumatur. Gorias will be destroyed by hurricane, Murias by tidal wave, Findias by fire, and Falias by earthquake. If we don't act, the fate will come to pass and leave us with no hope. Danu will be ripped from us."

"How have you come up with this knowledge?" Aunyia asked quickly and for a moment she almost lost her façade.

"I have dreams, Aunyia. Horrible, terrible dreams," Mia whispered and when Aunyia met her eyes a flash of confusion danced there. "There is more I must tell you. I have seen the weapons in visions, but as to where they are I do not know."

Her secrets were coming out. It was time to trust fully, yet she wouldn't pain Aunyia with the bloody vision of Aldrich. She would just pray that Horace kept his eyes on the Emperor. She told her of the Sword and how it came into her hands. When she was through, she was thankful to see that Aunyia wasn't cross with her.

"It's a relief to know we have one of the weapons. However, it will do us no good to tell another soul until we retrieve them all. It would draw unnecessary dangers to our mission. To you. We need you to be safe, Mia. You are the Bearer."

"I know. The only other who knows is Sierra, my priestess."

"Jacobane knows nothing?" Aunyia questioned.

"I haven't said a thing to him," Mia replied.

"Perhaps it is best left alone." Aunyia smiled, "You've grown fond of him as I said you would."

"I have," Mia blushed. "I love him and he loves me. It indeed is a miracle."

The women laughed and turned their attention to the beginning of a wrestling match. Mia dropped her jaw and pointed.

"My Goddess! Is that Cole!" Mia exclaimed as the brave knight strode proudly to his opponent who was head and shoulders taller than he.

"Why I believe you are right!" Aunyia grinned.

"Oh, he looks so little near to the Barbarian," Mia screwed up her face. "What has his arrogance gotten him into now!"

"The Tribes have agreed to negotiate their terms." Jacob's voice reverberated off the walls as he stood tall before the podium.

Every eye was locked onto him, some more interested than others. The Imperia Hall dwarfed any who stood beneath it. Jacob often wondered why such an enormous hall was needed to hold a council of maybe twenty Senators. It was a waste of space.

"And if they are not satisfied?" Aldrich asked Jacob wearily from his throne.

The Emperor's eyes twinkled beneath the lights, but his face was somewhat drawn behind his braided beard. Jacob thought him to look thinner. His majestic purple robes drooped on his normally sturdy build. Jacob decided he would see about it when the assembly was through.

"Then I'll do what I can to protect Vansant Summit." Jacob nodded to his brother. "I have hope that the Clawclan will aid me in my negotiations. The Wise Man Erikrates and the Clawclan Chieftain Ark have given me their support. However, if there is indeed a battle, they've told me they wouldn't involve themselves in it at all. I couldn't be angry because it is they who have homes in the Wildlands and they who would fall to the mercy of the other Tribes for such involvement."

"My High Prince, why don't you just give Vansant Summit to the Tribes and stay in Vhladic where it is safe. I seriously doubt that the Tribes are daring enough to assault the imperial city," a tall lanky Senator named Victros responded skeptically.

"The purpose of the wall was to protect the farmers and the lower caste people from such things. If I were to abandon Vansant Summit, what would become of those people beneath the angry Tribes? Are they not the ones who provide us with mead, crops, and fertile land?"

"To the south the fertile lands are vast," Vastadon added arrogantly. Jacob turned his head slowly.

"So leave the east for dead? No. I'd rather die with them than to abandon them to certain death," Jacob argued shooting daggers at his pious nephew.

"You would die and so would your princess. We don't want another war with the *magicians!* Better to sacrifice a few farmers and peasants than a whole nation," Senator Victros replied lazily.

"It takes nerves of steel to speak so prejudicially of the Thaumaturi when your High Princess is one!" Jacob rebutted forebodingly. He could hardly believe his defense. A year ago this day, the term *magician* wouldn't have fazed him. Things were different now. He had learned and loved. She was as much his life as his people.

"Hypocritical words you speak, Uncle!" Vastadon spat.

"You dare—" Jacob leaped from behind the podium.

"Enough!" Aldrich bellowed. "I support my brother in whatever he decides regarding Vansant Summit. After all, it was he who dealt with the Tribes while all of us quibbled about lesser things safe enough away from any real threat. Jacobane, if a battle is inevitable then I'll provide you with enough imperial forces to protect your home. That will be all of it." Aldrich waved a hand through the air indicating the end of the session.

"Such a fiasco could've been prevented, my lord Emperor," Vastadon added halting the Senators from their departure, "if you didn't push so hard for this union between the High Prince and Miarosa!"

Aldrich stared at his son for a moment and the entire Senate looked upon the scene with shock and silence. Jacob saw the desperation in his brother's eyes. Aldrich wanted his son's love more than anything in this world.

"I did what I did. I'm not obligated to explain to anyone, including you, my reasons for it. I've said it too many times. I'll not say it again!" Aldrich bellowed and was attacked by a series of coughs.

Jacob stepped down from the tier and darted to Aldrich's side. It was too late. His brother had sauntered off into solitude. Jacob spun angrily and his attention was drawn to the stony face of his nephew. Jacob tightened his jaw and clenched his fists against his instinctive reaction to strike the knave dead. He hadn't forgotten what his nephew did to Mia.

"Uncle," Vastadon lifted his chin and tugged his gloves down over his hand, "I told you we would meet again soon. It seems you have had some trouble in your little part of the world, but I'm sure the almighty Jacobane, Barbarian Savior of the little people will manage to save the day."

"Get out of my way," Jacob growled and pushed by him.

"How does the lovely Mia fair?" he taunted.

Vastadon's ice-blue eyes danced with maddening obsession when he spoke of her. For a brief painful moment the image of his nephew violating Mia sketched along his mind. He stifled a low roar and leaned in close to his nephew.

"If you even think about placing one little finger on her, I'll make sure you never open your eyes again." Jacob grinned wickedly and shoved by him.

He meant what he said. Aldrich wouldn't stop him this time.

CHAPTER THIRTY-FIVE

The Father

A horse drawn litter was sent to retrieve Mia from the Spa along with a hand delivered message from Jacob. It offered an apology and a promise to a night of privacy in his estate, Cordia Hall named in honor of his mother, in his courtyard garden at twilight.

Mia's mouth dropped when she was escorted from the litter. The estate was enormous and set widely apart from the rest of the city. Columns of gold rounded the marble entrance to the building. High arches adorned with pale silks and sparkling jewels dominated the vast architecture of the luminous structure. Acres of rolling green hills kissed with violet and white flowers surrounded the entire front. Two large figures of the Barbarian Gods—Lugh holding tight to an arrow in his right fist, a sword of fine gold dangled from his left and Dagda who held a sun designed staff above his head and a lion at his feet—erected from sputtering fountains. Pale shimmering lights added to the stunning appearance. Several guards clothed in imperial regalia awaited her in front of two large stain glass doors. They promptly drew the doors opened to allow her entrance.

The woman who rode with Mia, a noble Barbarian lady of about thirty and five who chattered endlessly the entire way, was restricted from entering. One of the guards had told her that no one was permitted entry on this night by order of the High Prince. Mia could've sworn she heard the woman huff sourly, but when Mia turned to bid her good day, she was on her knees, her auburn skirt fanned about her. She smiled up at her from behind thick lashes and retreated behind the glass doors.

Three maids garbed in matching sky blue frocks rushed forth, tight smiles on their faces, and crumbled to their knees before her.

"Stand up ladies," Mia laughed, "I have had enough of that for one day."

The women jerked up with practiced obedience and Mia smiled encouragingly.

The first servant maid, who was round with a graying bun atop her head and a pinched face, stepped forward and inclined her head.

"Welcome, my lady of the High Prince! My name is Drusilla and I'm his majesty's head cook. Although his majesty has prepared a rather enticing dinner menu for this eve, be sure to call on me if you become hungry before hand, my lady." She spoke fast and breathless, but she appeared to be the more experienced one within the presence of a royal figure.

Mia inclined her head, "*Gratsie*, Drusilla. I'll be sure to keep that in mind."

Mia's thanks drew a surprised look on the maids' faces and for a moment she thought them beside themselves with bafflement. What a sad thing to rile such surprise with a simple courtesy.

The second maid, who reminded Mia of the Spa servant—or should she say spy—Mina, stepped forward cordially. She was a pretty girl with creamy chocolate skin, slender and delicate, and about the same age as Mia. Her thick gold-streaked hair was wound in two loose braids. She spoke the language well, but it was thick with the same accent Mina had spoken with.

"I have yet to meet the High Prince, my lady, for I took on the service of Cordia Hall well after his majesty departed last time. I must say that I love—"

Drusilla nudged her nervously, "The High Princess doesn't wish to hear the ramblings of a servant, Kissa." The older woman tightly smiled, "I'm sorry, my lady. When I found her homeless on the street, I'm afraid I needed to clean her manners up a bit."

The one who was called Kissa lowered her blushing face like a child who just received a lashing.

"I welcome conversation, Drusilla. I want my maids to be comfortable around me so that they may speak freely with me in the privacy of my dwelling. I once had a woman who I loved as my own mother and showed her respect as an elder. She was my servant, but I appreciated her."

Kissa's head shot up and she beamed. Drusilla looked utterly confused and the third maid, who was a bit more boisterous than the other two giggled. She was a lean woman with a sturdy posture, about Mia's height—although most of the Barbarian women were tall, they usually stood only an inch or two above Mia's height who was tall among her kinswomen—and her ash hair was spiraled tightly around a spike-like hair adornment.

"Kissa is the housekeeping attendant this eve, and I am in charge of visitors and entertainment. It would seem that my talents are going to be useless tonight, so I will merely be the serving maid," the woman said.

"That is what you always do, you serving girl! Entertainment, bah!" Drusilla huffed in a husky voice, but nervously looked to see Mia's reaction from her outburst.

She was eased when Mia laughed at the jesting.

"Don't be envious, Drusilla!" the third woman frowned and then inclined her head to Mia, "My name is Phileta and I'm at your service! We have nicknames you know, if you'd like to call us by them!" she added excitedly.

Drusilla, whose cheeks became bright red, gasped at the notion. It seemed to Mia that Drusilla was the maid who kept them all in order, but it was probably with good intentions to make certain her friends stayed out of trouble. Mia liked all three ladies, especially since they didn't treat her as if she were a plague because of her race. Even in the warm faces of the Senate and the court servants, Mia could sense a certain edge. Not with these women, who two out of the three were of the Barbarian race.

"Forgive her, my lady!" Drusilla pleaded, "She's as stupid as an ox and is ignorant to her own offenses!"

Mia laughed loudly. The women blinked.

"I had no idea that anyone *could* take offense to conversation of endearments such as nicknames!" Mia exclaimed. "I love nicknames! I myself answer to a nickname. Tell me, and I shall call you by them, for you are my women here in Vhladic! It's only right for me to have such privilege."

Phileta jumped up and down and said, "Her majesty is most wondrous and fair. I've never served better than thee! Call me Leta, my lady. And she is Silla!" she pointed to Drusilla, "And we like to call her Sissy!" She referred to Kissa.

"Very well, my women! Now, would you show me to my room?" Mia was overjoyed with Leta's excitement.

They seemed to trample over each other for the benefit, but Mia willed them all to lead her to end the display.

The room was as stunning as the outer appearance with arched ceilings and bejeweled draperies and flowing purple silk. The black and white mosaic floor was covered with soft white rugs. Mia was beginning to learn how her husband favored the color white. It would be one of many small discoveries she would learn of her husband, each one like a tiny gift-wrapped surprise. The hearth in the room was shaped into the Imperial Family's emblem out of iron.

Mia danced around the room with delight before collapsing on the bed. She decided to lounge before she reunited with Jacob in his garden.

Once she woke from a brief nap, she refreshed herself before a scrolling mirror of polished metal and headed quickly to the garden.

Two sets of marble steps spiraled down into a garden circle. In its center, a life size statue of Ogma stood; his hands folded together cradling two scrolls plated with hammered-thin gold. The statue was enclosed with bejeweled columns and at the foot of the granite depiction of the God, an onyx encrusted panther fountain shot clear waters from its mouth into a thorn-shaped pool.

The cooling wind rustled the green and white flowered shrubs. The garden was the most beautiful sight she had ever seen. It was a garden that belonged to a very wealthy man. Jacob was that man yet he preferred to live simple in the country despite his riches. He explained to Mia earlier that had the estate not been a gift designed by his mother, he would've already sold it and purchased something a little less elaborate for his short visits to Vhladic.

Mia glided down the set of winding stairs and emptied herself like a child onto the plush jade grass. She spun in whimsical loops around the garden and hummed a made up tune into the twilight breezes.

She had never dreamed of being so happy. She had finally found a love so powerful, that it heightened her magical senses. He loved her back, a Thaumaturi. And he truly loved her! She had never been truly loved before. She lowered herself in a polished bench before the rushing fountain and silently waited for her husband to come as he promised.

A shadow caught her attention from the corner of her eye. It didn't alarm her, for there could be no possible way for an intruder to penetrate Jacob's estate after he issued strict instructions to his guards not to allow anyone entry on this night. It was their night.

She strolled across the stone path to where it looked to be the beginnings of a maze. She smiled softly. A lover's game, she thought. Pilasters holding large blazing sconces lined the walls of decorative stone. Mia followed the crackling sounds until her feet were soar.

"I give up, Husband!" she cried breathlessly. "Where are you hiding?"

No answer came. Mia laughed nervously and sprinted further into the stone maze. Abruptly the lit pilasters died down and she found herself lost in the middle of a moonlit puddle. She turned to retreat, but the flames were dousing out, one by one in a line toward the direction in which she came from. She drew her breath in sharply and swallowed hard.

"Jacob, this is no longer amusing!" Mia shouted nervously. "It is very dark!"

"Come forward," A whispery voice beckoned to her. "Come and see what you have come to see."

It was too soft to be noted as a voice. It was more like a hissing gust.

The vale between Mia's eyes creased, but oddly, the panic that was budding within her subsided into compelling interest. Her feet moved forward, as if guided by a daydream.

The walls of the maze dissolved around her as she came unto a glowing pool. Bubbles ruptured its placid surface. Mia peered inside.

A Stone with pale fire floated to the bubbling surface. Mia reached out to touch it. The image faded and she grasped nothing. She frowned and plunged her hand into the waters with a sudden and desperate need to find the stone. Something pulled her into the pool. She didn't fight the grip. She flowed with it until she fell onto golden hot snow, a substance the Murians called sand. She impulsively began to dig and dig. She raked her fingers into the fine sand, ignoring the singe of its texture, untouched by the ebbing waves of the sea. Another set of dark hands began to dig alongside of her, but she paid no mind to them. She wasn't sure what she was digging for. It only mattered that she found whatever lurked beneath the sandy earth. Pungent sulfur wafted up into her lungs. A shadow covered her back and the ground before her disappeared into its abyss.

She lifted to her feet and cast her eyes down the length of the beach. Rows of thin dark-skinned people were bent on their knees burrowing the sandy ground. Mia could see a trace of the beautiful people they once were. Their golden-streaked ebony hair was crusty with sand and their once cheerful faces were drawn and melancholy. They were humming lowly a song empty from a magic they once mastered. A magic of peace and love. Sihoma...

A violent wind sent masses of sand sailing across the shoreline. Mia protected her face and head between her elbows against the rapid storm. It evaporated quickly. The people were gone. She turned her eyes to the dark red skies. A mountain rose beneath a blacked-out sun and a river of lava tumbled from its cylinder mouth. Solar Eclipse.

Mia shielded her eyes from its brilliance and when she looked again, she was no longer on the chaotic beach. She was in a cell, a craggy cavern with rusted iron bars. No light gave way to her sight except the stingy sliver of moonlight that drew a line before her. At her feet, lay balls of tattered robes. She lowered herself to the floor and gasped when a wide-eyed child, silent tears falling down his gaunt cheeks, stared fearfully back up at her.

She took the child in her arms and searched frantically for a way out, to no avail. Soon she was surrounded by many children, their frail arms outstretched to her desperately.

"Who has done this to you?" Mia demanded half appalled and half sympathetic.

The children slowly split the circle in two and the child in her arms pointed toward the blackened wall. Mia lowered the child and advanced forward sliding her hand against the craggy surface. It became hot beneath her fingers.

The ground beneath her feet rumbled. She snatched her hand away and stumbled back toward the children. They didn't cry or didn't cling to her in fear. They simply stared ahead, their eyes black and sightless, their faces pale. The rocky surface split and a blinding crimson beam spat through the newly born gaping hole. The children fell to their knees around her.

The sound and feel of thunder shook her entire body. A dark and massive figure stalked forward until the blood red aura betrayed his darkened concealment.

Mia raised her eyes to the towering winged figure before her. His flashing eyes lightened with malicious delight and His lips split his face into a jagged smile. She had seen Him before in her dreams...her nightmares.

"My Mia," His wraithlike voice thundered with the quaking earth, "You have answered my call at last."

She didn't retreat. Instead she drifted closer to His spellbinding presence. Her feelings betrayed her and a hissing of great and dark promises entered her mind. The world would be hers and all who had caused her misery would fall to their knees before her in agony. The glory of a scorn and battered princess would come to pass. She smiled. Bile stroked her cheek.

"I can give it all to you if only you promise Me your love," He spun his glittering web of seduction planting a simmering kiss on her brow, "and the weapons that rightfully belong to Me."

She covered his clawed hand and drew it from her face. She met his eyes.

"No, Father," she grinned, "Never!"

Mia was sailing through the air from an eruption of waves. She was on the ground before the pool completely drenched and shaken from the vision.

My father has returned for me and he wants to drag me from my happiness into his bitter and horrendous plot! I don't think so!

She studied the pool's surface. It was once again placid. Then something very important dawned on her. Sihoma is a key to something more! Mia jumped to her feet and fled the way she came, praying to the Goddess she would find her way out. She collided into her husband. He looked down his nose at her. His smile quickly evaporated.

"My Gods, Mia, what has happened to you?" he asked urgently.

She couldn't speak. She hurled herself into his arms and allowed his warmth to shroud her. With his strength she could calm herself and collect her thoughts. She needed to reach Sierra in the Ogma Halls and pass along her vision to her. She couldn't do so now. There was no reason to alarm Jacob, or confuse him with things he didn't believe in. He was so eager to spend this first night in Vhladic with her alone. She decided to enjoy the night with her husband, and once the world was asleep, she would climb to the terrace and call upon Blodeuwedd. A visit from her was long over do and Mia wanted answers.

"I thought I would find you out here, but I stumbled into the pond. It startled me is all, love." Mia whispered forcing calm into her voice.

Jacob slowly tilted her face up and looked at her with concerned eyes. She could feel his heart pound against her wet chest. She felt so horrible telling him untruths, but it was merely to protect him.

"Come, you must change from these wet clothes before you become ill. The crispness of approaching autumn is in the air this night." he whispered.

Mia nodded and allowed him to cradle her as they returned to the hall.

Once she was fully changed into a white and silver stola, she made her way down into the garden where he promised to meet her promptly this time. The garden circle was as beautiful as she left it. This time Jacob had prepared a table beneath the diamond sky with jeweled candles and lavish dinner settings. The bronze table was decorated with roses—Mia's favorite flower ever since she first cradled the soft petals in her hand in Gorias—three plum candles danced gently, and silver dishes filled with fish, honey-dipped bread, grapes, a wheel of hard cheese, and flasks of wine. He slid a plush chair from beneath the table and held her arm as she lowered herself. He took his own seat and snatched up her hand in his.

The flickering flames lit tiny embers in his cerulean eyes. Not so long ago, he had selfishly hid his brilliant gaze from her, as well as his unconfessed love. Now she could see the clarity of his heart through the beautiful windows of his eyes. She couldn't breathe or live in this world without him and strangely, she somehow knew it from the moment she met him. Mia drew into her lungs the fragrance of roses and lavender oils from the burning candles.

"Everything is so beautiful. I have never known this kind of happiness, Jacob," Mia said lovingly touching his bearded chin with her free hand.

The ritual silver thorn that nestled within his neatly trimmed beard gleamed beneath the moonlight. It was an unusual kind of jewelry, an unheard of piercing in Thaumatur, but it had always looked appealing to Mia. She, however, noticed that none of the Senate took to wearing such battle memorabilia. The women had never worn such things either, although it was quite common to find them as brave a warrior as the men. Some even more so. It was in the nature of a woman to protect, just as the Great Mother has protected.

"I know, Mia," he whispered understandingly. "I was never one to accept such things for myself."

"I often fear every night before sleep finds me that I will wake to see that I had only dreamt such fortune." Mia looked away from him. "That I am home in Falias beneath the hateful eyes of Merle."

Jacob drew her face back to him, "Your fears will never come to pass."

Mia nodded and her thoughts drifted to a grave secret she could never tell him. If it would return to him by another's lips, could she not lose him? If he truly knew who her birth father was, would he love her still? After all, it was her father who was responsible for his mother's death and the death of so many more of his kind. Her vision had triggered the simple truth, because somehow she was face to face with her father. She knew it was him, she had called him *Father*. He had come for her and her gift to cease the weapons of Danu. She shuddered. If he returned from his banishment, there would be a chance the truth would come out.

"Are you cold?" Mia felt his warm hand press against her cheek as he spoke.

Mia inhaled deeply, "There is something I have been fearful to tell you about previously, Jacob."

"I too must reveal something," He replied quickly. "I didn't speak of this before because I wasn't ready to face it myself."

Mia leaned forward with great interest. His face became solemn, almost nervous with his confession. "Nothing you could say would ever change my love for you." she encouraged him.

"Aldrich has told me that he will name me his successor when the time is right." he paused.

Mia leaped up and threw her arms around him. "That is wonderful news, Jacob! I'm so happy for you!"

He slowly pulled her arms from around his neck and looked deep into her eyes.

"For us, Mia. You will be Empress," he said slowly enough to allow the title to sink in. Her face paled and a battle of nerves and joy clashed within her stomach.

"Me, Empress?" Mia murmured aloud. "Oh dear." She lowered herself into the seat. Her mind was blank.

"You are my wife," He laughed. "No other, even if I had a choice, would be known as Empress by my side."

"I don't know if I'd be any good at it."

"I'm not concerned with that. You have a heart that rejects no soul in need and the temperament of a stern leader. My concerns lie with the Senate and the Brotherhood. Not only will you be the first Empress since my mother, but you are Thaumaturi. I will fear for your safety. I only wish my brother didn't beg me so." His forehead creased with worry.

"Better you than Vastadon," Mia said sourly. "He would rule with a seductive and destructive hand."

"That is one good thing of it. The Senate would sooner see an Empress Thaumaturi as opposed to a Thaumaturi Emperor *and* Empress, but the Brotherhood may see such a successor a benefit. The High Chaplain, reverent or not, has been well-known for his desire to see things his way. The Senate would be more likely to look to him for advice if my nephew took the throne while some still hold respect for me."

Mia suppressed a smile. So Jacob didn't trust the chaplain. Perhaps he is more intuitive than she gave him credit for.

"The Chaplain doesn't seem right to me, Jacob. He intruded on me at the Spa this afternoon merely to bid me farewell. I was only concealed by my hands and the water," Mia sneered.

"He did what?" Jacob growled darting from his seat. "I'll see an answer to such disrespect!"

"It's not necessary. I have made myself clear to him," Mia soothed seeing her husband's fists tighten with anger. "Come, Jacob, let us enjoy our night together without the irksome ghosts of the court."

He grunted, but took his seat again. He ate until he became calm once more. Mia too nibbled on the honey-dipped bread and some cheese. It was delicious.

"So how did your meeting go today? Or assembly—with Senate?" Mia asked in between bites.

"It went as expected. The Emperor has offered his military up if war invades our home. The Senate, of course, impressed on me their disagreements. They think I should abandon the lands to satisfy the Tribes."

"They are foolish then. We would never do that," Mia replied.

Jacob put down his fork for a second and eyed her, "*I* wouldn't do that. Until this thing is settled, I plan to keep you here in Vhladic with your priestess and Kennick."

"You cannot be serious. I'll not stay here without you, Jacob," she argued but Jacob held a hand up to end the conversation and picked up his fork again.

"Forgive me, my wife. I hadn't meant to cut you off from speaking before. What is it you wanted to tell me?" Jacob asked.

Mia had almost forgotten her own secret. The fluttering feeling returned to her, but she swallowed back her apprehension. It wasn't her wish to ruin this night. However, she had no other choice but to tell him. She lowered the piece of bread she nibbled at and inhaled deeply.

"In the beginning, this marriage was something neither one of us wanted. Yet we embraced it anyhow. I'm thankful because of our reluctant decision," Mia paused and saw clouds of confusion hover about his face. "I want to explain to you why I made no attempt to talk Aldrich out of the marriage as I promised you."

"There is no need—" she waved a hand to silence him.

"I need to, Jacob," he nodded and she continued. "The very night after you revealed to me your brother's plan, I unearthed a deep secret Merle and Aiden had buried a long time ago. Upon Lucian's dying wish, I found my way to the south tower of the Winter Palace and entered a wing that held an enchanted mirror. When I was younger, I witnessed a murder. Before my very eyes, my mother was burned at the stake by the hands of my father's followers."

"What are you saying? That Merle isn't your true mother? I find that a relief," he smiled nervously.

Mia looked away, "It is by far worse, Husband. My true mother was Cassiandra DeBurke. Ahriman was my father, not my brother."

Silence. Not even the sound of the trickling fountain or the sputtering flames could penetrate the force field of complete silence. Mia turned her eyes back to Jacob. He didn't meet her gaze. His profile was vividly frowning. He slammed his fist on the table, kicked the chair from beneath him and turned his back to her. He sauntered a good distance away from her, his hands firmly placed on his hips.

"Who else knew of this besides your blasted kin?" he said slowly with an angered edge in his voice.

"My priestess," Mia replied softly and dared not mention the fact that Darius knew as well. Mia hadn't told the Mind Mage of it. He merely helped himself to her brain.

"I cannot believe you have kept this from me!" he snapped. "You might as well have taken it to your grave now!"

"I was afraid that you would be angry!" Mia cried.

"I *am* angry!" he retorted and flew up the garden stairs.

"I was afraid that you would no longer love me!" Mia bellowed.

He stopped in his tracks and peered down on her from the terrace above.

"I love you, Mia. It will not change. That is what angers me so. I'm in love with the daughter of my mother's murderer," he said coldly.

"I wish it were not so! I loathe the man although I have never met him," Mia retorted unable to hide the sting from his words.

She went to him swiftly and grasped his hand between hers. The scowl on his face loosened with her touch, but his ire remained. She refused to lose him now. Damn her father, damn her grandsire for forcing her to face an awful truth.

"I'm not like him. I'd never hate and kill and turn on my own kind or any kind as he did," Mia said her grip tightening on him. "Please, Jacob! Speak to me! I'd give anything to bring your mother back from my father's murderous hand! I'd take her place if I could. I'd do it for you! Because you are all I have and your happiness is all I live for!"

Tears streamed down her cheeks and the breeze caught a lock of her golden hair, pressing it against her forehead. She could see pain in his eyes. He couldn't forget what he saw when he was a child. The cruel murder of his mother haunted him and she had done nothing but resurface such pain. She embraced him tightly. "Forgive me, Jacob. Forgive me for my father's cruel murderous hand."

After a moment, he stroked her hair, "I blame not you. I'm just so angry that someone as kind and precious as you could be spawned from a creature like him."

They held one another for a while as the moon shone its light on them generously. They were the only two in the world.

"I think my father is hunting me, Jacob. I think my father sends the Demons after me," Mia whispered in his hair. A shudder went through her and he was prompted to draw her into him more.

"Over my corpse will he ever place a hand on you," he vowed. "I'm a child no longer."

He led her to the master chambers and guided her to the bed. The room was washed with a tawny hue that illuminated every part of his body with a warrior's fire. His eyes shined down at her with his need and she fell into his strong arms. She couldn't resist him, the feel of him as their bodies became one. A power beyond lovemaking and desire swept through her soul, joining them into one life force, one power, and one peace. It was as if through them, the world united. They made passionate love until they both collapsed into sleep.

Mia awoke in the darkness, slipped into her robe and returned to the garden terrace. It was time to summon Blodeuwedd. It was time for her to speak the entire truth. Blodeuwedd was perched on the balustrade when she arrived.

I was beginning to wonder when you would need me again.

"I need answers. I saw my father," Mia said flatly and folded her arms closely to her chest.

No, he wasn't Ahriman.

"What do you mean? He was before my eyes enforcing his will upon me, but I bested him. That's right. I've waited too long for this kind of happiness and I'll be damned if anyone is going to rip it away from me," Mia snarled.

You called him Father because he is in a sense your father. Bile, the Father God who long ago fell into corruption.

"We discussed this on one of our last meetings. We don't believe in such things!" Mia shook her head.

I know, but how can you honestly think that things are as we believe when you have seen for yourself things that are strange. For many years we didn't believe in Demons, yet is it not Demons that have made their presence known to you?

"Fine. Suppose what you say is true. Where do I go from here?" Mia asked.

It is time to come together with the Goddess' Circle. It's the only way you will be able to retrieve the next weapon. You need the bonds of your companions to move forward. You have isolated yourself for too long.

"So I just forget about the people who are imprisoned? Forget about what has happened to Diamond?" Mia shook her head. "I cannot do that, Blodeuwedd. I have to help save them."

You will save them! But you need the weapons to survive such a battle of liberation! You would be no good to the prisoners if you end up dead.

"I will beg Jacob to take me to the temple. I must feel what, if any, kind of magic is at work there," Mia said firmly. "Once the chance arises, I will come together with Cole, Horace, and Aunyia."

You must come together with more than the three. You have your own Bond to heal.

A wind swept through Mia. It turned her skin inside out and brushed her with infectious darkness. Something evil. Prophecy. Mia clung to the balustrade and shot her eyes to Blodeuwedd. The owl's eyes were wide and her head swiveled in rhythm with her frantic bouncing.

"Aldrich!" Mia cried his name.

The Emperor is dying! Blodeuwedd's voice shrieked and she was gone.

Mia fled to her husband and shook him from sleep. When she told him of her feeling, the vision the Demons had given her probed at her mind once again. They had shown her the death of the Emperor. A thousand wails invaded her mind, including her own.

They didn't linger to freshen. Within the half hour, Jacob and Mia sailed to the imperial palace.

CHAPTER THIRTY-SIX

Dark Magic

"I'm in no mood, Falcon!" Merle strode across the marble floor. "My son is an idiot, my staff is unbearable and I won't deal with an Elder at my door snooping around as if they could ever find anything out I don't want them to know."

Falcon inclined his head but didn't retreat from the chamber. Merle snapped her head to the side and met his slow gaze.

"The Elder who has come isn't from our Season House of the Sapphire Crest," he replied flatly. "The white robe *Enchantra* Grand Paladin is here and she won't allow us to turn her away."

"What?" Merle hissed and widened her eyes. "I'll not see *her*! Find out what she wants." Merle stomped her heel to the marble floor when her advisor didn't leave. He let out a long bored sigh and approached her.

"She has told me what she wants and, believe me, she'll wait an entire Moon Cycle before she retreats without answers." He shook his head and lifted her hand to his lips.

Merle, his lovely and cold queen, trembled for the first time since Ahriman's banishment. The woman was strong, intelligent, and entirely too confidant with her plans of vengeance. Her service to the Father God was unyielding, but she often forgot that, although her Power was unique and prominent, she was merely a mortal woman just like any other. She could be caught. She could be imprisoned. She could even be executed, even if a crime of multi-kingdom involvement was usually punished by means of incarceration within the Nightingale Prison. It was the intentional plan for the Legion's punishment, yet they were excommunicated from the moment they fled the Sun Knighthood military. That meant that Ahriman could never set foot back into Thaumatur without being identified and imprisoned.

Falcon himself was lucky. He escaped the trials of the Legion by the skin of his teeth and the thickly lined pockets of his garb. He couldn't help Ahriman, although he would've if he could. His master was ignorant and cocky. He had never made it a secret what he intended to do and that alone was his downfall. He would not've taken the precautions Falcon took.

Falcon studied the pale face of his queen. Even though she was a striking woman, she had aged over the past two Moon Cycles. Her face was unhealthily slender and her onyx eyes were clouded with insanity. She doubted her actions. He knew it as sure as he knew his own feelings.

"Does she suspect your dealings concerning Vansant Summit?" Merle asked nervously.

"Be at ease my queen. After I found out what I needed to know from the young and foolish Vastadon Delucible, I came in contact with a mere trembling. He was so fearful. Even if I wasn't entirely concealed, I doubt the boy could even begin to describe my face," Falcon smirked. "And I left him the impression that I was an Elder from the Order. Has it been that long? You couldn't possibly forget my skills."

She lowered her head, "I suppose you're right, Falcon. I'm just not up for games! What the hell does the witch want?"

"Karenna Bell wants to ask you some questions in regards to the marriage of your daughter to the Barbarian, My Queen. You must clear this up because the Grand Paladin will not accept me in your place. You know I wouldn't be here if she would," Falcon told her softly and kissed her frail fingers again.

"I know," she whispered and squeezed his hand gently. Falcon released her hand and she turned her back on him. She sighed heavily, almost defeated, and pressed her hands to her hips.

"I'm getting too old for this, Falcon," Merle began. "The games, the darkness…"

Falcon immediately placed a hand on her shoulder and whispered in her ear, "Then you should've never brought Ahriman into the world, My Queen."

Merle turned to face him, her eyes wide and her brows arched with perplexity. His meaning was clear. He wouldn't yield to the influence of the Order and as long as she stuck to the plan without wavering, he'd remain loyal to her. If she faltered, although he loved her and always would, he would walk away from her, leaving only the shadows of her tower to comfort her. She nodded, regained her posture and sauntered off to face the Elder.

He did his job. He pushed the child out of Merle and made her face what she needed to face. Bile help the *Enchantra* if she figures anything out. If she does, Falcon would make certain she wouldn't live long enough to tell about it.

He spun on his heels and followed his queen to the receiving hall. He had made certain that the servants understood not to impose on the meeting and he arranged for several of the finer whores to gather in Aiden's four rooms. He would be occupied for hours.

Grand Paladin Karenna Bell wasn't at all attractive in the face. She was a spinster who lived her nearly ageless life without a mate. Falcon had to admit that she was quite fit for her age. She sat elegantly in the high back chair before the hearth, her right leg swung impatiently. She leaned forward in liquid folds of white to her waist. Beneath her partial robe she wore snug white breaches and knee-high leather boots. When Merle approached, she swayed her head in the direction with unreadable eyes.

"*Enchantra*," Merle inclined her head and took a seat directly in front of her. Falcon stood behind Merle.

"Lady Queen of Winter," Karenna smiled and extended her hand.

Merle took it and released it quickly, "Would you care for some refreshments?"

"Nay, gracious you," Karenna waved a hand. "I've come to you for a report. I will make my business clear and brief."

"Very well, but I have little to say. I fear your report will be rather boring," Merle replied with a frigid smile.

"I doubt that," Karenna replied with a slight edge. "It seems you have sent our commanders and *Enchantras* into a whirlpool with your sudden interest in joining your daughter up with a Barbarian by matters of peace."

"Is it so wrong to give my daughter a better life? He wasn't just *a* Barbarian. He is High Prince and a good candidate for the native Emperor's throne." Merle replied smoothly.

"I'd be willing to accept that as an answer simply because you are known for securing such power. However, I think there is much more to it especially since your youngest daughter's birth was never recorded in the healing center's scrolls," Karenna replied a bit harshly.

"I had no need for one of your healers when I had one of my own to birth my child. I am a private woman and it is my right to choose my healing preferences."

"So be it, Lady, but I find it quite curious that you were willing to ship your last child off with a Barbarian well known for his bigotry." Karenna lifted her chin disbelievingly.

"Perhaps my daughter loved him. After all, he protected her for nearly two years as her personal guard. Constant companionship with two handsome people could spark a love interest," Merle answered immediately.

"Doubtful," the Elder sighed and leaned back. "Tell me what you know of the island."

"What island?" Merle smiled coldly.

"Sihoma. I know you know something. You have an advisor who is an inhabitant to this island." Karenna lifted her eyebrows.

"Sermino came to us many years ago. He was a member of some foreign tribe, but that is all I know. I didn't even know there was an island. Now," Merle stood hastily, "if we are finished, allow Falcon to accommodate you with whatever you need. I've been ill and cannot waste any time on secrets I have no knowledge about. Secrets you and your

Order seem to know all *too* much about and choose to selfishly hide them from the other divisions of rule."

Karenna Bell stood slowly and nodded, "I have been watching you. And someone watches your daughters. I know *your* secrets and I know you are meeting with the Necromancers of the Legion. You will never get a way with the treasures."

"I know nothing of the *weapons* and if you believe that I do, then why don't you prove it," Merle scowled. "Good day, Grand Paladin."

Falcon shot Merle a nervous look. Merle's face was a sheet of ice while she watched Karenna depart. Once the woman left within a flurry of white, she met Falcon's eyes.

"Make sure she and her elite never make it back to Tania's Citadel. Now I think it time we learn of this island she speaks so worriedly of. It's time to find those weapons!" Merle commanded and spun on her heels.

Falcon grinned.

That a girl. You have stepped up to your position.

He fled to his plain chamber east of his queen's, adjoined as a matter of fact for delightful ease, and flung open the cedar chest in the far corner. He hadn't opened it since his final day with Ahriman. He pulled out his chain mail vest, his black and navy blue breeches, and his cowl-robe marked with vipers of the Legion. The vipers brocaded on his robe were silver indicating the highest ranking commander in the Legion. He laced up his soft leather boots that offered comfort and quick stepping and streaked his face with charcoal spirals. His gauntlets were made of thick iron weighing down his pampered wrists. It indeed had been too long, he thought with a grimace. He found the eyes of the iron snake that marked his gauntlets and pressed them. Three spikes shot from each of his wrists instantly. Falcon smiled.

Once he was garbed, he peeled open the folds of his robe and inserted three daggers, one short sword, an onyx wand, and two curved blades. He tied a scarf around his mouth neatly and braided his hair tightly to his scalp for better concealing beneath the black bandana he wore under his cowl.

He dropped to one knee and placed two smaller daggers into each boot and closed his eyes tightly. He prayed to the Father God for protection and strength and rose to his feet. He wandered to the polished metal mirror and grinned beneath his face mask. He loved the way he looked in the Legion uniform.

Merle had entered before he noticed. Only she could sneak upon him so easily. Her dark eyes sparkled as she allowed them to wander over his form. She had always liked him in uniform too. Her cheeks reddened but her color quickly evaporated and she regained her expression of stone.

"How many?" he said through the muffle of the mouth scarf.

"Three knights, one advisor, and a governor I don't recognize," Merle replied curtly. "Kill them all."

"Very well," he replied and set about to the hidden passages of the palace.

It was dark, and the snow covered the ground in soft layers, not ice, thankfully. Falcon caught sight of his prey and he took them down one by one with silent precision. He made certain, once he had the Grand Paladin at his mercy, that she saw his face.

Even when he drove his sword through her heart, the woman made no change in her fearless expressions. Such a pity a woman of her nature was wasted on uselessness. But it was too late for that, now, wasn't it?

He marked the bodies with his onyx wand, singeing the flesh on the corpses' forehead with the markings of the viper. It would occupy the Order's time for many Moons.

He cast his eyes to the tree line and grinned. The Necromancers, part Demon and part mortal, pointed their scepters to the Agustu moon.

"Welcome back, Brothers! We have a war to invade!" Falcon called to them.

Thane, always dressed in oversized stolas of grey, was sister to Jacob's father, the last of his siblings still living. She had shrunk from age and shriveled from constant bitterness. Her hand was planted firmly on her bony hip and she stood in Jacob's path before the corridors of Aldrich's chambers.

"Your brother is too unwell for visitors," Thane replied slowly sweeping her eyes over Mia with clear distaste. "He has been struck with something the medics cannot even name let alone have a cure for."

"Aunt, I'll see Aldrich with or without your consent!" Jacob brushed by her.

After four strides, he spun on his heels. Thane was blocking Mia's path with a gnarled outstretched hand. Mia didn't force her way through the older woman, although she could've easily done so. Jacob tightened his jaw. He wouldn't leave his wife alone in this city. Not even within his brother's imperial palace. Thaumaturi were hated everywhere. The people were just better about masking it here in Vhladic. And with Aldrich unwell, Jacob was certain the High Chaplain oversaw the city. Hector would rule it as Luthros had. The thought of such a thing birthed a battle of mixed emotions inside his heart and his stomach. It was a feeling he fought all of his life whenever he was in Vhladic. It was the reason why he was slow to accept the idea of being Aldrich's successor.

He strived for his father's approval, but he valued his mother's compassion, even to those who sent her to her death. Until now, he was content in the country, a warrior and a leader, away from politics and royalty, and festering in his bigotry. But this woman, who he prevented himself from ever truly knowing, had awakened a side of him he never believed he had. He would die before he'd let harm befall her.

"If you must see your brother, so be it. But I'll not let this *magician* by!" Thane said sharply.

"She is kin to the Emperor by marriage, Thane. A marriage he himself arranged. She has as much right as I to see him," Jacob shot back. "Let my wife pass."

"She can wait for you in the temple," Thane ignored his words. "Now go before I change my mind about you."

Thane's ignorance caused him to stomp back. He towered over her, looking down the ridge of his nose. Thane didn't falter and looked up at him with her own challenges.

"It is all well," Mia intervened with a soft patient voice. "Aldrich is most important now. I won't have you waste such valuable time on a useless quarrel."

He shifted his eyes to her and his heart skipped a beat. She was beautiful in everyway. Her deep violet-blue eyes shone with genuine sorrow. It was clear to Jacob that she had pushed the ignorant remarks of Thane aside for the sake of the Emperor.

"If you must wait. I'd prefer you not go to the temple. Remain here until I come for you," Jacob caved in. Thane flashed him a wrinkled smile before he turned and walked away.

The Emperor's chamber was guarded by a mass of white clad imperial guards. They immediately stepped aside with one look from Jacob. He pushed through the polished wooden doors and was swallowed by inky-darkness. Two sconces on both sides of a thickly draped bed held torches with little life. For a moment his legs felt weighted down. The man, who he had not only loved as his Emperor but as a father and a brother, was within the neatly molded bed dying. How could it be this way? Jacob had always thought himself to die much sooner than Aldrich in battle. Aldrich was the best of them. He was so like Mother.

Jacob swallowed hard and went to the bed. He looked down on his brother with a heavy heart. Aldrich's eyes were closed. Beads of sweat dotted his forehead and drizzled down his cheeks. His breathing was laboring.

"Brother," Jacob whispered and lowered himself into the chair near to the bed.

Aldrich stirred, but his eyes remained closed. Jacob reached his hand to grab a cloth from the bowl nearby and wiped the sweat from his head. The man *was* dying. Jacob felt his brother's life evaporating. And Mia knew it. Jacob, for the first time, didn't question the mysteries of magic. He trusted his wife.

"I'm here, Brother," Jacob whispered again.

The corners of Aldrich's lips twitched up into a half smile. His eyes remained closed. This horrible moment was the first they shared privately between them since the night on the balcony in Falias. How long ago it seemed. How petty the arguments between them were. He'd give his own life to spare the man grasping for life beneath him.

"Jacobane," Aldrich's voice was merely a whispering wind. "You've forgiven me, then?"

"There is nothing to forgive, my lord Emperor," Jacob replied and brought his lips to Aldrich's signet ring.

"I've done things that shouldn't have been done. I have hurt those who I love most. But it was only a matter of peace that drove me," Aldrich whispered, "Have I become so arrogant that I am blind?"

"You are a good ruler, Brother," Jacob squeezed his hand gently.

Aldrich went into a seizure of coughs. Jacob steadied him with his strong hands.

"When I leave this world, how will I be remembered? As the man who destroyed his own people or the coward who has divided them?" Aldrich whispered sadly.

"You'll be remembered for what you are. A man who loved all people, no matter the case," Jacob swallowed. "They will recall your valor and determination."

"I wasn't a good father." Aldrich raised a shaky hand to silence Jacob's repose. "And I've hurt the woman I love. I should've brought her here and proudly married her before it became too late. You were right, Jacobane. I had wished to right my wrongs through you. I was selfish to place you in such a position. I was unfair to the princess too. She is special, you know…important."

"You must rest, Brother," Jacob said firmly.

"I'm sorry, Jacobane. If you wish to remain in Vansant Summit, then you are free from my will."

"You were right, Aldrich," Jacob told him and paused when the weak smile returned to Aldrich's face. "I have love for my wife and she is special. I know that now."

"You have come together?" Aldrich whispered. "Have you shared your secret with her? Have you told her she will be Empress?"

"I have," Jacob replied.

"The Gods work in mysterious ways," Aldrich whispered and sunk lower into the large pillows. "I long to see Miarosa. Have you brought her with you?"

"Yes. I shall get her at once," Jacob rose and left swiftly.

He passed the guards and stole away into a shadowed corner of the corridor. With the sight of Aldrich still in his mind, he lowered himself in a crouching position. Then he did something he hadn't done since he was a child. He wept.

Aunyia awoke to the sound of pattering feet below. She was in her wing, quite isolated from the rest of the palace. The noise indeed was loud to pull her out of sleep. She lifted herself from bed, careful not to disturb her younger cousin Ethane from her slumber. She tossed on her robe and tiptoed out of her chambers.

Aunyia listened carefully. The noise had stopped, but she wouldn't be able to get back to sleep until she found out exactly what caused it. The knight in her awoke. When she made her way through the wing and her part of the palace she came upon her Great Aunt Thane blocking the way to her father's apartments. Mia leaned against the arches of the outer doors.

"What is all the noise about? What has happened?" Aunyia asked urgently.

"Go back to sleep, you!" Thane pointed a crooked finger at her.

"I'll not Aunt!" Aunyia yelled.

Mia rushed to Aunyia's side. "Aldrich is ill, Aunyia," she explained and kissed both her cheeks.

"You *magician*!" Thane hissed. "You dare upset the First Princess!"

"Dare you insult my Aunt? Let me pass!" Aunyia exclaimed.

"No. I will not subject the Emperor to such disruption!" Thane jutted her chin.

"You," Vastadon hissed as he stormed through a wall of guards pointing a finger at his great aunt.

Aunyia inclined her head careful to keep her annoyance from spreading to her face. Despite the fact that she was never close to her brother and never desired to be close to him, she knew if anyone could get them through the stubborn woman it would be him.

"Vastidrich," she took his gloved hands in hers and kissed him formally before the guards and Thane.

"I'm afraid I cannot let either of you in. Your father is too ill and he already is visiting with Jacobane," Thane snapped.

Vastadon cocked his head at the old woman. "And you think you will stop me?" he laughed. "You have no right to. He is *my* father. Step aside."

"I'll not!" Thane's whole frail frame shook with anger and obstinacy.

The guards behind Vastadon shifted and a beautiful woman slipped through. The Viscount's daughter, Camille, strode to her husband's side and took his hand. She was garbed in stunning sparkles of mauve and her pale hair was swept into a rose-style bun. Curls strayed from the crown of her head. Vastadon and Camille made a beautiful couple.

Vastadon opened his mouth to rebut but stopped when his eyes fixed on something beyond Aunyia. Camille followed his line of sight and arched her platinum brows. Aunyia spun and looked at Mia whose went pale, attempting to shrink from the crowd. After several breaths he returned his attention back to Thane. Camille continued to stare.

"I see you have refused to let my sister *and* the High Princess in along with Jacobane. Could it be because we are all Thaumaturi?" He smirked evilly.

"Of course not!" Thane became flustered.

Mia tugged on Aunyia's arm and leaned into her ear, "Please tell Jacob I've gone to the temple. I don't think so many of us will gain advantage over this woman."

"Are you okay, Mia? Has my brother done something to you?" Aunyia questioned quietly because she had a sensation in her gut that forcefully told her that there was much more between Vastadon and Mia.

"I'm okay," Mia said quickly and glided past them.

Vastadon watched her leave. His stare was so deep it made Aunyia uncomfortable for his wife. Camille inclined her head to Aunyia and kissed Vastadon before following Mia's path.

"Excuse us, Aunt," Aunyia said and slid a hand through Vastadon's arm guiding him away from the ears of the others.

"Tell me, Brother. Is there something between you and Mia?" she asked.

He focused his ice-blue eyes on her. It was a look that would send a weaker person to their knees. He emanated power and she wondered if he too was a Mageborn. He drew his breath in and enfolded her in his arms. His breath was hot against her ear.

"You don't want to know, Sister," he whispered and spun her free from his cold embrace. He strolled back to Thane, shoved the old woman aside, and strode through.

"I told you. You couldn't stop me," he called back arrogantly. "Coming, Sister?"

Thane pressed a knotty hand to her chest and her face paled with shock. After a moment, Aunyia followed her brother to see their father. There would be time later to learn the details of Vastadon and Mia's strange and silent conflict.

Aldrich was alone when the two came through the door and for a brief moment she was bewildered. Thane hadn't lied because Mia's presence indicated Jacob to be there. But he wasn't there.

Aunyia fled to Aldrich's side and kissed his cold cheek. Her tears spilled across her father's face.

"Father, oh Father…" she wept whatever words she couldn't speak.

She couldn't lose him now that they were reunited after all of these years. Had someone hurt him? Could he be healed? She probed at her magic with little care that her brother stood not even a foot away from her. Heat rushed to her hands as she stroked Aldrich's cheek, but her magic wasn't strong enough. He was warded and debilitating from some magic disease. Aunyia grimaced. He was being deliberately murdered. She shifted her eyes to her brother, who took no care in hiding his impatience. And instantly she knew he didn't want their father to recover. He wanted the throne.

Vastadon turned his attention on her. She grimaced at him and as she moved to confront him, Aldrich's frail grip halted her.

"Daughter," he whispered. "I must speak with my son privately."

The caves were silent with the rising of the sun. The High Priestess awaited the return of Cole with some news. And to ease Alabaster and

Phoenix's patience, she arranged some small duties for them to do. Investigations in the House and inspections of the coasts dominated their time giving her space to work with Diamond. The two of them were off for sometime in Findias. Janella wanted Alabaster to take a break and return to his homeland. And it was a good enough excuse to see the Queen, Arabella. Perhaps she heard some news from her sister—niece....

Miarosa was always important to her. But it was even more personal now. She was the daughter of her sister, as Darius was her sister's son. She was dying inside not knowing what was happening in their lives now. She had kept her distance from the Wysteria Well. She couldn't allow herself the temptation with Diamond so delicate in her health. The Goddess had not spoken to her. Janella was fearful that she had done something to displease Her.

If only to receive word...

"Are you okay?" Diamond asked with concern.

"Aye," Janella answered quickly shaking the thoughts from her head. "How do you feel today?" She sat on the edge of the bed and stroked Diamond's locks.

She looked a little better this day, but it had taken much time for her to get to this point. Her memory was gone. She only knew her brother's name and her own name. Janella was slowly teaching her the things she had forgotten.

As if this tough and brave child hadn't been through enough!

"I'm okay," Diamond smiled child-like. "Will Phoenix come to see me today?"

"I'm sure he will," Janella replied and smiled brightly.

"Hello Diamond," King Valance said kindly as he came through the door, "How are you?" A smile played on her lips when he gently tousled her hair.

"Very well, my lord." She swung her legs off of the bed and looked at Janella with a twinkle in her honey eyes. "I wish to walk through the grove, my lady."

"Don't wander too far. You didn't break your fast yet." Janella cocked her head.

Diamond nodded and left them alone.

For a moment Janella contemplated spilling Darius' secret out. The pain of Cassiandra's death would be as unbearable for Valance as it was for her. But she also respected Darius's wishes to remain silent until he was ready. Janella forced a smile on her face and placed a gentle kiss on his cheek.

"Valance, have you news?" Janella took his hands in hers.

With a great sigh Valance said, "I am afraid it isn't good news."

"What is it then?" she became alarmed.

"The body of the Grand Paladin was found this morning. All of her guards and the officiator that accompanied her were also found dead. They were killed in the manner of Ahriman's Legion. The marking of the Necromancers was burned into their foreheads. Karenna hadn't mentioned to the Order where she headed."

"Oh my Goddess, Valance. Oh my—" Janella gasped and squeezed his hands.

She had never seen eye to eye with the stern woman, but her death affected her. Karenna wasn't a bad woman though a little misguided in her ideas. Her death would be a great loss to the structures of rule in Thaumatur. What shook her even more was the idea of the Necromancers daring return. Half undead and near invincible, they were feared by many.

"They've asked the Viscount to take her place, for she had no successor," Valance said grimly.

"The Viscount? That is absurd! He knows nothing of the delicate nature of the Elemental Rites and the true form of Power in an *Enchantra!*"

"I know. But I'm afraid I can do nothing about it. What I can do is see to your safety here now that the Legion has marked their return," Valance patted her hand. "I worry for you now that your knights are gone."

"Alabaster and Phoenix will return soon," Janella protested what she knew he would say.

"You know they must be free from any tied down responsibilities because they could be Called into duty by the Goddess at any waking moment. Let me set you up with two brigades from the Sun Knighthood for constant vigilance. One for the day and one at night," Valance said with finality.

"I suppose so, but please provide them with our rules. This place is sacred," Janella implored.

"I will," he laughed at her.

Abruptly, Janella hurdled to the floor. Her skull felt as if it was split slowly open with a spoon. Valance quickly supported her with his big arms. Blood poured from beneath her eyelids. Red was all she saw, pain was all she felt.

Death…Death

She was swimming in a blood pool and no matter how hard she tried she couldn't find an edge to hike herself upon.

Putrid death…flashes of gray robes…Barbarians dead all around her. From the crimson surface, a great glowing sword rose gripped in the fist of a woman.

Janella's legs were heavy and she could barely kick. She was sinking into the vat of blood… Drowning…

Mother…Father is dying….

Janella screamed and fell back hard against Valance. Sweat poured from her face, stinging her eyes. Her eyes and mouth were wide in shock.

"Aldrich is dying!" she wailed. "Bring me the last Earth Crystal."

The temple was large and beautiful, monstrous with its double towers glowing beneath the threads of golden sunrise. The first gates opened up into a reception pavilion draped with purple and green. The roof and pillars were yellow polished marble that sloped down the rear and was connected by a covered corridor. Mia followed the causeway to the open court of the temple within which stood an obelisk made of limestone. Huge onyx arched doorways rounded the circumference of the obelisk. Each door had its own symbol of a God on the face of the door, the center and fourth door was designed with the knotted triangle of the Trinity. Mia approached that door and traced her fingers along the indentations, looping around each knot. Although she didn't worship the Trinity of Gods, the feel of their emblem somehow gave her comfort. She said a silent prayer for the life of Aldrich to Danu *and* the Trinity.

When she finished, she pushed through the fourth door. The morning light streamed in through the slender windows cut into the roof giving the temple an ethereal presence. Three green carpeted aisles stretched down to three separate altars dedicated to each God. Gold statues rose behind large marble altars kissed by spiraling incense. Mia inhaled the spicy scents of the temple and closed her eyes.

Aunyia's question about her and Vastadon repeated in her mind over and over. Was it so obvious this dark connection between them? But Mia remembered the connection she too shared with Aunyia and the other knights. They sensed things that no one else could ordinarily know. She couldn't tell her how awful her brother was. Not now while her father lay dying.

"Miarosa Hilliard," A strong female voice caught her attention.

Mia spun and tilted her head. She drew closer and immediately recognized Vastadon's wife Camille.

Chapter Thirty-Seven

The Emperor's Son

It wasn't her fault, Mia reminded herself silently. *She is innocent.*

The woman before her wasn't the laughing arrogant woman she saw in the Gorias flirting with her future husband beneath the dazzling atmosphere of the ballroom. She looked tired. Scornful.

"Lady Camille," Mia nodded her head. "I'm afraid we haven't had the pleasure of formally meeting."

Camille snorted, but extended her elegant hand. Mia took it lightly in her palm and shook it.

"Yes, well, pity it took something awful to bring us together." Camille glided ahead facing the altar of Lugh. "And what an awful thing to happen during the first week of the Barbarian Gods' Celebration."

"I know. Aldrich is a good man. I pray for him," And Mia added, "To Danu and the Trinity."

"I wouldn't speak Danu's name so freely here. The Brothers and Chaplains might scale down from these great adorned walls and burn you alive at the stake," Camille replied haughtily.

The comment was meant in derisive jest, but she hadn't known how her words seared through Mia's memory. Her mother was burned in such a way. Hideously painful way…

Mia truly doubted Camille knew anything of that. She cleared her throat and strode up beside her.

"Aldrich has brought the races together fairly well," Mia spoke not quite sure what to say.

Camille nodded and for a long while, the two women were content in their silence. Mia often wondered about the kind of woman she was. She was more beautiful than any other woman she saw. How could Vastadon not be satisfied with her?

Camille interrupted the silence with a sob, "I hate it here."

It took Mia by surprise, but she was quick to encircle her arms around the woman's shoulders. Camille trembled with each sob and with each sob she nearly crumbled. Mia didn't know how to comfort her. It was strange.

"I hate the life that has been chosen for me," Camille continued through her tears and jerked her body from Mia's grip. "He pretends I'm you, you know."

Mia froze. It was as if she was thrown into a vat of ice cold water. *Goddess, no.*

"Every single night he comes upon my person, demanding me to fight him off. At first I'd thought it a little lover's game. But when it didn't stop after the third night, I truly began to fight him. He calls your name over and over again. Raping me, his own wife, who would give him whatever he wanted." The tears flowed from her eyes until she tossed them to the side angrily. "What happened to you that night happens to me over and over again."

"No!" Mia hissed and took hold of Camille's fisted hands. "We must stop him."

The thought terrified her. She couldn't imagine suffering that pain, that humiliation, and that degradation every single night. Guilt rode her blood and settled behind her anger. She wanted to kill him slowly. This beautiful woman didn't deserve such pain.

"He cannot be stopped," Camille said through clenched teeth. "He would kill my father and get away with it too. He has the power to do so."

"You cannot suffer this anymore," Mia snapped. "What if he goes too far and kills *you*?"

Camille ripped her hands away and threw her head back in bitter laughter. "Do you think I care if he kills me? I pray every night that he does. And do you want to know the crazy thing about it? I *still* love him. He *makes* me love him."

"Please, let me help you," Mia pleaded. The woman was abused and sick. She needed to help her. She was desperate to stop this tyrant she had unknowingly created.

"*You* cannot help me. It's too late for that!" Camille snapped. "*You* should be where I am now. It's *you* he hates and it's *you* he wants to hurt, not me. I married the wrong Hilliard!"

Insanity danced in her eyes and Mia believed she comforted herself with those last words she spat. She pitied her and wanted to force her hand to help her, but she couldn't lead a horse to water and make it drink.

"I want you to know, despite your confusion, that I'm here if you need my help," Mia offered gently.

Camille opened her mouth to respond but closed it quickly and smiled. She strode past Mia and kissed Jacob's cheeks. His eyes were heavy and his broad shoulders slumped. Mia was pained with his sadness as well as her own.

"I'm praying for your brother, my kinsman," Camille said sweetly.

She inclined her head to Mia and swiftly left the temple. Mia ran into Jacob's arms and held him close to her. His pain flooded through her pours and soured her stomach.

"I asked you not to come here, Mia," he whispered, "It's not safe especially now—now that Aldrich is ill."

"He will pull through, Jacob. He's strong and his daughter is a Healer. He doesn't reject magic as you," Mia smiled and brushed a strand from his brow, "Did you not see her?"

"No, I didn't—" Jacob responded.

"I'm here Uncle," Aunyia interceded floating toward them.

"Did you see your father, Niece?" he kissed her cheeks and she did the same.

"Yes, briefly. He wanted to speak privately with Vastidrich," Aunyia shook her head.

Jacob tensed, "I don't trust him alone with my brother."

"I know, but Father didn't dismiss his chamber guard. So be at ease," Aunyia soothed and met eyes with Mia.

"Can you heal him?" Mia questioned urgently.

Aunyia glanced at Jacob. He roamed down to the altar of Dagda and inclined his head.

"No," Aunyia replied. "Someone is murdering him and the sickness is warded from my magic."

Mia gasped, "Perhaps I can call on Sierra—the two of you—maybe even the three of us—"

Aunyia shook her head, "No. It's tied too deeply into him. I know what I must do to save him. We have an idea where the shards are and with that in my grip, my Powers to heal would multiply by the thousands."

"I want to help, Aunyia," Mia implored. After all, she had come to Vhladic with intentions on discovering what her duty was.

"Not now, Mia. Not in this. I need you to comfort my uncle for he will take it the worst out of all of us if my father should die." Mia thought she spoke too unemotional. The girl hid her hurting well.

"Very well, but there is something I need to tell you. I had a vision."

Aunyia nodded and listened closely as Mia told her the vision and her conclusions with Sihoma. She also decided to tell her of the attack in the forest and the vision of Aldrich's death.

"Visions are warnings, not facts," Aunyia replied sharply. "After all of this is done and my father is well again and he *will* be well again, it sounds as if we will have to find this Sihoma Island. I must go and meet with Cole at the inn. By the way, have you seen Horace?"

"You haven't? He left Vhladic nearly five days before Jacob and I," Mia queried.

"Perhaps he'll turn up with some useful information. He does the disappearing act often. He is well," Aunyia added when she noticed Mia's worry.

They embraced each other and Aunyia was off. Mia regretted she could be of no help. But her friend was right. Her husband needed her and she wouldn't leave his side. She went to him and placed a hand on his shoulder. Together they silently prayed.

The night had been a long one and Aldrich scarcely remembered when the first violent tremor seized him. He'd been slowly dying, and he hadn't realized it until this night. Over the past few months he coughed a little more than he should have and the fits only grew worse with blood in his phloem. He slept much more often, but with his stubborn will, he managed to push himself to the Senate assemblies.

And now, as death was nearing, he had but one desire. To see Janella one last time. To explain to her the truth of his intentions. To tell her how his ambition was to unite the two races underneath the rule of two good and fair people blended together so perfectly. To tell her how sorry he was that they weren't the ones to marry and accomplish such a goal. To tell her how much he loved her.

Aldrich raised his eyes to the stony face of their son. How could his son be so cold? Aldrich could feel his son's eagerness for the throne—for his death. He had Janella's eyes, though slight difference in color. Vastadon was tainted. Gods, he was destroyed. His son placed a heavy gloved hand upon his. He couldn't bear human touch, could he?

"I must ask you to—"

"You want the world to say that you are my successor," Aldrich whispered weakly. "And what would you do with such power, Son?"

"I would see that the Thaumaturi would be treated equally," Vastadon countered quickly.

"By what means? Blood shed? War upon Jacobane over a woman?" Aldrich paused. "Have you not begun already?"

"Jacob has poorly supported your beliefs. He must be controlled," Vastadon sneered.

"He has fallen in love with her. She has shown him the error of his ways," Aldrich said and felt the grip of his son tighten. "Would you destroy your own uncle and the woman you claim to love so much?"

"I wouldn't let harm befall her, but the war has already been declared. Jacobane will meet his fate," Vastadon hissed. "Under my rule the lands would become one."

"Under the Empire," Aldrich replied softly.

"Under *my* Empire," Vastadon corrected him.

"You will take the Thaumaturi freedom from them in exchange for their acceptance," Aldrich sighed.

"It's the only way agreeable in the Senate," Vastadon replied haughtily. "You have failed, Father. I will not."

"So you are quick to discuss alternatives with the Senate already?" Aldrich went into a seizure of coughs. "I don't know why you loathe me so, Son. I've tried to love you, nurture you and give you honor. Why have you become so bitter?"

"You made me bitter, Father," He hissed. "You have always loved Jacobane better than me."

"I loved you both the same," Aldrich interrupted. "It is you who have become so greedy that not even a father's love could be shared."

"And what of you, Father?" Vastadon growled. "You kept me apart from my birth mother and never told me who she was. If she lives. If she is dead. You kept that knowledge all to yourself." Vastadon tore his hand away. "You took my own sister from me before we had the chance to know one another. Now she, the sister I have never known, looks upon me with disdain. And you ripped the only woman who has ever looked upon me with the truth of her heart and twisted it into hate. You gave her to your *precious* Jacobane."

"She wasn't for you—" Aldrich responded.

"And she is for *him*? He cursed you for the forced marriage only to fall in love with her well after the contempt?"

"You used your magic in vain against her to influence her feelings and then you go and rape her!" Aldrich's voice gained some volume. "Rape her and leave her a destroyed mess? You call that love?"

"You made me what I am!" Vastadon thundered. "There was no other way to make her see. You left me with no choice, Father."

"See what, Son? Have you gone insane? Truly something is wrong when you refuse to see the immorality of your actions."

Vastadon smiled widely, "She needed to see how we were meant to be One. Her Power *needs* me for completion. Your Jacobane will never be enough for that purpose."

"Jacobane is my successor. He will become Emperor and Miarosa his Empress," Aldrich sighed into the silence. "You're not ready."

"You never loved *me*. *He* was more of a son to you," Vastadon bellowed. "I will have his wife as my whore and he'll be dead by the Moon's end. Name him if you will, but it won't be passed from my lips. From this room." Vastadon eyed the guard in the room before he returned his insane eyes back to Aldrich. He placed his gloved hand over Aldrich's ring.

"My poor doom-fated son, never touch me again," Aldrich replied and withdrew his eyes and his hand from Vastadon.

Vastadon lowered his head to his father's hand and spit on his signet ring.

"I will find my mother and know her love. You won't live long enough to keep us separated any longer," Vastadon said with horrible pleasure.

"I'm here, Son," A soft familiar voice sang from the shadows. A flash of green light expanded silently and retracted behind a slender figure garbed in burgundy robes.

Aldrich gasped and Vastadon wheeled around in awe.

Janella watched her son from a distance become a man much different than his father. Oh, how she wanted to embrace him and absorb all of the venom from his veins. Though she didn't think it possible to save him now, she needed to try. It was a mother's job to try. He had known of her. Who hadn't? She was the High Priestess of the Brosian Ministry. Yet their blood ties remained secret. She kept them secret to spare her children confusion and judgment.

"*You're* my mother?" Vastadon whispered. "It cannot be."

Janella floated toward him, but fought her wish to embrace her beautiful son. He inched away.

"I am," Janella said softly.

Silence befell them and she watched her son battle emotions within him. He straightened his posture and approached her warily. He then brought his gloved hand to her cheek and looked deeply into her eyes. She felt him groping her mind with magic and she didn't resist him. He was searching for the truth. Let him have it.

"Mother," he whispered and drew her into an embrace. "You've abandoned me."

"I didn't abandon you. I watched you grow and loved you always."

"As you love Anne?" She felt his embrace grow tight.

"Yes, as I love Anne," she replied and pried his hold around her open. She took his hands in hers and looked into his eyes. He was hurting and bitter. Resentful.

"Liar!" he hissed and yanked his hands from her, "Dare you lie to my face, Mother? You didn't want me as you wanted Anne. Is it not why you took her from me? Separated us?"

"No, I—" Janella tried to calm him.

"Then why did you leave me alone without a mother's love? You rejected me, so now I reject you just I have him," Vastadon sneered and pointed a finger at Aldrich.

A strange feeling soured her stomach and pain overwhelmed her from his remarks. "Aunyia doesn't know I'm her mother and I couldn't take both of your father's children from him. You were to be his successor. I couldn't rip such a thing from you and I would've had I taken you."

"It was my choice, Son. Blame me. Blame me for wanting my only son with me. Not her," Aldrich interceded weakly.

"Little does it matter now?" Vastadon grimaced. "If Father has his way he will put Jacobane on the throne."

"Things could change. Release this animosity that has poisoned you. Answer the Call to the Circle and swear your life into the hands of Danu. She will bring you peace." Janella so desperately fought the tears. She wouldn't appear weak before her son now.

"I have answered the Call," Vastadon said viciously. "I've taken the woman who belongs to me. We are bound together. But my father destroyed all of that. It's his turn to pay."

Janella stared at him. Why didn't she see it before? This madness came from a Bond between two Mageborns. Vastadon was Mia's Bond, not Darius.

"Don't say such things! You took that girl with hate in your heart. You violated the sacred Bond between you and turned it into something ugly. You destroyed it, not your father," Janella said sternly.

"It seems that you've made yourself clear, Mother. You never loved Anne or me above *Father*. And now I curse you to meet the same fate as *him*. The Empire will be mine and everything in it will yield to me. Behold your son!" He stretched his arms out beside him and scowled. Electricity leaped from his fingers to his eyes. "Behold what you have spawned." He swept from the room in a charge of lights and hate.

Janella ran to Aldrich's side and held him close to her bosom. All of the anger, all of the feelings of betrayal were erased with the mere sight of him. She couldn't condemn him, for he was not alone in his mistakes. She loved him and always would. They wept together for the son they had lost to the darkness. She slid into the bed beside him and held him until sleep conquered them.

Aunyia came through the receiving pavilion of the temple in the manner of a ghost. She felt someone watch her, but when she studied the area she saw nothing. She needed to think fast. She didn't want to lead whatever could be watching straight to her companion's hideaway. Something shuffled and across the way from the gates of the imperial palace, a circle of guards spilled through. Vastadon strolled with Camille on his arm out from behind the guards. They appeared to be arguing. Aunyia slipped back behind the curtain and waited for them to pass. She didn't wish to be hindered by a meeting with her brother.

"I spoke with her," Camille snipped, "right in the temple."

There was a long pause and Aunyia imagined Vastadon shot his wife one of his demanding looks. Of whom did Camille speak? Curiosity drove Aunyia to lean forward a little.

"So," Vastadon answered with annoyance. "What of it?"

"I wanted her to know what she has done," Camille spat.

"She has done nothing," Vastadon snipped.

"She has and now I'm made to suffer for it," Camille whined. "It shouldn't be so. The whore who married your uncle—"

"Never go to her again!" Vastadon hissed. "Or I will *kill* you and all you hold dear, Wife."

The conversation confirmed Aunyia's suspicions from earlier. Her brother had hurt Mia. And it was Aunyia's belief that Vastadon had something to do with their father's illness. He was a villain!

It was silent for a moment and when she was most certain they were gone, she slipped from the shadows and took the main street north.

"Sister!" Vastadon halted her flight.

Aunyia cursed before she spun around to meet his gaze. Fire was beneath his smile and in his eyes.

"Where are you off to in such a rush?" he circled her.

"I'm going to investigate the attempt on my father's life," Aunyia sneered.

"Oh," he drew out the word with exaggeration. "I *felt* you attempt to save his life, Sister. Your magic is strong, but it wasn't enough, was it?"

"You are behind this," Aunyia accused.

"How cruel of you to imply such things about me. I wouldn't kill my own father," Vastadon spoke smoothly. "What have I done for you to loathe me so."

Tiny sparks pricked her skin and crawled up her arm making her dizzy for a moment. She drew in her breath and pulled from the stones beneath her feet some magic to fight whatever was coming over her.

"I don't loathe you, Brother. I pity the person you have become." Aunyia walked away from him. Was he using magic? *Could* he use magic? That would only implicate him more. The sickness she tried to suck from Aldrich was magically woven into his body.

Damn him.

She would come back for him. But she needed to save her father first.

When she arrived at the inn she was pleased to see Darius and Horace among Mina and Cole. Tears nearly shoved their way through Aunyia's eyes when she embraced Horace. She slammed her lids shut on them. There was no time for weaknesses now. She needed to assemble her plan.

She clung to Horace regardless absorbing his warmth and drowning in his smell. It had been so many Moons since she held him like this.

"I'm sorry, Love," he whispered into her ear and stroked her hair. "I'm here now."

Aunyia broke the embrace and looked at Mina. "Do you have the plans and the map?"

"Yes," she hopped up and pulled a cylinder shaped container from her robe.

"My brother has magic. He tried to use it against me and I believe he is on to what we are about to do." Aunyia smoothed the parchment with her fingers until it reached a spot along the harbor. "So we must be careful."

"What is your plan?" Darius questioned.

"Tonight we go to the cave that Sermino has pinpointed on this map. Diamond told us the Stone is there along with the shards," Aunyia explained.

"Mia is the only one who can touch the Stone," Horace exclaimed. "I don't feel she is ready to—"

"She isn't." Aunyia crossed her arms over her bosom. "I'm not retrieving the Stone. I want the shards. They will save my father's life and that is the most important thing here."

Cole darted to his feet, "Then we must do whatever we can."

"Mina, I want you to go to the harbor here." Aunyia pointed on the map fairly close to their destination. "My personal fleet will meet you there with a ship to bring the prisoners back to Thaumatur."

Mina's eyes sparkled with tears and she placed a hand over Aunyia's fists, "You are truly going to free my people?"

"We will be there anyhow," Aunyia smirked. "Do you think I wouldn't?"

Mina smiled and inclined her head. "I will be there awaiting your command."

"Remember," Darius' said deeply. "How can you be sure this fleet of yours will not betray you to your brother?"

Aunyia grinned and grasped Darius' gloved hands. His lip curled and she laughed.

"Because the fleet is under the command of the Emperor's daughter. With my father ill, they won't falter in their orders."

CHAPTER THIRTY-EIGHT

Air Magic

Mia spent the entire morning shut away inside the chambers with Jacob. He was quiet and withdrawn. The pain of his heart ached within her so deeply that she couldn't part from his side. She embraced him, stroked his cheek, and smoothed his hair. She maintained contact with him at all times in hopes to draw some of his anguish into her bones so that he didn't bear the burden of it all on his own. It didn't take long for sleep to envelope them.

When Mia awoke, she stretched her arm aside and felt the silken sheets beneath her fingers. She turned her head and found the spot next to her empty. She decided to head down the stairs and into the dining area where her servants sat around the table chatting quietly. When Silla took notice of Mia, she jerked the women up from their chairs and bowed.

"Something from the kitchen, my lady?" Silla asked quickly.

"Yes, please, and once you come back, please sit with me. I could use the company of my women." She signaled for the other two to sit. The women did so quickly but they remained unusually silent.

"Has my husband left word on where he was going?" Mia questioned lightly.

"No, my lady," Sissy replied stiffly and averted her eyes down.

"Is something wrong?" Mia quirked an eyebrow. "You can scarcely meet my gaze."

The women looked at her and their cheeks flushed red. Leta leaped to her feet when Silla returned with a tray filled with tea cups and sweet buns. They were acting extremely strange. She knew if anyone would speak to her, it would be Silla.

"Sit, Silla," Mia ordered and the woman obeyed immediately. "Will someone tell me what is going on?"

Silla shot the other women a dirty look, but Mia lifted her hand in protest. "They have said nothing, Silla. Tell me at once."

Silla let out a sigh that jiggled her cheeks and she leaned back in the chair.

"Today, after the High Prince left, I was going to go into the city to the market to fetch some things for tonight's dinner. I wanted to make it special in hopes to cheer his majesty up. But the guards refused to let me leave. They told me that they have orders and that was all I needed to know," Silla clucked. "They weren't so friendly about it either, the oafs."

Mia darted to her feet and felt the anger rush to her face. "Why?"

"They wouldn't say," Silla said growing flustered.

"Well, we shall see about this. Dare they treat my women so?" Mia stormed from the kitchen through the atrium where the guards stood post at the door.

She stood directly in front of one. The man quickly blocked her way from the glass doors. Mia sneered, "What is the meaning of your treatment toward my women."

"Your Majesty," the guard spoke flatly, "The High Prince has ordered us to secure his home while he is gone. No one is to leave and no one is to enter. Including you and your women."

"Where is my husband? I don't believe you. He wouldn't allow you to hold me prisoner to our home," Mia shouted.

The guard remained silent giving no inclination that he even heard her words. Mia clenched her fists and hit her thighs.

"When he returns, I will make certain you are removed from my home, you bastard," she stomped back into the house and flew up to the chambers.

She searched beneath the bed, on the dresser, and anywhere she could to see if Jacob left her a note. There was no note. She ran to the terrace in a frenzy.

"Blodeuwedd!" Mia called to the skies, "I need you now!"

She had no other choice but to call upon the Great Owl. The guards refused to let her leave and gave her no answers. Panic gripped her and she didn't like the message her instincts sent her. When she looked down from her terrace, guards encircled the entire perimeter. Why were they treating her like a prisoner? Mia threw her hands in the air and growled.

"Blodeuwedd!" she cried angrily again.

No need to yell at me, the whimsical voice snatched her around. The owl perched on the bed post and her wings spanned out around her.

"What is going on around here? Where is Jacob? Is Aldrich alright?" Mia shot off the questions one after the other.

Hold on, Beauty, I'm no oracle!

"Maybe not, but you're on the outside! No one will tell me anything and they have me cornered here like a prisoner!" Mia tightened her jaw. "Help me get out of here!"

They keep you in here for your own good. They are heeding the orders of their High Prince. Don't grow nasty with them as you have earlier.

Mia bit her lip and blinked. Her words have a habit of growing cold when things didn't make sense to her. Perhaps that had come from living eighteen years of her life with Merle.

"Please Blodeuwedd. Is my husband well?" Mia questioned. "Why in the world would he have me locked up he—" Mia gasped and the owl's eyes flickered.

Mia didn't known where the feeling came from. She felt the blood drain from her face, leaving it numb. Vansant Summit was under attack!

"He went to fight!" Mia cried the realization aloud. "He has no chance against all of the Tribes!"

Mia went to her terrace and peered down again. One of the guards met her gaze and shook his head slowly. Mia raised a shaking fist and grimaced.

"Let me out of here at once before I beat you down!"

What can you possibly do to help your husband in a war? You are clumsy with a sword and useless with a bow and arrow. He wouldn't be pleased if you interfered with magic. You know how he feels about that. You would only be another thing for him to protect.

"You will tell me how to get out of here, now!" Mia charged Blodeuwedd, but stopped short when the owl's wings fluttered maniacally.

Beauty, your temper is horrible. You need to be calm if you want to figure out a way to get out of here.

"You are not going to help me?" Mia's eyes went wide. "Not even to give me a small clue?"

You are the daughter of the Tuatha Dé Danann! Can you not start acting so? You have four separate sources you can draw magic from. Air would be my suggestion. See I have given you a clue.

"I hardly know much about Air Elemental Rite! Could it not be Fire? Earth? Even Water?" Mia's head was close to exploding with desperation.

Air, Beauty, Air will aid you this day. Remember what I've told you thus far. Look at me and remember.

The owl was gone. Mia blew her temper and flung the toiletries off of the dressing table. The idea of being confined anywhere drove her mad. It hit too close to home and her days in Falias.

She inhaled deep steady breaths and released them until she felt her limbs loosen with ease. She wandered to the archway of the terrace and allowed the gentle breeze to drift across her face. It was chilled and refreshing from a morning of mostly rain. She silently prayed to Danu and willed her strength and courage.

Some soft hum reached her ears and ripped her from her focus. It was the tune of the Sword, only she *heard* it instead of *felt* it. Could it be Calling her as Nan said it would one day? She slid on her knees across the floor and yanked out the bottom drawer of her dresser. She tossed several clothing over her shoulder until her hand touched the bundle. The humming grew louder when she removed the Sword from the cloth. She stroked the amber encrusted hilt and a blast of magic flowed into her palm and throughout her body. The force was twice the powerful as it ever was in her clutch.

She gripped it between her fists and returned to the terrace. The air around the Sword whipped and charged. Her hair crackled about like a snare. Lightening streaked the sky and shot down into the Sword and through her. The answer came to her.

The streak of lightening receded and she brought the Sword across her other palm. She gasped. The Sword and her hands weren't there. She hurried to the polished metal mirror. She was invisible.

With a shrill laugh, she packed a few things and slung a sack over her back. She sheathed the Sword and tied it to her waist with a leather strap. She ran to the polished metal and was pleased to see that her additions to her garb remained invisible. She scribbled a quick note—she would be at least that courteous unlike Jacob—and flew down to the atrium. Before she snuck completely by the guard, she danced up and down in front of him. Damn fool couldn't see her, she thought somewhat maliciously.

She shoved out the door and turned around to see the guards' reaction. They jumped to attention with paled faces.

"Some say this place was haunted," one of the guards said in a shaky voice.

Mia laughed and headed for somewhere she could find a horse and change.

Damn the Emperor's daughter!

The High Chaplain slid from his altar and fled to Bile's temple. The bitch was snooping now. The most important thing for him to do was to retrieve the Stone. To hell with the shards. If he secured the Stone elsewhere, he could reform his connection with Bile. Half of the Pariah answered to him anyhow. He ordered the undead soldiers to gather as many of the Sihoman prisoners as they could and return them to the island quietly. They would create a new base there in the place that no other knew of.

His leverage with the strange natives of the island was easy enough. They would submit to anything even if he imprisoned only one. The peaceful group was loyal to their own. It was a pity that they couldn't be

Turned. Their innocence protected them during the earlier experiments. Yet it worked perfect because these Sihomans wouldn't oppose his troops in battle. They knew nothing such as war.

Sadly he needed to leave some of them behind. It was enough to implicate some evil force, but not enough to implicate him. He also sent some of the Pariah to resist the invading party to come.

Hector shifted his fingers before the center door, a spell for entrance, and ran through. He had no other choice but to do this. Bile would be enraged but the Darkgod would understand once He realized that his actions were necessary. This obsession with Anne devoured Him. Hector would think more carefully on choosing a better shell for the God. Mortal men were easily seduced with desire.

At the bottom of the cavern slope, he swung open the door and met eyes with his conspirator, the very man who informed him of the Emperor's daughter's plans. The man was robed, but his ice-blue eyes danced maliciously. They could belong to no other.

"Can you touch the Stone?" Hector questioned.

The man peeled his hood back and smiled. Vastadon DeLucible tossed his gloves from his fists and drove his hand down over the Stone. Hector studied him for any weakness, but there appeared to be none. He had the Power and it was strong. He could touch the Lia Fáil.

Hector opened the wooden chest carved with incantations and protection. Vastadon placed the Stone in the box and met eyes with him.

"I trust you can handle the transport," Vastadon said airily. "Now, I have taken care of my uncle. I trust you will complete the task in seeing me to the Emperor's throne."

"Yes, Lord Emperor." Hector swallowed his reluctance and lowered his head respectfully.

"Good. You have made the right choice because it is I who will protect your Brotherhood when my sister and her rabble find this place out," Vastadon sneered with the mention of his sister.

"What of your Aunt and her children?" Hector asked.

"It will be punishment enough for my aunt to see me ascend to the throne. Her children, I have grown rather fond of her oldest, and the youngest two are at a ripe age to be molded. If they return to Vansant

Summit, I am afraid there will be a little surprise in store for them," Vastadon laughed almost as hideously as Bile.

"And what of the High Princess?" Hector tried to conceal his desire. He didn't want this man to hold all the power in the Nations, though he had no choice. He would have to fight for his concubine much harder.

"Mia is safely tucked away. Clueless to what her beloved husband is headed into. Once it's done, I'll bring her to the throne as my mistress and I will make certain it is known to the world how she is nothing more than that. The Emperor's whore."

"She will be no one's whore. I doubt she will survive the attacks you have so delicately planned out. She went after him." he lowered his head. "Until we meet again, Emperor." And he was gone.

"Damn!" Vastadon hissed. He slammed his fist against the stone wall and went to assemble a brigade to retrieve the whore before she got herself killed.

The moon was full and the night sky was clear as they made haste from the inn. Aunyia contacted the captain of her fleet earlier during the afternoon to make a ship ready at the precise location in which Mina would await the freedom of her people. She crossed paths with Sierra and filled her in on the details of the plan. The priestess was a part of their Circle as well, but she wasn't a knight. Sierra would go home on the ship with the prisoners whether she liked it or not. And Aunyia made it clear when she began to protest leaving Mia.

The cave was located beneath a deep-set street so the ship wouldn't be directly accessible. She had made certain it was anchored as close as it could get. Her captain also arranged arms and a safe passage from the inn to the cave-mouth.

When they arrived at the cave-mouth, her captain slithered from the shadows and bowed before Aunyia. He was clad in his darkest uniform and several different sized blades gleamed along his belt beneath the sheen of the moon.

"Captain Lomious Biznee," Aunyia greeted him, "Have you manned the ship?"

"Aye, my lady, and I've brought some men to escort you on this crazy mission," The captain replied a bit snappish. "I'm concerned for your safety."

Aunyia sighed. He'd been around her much too often when she was a little girl and it didn't change when she returned as an adult. She was very close to her captain when she was a child. To leave him and her father at the same time sent her to Thaumatur a fountain of tears. She had thought him the bravest man in the world and when the bravest man in the world shed a tear at her departure all those years back, it worsen her own grief. The years hadn't changed him. He still looked upon her with the fear of a father for a daughter.

She smothered the urge to embrace him and replied, "The guards cannot go any further than the mouth of this cave. It would draw needless attention." She held a hand up to stop his reproach, "It must be done this way, Captain."

The big man grunted and a glint of concern stirred in his eyes. He obeyed and bowed before receding into the darkness with Sierra beneath his arm.

A moment later four guards stood at attention before them. They were the best of the best. The four men were concealed completely behind black form-fitted garb, only their eyes visible. Even their weapons were made from the finest ebony steel. They were ranked as *Fortfall* assassins, the most elite of an imperial brigade. These four assassins could encroach upon twenty armed men and best them.

Aunyia caught herself from chuckling. She didn't want to ease the moment of militia command, but her captain couldn't make his concerns more obvious than this.

"*Fortfalls,*" Aunyia nodded, "No one is to enter the cave after we go in. Await our coming with the prisoners. I trust your captain has informed you of the plans to see the prisoners to the ship and sail immediately for Thaumatur."

"Aye, Princess," they said in unison.

"Let's go!" Aunyia called to the others and gripped the sack hanging from her waist.

411

Her companions, like she, didn't wear the violet tunics of their Sun Knighthood. They were all dressed in black, but at Cole's insistence they wore their chain mail beneath the black robes.

Darius struck a flint against the stone and lit a torch. Only one would be lit to allow enough light to aid their vision to avoid any wandering eyes in the cave. Aunyia memorized the plans and the maps and followed the craggy paths until they reached a dead end where another cave entrance was supposed to be.

"I didn't expect this!" Aunyia complained searching the wall for a way through.

Cole grunted and pushed Aunyia aside. He lifted his sword above his head and struck the wall with it. "My magic did not form!" He frowned. He drove his sword into the wall again this time cracking the surface with his physical force. They all began to dig and slice through the wall until it was a gaping whole that led into a finely designed corridor. They stepped through and once Horace, who was the last in line, stepped through, the wall sealed up as if nothing dismembered its surface.

Aunyia quirked a brow and when she focused on her companions, they were all in battle stance, weapons gripped tightly in their hands.

The Pariah surrounded them. And Aunyia couldn't summon her magic. Something blocked her element. She gripped the double blades tightly and prayed to the Goddess that she would be of any help. She was no stranger to fighting, but fighting wasn't her strong point. Healing was. Earth magic was. And if she could manage to grip her magic, it would serve to be much more useful to them against the fifteen or so armed undead guards that surrounded them.

Cole immediately took his position before her, Darius behind her and Horace to her right forming a shield around her. Had Diamond been there, she would've taken up the left side. It was the first rule in battle to protect the Healer. But this Healer couldn't call her magic.

"Can *you* call your magic yet?" Aunyia murmured in Cole's ear.

Cole shook his head, "This place is warded. Get Back Aunyia!"

The guards tightened the circle around them, herding them back to back against each other. Cole swung his blade and took down two with one fierce connection. Darius fought fist to fist, kicking, and striking with his curved sword at precisely the right moment while Horace fought from his end. Whenever a guard came near, Aunyia drove her double blades into the enemy. She scanned the dim corridor for an escape route. Her eyes found a chasm in the wall. She began cutting her way through the guards. She felt them grab at her and rip her hair but they had made no attempt to wound her with their weapons. She guessed that they had their orders. Aunyia shivered and used the sensation forcefully in each sloppy stroke to open a path.

"There is a doorway ahead!" she shouted to her companions. "Try and hold them off while I clear the path!"

After three more fallen guards, Aunyia was able to get to her destination. She wheeled around and watched the last of the guards fall. Carnage circled the men. Mangled limbs and black blood pooled the floor.

Horace met eyes with her. "Let's get out of here before more of them come."

Thankfully the chasm wasn't completely dark when they stepped through. A torch or two flickered along the narrow walk space revealing an endless path that sloped downward. Darius had taken the lead, Cole right behind him. Horace stood behind Aunyia and reached his hand to her. She reached back and grabbed it clinging to it like a fearful child. Was she truly trembling? He stroked her fingers with his thumb. Even with the magic warded, she could still feel his spirit dip in and out of her body. He made her feel safe and he made her feel calm.

Soon the slope curved into a round platform. Four separate doors marked with strange carvings rounded them.

"Which door do we take?" Cole complained.

"This place is like a maze." Darius shook his head with annoyance.

Aunyia knew the Mind Mage's lack of magic drove him mad and every once in a while she *felt* him call to his element. Their connection to eachother could never be warded.

"Yes, but which door?" Cole snapped and lowered his blade to his side.

"I don't know—oh!" Aunyia gasped.

413

Horace was at her side and supported her by her shoulders, "What is it?" he commanded urgently. "What is happening?"

"I—don't know—" Aunyia struggled to breath let alone speak.

Something gripped her insides and it pulled her with a mixture of pain and exhilaration. It was magic, but not her own or of her companions. She cradled her stomach and Horace held tight to her. Her eyes began to roll back into her head with a mind of their own. Something was invading her body turning her skin backwards with tiny shocks. She swerved toward one of the doors. The door swung open and crimson light devoured her vision. Within a split second, she was sailing through the air and from Horace's clutch.

"Aunyia!" Horace's scream dissipated from her ears.

Her flight slowed down but her mind was too fatigued to focus on her passing surroundings. Whatever grasped her released her on a soft cloudlike carpet. The ground rumbled beneath her and when she turned into the crimson light she scrambled backwards until her back connected with cold stone. Before her the creature in which Diamond had described spread his lips in a jagged smile.

"My beautiful Anne," He spoke in a wraithlike voice that sent chills down her spine. "You have come to me at last."

CHAPTER THIRTY-NINE

Ambush

Word came. Erikrates head in a neatly tied up box. The rage had overtaken the grief when Jacob saw his closest friend mutilated and he left without leaving word about where he went. He fiercely ordered his guards to make certain his wife didn't wander off and possibly use her magical insight to lead her home.

He had suffered the loss of his friend. Had seen his brother clutch to life. He wouldn't lose her and if he died in this fight, he would die proudly, with honor, and at peace knowing she was safe.

He prepped the women and children on the safe passages that ran underground to the other side of the forest many times before. He reminded them of it and appointed Lucia in charge. She wanted to fight. It was in her blood for she was the first daughter of the Clawclan Chieftain, but Jacob forbade it. He assembled the men in the stables and discussed a war plan.

"How many?" Jacob asked Jovich as he mounted his steed.

"Not as many as we thought, but we are still out numbered. I do not believe we are up against all of the Tribes." Jovich too mounted.

"Good. Let's ride," Jacob commanded and sent his horse flying, the warriors in close tow.

They reached the battlements and Jacob gazed at the opposition for the first time. Battle raged in rushes of Tuskan war cries that seem to carry louder upon the late summer wind. Jacob scanned the enemy lines and saw only the flanks of the Tuskans and the Gravens. The war party indeed wasn't as large to Jacob's relief, but, as Jovich informed, they were still out numbered. With Jovich at his side, he galloped to the center of the battlefield and met with the Tuskan Chieftain Wolfstan and Hawk of the Gravens.

"It doesn't have to come to this," Jacob directed his words more to Hawk than Wolfstan. "We can still resolve this in a peaceful manner."

Despite the situation, Jacob had admired Hawk's intelligence and abilities. He was pure warrior at heart, but once a warrior has felt betrayed, that warrior becomes unpredictable. The Gravens were aggressive, but compromising to the matters of peace. He didn't want an enemy in Hawk and the loss of him left Jacob disappointed. It wasn't because he feared Hawk, but valued his determination and loyalty. Wolfstan, on the other hand, was a heartless, controlling, savage individual who cared only for the gain and the domination.

"It's much too late for that, traitor!" Wolfstan interceded with a roar.

Hawk pressed a hand against Wolfstan's chest pushing him back a little and drew closer to Jacob.

"We could've had this land long ago, Prince," Hawk began pacing back and forth. "But we respected you and we honored you. And we honor no one."

"I always said he wasn't to be trusted!" Wolfstan raised his clenched fist.

Hawk silenced him with a lift of his hand, "You've broken your promise, Prince. You left us no other choice."

"And what of Erikrates?" Jacob hissed, anger gaining momentum, "He's done nothing! Yet you murder him. Sent his head to my door!"

Hawk arched his brows, "Erikrates wasn't murdered by my hands. He has annoyed me with his desperate attempts to salvage his dear prince, but I wouldn't harm a foolish old man. To do that would be a great show of cowardice." Hawk turned his attention back to Wolfstan who was jumping out of his skin.

"Erikrates, dead?" the Tuskan smirked, "His life or death is meaningless to me. I cared nothing for him."

Jacob made a hasty move that was halted by the grip of his First Warrior. "Someone will pay for the death of him!" Jacob thundered.

"And you'll pay for bringing a *magician* to these parts as your wife!" Hawk pointed his sword at Jacob. He turned and called for Wolfstan to follow him.

The two parties returned to their warriors. And once Jacob set his eyes on the horizon, he howled.

"Onward!" Jacob bellowed and his warriors roared.

Jacob and his First Warrior charged full force down the hills leading the warriors into attack. The two bands of warriors crashed into one another in a bloody thunderous clatter. Steal upon steal, warriors fought and fell. Jacob cut one man down after another. His fierce warrior's eye was sharp and rapid to each oncoming attack. This was his home and in the name of his brother he would defend it. Aldrich would expect no less of him.

"Jacobane!" one of his warriors' bellow spun him around to a blind side attack.

The oncoming warrior let out a loud war cry and brandished two weapons, a huge sword and a huge axe. Jacob bent his body and set the warrior tumbling over his back. He drove a sword into his fallen enemy's skull.

The battle went on for hours, neither side giving in to defeat. Many lives lost. Both parties' were fatigued from the fight and the cries and action had slowed a pace.

Suddenly, the earth rumbled beneath their feet and an explosion of flames sent all warriors sailing through the air.

"*Magicians!*" several men cried.

Jacob was on his back. Something shredded his side and he stretched his hand out and saw blood dripping from his fingers. He rolled his head to the right. The smoke cleared and the last thing he remembered seeing was an army of gray-robed Demons floating across the hills.

What the hell was he?

The Demon-man crowded Aunyia against the wall and stretched His open hand out to touch her. She pushed her body back hard against the wall in hopes to somehow escape through the cold stone. She felt nauseous and dizzy. Had she somehow been drugged? Could the power of another's magic be so brutal and sickening? She twisted her head away from His slow gesture. His hand brushed her exposed cheek. She swatted His hand away, refused to meet his gaze lest she saw something she didn't want to see.

"Keep away." Her voice was dry and breathless.

Instead of backing away, the winged man leveled his body to hers and forced her to look at Him. His eyes flashed from crimson to jade and His face was strong and mortal folding into a paling frown. His touch strengthened whatever it was that birthed inside of her.

"I can give you anything you desire, my Anne," He whispered but even His whisper boomed throughout the room. "Everything you desire. You will be my queen. Surrender yourself to me, your Darkgod, Bile!"

Lust was in His eyes. She had known, had been warned of this entity's obsession, but it hadn't sunk in until this very moment.

"Set me free and give me the Stone and the shards!" she challenged with her strongest voice.

"You know I cannot do that and I know you could never touch the Stone. I cannot even touch the Stone now," He spoke as one would to a child. "And you also know I will not let you go."

He patronized her. She simmered and reached for her magic again to no avail. But her anger brought more life to her fatigued body. She met his strange eyes unflinchingly. "What do you want?"

"You. My rightful place in Paradise." He replied and grinned baring his sharp teeth. "You see, I've waited a long time for My release. Your Danu has buried Me into the world meant for those unworthy of Paradise. *Me!* I who have given life to Her children. I'm the Father to all no matter how Danu tries to erase Me from the minds of Our mortals. She has turned My own children against Me. Cast Me from My place by Her side in a feeble attempt to stop Me. It's time for Me to take My children back. I shall have My vengeance and when I do, My precious Anne, you will be at My side."

"You disgust me," Aunyia spat. "I will never betray Danu!"

He responded with a growl and hauled her to her feet. He dragged her to the altar where the shards glittered beneath the crimson glow of the pulsing room. She didn't see the Stone. It wasn't where she was told it would be.

Bile, with Aunyia still in his clutch, let out a shrieking roar and expanded his wings violently.

"The Stone! Servant!" Bile bellowed. "Show yourself at once!"

Aunyia didn't know who He summoned, but she felt the entirety of His rage when no one obediently responded. "Traitor!"

He spun on her. "Offer yourself to Me." He commanded sharply and swung His hand to the side.

A cloud of white mist gathered near to the floor and spiraled up to the ceiling. Horace stepped through smiling widely. Aunyia ran to him—Bile had let her go—and threw her arms around him.

"I love you," he whispered. "I know I haven't told you before now, but I love you more than life itself."

She tightened her hold on him and he gathered her close to him. Oh, how she longed to hear his words of love. How she needed him to be whole. He was all she desired.

Something jerked her from his arms and he faded into the smoky veil. Bile twisted her toward Him and scowled.

"Your love is a lie. He's a lie!" Bile thundered and shot his hand outward again. The rocks crumbled down where his magic struck. A gold hue exploded and Aunyia was no longer in the dark cave. She was near a river. She could hear its gentle rolling. The stars webbed the dark blue sky. *Vansant Summit.*

A female figure ran past her and a wave of hopelessness consumed her. She followed the figure down the length of the bank and watched as the sad woman approached another crouching form. Aunyia continued her advance but stopped at a good distance away from them. The two people fell into a deep and passionate kiss and when her vision cleared a little, her body ached.

Mia and Horace. No!
Aunyia's heart wretched. How could Mia do this to Jacob! How could Horace...

"They, who you trust, have betrayed you," Bile's voice hissed in her ear as the scene faded from her tear filled eyes. "They, who serve Danu and risk nothing while you risk everything, have found lust between them. I can promise you so much more than they. Vengeance, Power, elation."

Was it a trick? Could it truly have happened? Had a passionate love affair been conceived during Horace's solitude in the country? Aunyia was under the influence of her sadness and with the tidal wave of sorrow, her confinement to Bile's magic swept from her.

She swallowed hard and focused on the vows she had made to Danu before her brigade and before the High Priestess. No matter what, she wouldn't give in to evil and turn her back on those who trust her. Emotions couldn't cloud her judgment. She loved Horace and even if he did love another, she couldn't betray him to death. And death would come to him if she gave into Bile's darkness of vengeance.

He slid a hot hand up her arm to her shoulder. This time things awakened inside of her that made her lean back into the hard torso of the creature. His hand swept up from her waist and cradled her breast with the strength of a knight and the gentleness of a summer breeze. Her body tingled and her nipples hardened beneath his circling thumbs.

Another trick, her mind cried in repulsion. But her body rebelled against her mind indulging in the erotic feelings he forced into her countenance.

He pressed a lip to her ear and whispered, "Take the shard into your hands and give yourself to Me. I will not take away your soul like I did the others. I want you as you are. I need you. I love you, My Anne."

No one had ever said those words to her before. Could she be so desperate for such words? She spun her body toward Him and allowed Him to embrace her fiercely. His wings folded around her and His arousal was prominent against her flesh. Her mind went spinning against her movements.

He needed her. He was right. But it wasn't in the way He so deceptively tried to make it sound. Love is shunned by His evil kind. He didn't love her. He used her own desperate pleas for the words against her. He needed her blood to survive without the Stone. He needed the blood of a Mageborn. Suddenly the elated reaction of her body receded with the realization.

Two can play this game.

Aunyia slowly looked up at Him. His eyes went soft and dimmed. She forced down her disgust, laced her fingers through his hair and gently kissed His lips. He let her go and watched her glide to the altar. The shards gleamed hypnotically becoming brighter as she neared them.

She reached down and seized one with two hands. It exploded into a white and green ball around her fists. She stifled a gasp as the magic of Danu gushed through her body. Water, Fire, and Air flooded her veins until finally her own element, Earth encompassed her body. She smiled and said a silent prayer of thanks to Danu for the return of her magic. With her element she had the courage and strength to do what she needed to do. She turned and faced her enemy. He looked at her and smiled widely. She returned the malicious grin.

"Do it, Anne. Do it before it's too late," He commanded.

She nodded and said, "Come to me so that I may look into your eyes when you accept me."

In one swift motion, the winged Darkgod caught her up by the waist and lifted her into the air. Aunyia closed her eyes tightly and swallowed her fear. She hoped and prayed that what she was about to do would work. She would die happy if she could save her father's life. She needed the shards. It *was* what could save her father's life.

Goddess and the Trinity bless him and aid me!

She opened her eyes again. They were eye to eye. His grip tightened around her. She hesitated and He caught on to it.

"Pour your blood into me now!" He thundered.

For a moment His mortal face became translucent. Beneath the skin two thick horns protruded. The rippled veil of hair receded. Two slits replaced the sharp nose and where His chin began, His jaws hung. His teeth lengthened and, with a snap, his jaws disconnected.

The true face of evil contracted neatly behind His mortal mask again. Aunyia gasped. Fear had taken a stronger hold. He couldn't force her. If He could've He would've already done so.

The walls around them began to rumble and the craggy surface of the floor split into a gaping hole beneath His feet. Water bubbled up from beneath them and Bile extended his wings and soared high above the eruption. He howled as water splashed his skin. *Magic!* She could feel *his* magic!

"Aunyia!" Horace bellowed.

"Get back Horace!" She cried and wished she could turn her face to see him.

She was trapped within the grips of the angry Darkgod who held her captive. He roared, his true face again flickering from beneath his flesh and soared down upon the ground. He tossed Aunyia from His grip and she hit the wall hard. Her breath was knocked from her lungs. Warm liquid flowed from the crown of her head. When she came to, she saw Bile circling Horace. Horace held himself arrogant and fearless, his long sandy hair whipping around his face with the aura of Water Magic. But he didn't know just how dangerous this creature was. She had seen into the depths of the mortal shell.

"Stop!" Aunyia cried. "Don't harm him!"

Bile didn't back away. "It is too late for that, Bitch!" He hissed. "You had your chance, now it is time for one of you to fall!"

"Not him!" Aunyia cried.

She couldn't lose him. She loved him too much to allow his death. Bile spun on her. His approach was more rapid than methodical. He ripped her up by her hair and gripped her elbow pushing the hand that held the shard to her neck.

Horace howled and charged Him. He drove his sword straight through the winged man's torso. Black blood poured from the wound. Bile shook His head and spun His fist around knocking Horace across the room. Aunyia jumped onto the entity's back, the shard at his throat and kissed his cheek.

"Goddess rest your soul," Aunyia whispered.

In one forceful move, she slit His throat clean open with the shard. Rivers of blood spurted from His neck as He howled and spun maniacally tossing Aunyia to the ground. His blood dripped down her cheeks as she watched the repulsive body fall into the water filled earth. Just before His neck was submerged into the water, a fiery orb exploded from the shredded throat wound roaring and spinning above Aunyia's head. In an instant glimpse, she saw the face of Bile grinning before it exploded through the cavern roof and disappeared into the gaping sky.

Aunyia released her breath and ran to Horace.

"My Goddess, Horace," She took his face in between her hands, "I could've lost you."

"I almost lost *you*, Aunyia!" Horace countered urgently. "Don't ever do that to me again!"

She released him and he cradled her cheeks with his palms. His hazel eyes darkened with fear and relief at the same time.

"Now you know I cannot promise you that!" Aunyia smiled impiously.

He returned her grin with one of his own. "I love you."

Aunyia nearly wept with his admission. She lowered her mouth onto his and kissed him. It was a short kiss sweet with promise.

"What took you so long to say those words?" She playfully swatted his hand.

"You always knew." He winked and climbed to his feet, "It is over!" He embraced her but she went stiff.

"It's far from over Horace. The battle has just begun. Bile isn't finished with us yet." Aunyia shivered remembering the hideous face. "Where are the others?"

"When we followed you, we split up. I told them to keep an eye out for the Sihomans. This place has lost its Power."

"The Stone is gone. But I have the shards. Now we can restore the Season Temple. Give normalcy back to Thaumatur's climate. It's a start!" Aunyia handed him one of the shards. "When I touched it, Danu sent my magic flowing back to me. She protected us even when faced with an equally powerful God."

Horace jolted when he took the shard. It pulsed and churned with brilliant auras around his hand traveling up his arm.

"I feel it," he said with a breathless laugh.

"Now I know why the *Enchantras* are so desperate to regain the shards. We will have to tell them, you know. We will be the ones to reform the

Golden Skylight. I don't think they will be happy, but they cannot be trusted with the task. Danu has chosen us to take responsibility," Aunyia said.

"With the Stone missing, evil can survive," Horace shook his head.

The ground rumbled beneath their feet and rocks rained from the ceiling. Horace took hold of Aunyia's hand and fled from the cavern. They ran up the passage way, but boulders and debris blocked their path. They scanned for another escape route.

"Over here!" Darius called from the right. "Quickly!"

Aunyia glanced down the way she came from and saw the blinding red light expanding towards them. It swallowed the four encrypted doors and anything else in its path erasing all evidence of its existence. Aunyia shoved Horace ahead of her.

"Go, Go! Now!" she ordered.

The cavern was collapsing all around them. Aunyia called her element for protection. The rhythmic waves in her aura responded instantly. Aunyia tossed her arm over her head and glanced back to make certain the green shield she summoned indeed made a difference. The shield was in triangle form and its substance resembled flowing green water. She squeezed Horace's hand knowing he added his Power to the shield. Large rocks bounced off of the shield in green sparks but some of the little debris penetrated through scraping their cheeks and hands. It didn't hinder their flight. Instead they pushed harder ignoring the approaching crimson rays.

"This way!" Cole waved from an alcove in the cave and darted onward. When they met up with him he called back. "I found very few Sihoman and brought them to the cave's entrance so that Mina could gather them on the ship."

"Whoever stole the Stone must've received word of our unearthing and took most of the prisoners out!" Horace added.

"The Stone isn't here?" Darius questioned from ahead of them.

"No," Aunyia answered. "The shards were there. I have them."

They ran until they saw the brilliant sunrise penetrate through in rays of gold and rose. They raced until Aunyia found her feet dangling over the edge of a cliff. Horace grabbed her back before she toppled forward. Cole and Darius were gone. The sky was an endless blue and below, about fifty feet below them, the sea crashed against the rock in which they emerged from. Had Cole and Darius plunged into the water or to their deaths?

"*Goddess*," Aunyia swore.

She threw a glance over her shoulder. The shield was fading and the huge boulders spun violently against the green rush searching for a way through. The crimson light crept around the corner, hunting them slowly.

"We have to jump, Horace!" Aunyia cried and met eyes with Horace.

He nodded and tightened his hand around hers. "Point your toes straight down to break the water's surface!" He ordered her.

"Don't let go of me!" she pleaded.

"Never!" he said fiercely. "On the count of three, we jump."

Aunyia nodded, "One."

"Two."

"Three."

They threw their bodies off the ledge and not once did she let go of his hand. She felt the heat of the red light riding her back until her body broke through the surface of the water. She plunged deep into the depths of the ocean before she could begin to make her ascent back up. Both of their heads popped up and gasped deeply.

Aunyia returned her gaze to the cursed place they escaped. It was a mass of crumbling rock and flames. Slowly the massive peek sunk into the water's bubbling mouth, swallowing its evil.

Aunyia turned her back from the sight and searched the horizons of the water for Cole and Darius.

"Where are they?" she shouted and grabbed the medallion from between her breasts. All of the gems glittered with life. "They live, thank Danu!"

"We need to find them quick!" Horace hissed clinging to his medallion. "Look at it again!"

Aunyia did as he said and noticed that the opal stone that was placed in the center of the medallion's circle was paling. A chill crawled up her spine.

"Mia!" she cried and began swimming toward the shore.

She hadn't forgotten the vision she saw within the clutches of Bile.

Yet, as hurt as she was at the sight of Mia in Horace's arms, she didn't hate her. She loved her as if she were her true blood kin. And she knew Mia loved Jacob. She was her friend. But she still had to ask him for the truth.

They both pulled themselves from the water and onto the docks of the harbor. They were the only two rushing back into Vhladic. The port was teeming with frightened people trying to flee in congested vessels. It would be easy for the ship of Sihomans to blend in such hysteria and once they reached Murias, they would be safe. The Pariah wouldn't be so bold to invade the jurisdiction of Thaumatur.

Horace tossed his tunic off and snatched two woolen wraps from a vacant traders' stand tossing two coins in its place. Once they were able to get to the main street that would lead to the imperial palace, Aunyia halted.

"I need to ask you something, Horace."

His face had dried, but his hair dripped endlessly down his shoulders and onto his bare chest. His eyebrows knitted together and he folded his arms against him. "You can ask me anything. What is it?"

"When I was with Bile," Aunyia pulled the wrap closer to her to suppress a shudder, "I somehow saw—I—You and Mia, do you—?"

Horace laughed after a moment of gawking, "I love Mia as you love her. She isn't mine."

Aunyia nodded and lowered her eyes. Had he wished she were his? He lifted her chin with his strong fingers and stared into her eyes with deepness.

"And I am not hers," He whispered. "I am yours, love. Always!" She smiled and he kissed her quickly. "We must go and find them!"

"Do you know where they might've gone?" Aunyia asked as they rounded the gates of the temple. The crowd that wasn't leaving Vhladic poured into the temple crying pleas of salvation and penance.

"If they noticed the opal dim, then my guess is that they are headed to Cordia Hall," Horace paused and sniffed when he looked at the crowd surrounding the temple. "This is exactly what the Brotherhood wanted, wasn't it?"

"Their wish was granted." Aunyia said sadly.

Aunyia lead him to her uncle's estate set off the main road behind the imperial palace. When they came to the hall, they were stopped by two guards.

"The prince gave us orders. No one is to enter and no one is to leave," a guard explained with a military disciplined voice.

"I, daughter of the Emperor, command you let me enter. I feel that the princess is in danger!" Aunyia ordered.

The guard snapped his lanky head back and looked at her with more interest. When he realized she spoke truth, he inclined his head and apologized for his disrespect. He let her pass but held Horace from entering. Aunyia shot him a look telling him she would be okay.

"I will be right out." She ran up the stairway and crossed paths with a servant woman. She said her name was Kissa and it seemed to Aunyia she was stalling her from seeing Mia.

"I need to see the Princess at once."

Kissa lowered her head tiredly and said, "She's not here. But please, my lady, please she will be angry with me if—"

"Where *is* she?" Aunyia commanded and grabbed the woman urgently. "Where has my uncle gone?"

"The High Prince has returned to Vansant Summit," Kissa cried breathlessly. "He received word that his home was under attack by the Tribes. When my lady learned of this she followed him."

Panic seized her because she couldn't lose Jacob too. She couldn't!

"You *let* her?" Aunyia snapped.

"I had no choice. She was gone before I could stop her! I wish no harm to my lady. She is kind and gentle. She is my friend."

"Why did you not tell the guards?" Aunyia commanded again.

"Because she left me a note asking me not to. She knew with the Emperor ill that no aid would be sent. She knew the guards would only return her here to wait and suffer while her husband fought."

The last sentence was an echo in Aunyia's ears. She was down the stairs and out the door.

"We must go to see my father, Horace! My uncle and Mia have both gone to war! My father will send reinforcements. All I need is one word," Aunyia cried.

"The Emperor, you didn't know, my lady—" the guard drew her attention to him.

"What is it?" She ordered.

"The Emperor went missing three hours ago." the guard swallowed hard under her gaze. "Some say he left to die."

Aunyia stumbled back. Her senses went numb and her heart nearly exploded in her chest with grief. She fell to her knees and was hardly aware of Horace's embrace.

"No!" she screamed her eyes sprang tears, "No! He will die!" she cried over again. "I was going to heal him! I was going to save him!"

The shard fell from her hand.

CHAPTER FORTY

The Swordmaster

The fields were aflame. Thick columns of grey smoke rose from scattered burning patches. Mia's heart sank. She was motionless as if something bound her ankles and arms from moving. Where was Jacob? Her eyes followed the battered blazing surroundings. Several men were dead, rotting in crimson puddles of their own blood. The smell of burning flesh and hair was so strong that she almost became dizzy with repugnance. His people had fallen badly—*her* people—and she prayed that the women and children back at the dwelling were safely on the other side of the forest through the tunnels of escape Jacob had coached them on taking.

"Dear Goddess, please let my husband be well," she cried to the darkened sky and fell to her knees. She had pushed herself during the journey, taking not one moments of rest and arrived home in nearly half the time it should have taken.

Her legs felt like jelly and her head pounded, but she pushed to her feet and staggered through the field, tightly gripping her Sword. She was weak, she knew, but the pain was nothing compared to her fear. Suddenly, the smell of something familiar filled her lungs. It was so potent that it drowned out the stench of the air. A gentle breeze, so warm and so distant, threaded from within her, gaining strength as it rose and encircled her head. Her hair whipped about her, the feeling pushed her head to the side. She gasped.

Jacob was lying on his back with blood dripping from his head and nose. His armor was torn from his body and his middle was badly slashed. Mia ran to his side, dropped the Sword and fell to his side cradling his head upon her knee.

"Jacob!" she cried. His eyes remained shut. "Jacob!"

She struggled to pull his head up to her chest and curled her arms around him. She couldn't stop the flow of tears. She blamed herself, for the war had been all because he married her! He felt so cold against her, but she could hear the wisp of his shallow breaths. Swiftly she grasped her Sword and cut a piece of her chemise off. She sliced through his blood and sweat soaked tunic and studied the gash. It was bleeding profusely, and was gaping. She pressed the shredded piece of chemise against the wound to stop the flow.

"Please, you cannot leave me yet!" she cried over him and turned her head up to the sky angrily, "You cannot take him from me! I ask of You, I beg You for only this!"

The memory of him in her heart, smiling and holding her, gazing into her eyes with his passion, swam through her mind. It had taken them both so long to find acceptance and love, peace and joy. And now he clung to his life, and was losing his grip rapidly. She looked down into his face sobbing and his eyes fluttered open. He turned the corner of his mouth up into an attempted smile.

"Mia," his words were weak and hoarse, "I told you not to—"

Mia placed a finger to his lips, "You are weak. You mustn't speak."

"Leave," he slurred.

"I'm going to save you." She caressed his cheek.

"You cannot, leave before they return for you. Strange things— Strange creatures—"

"I won't leave you, My Love," her words were forceful.

"I'm dying, Mia. I will not live to take us to the throne," Jacob said slowly and desperately.

"I can heal you," Mia pressed her hand firmly on his wound.

"No magic, Love," Jacob pleaded. "What is to be will be."

Mia lowered her body over his, and bit her lip. Damn his stubborn will! His plea warded her from her impulses and when she reached for the Healing as Sierra had shown her, nothing came. She held him close, rubbing her hands over his skin vigorously to warm his body. He was so cold and he had lost much blood. He was dying. Her sobs choked her up on the thought. "I love you so!"

A chilled wind shot through the valley and hills, stroking the forest pine eerily. Something was watching. Something evil. Mia lowered her hands to her side and clutched the jeweled handle of her Sword. It vibrated and hummed beneath her fingers. She glanced down at Jacob and saw that he was no longer conscious.

Rage and blood darkened her vision when she sprang from her husband's bloodied body and spun toward the mountains. Three figures in the dark grey robes stood along the forest line. Their eyes were chasms of black and their gloved hands clutched scepters of pale iron.

Necromancers of the Old Legion.

They called to her through threads of stale air. She would go, but it wouldn't be to do their bidding. Their blood already marked the Sword in her mind. They underestimated *her* Power.

She hadn't even realized she was running. Crying and growling she took them out before they had a chance to raise their scepters and incantations. In one long swift stroke, she beheaded them, their severed heads cluttered before her. Black blood dripped from her blade and the putrid smell of death returned to her. She kicked the lifeless heads across the way.

For the first time since she arrived, she studied the corpse fifteen paces from her where one of the heads had landed. It wasn't one of Jacob's warriors, but a Tuskan warrior. Her breath caught. The valleys and hills were painted with the blood of the entire Tribe war party. Instantly she knew it was an ambush on both Vansant Summit and the Tribes. Her husband was set up.

Mia inhaled the heavy air and ran back up the hill. Jacob still lay bleeding, his body hardly moved. He was fatally wounded and wouldn't recover. Mia roared in anguish. Her legs collapsed bringing her to her knees. She gripped the hilt of the bloodied Sword of Light and pointed it to the sky. Black blood ran down the hilt and rained across her face. Her white garb was stained with the blood of the enemy and the blood of her love.

You have killed with the Sword of Light out of rage and anger. You are weakened, Beauty, tainted but not broken. Pull yourself up from the blood-puddled ground.

"Blodeuwedd!" Mia cried to the sky. "Come before me and witness my death! I will not live in this cursed land without him!"

The Great Owl remained hidden from her view. But her voice was sharp and angered.

Death is defeat! The husband you loathed and learned to love would be shamed to see you now. Taketh your life, you coward. Murder your husband's memory, defile his valor and allow his death meaningless.

Mia was heaving, her Sword still erected to the sky. Tears streaked her cheeks and mingled with the blood she had spilt and the blood of her husband. She wanted death. She didn't want to face the world with such hollow grief, alone, with no one to trust. A wave of black Power swept into her body. Her eyes felt cold and her heart was freezing. Curses spawned from her mind and nearly spewed out her mouth.

Voices and dark thoughts told her things. *Danu has betrayed you. She has always seen you suffer…left you with nothing. Turn from Her…*

"*Claimh Solais* has shown me the cursed path I have set for myself. I have been born from the wombs of beautiful dead queens and spawned of the first betrayals! The Lords of the Elements, my Forefathers, in their glass towers call me to my death! I am to die, for I am no savior. If I live, I'll seek my revenge and in that act, doom will come to this world!" Mia cried with the words of a thousand whispers in her head.

Fingertips caressed her cheeks. Razors sliced beneath the skin of her legs and arms. Something was inside of her, attacking her arms and hands with its malicious will. The voices spoke of a new world. One of darkness and Power. An existence she could alone rule and a God who would give a new life to her husband.

Fight the evil inside of you. Ignore the words hate and revenge has placed in your mind! The Power of the Claimh Solais is testing you! Sheath the Sword of Light at once, for riders approach. And get you to your feet!

"It must take me. I'm not strong enough!" Mia cried her voice was a tumble of insanity. "Don't let me become the dark! Claimh Solais turn on me! I command you!"

The sun blazed tip of the Sword didn't turn on her, although she struggled to twist it upon her. Madness and corruption flurried her senses. Death could only save the world from her dark curse.

The Claimh Solais was never yours to command! You are the Stone Mistress, the one who can change destiny! Jacobane Hilliard is the Swordmaster! It was he Claimh Solais chose to bear it as protector. You were just its Bearer as you will be for the other two weapons! It's the will of your husband that you live!

"Show yourself to me Blodeuwedd! Or have you abandoned me as Danu has!" Her voice was changing. It was wraithlike. "Bile, Father to all, has Called to me!"

The Great Owl screeched in horror and swooped down before her. A lucent light globed around the owl, and for a moment, the apparition of a white and silver clad woman with silver tresses stood before her.

Danu has blessed you with a child born from what many had thought an unattainable love and an impossible union of peace. The Marriage of the Sword is true. Do not believe She has abandoned you! You must have faith in Her love and compassion. Turn your eye from Bile, the traitor of Danu! You'll bring forth the slaughter of your husband's son that has yet to see the sun.

Mia closed her eyes and clenched her teeth against the sharp pains in her mind. She was with child? Her courses had come a little light, but she didn't think...

Blood trickled from her nose and eyes. The Sword was misused and she was being punished for it. She needed to fight. Blodeuwedd was right. Her child was a gift. His beautiful precious gift. She began to think of him and how it felt in his arms. She thought of the child that she now knew clung to its life within her.

"I will not surrender to evil. I will live for another!" she cried.

The droning voices drowned beneath the Power of her affirmation and the pain was gone. All was silent. Blodeuwedd no longer spoke to her and the apparition faded into a sparkling cloud.

*The Sword of Light, the treasure of Fire and Findias, has been cleansed...*the whisper was a whisping wind.

All fell silent as Mia closed her eyes tightly. Once her heart slowed its pace, she looked to where her husband lay lifeless. Numbly, she gathered enough strength to approach him. Severel moments of painful silence passed as she stroked his hair and touched his cold body. The Great Mother was above her, though she could not see her. She could feel the profusion of her love and elements.

"My duty with the Sword is done." she whispered as a burning tear slid down her cheek. "I have cleansed it and now return it to its master."

She opened Jacob's scarred hand and placed the Sword in his grip. She then crossed his arms across his torso. He looked like a true prince, and even in death she could see his beauty. "I love you my Barbarian Prince. I will always love you."

A cool shadow fell on her back and she was pulled to her feet. The strong hands secured her against a firm torso. She turned her eyes up. Vastadon's ice-blue eyes were filled with bewilderment. Fear couldn't even grip her for she was so weak. He led her away and she followed as if she herself was dead.

"You!" he pointed to a guard. "See the High Princess safely to my horse! And you two, go retrieve the corpse of my uncle for a proper burial."

An explosion sounded, followed by several cries.

"Lord Emperor!" a guard called, "I do not know what happened! Everything is an inferno here!"

Mia knew it was the final end. Her husband would have a proper burial, a great king's pyre, with the Sword of Light in his grip. Darkness invaded her.

CHAPTER FORTY-ONE

Shards of Hope

Mia jolted upright and for a moment she felt the comfort of her husband near her. But she wasn't in the fields of Vansant Summit and Jacob wasn't near to her. It wasn't all a bad dream He was lost to her forever.

The waking had brought back the ache and sadness. An old wound that would reopen and bleed with each dawn. A figure emerged from the shadows.

"We've returned you to Tania. The new emperor didn't like his prize ripped from him, but his stubbornness was nothing compared to his sister's." Darius muttered.

"New emperor?" Mia whispered.

Darius sighed and lowered himself beside her. "Aldrich has vanished and by now, the sickness that affected him, surely killed him. At least that is what has become conclusive in the Nations."

"No," Mia breathed, "Oh, Goddess…"

Mia's lips trembled and her eyes and lungs burned. She remembered Aldrich's kindness and his compassion, his evermore determination to summon peace between the races. How could fate be so cruel to take the lives of such good men prematurely? Mia slammed her fist on the table beside her and cradled her head between her hands.

"Aunyia grieves her father silently. She was always strong that way. I suppose it's the way of a Healer." Darius replied. "She managed to recover the shards and the Elders were not pleased when she told them that she'd personally see to their return."

"Damn the Elders and their feeble obsessions," Mia hissed. "My husband's body...the Sword?"

"I'm sorry, Mia, but Vansant Summit was devoured in flames. They were unable to recover him and the Sword has not been found. But a mourning ceremony for Aldrich and your husband was held in Vhladic the day of Vastadon's coronation," he told her softly. She had almost forgotten.

Vengeance and hatred soured her mouth with the news of Vastadon's succession. She hated him. She utterly despised him to the very last breath.

"I'm with child," she interrupted the seething silence. "I'm not certain how far."

"I know. It's three Moon Cycles and two weeks," Darius answered and knelt at her side. "I always know what happens to you."

Mia looked at him. What had changed? The last time she saw this man he had made himself clear. Yet hear he was by her side. Reaching out to her.

"You do?" Mia answered lightly.

"Yes," he answered, "And I want to help you, Mia."

"I'm afraid that there is no helping me now," Mia snorted.

"You speak as if you've given up!" Darius snapped. "The fight has only begun!"

"I'm tired of fighting!" her voice cracked. "I'm not strong without him!"

"You never needed anyone's strength! You must snap out of this and fight for that child within you!" Darius squeezed her hand.

"I cannot give this child anything close to what his father would've given him!" her eyes stung with fresh tears. "How will my son know how wonderful and beautiful his father was! How strong and brave he was to fight a war he couldn't possibly win to protect his people! My son was robbed that!"

"He will know his father through you! No one else could give him such a gift! Be strong and bring meaning to your husband's death else he died in vain!" he snapped.

Darius pulled her into his embrace while she wept. Her body trembled and she felt the surge of power between them.

"Take my strength. Take my strength, Sister," Darius whispered. "You must be strong."

Mia shot her head up and she arched her brows. Her heart sang with his confession and everything about his words hummed deep in her bones with truth.

"What did you call me?" she questioned needing to hear it again.

A small smile touched the corners of his mouth. He wiped the tears from her cheeks with his hand and stared deeply into her eyes.

"I was a fool not to see it before. I thought you remembered our mother's death and it hurt me to think you would deny her. I see now how cruel the world has been to you. How deceitful. I hadn't thought you suffered from the loss of Mother as I have suffered. I was wrong. Forgive me," he cupped her cheek. "Forgive me."

The image of a dark-haired boy before a blazing fire ruptured her mind. Instinctively she pulled him close to her and held him tightly.

"My brother, there is nothing to forgive," she whispered.

"You will never be alone again," he said in her ear. "We will fight together until the day comes when all who has betrayed us falls to their knees." He pulled from her embrace and flashed an unusual grin. "The Order anxiously awaits you. It's time you put your foot down."

Fifteen sets of eyes bore into Mia as she stood before the *Enchantras*. She couldn't focus her eyes on them, but beyond them with a bitterness directed aimlessly.

"Princess Miarosa Maladinto," Scatha greeted her in a warm voice.

She stood and extended her hand. Mia looked unflinchingly at the *Enchantra's* hand and lifted her chin. Scatha slowly withdrew her offer and lowered her body back down to her seat looking somewhat shocked.

"Hilliard," Mia said sternly. They arched their brows in confusion at her correction. "My name," Mia said impassively, "is Miarosa Hilliard."

Scatha shifted her eyes to her right and exchanged a look with the white-robed Viscount Eamon Birch, and cleared her throat.

"We are very relieved to see that you have returned safely. I'm speaking on behalf of the Order when I say that we are truly sorry that you had to endure such barbarism on your journey. But we do need to ask you for a report."

"A report?" Mia huffed.

"On what you learned. It has become apparent that the Barbarians within the vicinity of Vansant Summits were harboring the Necromancers of the Legion behind their infamous wall," The Viscount muttered.

Mia stared for a moment and then let out a loud maddening laughter.

"What is so funny, Princess?" The Viscount demanded.

"And where did you hear such tales, Viscount? From your son-n-law, perhaps," Mia shot back.

The Viscount's head recoiled as if he had been slapped. They darted their heads from one to the other nervously. Mia leaned forward slowly pressing her palms firmly on the council table.

"Innocent people died! They lost their homes! I know. I was there and what I saw was bloody carnage. Outlanders and Jacob's warriors died all the same at the hands of the Necromancers you set free when they should've been imprisoned or put to death!" Mia bellowed. "Where were you when this happened?"

"The Barbarian Prince was warned to leave. There is nothing we could've done," Birch hissed and leaped from his chair.

"The people had nowhere to go!" Mia retorted.

"The Prince should've remained where he was. He could've kept you in Vhladic!" Birch reproached.

"He tried to prevent me from leaving Vhladic! I chose to follow him, as I would have straight into the arms of death." Mia tightened her teeth.

"Precisely my point," Birch replied in a bored tone.

"Oh," Mia said withdrawing her hands from the table, "I see. So you expected my husband to leave his people behind?"

"What else could he do?" Birch threw his hands hopelessly in the air.

"He did what any good leader would do! He fought for his people! He fought, while you sat safe and warm behind your plans and schemes."

"We weren't about to alert the kingdoms into panic!" the Viscount thundered.

"Sit down, Eamon," Scatha snapped. "This council is being held for more important reasons than to quarrel. Now, Princess, the sooner we scribe the report, the sooner you can leave."

"You want my report? I'll give it to you. My husband died fighting a war he had no chance of winning. He knew nothing about the Necromancers and it's my belief that the Tribes knew nothing either. What I *do* think is that this tidy little Order of yours knew more of it than anyone. There are many well-kept secrets within this Order." Mia didn't forget what Horace had told her Moons ago about their knowledge of cruelty within the Brotherhood.

"You are presuming!" Birch interfered.

"Princess, did the Barbarian attackers carry any of the treasures?" *Enchantra* Emberlynn cut the Viscount off.

"The weapons, you mean?" Mia snapped her correction. "No."

"Do you know where the weapons are?" Emberlynn asked.

"I have my own conclusions."

"Tell us, so that we may guide you in your search!" the Viscount once again added angrily.

"I'll not tell you a thing!" Mia scowled. "You don't fool me. You used Vansant Summit as a stepping stone. You sacrificed it to better your knowledge of the enemy. You use me now. Don't think that I'm so naïve to your intentions with me. I know what I am. You are no better than those who oppose you. Power hungry for the missing weapons."

"We do what we must to protect our kind, Princess," Scatha said coldly. "We are issuing you an order."

"An order?"

"You have no idea what things you tamper with. The weapons could destroy our entire existence if they fall into the wrong hands. Demons and the dead could be unleashed," Emberlynn exclaimed.

"I am the Bearer. It's the will of Danu that I and I alone decide what happens to them." Gasps and cries circled around the table but she cut them off. "*And* I want no part of you or your Order. When I see fit, the weapons that fall into my hands will be destroyed after I have cleansed them from the poison you have pumped into them."

"You cannot...!" Viscount Birch paled.

"I can and I will. The weapons, at one time called treasures, can no longer be trusted in this world." Mia spun on her heels and strode from the pathetic audience to meet up with her brother.

Vastadon raced down the flight of stairs that led to the dark dungeons of Nightingale Isle. Agonizing moans and screams filled the air along with the foulest of stenches. As he passed by the prisoners bound to the wall with thick and rusted chains, he felt he might vomit from the hideous sight of them. They were barely clothed and looked as if they hadn't taken a washing for ages. The chains rattled with insanity as they pleaded for some form of attention. He ignored them moving through the hall rapidly until he reached the warden. The warden flashed his gruesome toothless smile.

"Decided to take an adventure in the bottom parts, lad?" he slurred morbidly. "Welcome to hell!"

Vastadon covered his scowl with a handkerchief as the warden swung open the gates to the holding wing. Before he stepped through, he drew back his hood and sneered at the warden. The smug toothless smile turned into panic.

"My Lord, forgive me. I didn't recognize you," he fumbled and bounced his body as if he was deciding whether to kneel or not. "What is your will, my lord?"

Vastadon waved an impatient hand to silence the guard and rushed down the lengthy aisle before him.

He reached the far end of the dungeon, in which holding cells lined both sides of the wall. He halted in front of the second to last cell and peered in through the bars. With a satisfied smile and a nod, Vastadon hurried back to the warden's gate.

"The prisoner I have just brought to you will remain nameless and faceless. He is to never receive visitors and if I find out that my orders have been violated, I will come for you when Thaumatur falls under my control. And what I will do to you is so horrific that I haven't the stomach to tell you. Is that understood?" Vastadon commanded smoothly.

The warden shook his scrawny body into a low bow, "You have my word, my lord."

"If you show me that you know how to follow orders properly, perhaps you may not be stuck in this," Vastadon slowly curled his lips as he glanced at his surroundings, "this place of employ forever."

"So gracious, wondrous, my lord." The pathetic man wailed.

Vastadon snapped his fingers and two guards appeared to escort him from the repugnant place. Just as he was about to make his ascent, he looked over his shoulder.

"You can make my prisoner as miserable as you wish, but make sure he is fed properly enough to ensure his survival in this blasted place. I want him alive and aware of what is going on. I want him to suffer seeing how everything he once held dear is ripped from him."

Vastadon swept from the dungeon.

EPILOGUE

Mia took in the scenery with awe. The streams rolled gently into a cerulean lake before the hills embellished with greens and vibrant yellows, purples, and pinks. She could see the golden citadel protruding from the center of the lake in a valley of rose gardens. The knights of the Circle stood on a dock made from wood that cradled the lake and several canoes.

"It is the only way to reach the sacred home of the Season Maidens," Darius whispered in her ear. "Come and let us return the shards to its proper place." Darius held his hand out to Mia and helped her into the canoe.

She inhaled the aromas of roses and spring and allowed it to rejuvenate her a little. The pregnancy mixed with the deep grief she was suffering took much strength from her body. But somehow, she knew she had to be a part of this. Even if she didn't have a hand in recovering the shards.

Aunyia, who also grieved deeply for the loss of her father and uncle, stepped into the canoe clinging to Horace's hand. Mia glanced behind her and saw Cole and Phoenix support Diamond into a canoe in which Alabaster sat. Diamond, Darius had explained, was suffering the loss of her memory from the imprisonment she suffered when she was in Vhladic. It was only one of many tragedies that branded a mark on their Circle. Vastadon had taken the Emperor's throne.

He will pay. I will see him to his knees before my life ends. By Danu I swear.

Mia rested a hand on her belly and allowed Darius to cradle her as they made their decent. He covered her hand with his own over her unborn child. He promised to be there for her. He promised she wouldn't be alone. He promised her the chance for vengeance. Someone would pay for their suffering. Someone would pay for what was done to their mother.

"No evil thoughts, now, Sister. The day will come," he whispered as if he could read her mind. After all, she couldn't forget that her brother was a Mind Mage. "Let us pay our respects to the Daughters peacefully."

As they came upon the garden patched shore, they climbed from the canoes onto a pavilion woven with grape vines and blossomed ivy. They made their way down the stone path in between pools of fountain waters and sturdy oak trees until they reached the column courtyard that lead to the entrance of the temple. Life-like fairies and mystical creatures made from amber and marble adorned the entry way and adorned the workmanship of the siding and arches. It was a place made from love and innocence, respect and honor. How could four weapons change the world so much?

They came into the altar room silently and bowed their heads with humble respect. Mia cast her eyes to the ceiling where brilliant rays from the sun spilled through. Below her feet, just to the right of her, she saw an amber sheet with two chunks missing from it.

"I thought it to be a skylight," Mia lifted an eyebrow.

"We are on the upper level of the citadel, Mia. We are where the Daughters have been paralyzed." Darius held his hand out.

Mia looked around again and gasped. Along the perimeter of the wall and in between pilasters of marble, four female figures were frozen in ice. Their eyes were sad and it looked as if they were weeping. Mia slowly approached the first maiden and stroked her hand along the ice prison.

The figure clad in navy blue velvet held her hands out with her palms facing upward. At her feet lay a scepter of silver and sapphire. Her pale blue hair hung loosely about her caped shoulders. *Skadi of Winter.*

The second maiden crossed both her arms over her chest. In between them she held a large staff made of fine silver and emeralds. She was garbed in robes of pastel pink and purple and her bronze hair was tied loosely in a river of curls that spilled over her shoulder. She noticed a tear was suspended down her rosy cheek. *Stara of Spring.*

The third maiden was garbed in a mid length dress of gold, her breast plate was made of amber. Her left arm was rested at her side while her right hand held tightly to an arrow. Her short pearl blonde hair clung to dark cheeks and her features were twisted with anger. *Chralam of Summer.*

Then, finally, the fourth maiden wore a one piece armor suit embroidered with brown and orange leaves. Her fiery red hair fell wildly about her waist. *Daphne of Fall.*

They were so sad. Trapped and alone. Mia understood their anguish.

By the time Mia was through studying the splendor and sadness of the Goddess's Four Daughters, her cheeks were wet with tears. Mia drew in her breath and faced her companions. "Give me the shards."

Aunyia withdrew the shards from her robe and placed them in Mia's hands. A wind collected at her feet and it spiraled upward whipping her hair about. Her skin was on Fire. Her fingertips absorbed the racing sensation and Water rushed through her body so hard that she gasped with elation. Her heart beat in rhythm with the Powers of Earth.

Her entire being was alive with the magic of all Elemental Rites. The Elemental Rites in which only she possessed through her birthright as the daughter of the Tuatha Dé Danann.

She met eyes with her brother. His face was frozen with awe.

"Your aura—" Darius pointed.

Mia looked at her legs to see that she was engulfed in an aura of colors.

The entire Circle linked hands around her and began to pray to Danu in soft uneven voices. Mia knelt before the skylight and placed the shards in their proper spot.

A blast of golden light shot up from the completed Golden Skylight weaving threads from Mia to the linked hands of the Circle. The essence of every single knight in the Circle whipped through her as if they were inside of her. They were becoming one.

You need the bonds of your companions to move forward. You have isolated yourself for too long. The whimsical words the Great Owl had once spoken to her echoed in her ears.

The ground shook violently and the ice around the Daughters began to melt, freeing them. Their lifeless bodies gasped with the first breath of their freedom. They stepped in unison from the statues that now replaced their prisons.

And then the light and the tremors were gone. The Daughters gathered around Mia. Their omnipotent presence drew the entire Circle to their knees.

"Rise, Daughter of Tuatha Dé Danann." Skadi's voice hummed throughout the temple. Mia obeyed immediately and inclined her head with respect.

"You have freed us," the gentler yet ethereal voice of Stara sang, "All of you."

The entire Circle remained on their knees and lowered their faces to the ground deeply when the Spring Daughter spoke of them. Chralam placed a soft hand on Mia's bowed head and smiled widely.

"We are so proud of your accomplishments, Bearer," The Daughter of Summer whispered and sparkles fluttered from her lips.

"Forgive me, Holy Ones, but I'm not the one who retrieved the shards. It was my companions of the Circle who took all of the risks and overcame their fears in the face of evil. I'm not worthy of Your blessings," she replied humbly.

"We know of their risks Princess and to them we bestow our blessings as much as we bestow them on you," The Fall Daughter giggled. The sweet laughter sounded as if a chorus had sung from Heaven. "You have overcome the tests and yet you didn't give into the evil as you could've so easily done. You have endured much. And because of the sacrifices you and your companions have made, we will reward you for your loyalty."

They drifted from Mia like beautiful white clouds and slowly floated around the Circle of kneeling knights. They halted before Diamond. Stara cupped her chin and brought her to her feet before them. Diamond was a medium sized woman, but she looked to be the size of a child in the mists of the Daughters' giant stature.

"Close your eyes, Lady Knight," Stara whispered. Diamond's honey eyes widened before they slammed shut.

Stara leaned over and placed a kiss on each eye, followed by the other

Daughters. When they were through with their blessing they bid the knights to rise. An orb of purple expanded around Diamond's entire form, webbing gently through her fingers before ebbing into her body.

"In the name of Our Mother, Danu, we call the return of this knight's memory and the healing of her womb," The Daughters cried in harmony.

Goosebumps traveled up Mia's arm when she heard the words of the wondrous Daughters. What they gave Diamond was a miracle. She heard the knights in the Circle gasp and sob.

No more will you suffer, Diamond! Mia's mind cried out, *No more will you be caught in an endless cycle of the Change.*

Diamond opened her eyes and started. She looked somewhat baffled and when she realized she was in the presence of the Daughters, she crumbled to her knees before them.

"It is alright, Diamond," Daphne chimed in. "You may rise."

Diamond leapt to her feet, but she was still vividly bewildered, "What has happened—How the hell-?" She covered her mouth well after the swear word left it. A chorus of sing-song laughter filled the room.

Cole took hold of her hand and murmured from the side of his mouth, "I will fill you in on it later."

"We must part ways, now. But know that we have faith in you and will be by your side every step of the way." Skadi opened her arms beside her and glided backward.

"It is only the beginning of a long and trying road," Chralam added as she too receded.

"But once you find the weapons, we are most certain the Daughter of Tuatha Dé Danann will cleanse them from the actions of greed and renew the purity of Danu." Stara centered herself between Chralam and Skadi.

"Until the day comes when the world calls upon you once again." Daphne smiled and turned to face her sisters.

Stara and Skadi giggled and disappeared in a cloud of sparkling mists. Chralam inclined her head and passed a golden harp to Daphne.

"I am afraid you are the first one to work." Chralam smirked in the way of jesting between two sisters. "I have an entire year to rest before Summer calls me down to do my duty. Autumn is calling, Sister."

"Ah, it figures," Daphne huffed and took the harp. Chralam waved and vanished in the manner of her other sisters. Daphne returned her attention to the Circle.

"May Danu bless you, the Circle of the Goddess." Her blessing was like thunder and she zoomed in a flurry of autumn vibrancy to the skies.

Mia and the others sauntered out of the temple courtyard and studied the surroundings. Although the roses remained before the gates of the temple, the oak trees and hills were vibrant with the luminous colors of Fall. The air was crisp with a refreshing snap and the aroma of apples and cinnamon.

"At last we have given back the normalcy of our season cycles. Blessed be," Aunyia whispered and Mia embraced her.

A small smile played upon Aunyia's lips. It was the first smile she had seen on her face for days. The Emperor's daughter would heal as she has healed so many others. She would survive her grief because she knew what her purpose in Thaumatur—in the world—was. And as long as she could help save others, she wouldn't give up. Mia admired her and loved her dearly.

They came upon the dock and when they unloaded, Mia was met with a warm embrace from Nan. "Oh, my beloved foster mother, how I have longed to see you!"

"Come, now, my little rose, let us go home," she whispered in Mia's ear. It was then that Mia had realized that "Home" was not a single place, but the people in which surround that place. Nan had been one of those people.

Mia nodded and said her farewells to the other knights. It wasn't goodbye. She knew they would come together soon. She would keep herself healthy and nurtured and would wait for the birth of her son. She vowed to see the mission through in honor of her beloved Jacob, the very man who taught her of courage and love. She was no longer the fearful Winter Princess.

When Darius was through with his farewells, he came to her side and took her hand. Nan encircled her waist and together they made their way home. Mia threw a glance over her shoulder one last time and smiled. Perched in the highest oak tree across the lake, Blodeuwedd flapped her white wings joyously and took flight into the skies.

Silent tears rolled down Mia's cheeks with the first feelings of joy since the day she lost her husband. She ran a hand over her swollen womb and realized there was something much more than joy. There was hope.

The End

Don't miss the second book in **The Treasures of Danu** *series coming soon. What secrets will be uncovered in* **The God of the Spear?**

AUTHOR'S NOTE

It is not my intention to recreate actual Celtic Mythology from the Book of Invasions. Here are some factors of the legend.

The Tuatha Dé Danann ("People of the Goddess Danu") was a mythical race who settled in Ireland before the arrival of the ancestors of Gaels. The Dananns were descendants of the goddess Danu of whom Her son Dagda powerfully leaded.

The **Tuatha Dé Danann** (Pronunciation: thoo'a-haw day dah'-nawn) were considered gods of the Goidelic Irish. They came to Ireland from four cities in the North; Murias, Falias, Gorias and Findias, bringing with them The Four Treasures. Of them the Stone of Destiny (Lia Fáil) in which would determine the destined ruler, was sent forth from the Druid Morfessa who lived in Falias. From the Druid Esras of Gorias was brought the Spear (Gae Assail). No battle was ever unrelenting against it, or against the man who held it.

From The Findias Druid Uscias was brought the Sword of Light. Once it was drawn from its deadly sheath, no one escaped from its will, nor resist its will. No one ever escaped from it once it was drawn from its deadly sheath, and no one could resist it.

From Semias of Murias was brought the Cauldron, the Undry Cauldron. The bottomless cauldron was capable of feeding an army and those who accompanied it was never left unsatisfied. It is said to behold the power of raising the dead.

For *Ami Kathleen* upcoming news and sneak peaks, please visit:
http://TheProphecyNow.bravehost.com
All animals are angels. Please do not forget them. Find out how you can help.
http://www.animalcharitiesofamerica.org/
To help for free, please click:
http://pets.care2.com/

Printed in the United States
71034LV00004B/59

9 781424 128464